Then Comes Marriage

Christie Ridgway

Then Comes Marriage

AVON BOOKS

An Imprint of HarperCollins*Publishers*

AVON BOOKS
An Imprint of HarperCollins*Publishers*
10 East 53rd Street
New York, New York 10022-5299

For Susan Crosby,

with love

Acknowledgments

My gratitude to the usual suspects: Teresa Hill, Barbara Samuel, and Elizabeth Bevarly.

Thank you also to the talented and funny Avon Ladies, who prove that "networking" can be so much more.

Special thanks to the loyal writers and friends of Romex, who are willing to talk craft and dispense comfort with equal enthusiasm.

No Christie Ridgway book is ever completed without the love and support of my husband and sons. Guys, your favorite stew and those home-baked snickerdoodles are coming, I promise. You're the best.

THE HEIRESS WEDS THE ENIGMA

Yep, yank out your hankies, hunks of the world. Honor Witherspoon, America's wealthiest daddy's girl, now sports Tiffany on her left finger. Who's the lucky guy, you ask? None other than high-tech hottie Bram Bennett, the founder of Enigma Company, and the man who develops security devices that keep superstars, princes, and presidents safe.

Following her kidnapping last spring, heiress Honor moved to historic Hot Water, California, where she popped a prime piece of Gold Rush–era real estate into her Prada handbag. **Celeb!** has now learned that purchase was brokered by Big Daddy Witherspoon, who bought Bennett's locally based Enigma Company at the same time. Was daughter Honor part of the deal?

According to a source in the county courthouse, just moments before the ceremony the bride introduced herself to the groom. Could it be they'd never met before the "I do's" commenced? "They didn't kiss, once pronounced man and wife," confided our person-on-the-scene. "They just signed the marriage certificate, then insisted that a copy be faxed to the residence of the bride's father."

When asked what the newlyweds did next, our source seemed even more bewildered. "I watched them out my window. After they left the building, they spoke briefly, then climbed into separate cars and drove off in different directions. What could it mean?"

Celeb! wishes it knew an answer to that one! But strange doings seem to be the norm in this colorful California town, because little green men may be among the first to congratulate the bride and groom. We kid you not! Hot Water is not only the site of the most intriguing celebrity wedding of the year, but of UFO sightings too. Word is spreading that a flying saucer will return this fall and the press and the curious are flocking to Hot Water, guaranteeing an autumn to remember.

Celeb! **is always seeking tips! If you have any scoop on the Witherspoon-Bennett wedding or if any big-eyed, pointy-eared little men come knocking at your door,** *Celeb!* **wants to know! Call us at 1-900-555-0155. ($ .99 per minute, average call 5 minutes.)**

Chapter One

*H*umming "Here Comes the Bride" to bolster her flagging spirits, Honor Witherspoon marched toward the emphatically closed gate in the twelve-foot-high rock wall surrounding the home of her brand-new husband.

There was some doubt in her mind that he would let her in.

Honor blamed that doubt on the grim set to the groom's hard mouth and the icy green of his eyes during the brief ceremony at the courthouse that morning. Or maybe it was because of his obvious impatience with the county clerk, who then took her time faxing the proof of marriage Honor's father had required.

Certainly the doubt's seed had flowered when Honor had volunteered to retrieve her belongings from her small rented cottage alone. So as not to inconvenience her husband any further, she'd explained at her most charming. If she'd expected him to politely insist he accompany her (and she had), then his instant grunt of agreement would have rendered immediate disappointment—except that she refused to acknowledge so negative an emotion.

However, if she'd known her car would choose this afternoon to have a cardiac arrest, she would most certainly have demanded his escort, or at the very least she would have worn flat shoes and blue jeans. But lacking psychic powers or mechanical know-how, she was left to make the trek from disabled vehicle to isolated destination in sandals suited only for starring in *Vogue* layouts and Rodeo Drive window displays.

Every time she planted a foot, her three-inch spiked heel wriggled as it tried to find purchase in the thin layer of dusty needles and candy-corn-colored leaves that had fallen from the pines, maples, and sycamores lining the long private drive. With every step the monogrammed tapestry suitcases she gripped in each fist swung awkwardly as she tried to prevent their overpacked weight from creasing the elegant yet understated Oscar de la Renta shift she'd selected as post-wedding wear.

Not until every little piggy was squealing in pain did Honor at last reach the unwelcoming, still-closed gate. She dropped her luggage in a puddle of shade and flexed her cramped and sweaty palms. Then she hooked a pinkie over her wraparound sunglasses and slid them off to study the button an arm's reach away. It was nearly hidden in the rockwork beside the gate, which was twenty fierce-looking feet of peeled logs lashed tightly together with iron bands. She presumed pressing the button would alert Bram Bennett to her arrival at the house the locals had nicknamed—very aptly, it seemed—the "Fortress."

Honor dropped her sunglasses atop a suitcase to reach for the tea-sandwich-sized purse slung bandolier-style across her breasts. No reason not to take a few minutes and undo some of the damage done by the early October warmth, she told herself. It wasn't stalling, or anything cowardly like that.

But then she hesitated, wondering if her new husband's obsession with security didn't mean cameras installed at his gate. Thinking that it probably did, she snapped the purse shut.

"You don't want him deciding you're shallow or silly or vain," she muttered to herself. Though was it really so shallow or silly or vain to want one's husband to think one was . . . presentable?

No, it was *dumb,* she thought, answering her own question. Her new husband didn't give a flying fig whether Honor looked presentable, pretty, or outright ugly. Her father had forced them to wed.

As she made herself step up to the button, she smothered a small pang of regret. Though she'd harbored the usual white-lace-and-promises wedding fantasy, in the grand scheme of life's thunderbolts an unwanted marriage wasn't *that* bad. Eventually her father would see reason and allow them to dissolve it. Until then, she would convince her husband to look on the bright side of the situation as she did: It was an interesting way to make a new acquaintance.

Without further hesitation, she punched the button with a freshly French-manicured nail. Nothing happened.

Accustomed to the uncooperation of anything electrical, she released a short sigh and poked the button once more. Still nothing happened. Honor huffed a second time.

Then, from the bushy undergrowth nearby, came a loud rustle.

Her heart bucked hard. The rustle sounded again—someone was moving up behind her! Pulse accelerating to freeway speed, she whirled to confront—

Nothing.

The panic dissipated slowly. Too slowly. Annoyed with herself, Honor spun back and plucked off a sandal, giving it a last chance to prove worthy of its designer price tag—she used the painful thing to whack the balking button.

Something rumbled, soft but deep.

Honor's heart tripped again, but then she realized the noise was the sound of the gate sliding open. In the time that it took for her to step back into her sandal, though, the contraption of peeled logs lurched off its track and abruptly stopped, leaving an opening of eight askew inches.

Shaking her head, she stepped to it and squeezed through. Quick impressions bombarded her: more trees and a winding stream; a rustic house of rock and logs, its Daniel Boone–style fashioned on a Paul Bunyan scale. Then, over the cheery gurgle of that stream splashing over stones, came a deep, threatening growl.

Honor froze as the growl sounded again. Woods, log house, stream, all led to one thought: *Bear.* Her head snapped right. She gaped at a snarling creature eyeing her from ten yards away, and her second thought was even more startling.

Scooby Doo?

Scooby Doo. The prerequisite huge head, perky ears, large size. But while cartoon character Scooby smiled when he opened his mouth, this, this . . . thing was *baring* its metal teeth at her. Metal teeth, because the whole darn dog was exactly that. Made of metal. It appeared to be an overgrown, homelier version of the robotic dogs that had been the hot kids' toy three Christmases back.

Before she could grasp the situation more fully, the huge creature slowly started toward her. It rolled along the flagstone drive on little wheels attached to the end of its long metal legs. Still emitting that low, threatening *grrrr*, its mouth opened and shut, teeth snapping like the jaws of a trap.

Her gaze glued to the approaching figure, Honor cautiously stepped back. "Nice boy," she called out. "Nice, nice boy."

The metal thing paused, then gave an even louder snarl, amber lights glinting from eye sockets in its huge, pewter-colored head.

Honor swallowed, sensing the timber gate behind her and its skinny opening to her right. Should she go?

No. Her palms pressing against the peeled logs behind her, she held her ground. She'd survived monsters far more terrifying than this during the kidnapping.

The satanic Scooby edged nearer, now a mere eight feet away. Honor crowded closer against the gate, quickly searching her mind for tips about confronting strange dogs and wondering if said tips applied to strange *cyborg* dogs.

Then the thing gave another throaty growl. It seemed to gather itself to spring. Honor threw up her arm to protect her face and braced for impact.

Instead, the only thing that hit her was the resounding crash and clatter of metal hitting flagstone. Her arm dropped, her eyes opened, and she looked down to find a heap of cyborg Scooby at her feet. The creature lay on its side, its amber eyes flickering to opaque black screens. It gave a jerk, a whimpering moan, and then went motionless.

Stunned by the sight, Honor was still staring at it when a pair of scuffed, rugged boots strode into her field of vision and halted beside Scooby's slack-jawed metal snout. Honor lifted her head.

Her new husband had changed clothes since the wedding too, out of a sober suit and into washed-to-the-point-of-whiteness jeans and a plain T-shirt. Both well matched the offhand air of his worn footwear. The only thing the least bit spiffy-looking about him was the streamlined palmtop computer he held in one hand. Bram Bennett obviously hadn't cared about dressing to impress *her*.

Self-conscious heat rolling up her neck, Honor straightened her spine and resisted the urge to smooth the wrinkles in her linen dress. She resolutely pinned on a friendly smile. "Hello, Bram. As you can see, I made it."

His gaze moved slowly off the mangled metal at her feet to meet hers. The angles and planes of his face hardened with unmistakable *un*friendliness and his eyes went arctic. "You . . ." he said, his rough voice making the words as abrasive as sandpaper against bare skin, "you killed my dog."

FOLLOWING Bram's stiff back in the direction of the house, Honor faced the fact that his accusation of crime against canine probably indicated he wasn't on the same why-can't-we-be-friends page that she was.

Still fixed on the goal of getting him there, though, she allowed herself a single sigh, then spared a glance over her shoulder at the heap of metal still lying by the gate. "I'm, uh, sorry," she said.

Again.

He grunted in reply.

Again.

His crisp footsteps snapped against the wooden slats of a footbridge that crossed the stream running through the expansive, tree-dotted front grounds. Beyond the five words earlier, he hadn't said anything at all. He'd silently retrieved her suitcases after her brief explanation of her carlessness. He hadn't commented on the off-kilter gate either, just muscled the heavy thing back on its track to slide it closed.

Though Honor had jumped at the loud, final-sounding clang of the heavy gate locking behind her, Bram had brushed by her without a word and strode toward the house. Apparently, bringing a new wife into his life didn't cause the merest ripple in his still waters.

She gave another guilty glance at the remains of cyborg Scooby. "That, um, thing back there," she began, trying to sound supportive. Upbeat. "It probably just needs a new battery or something."

Turning his head, he sent her a long, cold look.

Refusing to be squelched, she took another stab at starting conversation. "So . . . um . . . what do you call it?"

They were climbing the front steps to the porch now, a half dozen of them that were long stretches of smooth wood with rugged stone piers on either side. "Its name is Fifo," Bram answered.

"Fifo?" Now that her husband was finally making noises beyond grunting, she didn't think she should laugh. "As in *Fido*? It has an actual name? But . . . but what exactly is its function?"

She herself had always dreamed of having a dog, some needy mongrel to love, but she didn't think that was Fido's—er, *Fifo's*—purpose.

Bram set her suitcases near the double front doors and reached into his pocket to retrieve his custom-looking palmtop. "Its name, Fifo, is a computer programming term that stands for 'first in, first out.'" He glanced at her. "As to its function, it's security, of course. It's the first generation of a robotic guard dog I'm developing."

"Ah." Honor nodded, stifling a second urge to laugh. A robotic guard dog? But Bram was perfectly serious, that's for sure. Bram Bennett was always perfectly serious. Even though she hadn't been in Hot Water long, town gossip and her own brief observation confirmed that. "A guard dog. I suppose the ordinary Doberman or German shepherd variety is too—"

"Unpredictable. They can't be completely controlled." He turned away and pressed something on the handheld unit that caused the front doors to swing silently open. Then he grabbed up the suitcases and stepped through. "Close them behind you, please."

Palms going clammy, Honor stood where she was, eyeing the interior. It appeared positively murky in contrast to the bright sunshine outdoors, too sharp a reminder of the wine cellar that had recently served as her dank and dark personal hell.

After a moment, Bram reappeared in the doorway, shadows casting a diagonal slice of darkness across his face. "What's wrong?"

She stared at him, noting his ruthlessly cut dark hair and the equally ruthless angles and planes of his cheeks and jaw. Though she'd occasionally glimpsed him from afar about town, their wedding had been their first actual meeting. Since her father had coerced them both into nuptials during a three-point, three-way conference call, today was the closest she'd ever been to Bram's six-plus feet of lean, hard body.

It didn't take much imagination to picture him in camouflage paint, moving stealthily through a danger-filled jungle. He was attractive, she supposed, if one wasn't intimidated by all that stony commando coolness.

Which of course she wasn't.

She wiped her palms on her dress. Pinning on another social smile, she tried to forget intimidation and imprisoning darkness and follow him into the shadows.

Only to hesitate again.

His dark brows drew up and something suspiciously like a sneer curled his upper lip. "If you're waiting for a red carpet, princess, I didn't have the time to order one. Your daddy's ultimatum caught me by surprise."

Princess. Honor flushed at the little dig. "My father caught me by surprise too."

"What, he doesn't buy you every cute little town you get a hankering for?"

Honor felt her cheeks go hotter. After the kidnapping, Warren Witherspoon hadn't protested when she moved to this tiny town in northern California. In fact, he'd even bought two stakes in the community—Bram's company, Enigma, and also the town's six-block historic district, which was now hers to manage. But when a foreign ambassadorship had been offered to him, her father's imminent move out of the country had made him obsessed with Honor's safety.

In his typical bullheaded, feelings-last fashion, her father had promised to be the economic ruin of the town if they didn't wed. Couldn't Bram see that she'd been as neatly trapped as he?

She tried another smile. "It's only going to last a few months, I swear. Three months, four tops."

"That long?"

Something about his cynical expression made her reckless. "Six weeks, then. In six weeks he'll know as I do—that in Hot Water I'm perfectly safe. Until then . . ."

"Then until, what—mid-November?—you plan to intrude upon my privacy and solitude."

Again, his put-upon tone stung. "You should have chimed in when I was trying to convince my father you could handle the job *without* me living at your house and *without* us being married," she said. "That was not the time to hone your strong and silent act."

The angle of the sun had changed. Bram's face was now completely shadowed and his voice was harsher than before. "Your father mentioned that a man would go to any lengths to protect his wife. Not only couldn't I counter that argument, but I have some . . . compassion for it."

Honor's heart squeezed and her irritation evaporated. Bram had a very good reason for that compassion. "It won't be so bad," she promised, rubbing that sympathetic ache in her chest and thinking of the friends angle again. "I have it all figured out."

He shook his head. "I just bet you do," he muttered, then disappeared inside.

Honor peered once again through the yawning, dim doorway. Ignoring the anxiety trying to clutch at her stomach, she inhaled a fortifying breath and straightened her shoulders. Hadn't she just declared herself perfectly safe in Hot Water? To the depths of her soul she believed that. It was, perhaps, the only belief she had faith in anymore.

With one determined stride, she crossed the threshold.

It took a few more steps for her eyes to adjust to the change in light. Once they did, she found herself stunned for the second time that day. Nobody in town seemed to have firsthand knowledge of Bram's home, so she'd assumed it would be as cold and uninviting as Bram himself. But instead, the decor was just plain unexpected.

Like the outside, the interior walls were honey-colored log, the chinks between them sealed with a material of matching color. To the left of the small foyer was an informal dining area filled with a rustic French farm table. Through a doorway beyond it, she glimpsed a large kitchen, complete with copper pots hanging from an iron rack.

Bram had turned right, though, and Honor followed him now, into what she'd term a "great" room. It had soaring ceilings, with windows stretching from the hardwood floor to reach heavy, exposed beams. The expanses of glass let in light and wide views of the trees, stream, and a massive back deck with more forest beyond. The furniture was big too, heavy pieces velvet-upholstered in shades from sand to goldenrod. Their color warmed the room and their size went well with the mammoth stone fireplace anchoring one wall. Framed above it were two brightly colored, intricately embroidered Chinese robes, probably gained from some long-ago barter between a Chinese immigrant and a Bennett ancestor.

Honor drew closer to them and the mix of objects on the thick, log-slab mantel below. A gold miner's pan, metal sides battered and pocked with use; a hand-lettered sign, red paint faded and flaking, that

read, BENNETT'S DRY GOODS, EST. 1853; a framed photo—
the original of a copy she'd seen in tourist brochures—
that depicted downtown Hot Water in the height of its
gold boom.

Like many citizens of contemporary Hot Water,
Bram's connection to the town went back over 150
years, and it appeared his collection of memorabilia
did too. That sense of continuity and deep-rooted belonging was the basis of the town's appeal to her.

She turned toward Bram. "Your home is beautiful."

If she thought her admiration would ease the strain
between them, or at least bring some warmth to his
cool green eyes, his grunt of response told her different.

"Come on." He started moving again, without even
pausing to see if she followed.

For a moment, Honor didn't. But then she smoothed
her frown away and hurried in his wake. His unfriendly mood couldn't make her regret her decision to
move here or to marry him. She was willing to do
whatever it took to stay and make a place for herself in
Hot Water.

He'd disappeared down a hall and she caught up
with him at the first doorway leading off it. "My office," he said, nodding his head toward the half-closed
door, then striding on.

When he halted the next time, he set her suitcases
down. Assuming they'd reached her bedroom,
Honor's heart lifted in pleasant expectation. She even
felt her mouth curve in a smile. Based upon what she'd
already seen of the house, she looked forward to comfortable surroundings for her temporary stay.

Not to mention that unpacking her luggage would
give her a brief break from Mr. Personality.

Taking in her cheerful expression, one of Bram's

brows slowly lifted. "And here, here is the master suite . . . my bedroom," he said, with one hand making a welcoming gesture at an ajar door.

Honor froze. He expected her to sleep with him?

No. *No.* Her smile slid away. Her belly crawled after it as the unwavering look in his eyes confirmed the truth.

A slimy chill slithered over her flesh. Dirty words rushed into her head, a memory—but stronger than a memory, rawer—of crude whispers describing even cruder acts. Over them she barely heard Bram's voice.

"You said it won't be so bad. You said you had it all figured out." His expression turned frigid and his voice lowered to an even rougher rasp. "Maybe I have it all figured out too."

He expected her to sleep with him.

Chapter Two

*B*ram watched Honor's silvery eyes widen and her creamy skin go paler. Damn, it felt good to ease his anger by rattling the spoiled little rich girl. He was going to keep rattling her too, until she realized that bunny-hopping back to her party life in Bel Air or Beverly Hills or wherever she came from would be a hell of a lot more fun than invading *his* life.

Fun was what she was after, of course. He'd met women just like her during his college years at M.I.T. After a drive from one of the seven sister colleges such as Bryn Mawr or Mount Holyhoke, they'd step out of platinum-colored sports cars wearing their politically incorrect mink jackets, old-money honeys so jaded that they'd turned to luring eggheads away from their PCs for novel entertainment. He'd seen through them then, just as he saw through Honor now.

She didn't belong in his house or in his town.

So yeah, this marriage was going to be temporary, she was right about that. Still, he could kick himself for selling Enigma to Warren Witherspoon in the first place.

Last summer, he'd sought to free himself from all his head-of-the-company hassles. By staying on as an R&D consultant, he'd thought to keep a hand in Enigma, but from behind the thick walls of his home.

He'd never suspected he'd set himself up for being forced to choose between a wedding or ruin. So even though he'd vowed never to marry again, he'd chosen the wedding. Not that this marriage would *really* count, he assured himself. It wouldn't last long enough.

Six weeks, she'd promised. He predicted less.

Because before he let Honor upset his life with some passing fancy for his town, he was going to shake her up. Shake her loose. Freeze her out. Whatever was necessary to get her to leave his home and Hot Water forever.

He edged one brow higher. "Do you have an objection to me exercising my conjugal rights?"

She swallowed, and he followed the movement with his gaze, dispassionately assessing the slenderness of her neck and the fragility of her collarbone that created a sharp dip where her pulse beat rapidly against her skin. She was a small woman—delicate, even—but with more-than-adequate curves on top. Great legs.

Then there was the face. Jesus, what a face. Beneath shoulder-length dark hair was a wide brow, wide-set, heavily lashed silver eyes, short nose, full-lipped mouth. Her chin was shallowly dimpled, as if some man had lightly pressed a finger there, leaving his mark on her forever.

Bram considered a moment, evaluating her body's effect on his. Despite the coldness of his anger, there was a hot stir in his blood and a heaviness between his thighs, all thanks to Honor's tight curves and arresting face.

Hell, maybe he *would* go to bed with her.

Except that in recent years he'd made it a rule never to have sex with someone he planned on seeing the next morning. And, damn it all, he didn't think there was a hope of getting rid of her quite *that* quickly.

She wiped her palms on her dress, a silvery-colored, short, and sleeveless garment that revealed those slender legs and slim arms. The color made her eyes stand out like top-quality diamonds in her now-apprehensive face. "Bram . . ." She swallowed again.

Besides, Bram acknowledged, judging from Honor's appalled expression it didn't look as if she were too keen on the idea of going to bed with *him*.

Which meant getting her out of his life might be even simpler and quicker than he'd hoped. He crossed his arms over his chest and leaned against the wall behind him. "I repeat. Do you have an objection to me exercising my conjugal rights?"

Her eyes widened and her mouth worked, but no sounds came out. For a second her obvious alarm made him almost feel sorry for her. But then he forced his mind back to her wealthy-heiress whims, this damn marriage, and last but maybe not least, the damage she'd done to Fifo.

With his foot, he nudged the door beside him open. "There's plenty of room in the closet."

Her little tongue darted out, wetting her bottom lip, and the unconscious gesture fanned the sexual heat in his blood. His cock hardened and he started feeling sorry for *himself*, shackled for even a short while to a piece of prime-cut temptation that he would never taste.

"I think you'll find some empty drawers too," he added.

Color bloomed on her cheeks, then her eyes narrowed. "You're kidding around, right?"

He gave her a pitying look. "Didn't anyone tell you I don't kid around?"

She didn't hesitate. "Well, sure."

Her instant agreement strangely rankled. "Yeah?" He frowned. "What else did people tell you about me?"

" 'People'?" Now one of her dark, feathery eyebrows rose. " 'People' as in my father or 'people' as in the people in town?"

Though he didn't really care what anyone thought of him, he found himself answering, "Both."

She shrugged. "During negotiations to buy Enigma, my father complained you had an inflated sense of your own self-worth, which coming from him is the highest of praise. The people of Hot Water say . . ."

To hell with it. Fine. He was willing to admit he was as curious as the next man. "They say what?"

One of her shoulders lifted in a half shrug. "They say that you spend too much time by yourself."

Bram flinched. To take revenge for the minor, though unexpected hit, he set his face in even more implacable lines. "Then they'll be happy to find out you've moved in." He waited a beat, nudged the bedroom door wider. "With me."

"I won't," she said quickly.

"Oh, yeah?" He reached toward her face, meaning not to touch her, merely to rattle her more. But with his fingertips an inch from the warm color on her cheek, her skin seemed to draw his hand. Against his will, he made contact. A static shock snapped at him and he yanked his fingers away.

Her face had paled again but her gaze was rock-steady. "I won't move in," she repeated.

He set his jaw. "But sweetheart, you promised Daddy."

"Don't—"

"Don't what?" It was going to be child's play to scare her off, he decided. Bracing himself, he reached out and calmly caressed the side of her face. There was no jolt this time, just the sensation of velvet warmth. "Don't get something out of this situation that *I* want?"

Honor stiffened, then her eyes narrowed again. "But you don't want me," she said, her voice quiet. "I know that."

With her nervousness on a definite wane, he saw something else in her expression. Pity? Damn her.

"I wouldn't be so sure." He pushed away from the wall and leaned closer. The pad of his thumb deliberately cruised her cheek again, then lingered above that shallow dent in her chin.

A low hum of—more anger, he supposed—began vibrating through his body. "Maybe I want this to be mine," he said under his breath, pressing there.

She jerked her face from his touch. "And maybe you only want to punish me for what's gone."

Startled by a second on-target barb, he backed away from her. "Yeah," he said harshly. "What's gone is life like I know it."

In two strides he was across the hallway. With the flat of his hand, he slapped the door there, shoving it open to reveal the spacious guest bedroom. "This is where you'll stay." He was no longer in the mood to bully her with threats of sex.

He picked up her suitcases and strode into the room to dump them on the four-poster bed. "Bathroom's through there," he said, gesturing toward another door. "If you need something you can't find, ask me. Or Mia. She cleans and cooks for me a few times a week."

Honor slowly entered the room, her gaze roaming over the log walls and the small fireplace. "Thank you," she said. "I'm sure I'll be fine."

Bram grunted. Now that he'd let her off the hook of sleeping with him, her uneasiness appeared gone altogether. Dressed like a million of Daddy's bucks and wearing her debutante beauty like a crown, she explored the room.

Bram watched her, her every graceful movement grating against his nerves. He'd only built the house a couple of years before, so no woman had ever lived in it. Not one had slept in this room or in any of the others. Even when his mother visited, she preferred staying closer to town. The isolation depressed her, she said, her tactful way of saying *his* isolation depressed her.

Honor stopped before the double French doors that led outside to the back deck. "It's lovely." She smiled at him.

He grunted again. Damn, the room already smelled different. It smelled of Honor's perfume, a rich-girl scent that made him think of diamonds again, diamonds on pampered, naked flesh.

Christ. It was an image that didn't belong in his mind any more than Honor belonged in his world.

Irritated with himself, he shook his head, trying to clear it. "Just what the hell are you doing here?" he muttered.

"It's going to be okay," she said, smiling again as she moved to the bed and opened a suitcase. "You'll see."

Her optimistic attitude only made him angrier. He liked to control his world, but right now he felt as manipulated as a marionette. "How the hell can you be so damn cheerful about all this?"

Her head was bent over layers of clothing. "Because gloomy is so damn boring."

Disconcerted, Bram blinked. Gloomy? Boring? "Is that what people say about me in town? That I'm boring?"

Honor glanced at him, then shifted her gaze back to her suitcase. He stared as she started drawing, magicianlike, a swath of red silkiness from its depths.

Then she yanked, and the red garment swung free in her hand. She shook it out, a nightgown that was nothing more than two sheer triangles on top attached to a long column of more sheerness. His body started humming again; more heat rushed through his veins.

As if completely unaware of what she was holding, she casually looked over at him. "The people in town don't say you're boring, Bram." She flashed him another of those blinding smiles of hers. "*I* do."

He jerked back. *She thought him boring.* Speechless, and more annoyed than he cared to admit, Bram bailed out of the room before she could draw more blood. *Boring?*

In the welcome dimness of his office, he flipped on his computer monitor, calling up the game he'd designed during the endless days and nights of that summer eight years before. Later, he'd tried burying the horror by building a company that specialized in personal security devices, but those first months he'd built this game. Neither, of course, had brought him any measure of peace.

The word "ENIGMA" blazed across the black screen

like lightning, then the image changed to a shadowed maze with dungeonlike walls. The dark-cloaked figure of the player started roaming, his wandering movements growing more anxious as he tried to find his way to the dark, calming center of the maze. Bram focused intently on the game, using it to wipe clear his mind as he caused the cloaked man to dodge arrows that suddenly sprang out of walls and to leap over trapdoors that appeared without warning beneath the player's booted feet.

Bram was doing well, maybe his best game ever. Then, without warning, Honor invaded his head. Her smile. That damn red nightgown.

He missed the trap yawning beneath the player. The cloaked figured dropped.

Bram's pulse jumped and his fingers tightened on the controls, trying to recoup by scrambling the dark man back out of the hole. It was too late. The player disappeared. The maze exploded into thousands of glittering stars.

A door away, Bram heard a thump. Honor leaped into his mind again, her smile, her perfume. The way she was already screwing with his life.

And *he'd* wanted to rattle *her*.

He grimly calculated the current score.

Heiress, 1. Enigma, 0.

*H*ONOR continued unpacking, her tension slowly draining. Now that Bram had left the room, her heart no longer drummed against her chest. There seemed to be more air to breathe.

She supposed calling him gloomy and boring wouldn't endear her to her husband, but she'd only felt relief when he'd stalked off. Though it hadn't taken her many minutes to figure out he'd thrown those "conjugal rights" in her face to unsettle her, it had worked.

Even once he'd shown her to the guest room, she hadn't been able to relax. Oh, she'd tried smiling, but his gaze had followed her too closely, the attention making her stomach jittery and her flesh feel hot.

She definitely needed a break from him.

"Honor."

She jumped, then swung around to face Bram. Framed in the doorway of her bedroom, he was all covert commando again, his green eyes cool, his face impassive. Whatever feelings he had for her or about their situation were secreted away inside him. Still, she felt her heart knock hard against her chest.

One of his dark eyebrows winged up. "Honor?"

Something must be showing on her face. She had no idea what it might be, exactly, and hoped he didn't take it for attraction. No doubt he *was* a great-looking man, all the requisite masculine topography paired with the angled face and its sensual mouth and icy eyes. But she'd never been bowled over by beefcake, and considered herself immune altogether since the kidnapping.

His other eyebrow rose. "Are you all right?"

Oh. *Oh.* She was staring. Not speaking. *Still* not speaking. She cleared her throat, hoping she wasn't blushing again. "Yes. Yes, I'm fine."

"I wanted you to know I'm going out," he said.

"Going out?" Honor's gaze shifted to the windows of her bedroom. *Ah.* It was nearing sunset. "Okay, right."

"If you'll give me the keys to your car, I'll take a look at it before I leave."

She nodded, grabbed her keys off their place on the dresser, and tossed them over.

Then he drew his fancy palmtop from his front pocket. "The security system will be armed. The doors, the windows, the gate. But if you need to, of course, call 911."

The thought of making such a call briefly screeched across her peace of mind like fingernails against a chalkboard, but Honor had faith she was safe in Hot Water and she didn't hesitate to tell her husband so.

"Bram. The kidnappers who took me were arrested," she said. They'd been four criminally bored young men, college students looking to ditch finals and fund a high life in Europe. "They confessed, pled guilty, are locked up. Despite my father's concerns, I don't need protection."

She saw his fingers tighten on the palmtop. "And yet we're married."

"And yet we are," she conceded, and, grimacing, waved a hand. "By all means, then, go ahead with the force field."

He paused in the doorway.

"Something else?" she asked.

"Help yourself to anything you want in the kitchen. I don't know when I'll be back."

"That's okay," she said, shifting her gaze off his face. *Because I do.*

She knew Bram had a previous appointment, during which he would probably explain his marriage to Honor. It wasn't real, she supposed he'd say. The vows didn't matter, because he cared nothing for the bride.

Whatever his explanation, Honor knew he wouldn't be back until after his daily visit with the woman he loved.

With his first wife.

At her grave.

* * *

V̶ERY early the next morning, Honor tiptoed past Bram's closed bedroom door, heading for the kitchen. There, she found a brewed pot of coffee that he'd apparently preprogrammed the night before.

A thick mug in hand, Honor approached the countertop where the futuristic coffeemaker sat, two rows of lights glowing on its complex control panel. Despite their all-systems-go green, she counted to three, gulped a breath, then cautiously reached for the pot, wincing as the machine malevolently hissed when her fingers found the handle. The lights on the panel flashed red as she quickly poured, and she didn't exhale until she'd slipped the pot back into place.

The machine hissed again, then groaned. The lights on the control panel blinked out.

"Oh, shoot." Honor scurried away from the now-defunct appliance. Later she'd deal with it, once she devised a way to approach Bram about the phone call she'd received while he was out the night before. He wasn't going to like it.

The call had gratified Honor, however, and even now made her grin. In less than six hours, the news of their marriage had spread through the community grapevine. Just a day ago, Hot Water had been buzzing over a local man's claim of contact with a UFO. Now she and Bram were the talk of the town.

When she'd moved here, she'd counted on the small-town, your-business-is-my-business nature of Hot Water. She wanted—no, *needed*—to live someplace where people cared about what she did. Where in time, she hoped, people would truly come to know and care about *her*.

The distant sound of a door opening and closing

startled her, and coffee sloshed onto her fingers. *It's only Bram,* she reminded herself. And then an entirely different set of nerves fired off. He was making her jittery again.

But she forced herself to head toward the noise anyway. There was no point in stalling now that he was awake and moving about. She'd find him, get the entire phone conversation off her chest, and then . . .

Duck.

No! Chiding herself for such negative thinking, she strode off. By tackling this problem together, they could make a positive start to their situation.

That thought held her for the two minutes it took to find him holed up in his office. An apt phrase, "holed up," because the room's overhead light was off and heavy drapes were pulled across the windows. She might have strolled right by without detecting him, except she heard his muttered curse through the half-closed door.

"There you are!" Her voice sounded falsely cheerful even to her own ears as she slipped inside.

At the far end of the large, shadowed room, he was bent over a long table. A thin tool in hand, he worked on a piece of fist-sized machinery lit by the spotlight of a work lamp.

He didn't bother looking up. "What do you want?"

He didn't bother softening his irritated tone either. Ignoring it, Honor walked farther into the room, pausing beside the long set of windows. Grasping the edges of the drapes, she dragged them apart, breathing easier once the room was filled with more light. Her back to Bram, she let the sun warm her face as she gazed out at the expanse of morning sky.

"Did you consider I might like it dark?"

She'd considered it, but closed doors and darkness made her hear the echo of coarse threats and made her taste the acid flavor of fear.

"I'm sorry." She turned toward him.

He was bent over his project, so she took a moment to acknowledge he had one of those hard male backsides that looked their best in worn Levi's jeans. But then she noticed his hands shifting deftly. The small movements flexed the ropy muscles in his arms and through the thin material of his T-shirt she could see broad, well-defined muscles playing across his back too.

Some activity more strenuous than lifting screwdrivers created those wide shoulders and lean hips. Her gaze slid again to his long, agile fingers. With the room now sunlit, she had a better idea of what he was laboring over.

To Bram's right, at one end of the table, he'd laid the metal dog's body—er, carcass?—on a fuzzy blanket. Based on the yawning cavity in its big skull and the size of the project spotlighted at the opposite end of the work surface, it appeared her husband was tinkering with the brain of his robotic dog.

The dog he'd accused Honor of killing.

Guilt swept through her again. "I'm *really* sorry." Her stomach sank at the notion of presenting him with yet another complication.

To play for time, she circled the office, passing a massive desk topped by a computer, then a leather couch and matching leather chair positioned at angles around a woodburning stove. Built-in shelving filled every inch of free wall space, and Honor's gaze snagged on one of the few framed photographs among the obsessively neat stacks of books and files.

Her chest tightened even as her hand lifted the frame from its place. The photo was a candid shot of a round-cheeked brunette in her early twenties, her soft hair in frothy curls around her face. She had the cherubic look of someone who would die too young.

She had.

Honor swallowed. "Your wife?" she asked, glancing over at Bram.

Though he grunted an agreement, he was staring at the palmtop in his hand. Frowning, he looked at the window, jabbed at the device, then looked up at the window again. Nothing happened. He jabbed once more.

"How old is she here?" Honor asked.

He glanced at her, jabbed the device again without result, then strode to the windows to manually drag the drapes closed. Back at his worktable, he lowered his head over his project. "Twenty-four," he muttered. "Forever twenty-four."

Honor lifted the frame closer, studying the photo in the dimness. Eight years before, Alicia Bennett had been driving some neighbor kids into town when she was stopped by a carjacker on an isolated road. While another town resident who happened along—Dylan Matthews—had rescued the children, Alicia herself had been dragged into the adjacent woods by the carjacker.

She'd been found three days later, dead.

No longer able to meet the dark eyes in the photograph, Honor set it carefully back on the shelf. Then she turned to Bram, knowing it was time to get the problem off her chest.

"What do you think," she said, hoping to ease into the conversation, "about parties?"

"I don't think about them at all."

Well, she should have seen that one coming. According to town scuttlebutt, since his wife's death Bram had retreated from any and all social events.

Honor crossed to the windows and fiddled with the drapes again, pulling one side halfway back. A shaft of yellow sunlight glowed against the hardwood floor and lifted her mood. "Parties can be fun."

Light. Laughter. People.

Life.

He glanced at her over his shoulder, frowning as he caught sight of the half-open drapes. "Sweetheart, if you're looking for a wild social whirl, then you're living in the wrong town. This is Hot Water, not Hollywood."

She shook her head. "I don't need a whirl, but—"

"Listen, princess, I hear you." He straightened, turning away from his work to face her. "You're bored. So let's put an end to your playing small-town girl right this instant. Call Daddy and tell him you've changed your mind. I'll drive you to the airport in Stockton myself. Hell, I'll even take you into San Francisco if you want an international flight."

Honor gaped at him.

He grabbed up his handheld computer and aimed it at the drapes. "You can hire yourself a bodyguard and be back to the high life in less than twenty-four hours."

Still staring, she watched him jab at the handheld again. His frustration obviously grew with every moment the drapes resisted his remote command and stayed stubbornly open.

Bram thought she was spoiled, Honor realized, the truth slowly sinking in. Flighty. A party girl who didn't know her own mind.

Her hands clenched into fists. She'd thought she understood his anger the day before. She'd assumed it was a spillover from what he felt toward her father for forcing the marriage on them both.

She'd thought he was angry at the circumstances, but now it was clear he was angry with *her*. And it was very clear that he'd made unflattering assumptions about her character and commitment to Hot Water. Just like so many before him, he didn't bother, didn't *care*, about getting to know who she really was.

Her temper heated and she stoked it, telling herself she was insulted, not injured. He didn't like her. And you know what? She particularly didn't like *that* about *him*.

He expected spoiled? Oh, she'd show him spoiled.

Relaxing her pose, she tried sounding calm. "I was talking about parties, Bram. I didn't say anything about wanting to leave town."

The man even had the bad manners to look disappointed at that. "Well, then, I already told you. I don't do parties."

She lifted her eyebrow in a mild challenge. "There you go, boring me again."

He sent her an unsurprised but impatient look. "Yeah? Well, I'm the man you married, not entertainment, princess."

Princess. Oh, it was all so very, very clear to her now. Instead of a partner in this predicament, Bram considered her nothing more than a royal pain in his butt.

She managed not to gnash her teeth, though, instead releasing a long, disappointed sigh. "Did you hear that popping sound? You burst my bubble, Bram, and now my girlish dreams are dying. I always thought a husband *was* entertainment."

"Not this one."

No, this one was a piece of work who didn't realize

Honor needed Hot Water like she needed her heart to beat. So too bad, but *he* wouldn't run her off either. She smiled sweetly at him. "C'mon," she wheedled. "A party to announce our marriage."

He looked at her warily, as if sensing a trap. "The Hot Water grapevine will take care of that."

"Oh. Well." She attempted a pout. Though it wasn't her nature, she figured he expected it.

His gaze narrowed on her lips. She felt heat again, not of temper, but *there,* as if he were touching her mouth. Tingles fanned across her face and lifted prickly trails down her arms. Annoyed, she briskly rubbed them with her palms.

"Are you *sure* we can't have a party here?" she said, trying her best to sound as if she expected to get her way. "We could open up the house, invite in all your friends—the whole town, in fact—"

"We're *not* having a party," he declared, his expression adamant. "We're *not* letting the town—or anyone—in."

"Oh. Well, okay." She suddenly capitulated, knowing she had him right where she wanted him. "If you say so."

With a smile, she headed for the door, putting a princessy, spoiled swing in her walk.

Her hand on the doorknob, she paused and looked back at him. Still standing beside the table, he was eyeing her suspiciously, which didn't surprise her. But then, *she'd* never sold *him* short.

She tried to look impeccably innocent as she met his gaze. "So I guess that means we don't have an excuse to avoid the big bash your friends Dylan and Kitty Matthews called me about. They're throwing it tomorrow night, to, um . . . commemorate our marriage."

As he gawked at her, his awesome backside dropped to the tabletop. He yelped, lifted, then grabbed the screwdriver from its unfortunate location.

She hoped it hurt like heck, even as she smiled at him again. "Seeya," she said, then left.

Let her darling husband stew on that awhile. She was saving the part he'd *really* hate for later.

Chapter Three

*B*uttoning his shirt, Bram cursed as he caught sight of the clock. They were going to be late for Dylan and Kitty's party and he could only blame himself. He'd stayed longer at the cemetery than he'd meant to, slowed down by the leaden weight in his chest and a throbbing headache.

An echo of it clanged inside his skull even now, and he rubbed at his temple with the heel of his hand. He didn't want to attend a party. He didn't want to socialize.

Even more, he didn't want to spend the evening with Honor. The spoiled little witch had played him for a fool with all her talk about "fun" and "entertainment." Like a red flag, she'd waved the idea of a party in his face, when all the while there was an invitation on the table that she hadn't refused.

That he couldn't refuse, either. With or without Honor's interference, this was one event he couldn't skip. One person he couldn't snub.

Dylan Matthews, Bram's closest childhood friend,

had blamed himself for Alicia's death. Though he'd rescued the children who'd been with her, it wasn't until this past summer that Dylan had returned home and forgiven himself for not saving Bram's wife.

So, as much as he valued his solitude, he couldn't give Dylan an excuse to slide back into that ill-gotten guilt. Not when Bram knew that the man to blame for Alicia's death had died in a shoot-out with the authorities that same summer eight years ago.

Still, Bram would make sure Honor realized that his attendance at the party didn't mean she had the upper hand. Tonight, none of her sweet smiles, not one of her pretty, pampered pouts would soften him, distract him, get under his skin. Tonight he'd show her he wasn't a man who played games by someone else's rules.

With long strides, he crossed to his bedroom door and pulled it open. All at once, his feet, his mind, his internal organs, maybe, seemed to cease working.

Across the hall, Honor's door was open, the room glowing a soft gold from the light of the lamps on either side of the bed. Her skin glowed too, miles of smoothness displayed in a short, off-one-shoulder dress that appeared to be alternating slashes of black silk and black lace. Seated on the edge of the mattress and facing the door, her head was bent. She pursed her pretty mouth as she drew a sheer black stocking up her arm.

Bram had never seen a woman perform such a private, totally feminine act. If Alicia had ever worn pantyhose, let alone stockings, the memory was gone. And since her death . . . well, since her death the very few women he'd been near had only taken their clothing *off*.

So not one had ever slipped the gathered sheerness

from her slender hand. Not one had ever afforded him a glimpse of sweet, plump breasts glowing in the lamp-light as she leaned farther forward to point her pink-tipped toes through the circle of delicate mesh. Not one had smoothed a stocking up her slender ankle, rounded calf, over a knee. Never had he watched a woman casually draw up the hem of her dress to adjust a band of black lace against her smooth thigh.

That humming . . . vitality buzzed through him once again.

His gaze stumbled over the four inches of pale skin beyond the edge of her stocking to fix on a fascinating glimpse of pink satin panties. Maybe he made some sort of appreciative sound, because Honor suddenly yanked down her skirt and jumped to her feet.

"What do you think you're looking at?" she said, two spots of color high on her cheeks.

For a moment, Bram wondered if she really wanted him to state the obvious. Then he dragged his brain out of his pants, shaking his head to start it working again. "For God's sake, Honor," was the only response he could manage.

"What kind of answer is that?" she asked, crossing her arms over her chest.

He tried not to stare at her round, naked shoulder and wonder what she wore beneath the dress besides those panties and seduce-me stockings. "I . . ."

The foot of her still-bare leg tapped. He couldn't help but note that her toenails were painted the color of pink satin. She inhaled a quick breath through her nose and her face went redder. "Listen, buster. I . . . I don't like the way you're looking at me."

" 'Buster'?" Whether because he felt guilty or blame-less, he didn't know, but she was starting to piss him off again. "Let's get something straight here, princess. You were the one who left your door open."

Her foot froze, midtap. She opened her mouth, closed it.

Hah. No snappy comeback now, he thought, congratulating himself. Obviously this was just another of her spoiled-girl diversions, one he'd caught her at in midplay.

He hardened his mouth. "I don't know if you're an exhibitionist, princess," he said, his voice cold, "or if this is merely an attempt to befuddle me, but in either case, I'm *not* playing along."

Without another glance at her, he turned. "Come on. We're already late."

His palmtop in hand, he waited for her at the front door. When she finally stalked toward him, wearing both stockings and a pair of sexy high heels, he could feel her fuming. Well, that was just fine with him, he thought, ignoring the way the hair on his arms rose at the sight of her silky legs and those fuck-me-in-the-penthouse shoes. Her mood fed his, and it made a hell of a lot more sense to be angry with her than aroused by her.

Once on the driveway outside the house, he used the palmtop's thumbwheel to display the icons for the main security menu. He pressed the touchscreen to arm the house's system, then, walking to his nearby SUV, he pressed it again, selecting the icon that would release the car locks.

He didn't hear the telltale clicks. Frowning, he continued toward the vehicle. As Honor caught up with him, her elbow knocked lightly against his. An electrical shock burned up his arm. Grimacing, he pressed the touchscreen again.

No clicks now either, unless you counted the mad squeak of the windshield wipers as they suddenly came alive, frantically sliding back and forth along the dry glass.

"Shit." His fingers fumbled in his hurry, and instead of turning them off, his new entry caused the hazard lights to flash and the horn begin to beep. In the distance, Bram heard the half-repaired Fifo barking.

Honor scuttled closer to him, clearly apprehensive. "Is your dog loose?" She had to raise her voice to be heard over the noise.

Bram shook his head, fighting with the handheld, and fighting off a breath of Honor's rich-girl scent that was threatening his concentration. "No," he yelled back. "Fifo still isn't—"

The car went silent and inactive. "—working right," Bram finished, lowering his voice in disgust. "Just like everything else around here."

Shaking his head again, he dumped the handheld in one pocket and slid his keys out of the other. Then he opened the passenger door for Honor, shutting it behind her. Once he was in the driver's seat and had shut his own door, her scent hit him again.

In such close quarters, the luxurious, ultra-feminine smell acted like a slap. His headache vanished, but it brought his body to sudden alertness, to a keen awareness of Honor—those shoes, those legs, that skin—just inches away in the intimate darkness. In his mind's eye, he saw her slowly drawing on that stocking, the backsides of her thumbs running up the smooth warm flesh of her outer and inner thighs.

Before he could stop himself, he sucked in another long, addicting breath. It acted like a fuel, taking him to an aching, full-on arousal. Cursing inwardly, he shifted on the leather seat to adjust the fit of his slacks. Hoping like hell she had piss-poor night vision, he started the car and headed toward the party.

His house was situated at the end of a private lane off a country road outside of Hot Water. It was only a short drive, however, to the residential area of the town proper. He directed the car over the hilly terrain, along the narrow, crooked streets that had once been miners' trails but now led past established gardens and well-kept, Victorian-era homes.

The oldest buildings in town dated back to 1849 and were a mix of gingerbread storefronts and rustic structures built with hand-shaped bricks and native stone. In the early years of the Gold Rush, the mining camp of Hot Water had been busy, thanks to the seemingly limitless supply of gold in Piney Creek, as well as the steaming spring that bubbled in the nearby hills.

Yet when the gold had finally died out, Hot Water had not. The miners' tents had already given way to homes built for the families that followed them, and because of its central location in the Mother Lode country, the town continued to prosper.

Hot Water's history was a point of pride for its citizens, Bram included. He, like so many others in the area, was a direct descendant of those who'd survived in the rough, wild land. But surely, *surely* it could only hold a short-term appeal for a trust-fund bunny like Honor.

The comfort of that thought evaporated as he neared the large house that Kitty and Dylan were rehabbing. Cars crowded the street. Christ, he thought, people really were here for a party. His hands tightened on the steering wheel, a fingernail away from U-turning back to solitude and sanity. He didn't do parties.

But there was Dylan to think of.

And running away wouldn't mean escape from the woman by his side. Resigned, Bram found a parking spot, then jumped from the car, automatically moving around to Honor's door. She was already standing on the curb when he got there, a soft shawl-thing wrapped around her body. But her legs were covered in nothing but fine black mesh, miles of them that he knew began in pink silk the color of a blush.

The memory set his hackles rising again and in the meager moonlight he pinned her with his gaze. "You're on your own, party girl. I'm finding a corner and planting myself there." He grabbed her elbow, ignoring another hot jolt as he hauled her forward.

She pulled her arm from his grasp. "Bram."

Laughter erupted from the house, rippling through the night air. He turned his head toward the noise, and through the lit windows watched the chatting, exuberant guests. So much talk. Now more laughter. The clamor unsettled him, maybe because it sounded vaguely foreign, like a language he'd previously understood but couldn't interpret anymore.

Since Alicia had been murdered, so little of the world made sense to him.

"*Bram.*"

"What?" He turned his back on the house.

She hesitated, her naked shoulder peeking out from the shawl to lift, then fall. "There's one thing you should know. . . ."

He heard more laughter, but he found himself distracted from it by Honor's face, the meager moonlight enhancing those starlight eyes and night-dark hair. Without thinking, only wanting to touch something so pretty, something so warm and so close, his hand lifted toward the velvet skin of her cheek.

Then he remembered the last shock she'd given him. Shoving both fists in his pockets, he forced his mind back to what she'd said. "One thing? What one thing?"

"Well, um . . . as you anticipated, the town gossip mill has ground out an account of our wedding, that's all." Her gaze cut away from his and she shrugged again. "Including a motivation for our marriage."

A chilly blast rushed across the back of his neck. "Motivation?"

She looked up, the quarter moon's light catching in her silver eyes. "A slight variation on the real story."

That bad-omen chill blew over him again. "Define 'slight.' "

"Uh . . ." She bent her head to study her shoes.

"*Honor*." In his pockets, Bram's hands clenched tighter.

"It's your own fault, you're going to have to admit that." She looked up, defiantly meeting his gaze. "Because the town knows how private you are, apparently no one thinks it's odd that we married when we'd never actually been seen together. It's assumed that we were, um, well, carrying on behind closed doors."

"*What?*"

"When Kitty called last night, it was clear that she and everyone else thinks we married because we didn't want to spend one more hour apart. Why do you think she and Dylan are throwing this party?" Honor let the question linger for a moment. "The whole town believes we've fallen wildly, madly in love."

He stared at her, capability of speech, of movement, stunned straight out of him. In love? Were these people nuts? They should know that he'd rather be slow-broiling in hell than be in love again.

"And by the way . . ." Honor leaned close, as if she had a secret to share. Her rich-girl scent reached him a mind-numbing millisecond before her words. "Everyone is very, very happy for both of us."

By the time Bram stomped his way to Kitty and Dylan's front door, he managed to rediscover his voice. "I can't believe the gossips concocted such a load of bull," he muttered, casting a dark look at Honor.

"I think it's kind of sweet," she said.

"Sweet!"

She shrugged. "I have a thing for happy endings. So does Hot Water. How were *you* going to explain our marriage?"

He opened his mouth, closed it, his disgruntlement growing. He *hadn't* thought about explaining their marriage, and if he had, he would have thought about not explaining it at all. Because in his old life, the life of privacy and solitude that was looking more like paradise by the second, he didn't explain himself. He didn't go to parties. His dog worked, his car worked, and his brain stayed firmly above his waist at all times.

In his old life, he wasn't married to a woman who seemed as determined to like Hot Water as he was determined she would leave it.

Irritated even more, he scowled at Honor again. "I'm going to clear this up as soon as we get inside."

Something flickered in her eyes. She looked away.

"What now?" he demanded.

"I didn't say anything."

She didn't have to. He ground his back teeth together, certain there was something else on her mind. "Spill it."

"It's nothing to do with you." She wrapped her arms around herself. "It's just that . . . that once people find out my father—and by extension, me—forced you into the marriage, they won't accept me as quickly or easily as I'd hoped."

"For God's sake," he muttered. Even as he told himself her relationship with Hot Water was *not* his problem, he had to acknowledge she was right.

Though the town welcomed tourists, over the years it had spurned other wealthy outsiders who had traipsed in, eager to buy a piece of it. None of them had stayed. When the townspeople found out Honor had forced a Bennett into marriage . . .

"Damn it," he spit out, disgusted by his unwarranted prick of conscience. He should welcome her distress and hope it sent Her Pampered Highness hightailing it back to L.A. "Why are you here anyway? It can't be what you're used to. The town is remote, the people nosy, and the only thing that ever changes is the date on the calendar."

"If you really want to know," she answered quietly. "That *is* why I'm here. I've had my fill of changes."

He snorted. "Yeah? Those upgrades from gold to platinum cards wore me out too."

"Between age five and eighteen," she said, her voice going quieter, "I went to seven separate boarding schools. Not to mention a different camp every summer."

He stilled. "What the hell were your parents thinking?"

"My mother died when I was four. I suppose my fa-

ther was thinking he had no idea what to do with a little girl." Honor shrugged. "So he kept trying out new
things."

"I hope you pitched a fit or two."

She shook her head. "Not one. He was the only . . .
connection I had. I don't think I dared risk it."

"Jesus—" Bram started, then caught himself as he
realized she was playing him like a harp. He crossed
his arms over his chest. "What does all that have to do
with living in Hot Water?"

"I've been the new girl a thousand times. I always
said the wrong thing or went about things wrong or
didn't wear the new uniform quite right. I never fit in. I
never belonged."

"So now you think you want to belong *here*?" It still
didn't make any sense to him.

"Here is perfect," she replied. "A small town with
long-held traditions. Heritage Day in August. The excitement of the high school football season and the
Homecoming game. Christmas customs. I want to be
part of all that."

Bram rolled his eyes. "Hot Water is a place, not a
Frank Capra movie. The 'Christmas customs' are not
that—"

"They have to be better than Witherspoon rituals.
One December twenty-fifth my father and I met for an
hour in the de Gaulle Airport to exchange gifts. Another year I flew from school in Vermont to L.A., only
to discover my father and I had our signals crossed. He
was holidaying in Bampf, not Bel Air. It was too late to
get a flight, so . . ." She shrugged.

An image of Christmas in Hot Water popped into
his head. Lights strung up throughout the town. Shop-
keepers passing to husbands the hints their wives had

dropped. The local fraternal organization, the Independent Order of Odd Fellows, decorated an outdoor tree by the—

Bram put a halt on his sentimental wanderings. The woman was doing it again, damn it, getting under his skin in order to get her own who-cared-why way.

"Yeah," he said, his voice dry with cynicism. "I understand it all now. The Poor Little Rich Girl. As a matter of fact, princess, I read the book."

Her body stiffened. "I didn't tell you so you'd feel sorry for me—" she began hotly, then broke off, shaking her head. She let out a laugh that sounded half amused, half ashamed. "Oh, fine, maybe I did."

Setting his jaw, he spun away from that face and that oddly sweet laugh, more determined than ever to set the record straight about their marriage. He lifted his fist and pounded it against the door.

Kitty Wilder—no, Kitty *Matthews*, since she was recently married to Dylan—opened it and gazed on them with patent delight. "You're here!"

She gripped them each by a wrist and pulled them over the threshold and into the foyer. Her long blond hair swirled around her shoulders as she quickly kissed Bram's cheek, then Honor's. Her smile went wide as she stepped back to survey them. "You make a fabulous couple."

Bram took a breath. "About that—"

"For a while I thought you'd never open yourself up again, Bram," Kitty said, sobering. Her voice turned husky and her blue eyes went suspiciously bright. "I'm so glad you did."

"Listen, Kitty," he started, then stopped. "What do you mean, 'open yourself up'?"

"Oh, don't listen to me," she answered, laughing

even as she wiped away a tear with a hand that bore a shiny gold wedding band. "Dylan calls me a sappy romantic, and I suppose he's right."

Bram glanced at Honor, but she was no help. "Kitty, we need to—that is, I need to—"

"Rescue the party," his hostess finished for him, grabbing their wrists again. She towed him and Honor in the direction of the living room. "Emily Murphy brought a date who's giving lectures instead of politely mingling."

Before Bram could take a breath, he was facing a roomful of forty or so people, most of whom he'd known his entire life.

"Hey, everybody," Kitty called out. She forced Honor's hand into his. "It's the bride and groom!"

A ragged cheer erupted. Then, before he could explain the true nature of the marriage, everyone rushed forward, all of them talking at once. His slack grip on Honor's fingers was broken and they were separated. Heavy palms slapped his back. Women kissed his cheek. A champagne glass was shoved in his hand.

Bram couldn't seize control of the situation, let alone make sense of it. Half of the group in the room had worked for him at Enigma, a few when the company was little more than his desperate need to lose himself in work. The rest he'd known for years as well, but he couldn't recall a time when these people had appeared quite so enthused around him. So happy.

His gut knotted. Oh, hell. They were happy *for him*.

Honor was right. How gloomy, how boring *had* he been all these years?

He tossed that thought aside, and his gaze snagged on a familiar figure striding into the room. "Dylan," Bram yelled, in desperate need of a moment's relief from all the good-natured, embarrassing chatter. He pushed through the knot of well-wishers.

Bram's breaths came easier as he moved toward his oldest friend. Seeing Dylan recalled the Bram who he had once been, the Bram whose thorniest problem was a recalcitrant bicycle chain and who needed only explain simple things like late homework and broken curfews.

Dylan grabbed Bram's hand, pumped it, smiling an all-out grin. "You dog. I told Kitty I wouldn't believe the news until you showed up at the party. And here you are."

"About the party. You have to help me clear up . . ." He gestured with his hand, sloshing champagne across his wrist.

Dylan grimaced and plucked the glass away. "Come with me and I'll get you a drink more substantial than that bubbly shit."

Following his friend, Bram welcomed the chance to escape the crowd. He'd wet his whistle with something other than champagne, then enlist Dylan's help in untangling the marriage story.

He glanced around as they moved in the direction of the kitchen. Most of the partygoers were gathered around Kitty and Honor, so a stranger—a young man with a messy tangle of hair and a straggly soul patch—standing by himself at the fireplace caught Bram's attention.

"Who's that?" he asked Dylan, nodding in the kid's direction.

Dylan snorted. "Emily Murphy's latest odd choice. One of Beau Caruso's people."

Bram frowned. "Mia's dad?" Mia cleaned and cooked for him part-time, but she was quiet and rarely mentioned her father. "He has 'people'? I thought he was a mostly retired painting contractor."

Dylan pushed open the swinging kitchen door and gestured Bram inside. "You know what Beau's been going around spouting, don't you?"

Bram shook his head.

Dylan's eyebrows rose. "That's right. You really do live in a cave. But Honor will change that."

Bram opened his mouth to deny it, then closed it again. In a minute he'd tell the truth. *It's a marriage of co-incidence*, he'd say, her rich-girl whims bisecting with his sense of responsibility to the town. "What's this about Beau?"

"He says he was abducted by aliens."

Bram gawked at his friend. "What?"

"A few months ago he went off on one of his toots, then showed up at the county sheriff's at midnight, drunk as a skunk and claiming he'd seen a UFO and had been abducted by aliens."

"*Aliens?*" First heiresses, now aliens. And he'd just told Honor the town never changed. "What the hell is happening around here?"

Dylan shook his head. "I only know that Beau claims a 'close encounter' on Gold Dust Road."

Bram frowned. "Enigma has property along Gold Dust Road. There's nothing out there but empty fields."

"If you ask me, Beau's head is empty too. But he's got himself a website now, not to mention more than a few followers like our buddy out there. They're certain the mother ship is coming back to Hot Water." Dylan grinned. "Can you believe it? A UFO."

A UFO. Bram was still trying to wrap his mind around the ridiculous idea as Dylan opened the refrigerator and drew out a couple of long-neck beers. Leaning against the appliance, he shoved one at Bram. They simultaneously twisted off the tops, then tilted back the bottles.

Bram downed half his in one swallow, then met Dylan's gleaming eyes. His friend lifted his beer in tribute. "This marriage business gives a man a mighty thirst," he said, his voice full of laughter. "I know that's true."

Oh, hell, Bram thought. He'd been distracted by the crazy notion of UFOs and aliens. "Dylan, about that—"

"Wait." Dylan's expression turned serious. "First let me tell you how glad I am about all this. I—" He broke off, downed some more of his beer, then smiled ruefully. "I've felt a little guilty, being back home, being so happy with Kitty, knowing that—"

"Alicia's death wasn't your fault," Bram interrupted, his gut coiling. He hated Dylan's doubts as much as he hated the questions that tortured himself. "I never thought it was."

"But—"

"Can't we talk about something else?" Bram's gut twisted tighter. Nothing Dylan could say about Alicia's death could help either one of them.

Dylan's expression lightened. "Yeah. Okay. But I've gotta tell you that knowing you have Honor, knowing that you found love and married again, it's . . . it's going to make it a hell of a lot easier for me to enjoy *my* life and *my* marriage."

Bram's hand contracted on the sweaty bottle. He opened his mouth, but then couldn't speak, not with the suddenly clumsy tongue he found there. Squeezing the bottle in his fist even harder, Bram tipped back his head and drained the rest of the beer.

But he still couldn't talk, not even when Dylan told

him they had to get back to the party. Instead, he obediently trudged out of the kitchen. There would be no en-
listing Dylan's aid now, because there was no way
Bram could face Dylan one-on-one and tell him the
truth of the Bennett-Witherspoon wedding. Not when
the other man had just said Bram's marriage made Dylan's own happiness easier to enjoy.

Bram would break the news to Dylan at the same
time he told all the other happy partygoers.

Shit.

"Shit," Dylan echoed as they reentered the living
room. "Emily's weirdo date is at it again."

The other guests were gathered near the fireplace at
the far end of the long room, listening politely to the
odd young man.

"I'm only a simple courier, of course," he was saying. "The one who has seen them, spoken with them,
and actually heard their message for himself is Beau
Caruso."

Despite the curious words, Bram's attention wandered until he found Honor. She was standing at the
edge of the group, looking as natural sipping champagne as other women looked drinking diet soda. The
other guests had left a bubble of space around her, giving the impression she was alone in the crowd.

The new girl, Bram thought, then immediately
cursed himself for it.

Dylan's voice lowered. "Who would have guessed
I was playing matchmaker when we were locked up
together?"

Bram glanced over. His friend was looking at Honor,
of course. After leaving Hot Water, Dylan had joined
the FBI and then several months ago been part of an attempt to rescue Honor from her kidnappers. At the

time, Bram had given the widely publicized story only cursory attention, but he knew that when the attempt went awry, Dylan had shared her captivity for four days until they were both successfully freed.

"You must have said something that made her fall for the town," Bram said. "I'll give you that."

"She was pretty desperate for a distraction. Suddenly I found myself telling her everything about Hot Water," Dylan admitted. "She was fascinated."

"See?" Bram pushed away thoughts of Honor's desperation even as a knot twisted in his belly again. "It was Hot Water. You didn't make her fall for *me*."

Dylan grinned. "How do you know I didn't tell her about you too? Do you think you could possibly work this fast on your own?"

"Believe me, I *know*. You didn't make her fall for me."

Dylan shrugged, still smiling. "I suppose you do. You're her husband, after all. The man who's in love with her."

The knot in Bram's belly jerked tight. *That's it*, he thought. He couldn't keep the truth to himself a second longer. "Listen, you need to understand—"

"Hey, everybody!" Kitty stood in the doorway that led to the dining room and clapped her hands, then used them to beckon the crowd forward. "It's time for cake. It's time for a toast to the bride and groom."

Dylan immediately hurried to help his wife. Bram didn't hesitate either, joining the wave of people following their hostess's directions. He even made it a point to glance around and catch Honor's eye, letting her know with a look what he was about to tell the crowd. She responded with an accepting half shrug, the ends of her dark hair sliding over that one bare, smooth shoulder.

Lust came out of nowhere and jabbed him with another hot-wire poke, but he ignored it.

As his elbow jostled that of the soul-patched "courier" on the way into the dining room, Bram's determination redoubled. With his world going crazy around him—UFOs and heiress love-brides!—it was time to restore at least partial order.

It was time for the truth.

Chapter Four

*B*ram's world cartwheeled again, though, when he was ushered toward the cake Kitty was serving. It was a *wedding* cake, two round tiers complete with white icing, white icing roses, and topped with a bride and groom. The small plastic figures were dogs—dogs!—one a morose Great Dane-ish type, the other, complete with gauzy veil and pink-tipped toenails, a snobby-looking, fancy-clipped white poodle.

Beside him, Honor took one look at the absurd sight, then quickly drained the contents of her champagne glass and half hiccuped. "Oh, my."

My God.

He resisted the urge to close his eyes and pretend he was somewhere else. Suppressing a sigh, he cast a questioning look at Kitty.

She beamed back at him. "The cake was made specially for you, Bram. Annette and Joan wanted me to express their congratulations and hopes for your happiness."

Then she colored and made a quick gesture at the

unexpected bridal couple perched in the icing. "Sorry about the pooch cake topper, though. Old Mrs. Percy came in the bakery when I was picking up the cake and she insisted I wait while she went home for it. It's good luck, she wanted me to tell you. It topped her own cake in 1962, when she wed Mr. Singer. She said he was the best husband of the four she married."

Bram shook his head. "I'm . . ." *Screwed*, he thought. This was what happened when you let feelings in. When you allowed yourself to care about people. You agreed to go to a party, and then you were presented with a cakeload of more complications. "I'm . . ."

"Overwhelmed," Honor inserted. "I'm sure Bram will take the time to tell Mrs. Percy how much he appreciates her thoughtfulness."

Yeah. Right after he explained to her that she'd shared her family heirloom to celebrate a marriage made at the end of an economic shotgun.

Sure, he'd talk to Mrs. Percy, and then he'd have a word with Annette and Joan at the bakery too. His mood going darker, he studied the still-smiling Kitty. Of course, that would be *after* he told his oldest friend's wife—who was right this minute wearing her sappy, romantic heart on her sleeve—that there wasn't any good reason to throw a party, let alone serve a wedding cake, with or without plastic dog-groom and dog-bride.

Kitty moved off to round up a few straggling guests while Dylan circled the room, a champagne bottle in each hand. He was topping off the glasses of forty happy, chattering people who—maybe—wouldn't be so very disappointed when Bram explained how things really stood. But there still would be Dylan to look in the eye, the man who had wrongly blamed himself for Alicia's death. The man who had just confessed he would be more comfortable with his own happiness since Bram was married to Honor.

He swung around to glare at her, the cause of all this mess. She was busily working on another glass of champagne, probably trying to numb herself for the moment of truth ahead.

Noticing his regard, she lowered her glass an inch. There was a drop of liquid on her lower lip and her tongue found it. "Nice party, huh?"

He grunted in response.

She gulped another swallow of champagne. "Of course, I suppose you'd rather be home waxing your dog."

His attention jerked from her mouth to the words that had just come out of it. *"What?"*

"Fifo," she explained, all innocence. "You have to care for him more like a car than a real canine, right?"

He narrowed his eyes. "Hah, hah."

"Seriously, though, it could be a marketing point. Why take your beloved pet to a dog groomer when an auto detailer will do?" A little laugh escaped her mouth that was half giggle, half hiccup.

He shook his head. "Have you had too much champagne?"

"Probably. I'm always nervous at parties. I want people to like me." She let out another giggly hiccup, then leaned close and stage-whispered, "I wanted *you* to like me. Can you believe it?"

He shook his head again. "No more for you," he said, reaching for her glass.

She held it out of range. "Champagne is a girl's best friend."

"I thought that was diamonds."

She frowned as if struck by a new thought, then held out her left hand. "You didn't give me one."

No, but her father had had the gall to send them his-and-hers platinum wedding bands. Honor's circled her ring finger. Peering over at Bram now, her frown deepened. "You're not wearing yours."

"I work with my hands," he replied, then kicked himself for bothering to explain. He'd never worn a wedding ring before and he didn't want to be married now.

Honor gave the sage nod of the tipsy. "And you work with your mind too. Don't forget your mind. But what about your heart?" She tipped her glass, drained it, then smiled up at him. "Oh, that's right. You don't have one. Just like your robot."

He smiled back. Grimly. "Thank you."

"Powered by the Jarvik-7," she said, her sloppy gesture causing her beringed left hand to brush his chest.

He pushed her fingers away. They seemed to burn.

"Jarvik-7?" It was the name of the first human-tested artificial hearts. "You surprise me, Honor."

"You surprise me too." She leaned confidential-close again. "I always thought you nerdy guys didn't have good bodies." Her hand gestured carelessly once more.

Bram leaped back, as much to get away from the po-tentially electric touch as the insult. *Nerdy?* But before he could think what to do or what to say in response, Dylan called out.

"A toast," he said. The room hushed.

"Whoops," Honor's voice broke into the quiet, and she lifted her glass. "I'm empty." Her bright smile looked fuzzy around the edges. "More, please."

Bram narrowed his eyes. Had he thought her tipsy? Hell, she was speeding straight toward drunk.

He watched Dylan refill her glass, which she slurped half down even before the other man ended his brief best-wishes speech. "To Bram and Honor!" Dylan finally concluded.

Honor obediently chugged her champagne, then hiccupped again. She grabbed the table as she wobbled on those ridiculously sexy shoes. Rolling his eyes, Bram moved closer, preparing to save her from falling face first into the cake.

Nerdy insult or not, there was Mrs. Percy's Great Dane and the poodle to think of, after all.

"Kiss, kiss!" someone yelled. "Come on, Bram, kiss her."

"Yeah, a kiss!" The rest of the guests took up the chant.

Honor's spine straightened. She swayed a bit, but he could tell she was suddenly on alert, her champagne-dulled brain preparing for Bram not to kiss her, but condemn her. Her body half turned toward his, and his gaze landed on her profile with its perfect nose and stubborn, half-dimpled chin.

He didn't need to see her eyes to imagine them, their clear silver the color of starlight. *Here is perfect*, he remembered her saying, those eyes shining.

"Oh, hell," he muttered, making a sudden and unjustifiable decision.

He wasn't giving up on regaining his solitude, and he didn't care a whit about Honor, but all at once he found he didn't care for making her life with the townspeople difficult either.

Braced for another static jolt, he put his hands on her

shoulders and turned her toward him. But instead of a shock, he felt a shiver. Her shiver. She looked up, uneasiness and confusion written across her face. Breathing deep, he leaned over her.

She stiffened, bowing her body away from his.

He tightened his fingers and hauled her nearer, bending his head to bring his mouth beside her ear. "I thought you said the town thinks we're wildly, madly in love," he murmured.

Under his hands, another shiver shook her body. "Wh-what are you saying?" she whispered.

"I'm saying you better make this look good."

Then he pulled her closer and slid his lips from her earlobe across the soft velvet of her cheek. He heard her quick, indrawn breath, and then he found her mouth.

Her lips were smooth and cool and he angled his head to rub his against them. To warm them up, he thought vaguely. Her body was still stiff beneath his hands and he suddenly wanted to change that too. He gentled his touch, palming her shoulders instead of gripping them, but he hardened his mouth, wanting, demanding, needing . . . needing to make this look good.

Yeah, that was it.

Her body slowly relaxed against his, as degree by degree her mouth softened. Heaviness gathered at Bram's groin as he ran his tongue over her lips, pushing against them, pushing between the seam to enter her slick heat.

She tasted rich. Expensive and exotic, like desert-dry champagne and delicious, unfamiliar fruit.

His tongue brushed against hers and he tasted something else, something hidden and hot, but that pulsed with energy. Her body started to finely tremble, as if charged. He kissed her deeper, that dark, hot energy of hers bursting on his tongue. It surged through his bloodstream to carry a startling message.

Inside his pampered, uptown bride was passion. Electricity. Sex.

Untapped sex.

His lower body got the news first, surging toward readiness. He yanked her against him, instinct demanding to discover more, to bring to light what she was hiding. He withdrew his tongue, thrust inside again, and—

She shoved him away.

They stared at each other, both of them breathing hard. In the distance, Bram heard enthusiastic applause and a couple of catcalls. His blood was still pumping like a madman's, unwilling to accept that there was nowhere for this kick-ass-quick, savage arousal to go.

He rubbed his palm over his face and turned toward the admiring crowd, trying to cool down, trying to think, trying to convince himself he hadn't made a colossal mistake.

Because he hadn't only tasted Honor's naked, electrifying passion.

He'd also tasted panic.

No! That made her vulnerable. Breakable. Unprotected.

He refused to let those perilous ideas take root in his mind, because, even worse, they might make her need him.

THE loud morning calls of the birds added an unpleasant countertempo to the faint pounding of Honor's too-much-champagne headache. She tried ignoring them both and sat down at the small desk in her bed-room, hoping to lose herself and the memory of that kiss in the stack of paperwork in front of her.

That mistaken, magnificent, hot, hopeless kiss.

Rubbing her temples, she focused on the reports. The paperwork described the day-to-day details of running Hot Water's Old Town, the six-block tourist at-traction that her father had purchased and would be Honor's to manage when it opened on Memorial Day.

After college graduation she'd joined the Wither-spoon Corporation at her father's insistence. Because he wanted her to learn from the ground up, she'd spent the last few years taking short-term assignments at a succession of Witherspoon holdings. But there had never been a more fitting job for her than this. The tourist attraction re-created life in a Gold Rush boom-town of the 1850s, so she would be responsible for pre-serving the history of the very place where she wanted to dig her own roots deep.

One of the trauma counselors her father had dragged her to after the kidnapping decreed that Honor now had a "heightened fear of abandonment"—it was only natural, the woman had said. But whatever the diagnosis, Honor knew the cure was to be con-nected, to belong, to never again experience the deep, lonely despair she'd felt while waiting helplessly in that darkness.

When Dylan had described his hometown, she'd known that in Hot Water she would find what she needed.

Of course, she'd never expected Bram. Or last night's kiss.

He'd been motivated by an unexpected streak of kindness, she was sure, and she'd been too surprised to fend him off. What had startled her next was her own response. There had been an initial, stomach-clenching disquiet, but then his mouth had honed in on hers and she'd lit up. The heat had flashed over her and she'd been so shocked by the sensation that she'd wrenched away.

Her faced burned at the memory even now. Not only was it confusing to find herself feeling so suddenly sexual, but it was embarrassing to feel so *overwhelmingly* sexual toward a man who didn't even like her.

They hadn't discussed the matter at all.

After their embrace last night, she'd been too dizzy and too tipsy to do more than eat her portion of wedding cake and then collapse gratefully in Bram's car when he said it was time to go.

The distant clatter of dishes reached her ears, signaling someone was moving about the kitchen. She blinked and glanced across the hallway to his closed bedroom door. Somehow he'd gotten past her.

Though she was nervous about facing him, she had to thank him for the kiss. And then there was that other, hazier memory nagging at her too. She was pretty sure she'd insulted him last night. And maybe his dog. She knew she'd called him a nerd.

Wincing at the recollection, she pushed out of her chair and headed for the kitchen and Bram. Yes, indeed. She had to make amends.

But it wasn't Bram she found in the sunny room. Instead, Honor encountered a dark-haired young woman, her voluptuous body enveloped in a floral apron. Pausing in the act of pouring a mug of coffee from that George Jetson-esque coffeemaker, she looked up and gave Honor a diffident, though friendly, smile.

"Good morning, Mrs. Bennett."

Honor stifled the impulse to look around for the "Mrs. Bennett" the other woman had addressed. Of course, it was Mia Caruso in the apron, Bram's part-time housekeeper. Of course, "Mrs. Bennett" was none other than Honor herself.

"Please, there's no need to call me that," she said quickly.

"Ms. Witherspoon, then?"

She shook her head and leaned forward to accept the steaming mug offered to her. "Honor, please. And you're Mia, right?"

The housekeeper smiled again, her white teeth a pretty contrast to her golden-hued skin. "Yes. We should have met last night at Kitty and Dylan's, but my father received some unexpected visitors and I stayed home to help serve refreshments."

"Ah." If Honor had the relationships right, Mia's father was none other than Beau Caruso, alien contactee. Hmmm. Was it possible that the "unexpected visitors" had arrived from another galaxy?

As if reading her thoughts, the outside corners of Mia's brown eyes tilted up in quiet amusement. "In case you're wondering, they looked like your normal, carbon-based life-forms to me."

Honor laughed and took a few steps to pull out a stool drawn up to the long butcher-block island. "You caught me. I met an admirer of your father's last night and heard a little about his . . . beliefs."

"I understand." Mia turned to fetch sugar, creamer, and spoon, which she set in front of Honor. "Would you like something for breakfast?"

"Oh, no, thank you." The first sip of hot coffee almost burned away the last of her headache, but she wasn't quite ready for food. "I can help myself later.

Though you wouldn't happen to know if there's aspirin nearby?"

Mia crossed to a cabinet. Her hair was glossy and waved down her back. With her golden skin and abundant hourglass figure, she looked as if she belonged in Tuscany, raising a brood of laughing bambinos. Honor could almost hear the accordion music her mustachioed Italian husband would play at night, happy chords that sang of the most basic of joys. Home. Family. Love.

All the basic joys that Honor hoped to find in Hot Water.

Mia returned with a bottle and shook two tablets into Honor's cupped palm. "I hope you're feeling all right."

Honor couldn't keep herself from smiling again. If Mia looked like a Tuscan beauty, her instant, natural warmth was like a beam of Tuscan sun. "I'm fine. Just a bit too much champagne last night."

Mia nodded with sympathy. "I had an experience like that myself a few months back. Silly me, thinking a celebration *required* champagne. Bram suggested Dom Perignon, and I liked the taste, but by the next morning I could only think it was a horribly expensive headache."

Dom Perignon? It must have been a big something to celebrate, Honor thought. She opened her mouth to ask what, but before she could get the question out, Mia surprised her again by sliding a gift-wrapped box her way.

"This is for you," she said, her smile very shy. "A bridal gift."

Guilt pinched her. "Oh, Mia, you shouldn't have . . ." Honor began, but, worried she might appear ungracious, she shut her mouth and unwrapped the box. Her eyes widened as she lifted a filmy, barely-anything white nightgown from a bed of tissue paper.

Mia's cheeks were red. "I hope you like it. It's something I would give my eyeteeth to be able to wear, but . . ." She glanced down at her rounded curves and shrugged.

"It's beautiful," Honor replied, touched by the thoughtful gesture as well as Mia's self-consciousness about her lush figure. "Thank you very much."

"I'm so happy for Bram," Mia said.

Honor lowered her eyes and was silent for a long moment. Keeping her gaze on the nightgown, she slowly folded it, then carefully returned it to the box. How alone had Bram been?

"We haven't had much time to get to know each other," Honor finally said, glancing up. "Can you tell me what his life was like, um, before me?"

"There was only Enigma," Mia replied. "He tried to bury himself in it."

Honor ran a finger along the edge of the gift box. "Then maybe it was a good sign that he sold it to my father."

Mia crossed with the coffeepot to refill Honor's cup. "I think he gave up believing that the company would take away his pain," she said matter-of-factly. "He's only become more isolated since."

Honor rubbed at the sudden ache in her chest. "You're an astute judge of character."

"Oh." The younger woman flushed, as if suddenly realizing she'd been discussing her employer with his wife. "I shouldn't have said anything, especially when I like to stick close to home myself."

Taking pity on her, Honor changed the subject. "Then the men must be lining up at your front door."

Mia blinked big brown eyes, looking startled by the very idea. "That's very kind of you to say, but no." With quick footsteps she hastened to the sink. "Let me just say again how happy I am that Bram took another chance and brought a living, breathing woman into his life."

For six weeks minus two days, Honor thought, remembering her rash promise to him. But surely she couldn't be the first woman he'd been linked with? Rearranging the nightgown in the box, she fussed with the tissue and debated the line between curiosity and gossip.

With her gaze still trained on the present, she finally gave in. "Wasn't there . . . hasn't he had someone else, some other woman in the past eight years?"

When Mia didn't answer, she glanced up. Instead of the housekeeper's brown eyes and shy smile, it was Bram who was staring down at her. Honor looked wildly about, but Mia was no longer in the kitchen. A telltale heat crawled up her neck.

Bram appeared cool as always, though, his hair shower-damp, his green eyes expressionless. As he slowly folded his arms over his broad chest, she searched his hard-edged face for that kindness he'd shown the night before. She was supposed to be making amends, remember?

"Exactly what about last night's kiss," he asked, one eyebrow lifting in that humorless way he had, "makes you think I'm out of practice?"

BRAM watched Honor, enjoying her discomfort as a second flush of embarrassed color washed over her face. She deserved the feeling, damn it, for trying to pump Mia for information about him. "Well?" he prompted.

Obviously trying to avoid answering, she slid off her stool and walked away from him, toward the kitchen sink. Bram's body jolted, and he swore silently.

She wore a clinging, raspberry-colored top that encased her body from shoulders to wrists and neck to waist. But it did nothing to cover a six-centimeter strip of bare skin between the bottom hem of her shirt and the band of her hip-hugging jeans that might, *might* be big enough for a three-inch zipper.

From his backside perspective, the pants scarcely covered the cleft in her pretty round ass. *Christ.* He closed his eyes, trying to imagine himself back in the freezing shower he'd just climbed out of.

But his eyes popped open again, in time to see her stretch for a water glass. The hem of her top rode higher, revealing the naked curve of her waist. Bram jammed his fists in his pockets and curled the fingers of his right hand around the hard case of his palmtop.

Then Honor spun around, leaning against the sink. Her face was still pink and she didn't quite meet his eyes. "Well, uh . . . about the kiss . . ."

His gaze ran from her flushed face down to the slice of belly revealed by those outrageous jeans, snagging on the tight whorl of her navel. He'd never noticed how sexual a belly button could be. It was tight, like a woman's aroused nipples, but closed, like her soft center folds before a man had parted them with his fingers or his mouth or his— *Jesus Christ.*

He shook his head to clear it. What had she just said? The kiss. That was a hell of a topic to sharpen his mind on. He remembered the order of her reaction: alarm, then fire, then back again to something close to fear. Yet under it all, that needy, electrical pulse of sex.

But he'd promised himself not to think of any of it, so he set his jaw and tried to appear as unaffected as a sleepless night and a cold shower could make a man. His brows rose. "Ah. So you *do* have a complaint?"

She put the water glass aside and tugged on her top, pulling the stretchy fabric down. Her wet tongue slid out to lick her lips. "No, of course not. I, uh, wanted to say it was very considerate of you, uh, under the circumstances. Thank you."

Thank him? He set his back teeth. She better not be thinking he was now reconciled to some touchy-feely, nicey-wifey temporary marriage. He was still bent on finding a way to get rid of her quickly, so he sure as hell hadn't kissed her to earn her gratitude. He'd kissed her because . . .

Maybe because the party had been so noisy. So full of expectant faces. The voices, the laughter, the smiles, he'd felt them hammering at him, trying to chip away at his defenses.

It had unbalanced him, unsettled him, because he couldn't afford that kind of damage. The barrier he put between himself and everyone else was how he endured, damn it. And enduring was the best he hoped for—except at twilight, when he still allowed himself to beg for peace.

"Don't get the wrong idea," he snapped, holding tight to his anger. Last night was all Honor's fault. Her passing fancy for a bucolic life in his town had dragged him to that noisy party and back to the noisy, hazardous world of expectations and emotions. But, damn it, the next time he wouldn't let her get away with it.

The next time he would just say no. "I didn't do it for you."

"Oh. Well." Her face fell from an awkward earnestness to . . . he didn't know what to call it.

And he didn't want to know, because despite his stupid lapse in judgment the night before, he didn't want to spend his time or energy deciphering her moods. Without another glance at her bewitching face or her distracting body, he stalked out of the kitchen and escaped through the front door.

Sliding his palmtop from his pocket, he tapped on the touchscreen as he strode down the driveway. To his right, one of the doors of the four-bay detached garage opened and Fifo rolled out, its gait smooth, its amber-colored motion sensors blinking like eyes. After repairing the Honor-induced damage and adding a few enhancements, Bram had finished reassembling the robotic dog following last night's party.

He touched the palmtop again and Fifo accelerated, racing down the driveway toward the front gate at its top speed of fifteen miles per hour. Its metallic snout an inch from collision, Fifo smoothly turned and rushed toward Bram. Reaching his feet, the dog paused, settling back on its haunches with a creaky squeal.

Frowning, Bram put the robot in standby mode and squatted to inspect the hip hinges. Then the faint rustle of something moving in the brush beyond the rock wall made him go still. He turned his head toward the noise and heard it again, now farther off.

"Is Fifo all better now?" Honor's cheery voice drifted toward him, an instant before a breath of her luxurious scent floated by.

Ignoring her, Bram cocked his head in the direction of that rustle. When it faded away, he grimaced. Over the last week, both he and Mia had spotted a stray dog in the surrounding woods. If it hung around much longer, he would have to catch the thing and get it a home away from here.

"Is Fifo all better?" Honor repeated, coming closer.

Bram glanced over at her, only to find that his position put him eye level with that disturbing slice of bare belly skin. Tension gripped his neck. He grunted at her, then used the palmtop to trigger the outdoor security cameras along the wall. Though he rarely activated them during the day, especially when he was at the house, something about the rustling bushes and that glimpse of Honor's pale flesh made her seem too . . . He refused to even think the word "vulnerable."

"What do you want now?" he muttered, standing.

"I wasn't sure we'd finished our conversation."

He glanced at her. She'd slipped some trendy, rimless sunglasses on her short nose. Like her top, the lenses and the stems were raspberry-colored and her mouth was painted raspberry too. She looked like the sweetest, smoothest, most expensive item on the dessert cart at some ritzy five-star restaurant.

Which made him think of the primitive burn of her kiss, its desperate aftertaste, the almost-frightened bite of her fingers when she'd pushed him away. "We are definitely done with that conversation," he replied, shoving it out of his mind again and returning his attention to Fifo.

He switched the dog from standby mode to active. With another squeak of joints, it straightened all four legs, then shifted to face Honor. Sunlight glinted off its teeth as it opened its mouth and emitted a low growl.

Honor stepped half behind Bram. "That dog hates me."

"Of course not." Frowning, Bram touched an icon on the handheld's screen to display the program that controlled the robot. "It wasn't supposed to do that. I added some new features I haven't completely debugged yet." He rotated the handheld's thumbwheel to scroll through the lines of code.

Its light sensor eyes still fixed on Honor, Fifo responded with a short hop forward, snarling.

"I'm telling you," Honor said, her voice wobbling a little. "He dislikes me."

Bram rolled his eyes. "It's a security device, Honor. A machine." Still rotating the thumbwheel, Bram scanned the program, trying to see where he'd gone wrong. Fifo let out another snarl and snapped its teeth.

Honor scuttled directly behind Bram. Feeling a tug at the back of his jeans, he glanced over his shoulder to see her peering around him at Fifo, her eyes wide over those froufrou glasses. One of her manicured fingers was hooked on Bram's belt loop. He told himself not to notice.

Fifo snapped again.

Her finger flexed in response, tugging on his pants. "Bram, seriously. That dog distrusts me."

He lost his temper. It was everything: the sleepless night, the bugs in Fifo's program, Honor's hold on him, her skin, her mouth, her scent. Her scent. Her skin. Her mouth. Her hold on him. That kiss.

That goddamn kiss that made him feel carnal and maybe even curious, but that wasn't going to make him care.

He spun to face her, his voice cold and controlled, even while he thought the top of his head might explode. "Fifo is made of titanium and processors. Circuits and screws. It doesn't hate you. It doesn't dislike you or even distrust you. It doesn't feel anything for you at all, do you understand?"

She took a step back.

But he wasn't relenting, not when she was churning up a thousand unwelcome sensations inside him. Even as he fought to master them, he strode forward to shove the palmtop in her hand. "It's all right here. Circuits and processors. Motherboard and microchips. Zero feelings. None. The dog's not controlled by any emotion it feels for you, but by the handheld." He curled her fingers over it. "See for yourself."

She stared at the electronic device as if she'd never seen one before. Gingerly cupped in her palm, she held it away from her body. "This isn't a good idea, Bram."

"It's a great idea," he said roughly. "You need to understand. *No* feelings."

"*You* don't understand—"

"Press the icon on the bottom right of the touchscreen and the dog will sit for you," he commanded.

"Bram—"

"Press it!"

Biting her lip, she obeyed.

But instead of resting on his haunches, Fifo spun a three-sixty, then beelined for the gate.

"Damn it, Honor, I said the icon on the bottom right."

"It *was* the icon on the bottom right!"

Bram shook his head in disgust, but he merely watched Fifo barrel toward the gate, knowing from the test he'd run just minutes before that at the last instant the dog would sense the barrier, pivot, and then return their way.

So Bram wasn't the least bit braced when that detour didn't happen. He wasn't the least bit braced for the earsplitting crash that followed either.

"Oh, no." Honor moaned.

Frozen, Bram just stared.

Honor ran past him toward the metal disaster lying on the driveway, holding out the palmtop and madly pressing the touchscreen as if she were speed-surfing through television channels. "Wake up, Fifo! Wake up, puppy!"

Skidding to a halt at the remains of the dog, she glanced back at Bram, her sunglasses slipping down her nose. "I think he's okay." Still pressing the touchscreen indiscriminately, she looked back down at the dog. "I think he's just taking a catnap or something."

A catnap?

Dumbfounded, he continued to stand there, watching her fingers tapping frantically. Then his brain finally reengaged as an electronic hum penetrated his half-paralyzed consciousness. "Honor, the handheld. Don't push—" Too late.

Movement caught his eye. He turned his head to the right to see the four garage doors slowly begin to open, one after the other. Then they slammed down, opened slowly again, slammed down.

A loud pop-hiss sounded, like a caseful of beer cans simultaneously opening. Across the front grounds, the automatic sprinklers jumped to attention, then started spraying. One of the programmed arcs was off—of course—so that a cold swath of water slapped Bram in the face.

At least it woke him up. He strode toward Honor, who was still holding the palmtop and still standing over Fifo. Christ, he thought, the pressure in his head resurging. She was still pushing touchpoints too. Suddenly the peeled-log gate behind her rumbled, preparing to move.

A premonition prickled the back of his neck. His mind leaping back to that suspicious rustle, he started to run as the gate began to slide open. "Honor!" he yelled.

The gate rocked off its track to stop partway open. Bram continued forward, vaulting the last few feet to put his body between hers and whatever had made that ominous rustle he'd heard earlier.

On his same trajectory, a huge, shaggy form tore through the open gate and collided with him, knocking him backward. Bram landed on his ass, three yards from Honor and Fifo. The collision couldn't have dazed him more than a millisecond, but by the time he scrambled to his feet to save her . . . Honor was fine.

With her hands buried in the unkempt fur of the damn dog he'd been spotting in his woods, the dog that had just flattened him, Honor was not only fine, but smiling. At the dog. Talking. To the dog.

The same ugly beast that could have knocked him unconscious without, apparently, his days-old wife even noticing.

"Who's this?" she asked, still gazing at the beast in delight.

Bram began brushing himself off. "A stray dog that's been hanging around." He gave it a sideways glance. "Or maybe it's a small moose."

"A stray?" Honor echoed.

Oh, no. *No.* He didn't like the sudden, instant, *happy* speculation in her voice.

"As in an animal without a home and someone to belong to?" she continued, a radiant smile kicking up the corners of her mouth. "A pet. I've never stayed in one place long enough to have a pet, but I've always wanted one."

Oh, no, no, no, no. So she'd never had a pet, thanks to that erratic childhood of hers. That didn't mean he had to let her introduce yet more chaos into *his* life. More expectations. More emotions.

A pet. A *dog*. He wouldn't agree. She wouldn't dare ask.

"You won't mind, right? I can keep him, can't I?"

Bram opened his mouth to refuse, just as the hulking, hairy stray whined, then lowered his massive head to run his long tongue over Fifo's smashed snout. Honor beamed down at the animal, then back up at Bram, her starlight eyes shining.

No. She could not keep that ragged, beastly invader. No.

But even though he didn't care about her feelings, and even though she'd ruined his night, his day, and now, once again, his dog, he couldn't push that single, simple, two-letter word past his lips.

Chapter Five

*T*HAT afternoon, Honor peered out her bedroom's French doors, smiling with happiness as she caught sight of her new dog—she'd named him Joey—bounding through the woods beyond the back deck. Not only did she have a town now, she had a dog! Something warm and furry and all her own.

That thought was almost as startling as the fact that brooding Bram had actually agreed she could keep the animal, albeit outside, despite the electronic havoc she'd wreaked. Likely he'd been too stunned by her effect on his technology to truly understand what he'd been agreeing to.

Which was exactly why she'd chosen that moment to ask.

She wondered, though, how long it would take Bram to deduce that the electronic glitches that occurred with regularity around her were more than mere coincidence. If she wore a watch, the time ran fast or slow. Unceasing cell phone static had caused her to give them up altogether. The truth was, she'd created at least one memorable mishap with most kinds of electrical devices.

Her father's assistant, Josh McCool, laughed about it and claimed she made ACs run DC and DCs run AC. But she wasn't sure Bram Bennett would find it quite so amusing.

He continued to surprise her, though. There was that kiss last night. Then the dog this morning. Because her car was in the shop, he'd even agreed to give her a lift into town so she could purchase canine provisions this afternoon.

When it came to this man, she cautioned herself, she'd better be prepared for anything.

But Bram's unpredictability wouldn't worry her. She had a town, she had a dog, and she had a healthy *carpe diem* attitude toward life. The therapist who had hung that "fear of abandonment" label around Honor's neck had noted that too—with approval.

As Honor had told Bram when she moved in, she *did* consider gloominess a waste of time. After those days held captive in tomblike darkness, she had emerged knowing time was too short to postpone living.

Humming to herself, she peered out the French doors again, noting the leaves drifting down from the sycamores and maples like red-and-gold paratroopers. The sight made her give a second thought to the silk T-shirt she was tucking into her jeans. Joey had branded her other top with muddy paw prints earlier, but maybe something warmer than a thin shirt was called for.

She crossed to the dresser, pulled out a navy blue cotton knit sweater, then slipped off her shirt. Still humming, she struggled to poke her head through the sweater's tight neckline.

"Honor!"

Bram's irked voice startled her into thrusting her head through, but then his disapproving scowl paralyzed her. Wearing black jeans and a black T-shirt, he stood in the hall between their rooms, a denim jacket in his hand and the scent of spicy soap wafting from the open door behind him. He was staring at her.

"What the hell do you think you're doing?" he asked. His gaze ran from her face, to her belly button, and then halfway back up.

Honor blinked, the situation coming into focus.

"I asked," Bram ground out again, "what the hell do you think you're doing?"

If his look had been sexual, she would have been spooked. If his look hadn't been so angry, she would have been mortified and immediately covered herself. But instead she bristled at his rude tone. Kiss or no kiss, dog or no dog, she couldn't forgive him *everything*. "I believe it's called dressing," she said through her teeth.

She figured he could see that. She was standing in her bare feet and wearing the same pair of low-riding jeans she'd pulled on that morning. He was reacting to the fact that she wasn't *finished* dressing, of course, so that he'd managed to catch her in her satin demi-bra, her sweater still bunched around her neck.

It was the annoyed look on his face that motivated her to do nothing about covering the skin he was ogling with such irritation. Because it was patently clear he believed—

"You're trying to tease me."

That.

Jerk. Arrogant jerk. An arrogant jerk who was willing—no, *wanted*—to think the worst of her.

"Oh, yeah. That's right," Honor said, each word dripping acid. Under his ill-tempered gaze, she finally moved, slowly pushing her right arm into its sleeve, then her left. At that point she stopped, holding the bunched hem of the sweater in her fists.

She left it there, right above the cups of her low-cut bra. "I've been waiting all day for you to catch me." When the mocking words were out, she inhaled deeply to maximize her cleavage. Take that.

Snap.

It was almost audible, the sudden switch in his mood from irritation to arousal. His nostrils flared and all at once the tension in his body was no longer mad— but male. His gaze washed over her, this time leaving hot tingles in its wake.

Honor's fingers tightened on the hem of her sweater. Her stomach muscles tightened too, preparing for panic. Instead, a sexual spark struck inside her and from across the room his suddenly harsh breath blew it to a flame. Desire heated.

Honor hadn't known that a man's look could be so physical. She felt it against her skin, licking over her midriff, stroking the rising flesh of her breasts. Bram would see that her nipples had tightened in response. She felt them pressing against the fabric of her bra.

Then his gaze lifted from her breasts to meet her eyes. Awareness, Honor thought, sexual awareness was palpable too. They stared at each other as another wash of goose bumps broke out across her breasts and skittered down her belly to all the private places below.

Honor's inner muscles clenched. She instinctively shifted to press the insides of her thighs together, holding on to the warm, tingling fullness she felt there.

A man could bring her to this with just his eyes, she thought, more amazed. *This* man could.

Nostrils flaring again, Bram took a slow step toward her.

But at the clap of his boot heel hitting hardwood, the flame inside Honor snuffed out. Her sexual spell shattered. Goose bumps transformed to chills, crude male voices sounded in her head, using crude male terms to describe her body and what they planned to do to it.

She yanked her sweater down, stomach now churning. On shaky legs, she spun away from Bram and rushed to the dresser to pick up her hairbrush. With a short, jerky stroke, she pulled it through her hair.

"I undress at eleven P.M. if you want to be on hand for the next show." She didn't look at him.

But she knew when he left. One minute he was there, sending out wave after wave of Y chromosomes. The next he was gone, leaving his spicy scent and that sexual awareness lingering in the air like smoke.

Relieved to be alone, Honor closed her eyes.

She stroked the brush through her hair more gently until her heart rate slowed to normal. Then she slipped into her shoes, picked up her purse, and walked to the front door. Pulling it open, she saw the SUV sitting in the driveway, Bram behind the wheel, waiting for her. This time he didn't surprise her.

Despite condemning her as a tease, he wasn't one to renege on a promise. This was the same man who visited his wife's grave every night, after all.

And she wasn't surprised either, that even after what just happened he was his customary silent self as she climbed into the passenger seat, then automatically rolled her window halfway down. But overlooking the incident suited her fine too, because when she'd told herself to be prepared for anything when it came to Bram, she'd never expected "anything" to include sex.

Oh, the sexual disquiet she understood, she'd been dealing with that for months, but not the sexual desire. She needed silence and breathing room to get over them both.

So, for once grateful for Bram's taciturn reserve, she closed her eyes and tried fixing her mind on other thoughts: sloppy dog kisses, Mia's warm smile, a two-tiered wedding cake that had made her feel so welcome.

Bram started the engine and smoothly put the car into gear. As it accelerated forward, he spoke. "What happened?"

Startled, she opened her eyes and slid him a look. "Huh?"

"Something happened to you." He was gazing out the windshield, his face expressionless.

Honor stared at him, nerves jangling. "What do you mean?"

"Somebody hurt you or scared you or—"

"I don't know what you're talking about." Why was Mr. Antisocial trying to delve inside her now?

He took a left turn on the narrow road that led toward Hot Water. "Honor, don't try to deny it. I saw your face."

"You saw my bra," she retorted, hearing the panic edging her voice. "*That's* what set you off."

"It set you off too," he said flatly. "Tell me what happened."

Shaking her head, Honor laced her fingers, trying to wish the conversation away. There were secrets that even the therapists hadn't uncovered and Honor wanted to keep it that way. "There's nothing to tell."

"Honor—"

"Can't you leave me alone?" she snapped. Afraid she'd betrayed too much already, she forced softness into her voice. "I'm sorry, but there's really nothing to talk about."

"I'm not buying it. After what just happened in your bedroom, I'm *positive* there's something we need to talk about."

Her muscles tightened and she swallowed, trying to resist his unexpected insistence.

"I thought you did it to amuse yourself. To get a reaction out of me." He glanced over at her. "But that isn't the case, is it?"

Give him something, she thought quickly. *Give him something to chew on and then he'll leave you alone.* "I suppose it was bound to come up sooner or later," she said, trying to sound nonchalant. "I don't like closed doors."

He took a moment to absorb that. "Why?"

When she hesitated, he sent her a sharp look. "Tell me, Honor."

Frustrated with him, she made a swatting gesture with one hand. "It's no big deal, okay? The men who kidnapped me locked me in the trunk of my car. Then they drove it to the house where I was held in a dark wine cellar."

When he stayed patiently silent, she connected the dots for him. "So I haven't quite yet lost this little aversion I have to darkness, closed doors, and close spaces. Satisfied?"

"That's why you leave your bedroom door open."

"Yes." She looked away, out the window. "And a light on at night. I've gone to bed after you and gotten up before you, hoping you wouldn't notice."

He was quiet for several moments. "All right. I'm sorry for how I reacted."

"Apology accepted." Okay, that wasn't so bad. She could relax now.

"But there's something more," he went on, sending her a quick, piercing look. "Something more than closed doors."

Her muscles bunched again and a flush shot up her neck. "I don't know what you mean," she denied. "There's nothing else."

"Something about men . . . or me? Maybe it's the way I look at you. The way I kissed you."

Oh, she liked the chilly Bram much better than this chattier version. Pressing her lips tightly together, she turned her head and gazed out the window again, trying to focus on the passing countryside, golden in the afternoon light.

"Honor? Ignoring me won't work."

Well, something had to, because she had her reasons for keeping things to herself.

Making a ladylike sandwich of her hands in her lap, she lifted her chin and gazed at him coolly. "Really, Bram." She strengthened her bluff with generations of well-bred Witherspoon hauteur. "I have no idea what you're talking about."

He let go a humorless laugh. "Give me a break, princess," he drawled. "You're going to have to do better. Are the men you usually spend time with cowed by that you're-a-spider-beneath-my-shoe kind of talk?"

At his derisive tone, her temper flared. Jerk. Arrogant, insulting, *male* jerk. "Fine," she spit out. "You want to know about the men I usually spend time with? Just lately they've been men who talked to *me*. About their sick sexual fantasies, starring *me*."

Regretting her outburst instantly, she squeezed shut

her eyes and knocked the heels of her hands against her forehead. *I'm an idiot*. It had taken Bram—what, all of two minutes?—to provoke his way past her defenses.

But it wasn't satisfaction on his face as he wrenched the wheel and pulled to the side of the road. She didn't know how to label his expression, but his fingers were white-knuckled as he gripped the key and turned off the car.

Sucking in a sharp breath, he looked over at her, a cold fire in his green eyes. "Was it only talk, Honor? Or did they touch you too?"

She shook her head. They hadn't touched her body. Only her mind, her sexuality, and her sense of security.

"But you thought they would."

One shoulder lifted. "As time went on and negotiations stalled, I occasionally . . . considered the possibility."

"Negotiations stalled," he muttered. "Jesus Christ."

Unsure how to respond, she lifted her shoulder again. "So let's just say the experience has made me a little edgy."

"Edgy," he repeated. He ran his palm down his face. "Edgy how, exactly?"

A cold shudder ran down her spine. See, that's what she got for talking about it. "Why should I tell you? And why do you want to know, anyway?"

"Because you live in my house, damn it, and despite what you might think, I only like to terrorize young women during the months of March and May."

She closed her eyes, opened them. "If you must know, certain looks, certain kinds of touches, personal ones . . ." *Intimate ones*.

"I know the kind you mean," he said, his voice dry.

Her blush reheated. "They make me hear their voices, their words, in my head."

"So certain touches, looks, they make you afraid."

She didn't want to ever be afraid again. "Edgy," she corrected.

"All right." He scrubbed his face with his palms again. "Tell me everything, from the beginning."

"About the kidnapping?" She suppressed another shudder. "I don't talk about the kidnapping."

He threw her a frustrated look. "Why not?"

"After my rescue, I talked to the FBI, I talked to the police, I talked to lawyers and crisis counselors and trauma therapists. But I'm done with that. Now I don't allow the SOBs who took me any more power over me or any more time in my head and in my world." That was how she protected herself. That and coming to live in Hot Water.

A muscle kicked in his jaw. "But there's still those doors you can't close."

She hated that he mentioned them. "Soon I'll be able to."

"And what about sex? Will you be able to do that soon too?"

Her head jerked up, even as she recognized he was trying to antagonize more information out of her. "That's none of your business."

His half-smile was mocking. "Really? But I'm the one who's madly in love with you. Your husband, re-member?"

Her husband. That was his best shot and he'd taken it.

For the first time since moving to Hot Water she felt her optimism waning. She'd thought marriage a small price to pay for making a place here, but it did not bode well that the man she'd married ignited her libido despite those voices in her head.

"This is turning into a disaster," she muttered.

He stilled, then lifted one eyebrow. "Did I hear you say 'disaster'?" With a quick flip of his wrist, he started the engine and steered the car back onto the road. "You'll really have me reeling, princess, if spilling your secrets rips off those rose-colored glasses you wear. Aren't you the same woman who came traipsing into this marriage with a smile on her face? Where's my Pollyanna bride?"

" 'Pollyanna bride'?" she echoed, grateful to see the feed store just ahead. She couldn't wait to be dropped off there. Time and distance from Bram would allow her to smooth over the layers he'd so ruthlessly peeled back. "More like the Bride of Frankenstein."

*N*ow that Bram had wormed Honor's secrets from her, she thought he'd be satisfied with his victory and withdraw. But she should have guessed he'd be perverse about that too. Probably as punishment for the Bride of Frankenstein insult, he went lichen on her, not only parking the car in the feed store's lot, but following her inside the barnlike structure too.

What he'd baited her into confessing hovered just as closely. Though she was certain that in time she'd feel normal about darkness and closed spaces and maybe even about sex, talking about her fears only made them weigh more heavily.

The bells on the feed store's door jingled as she pulled it open before Bram could, still hoping to outdistance him. But two strides over the threshold, the warm, oaty smell of the store's interior struck and she found herself halting to inhale another long breath of the foreign scent. Her gaze ran over the aisles that towered with equally foreign goods. Signs pointed the way toward horse tack, gopher traps, and llama chow.

Breathing in again, her mood began to lift. As unfamiliar as the store smelled, there was an earthy goodness to it, an earthy goodness which she recognized as the essence of Hot Water.

She continued to look about the shelves with their uncommon offerings. This was why she'd moved here, she thought, for critter kibble and duck feed and an entire display of poultry incubators.

A town that nurtured its baby chicks would nurture Honor too, she was counting on that. If Hot Water couldn't provide her with a normal, happy life, then no place could.

A voice drifted from somewhere amid the aisles. "Can I help you find something?"

"We'll be fine, Dave, thank you," Bram called back.

She glanced over her shoulder at him. "*I'll* be fine. Why don't you wait for me in the car?"

But just then, a portly bald man turned the corner of a nearby aisle. "Don't you be running off now, Bram Bennett." Though he balanced a massive bag of animal food on his shoulder, his face didn't show the slightest strain.

The bag slapped the nearby countertop with a thud, then the man came forward to extend his palm for Bram's handshake. "I thought I recognized your voice. I can't remember the last time I've seen you face-to-face. It's been too long."

Dave's eyes then lit on Honor and he grinned. "And this must be your bride. Introduce me," he demanded.

She was forced to sidle closer to Bram, but she managed a smile as he performed the introductions. After accepting the store owner's good wishes, she was saved from further small talk when a committee of high school kids arrived in search of straw bales for their upcoming Homecoming dance.

Hoping to escape Bram, Honor took advantage of the diversion to dash down one of the aisles. But he caught up to her quickly.

"Honor," he started. "About before—"

"Please," she said wearily, her spirits plunging low again. Didn't he get it? "I've already told you things I've not told anyone else. Isn't that enough?"

Some emotion softened his usual stern expression, but then it was gone so quickly she thought she'd imagined it. "Over here," he said, his long fingers grabbing hold of hers. He didn't allow her to pull away, but instead tugged her in another direction. "You need to see this."

She was too worn down to protest. His touch impersonal yet implacable, he towed her toward a plywood partition that separated the right rear corner of the store from the rest of it. Twitterings, cheeps, and the sounds of fluttering wings filtered through the thin walls. Bram led Honor to a screened door, then dropped her hand to usher her through. Before her was a narrow, sawdust-covered aisle, bounded on either side with large and small wire enclosures.

Honor gaped at the sight of birds of all variety and hue. Inside one cage, a swarm of finches hopped from perch to perch. In another, quail scratched at gravel. She gazed on long-tailed pheasants, noisy parakeets, and a flock of yellow canaries. Next to a cuddly crowd of fuzzy chicks, two ducks swam in a plastic kiddie pool.

Nature. Animals. Life.

Maybe Bram understood more than she gave him credit for. She glanced at him, but his face revealed nothing.

A speckled, gold-and-brown feather floated past her nose, and despite Bram's cool eyes, her mood rose with it. Surrounded by the peeps, squawks, and honks of cheerful bird chatter, she followed the twirling and rising bit of plumage all the way down the aisle.

Inside the last enclosure, a rooster paced, his upstanding tailfeathers quivering with each aggressive stride. His red coxcomb reminded Honor of a man's hair, disheveled by impatient fingers.

Noticing her, the rooster turned. He arched his neck and stared at her with one suspicious, beady eye. Then he stalked toward her for a better look, cloaked in a half-arrogant half-angry air she was becoming more familiar with by the hour.

A half-arrogant, half-angry, and all-male air that was just like her husband's.

She couldn't hold back her grin.

"There it is."

Honor looked at Bram. "There's what?"

"Never mind." He shook his head, but didn't take his gaze off her face.

That hot, sexual flicker once more came to life in her fickle belly.

Her smile dying, she whirled away from the rooster. And from Bram, again desperate for distance from him and the confusing responses he set off in her. "I want to find those dog supplies."

Hurrying away from the bird aisle, she barely avoided a collision with a thin young man striding from the opposite direction.

"Excuse me," he said, raking a hank of messy hair off his forehead.

Honor recognized Gil, the self-described "courier" for Mia's father, the self-proclaimed alien contactee. "It's quite all right."

The scruffy hair beneath the young man's bottom lip wiggled with his distracted half-smile, then his gaze sharpened. "You're Honor . . . Bennett, right?" He looked over her shoulder, and she could feel Bram's presence behind her. "And your new husband."

Honor nodded. "Nice seeing you again."

When she made to move around him, though, he stepped into her path. "Wait." He grabbed her shoulder.

Honor jumped, startled by the unexpected touch.

Bram instantly slid his arm around her waist and pulled her away from the other man, then just as quickly let her go. "What is it you want?" he asked Gil.

The "courier" didn't seem to notice their unfriendly reactions. His face lit up in a beatific smile. "You need to mark your calendars. Beau remembered more about his abduction and now we've determined The Date."

Honor glanced up, but Bram's blank face was no help. "Um, The Date?"

"Of Their next visit." Gil smiled again. "November fifteenth."

"So they're definitely coming back?" Honor asked, not quite sure how to respond.

"Oh, yes," Gil said. "Definitely coming back, and definitely coming back to Hot Water. We expect hundreds to make the pilgrimage here in the next few weeks." With another distracted smile, he hurried off.

Honor turned to Bram. "Hundreds? Do you really think hundreds will come here to meet aliens?"

He made a sound of disbelief. "Please God, no. Especially when the only alien I've seen around Hot Water is you."

She ignored him, mulling over the possibilities. She wasn't her father's daughter for nothing. "Maybe I should open up Old Town. People interested in aliens are probably interested in history too. Perhaps just a few buildings, or—"

"No." He grabbed her elbow and towed her across the cement floor. "I'm telling you, the 'hundreds' aren't going to happen. Even if they do arrive, I wouldn't want you exposed like that to a bunch of strangers."

"Exposed?"

Grunting, he stopped halfway down a long aisle with a mind-reeling selection of canine merchandise. "Here, you'll definitely need a flea treatment."

Honor didn't glance at the box he shoved in her hand. "What do you mean by exposed?" she insisted.

He restlessly perused the items on the shelf, picking up and inspecting one after the other. "Never mind. You'll be out of my hair by November fifteenth, right?"

"I told you, I'm safe here," she hedged, remembering those mere six weeks she'd promised, yet loath to confirm them again.

His eyes narrowed, his attitude once more that of the ruthless man who had probed her secrets. "Regardless of that, between now and when you go, you'll do as I ask."

Honor backed away at the flat conviction in his voice. "Bram . . ."

His eyes flickered and then he quickly pulled something off the shelf. "Here," he said, pressing it into her free hand. "A book on dog training, though with that stupid mongrel of yours it's probably a waste of time."

"Stupid?" She bristled, immediately diverted by the insult from the talk of strangers and safety. "My dog isn't stupid."

Bram sent her a look full of compassion. "Your dog wears stupid like a crown. I caught him slurping kisses all over Fifo's metal casing. Obviously he thinks it's alive."

Since she'd seen the sight herself and guessed the very same thing, Honor had to smile. "I think it's sweet."

"There you go again." Bram shook his head. "'Sweet.' You're nuts. Why don't you save time and admit right now that the dog you've decided to adopt is good for nothing?"

"Who said he has to be good for something?" Miffed, she jammed a hand on her hip.

"Oh, so you want him for his handsome appearance alone?" Bram asked.

Thinking of Joey's half-moose, half-mutt looks, Honor had to laugh. "Okay, fine, maybe he's not the most beautiful dog in the world, but he fits right in with . . . with . . . our household. Come to think of it, he reminds me quite a bit of you."

"I'm afraid to ask."

"He's a bit of a mystery, of course." She pursed her lips, enjoying the mildly irritated look on Bram's face. "And he's dark, like you. And big."

He crossed his arms over his chest. "Yeah? Well, I think he's a lot more like you. Guess how."

Surprised, she tried to think. "Good-natured, maybe? And . . ."

"Obedient?" Bram supplied.

She stifled a snicker. "Oh, I see. An underhanded ploy to get me to obey your every command, is that it? I believe you just declared him untrainable."

"Okay, fine," he conceded. "You're definitely smarter than the dog."

She laughed again.

"Prettier too." His hand reached for her cheek, as if he were going to touch her.

Without thinking, Honor backed away.

He casually pushed his hand into his pocket. "Yep, I do think that dog is as dumb as they come. But maybe you'll prove me wrong."

Now that she was safe from another of his touches—she hadn't known whether it would ignite apprehension or passion—she could breathe again. "Maybe I will."

His eyebrows rose in speculation. "Really? Then I dare you. If that dog learns to do anything the least bit useful, I'll . . ." He seemed to be trying to decide.

"Give him his first flea bath?"

Bram shook his head, looking at her in pity. "You're not thinking big enough. I'm going to be very, very impressed."

Honor surveyed the products on the shelves, unable to hold back another grin. "Brush his teeth? Cut his toenails? Clean his ears?"

But he told her she was still thinking too small. They bickered about the terms of the silly dare all the way through the rest of the shopping and then during the car ride home. Every thirty seconds or so, Honor found herself smiling. Smiling at Bram, or at the thought of trying to teach her dog Joey a trick, or just at life in general.

It was almost hard to believe that the drive *to* the feed store had left her feeling so miserable.

Bram pulled the car in front of the house, and they unloaded her purchases. Then, as he was climbing back into the driver's seat, it suddenly dawned on her.

"Wait a minute." Bemused, almost . . . charmed, she pulled open the passenger door and met his inquiring gaze across the seat. "I know what you did," she said.

His brows rose. "My first inclination is to deny everything, but—"

"You cheered me up."

"No way." He appeared almost offended.

Not fooled, she shook her finger at him. He'd taken her mind off her fears with those birds and all that ridiculous talk about her dog. "Yes, way."

"Not me. I'm gloomy and boring."

But even his denial made her smile.

"I have it on the best authority," he continued. "Gloomy and boring is no good at all for cheering people up."

She tried to look serious. "You forgot brooding."

He blinked. "You never said brooding." His brows lowered. "I *don't* brood!"

"Take it from me, Bram, you brood." Before he could protest further, she shifted her hold on the door. "As a matter of fact, if you were a chicken we'd be overrun in eggs."

Without giving him time to respond, she slammed it shut, and wasn't surprised when he immediately swung the car back toward the front gate. It was nearing twilight, after all, and Alicia was waiting.

But Honor's heart stuttered in her chest and she

nearly fell over in a faint when she caught sight of his face through the windshield. He was smiling.

Bram. Smiling.

Just like that, the spark inside her flared, caught, became a fire. Then her whole body heated with desire and Honor could only tremble as she watched him drive away.

It was getting worse. This time, it had only taken his smile.

Her legs wobbly, she finally turned and made it into the house, not even wincing when the heavy front door closed behind her. She could hear the whine of the vacuum in the distance, but avoided Mia by ducking into her bedroom. In the mirror hanging over the dresser, she stared at her flushed-cheek reflection.

She'd been certain the kidnapping had extinguished any and all passion she'd ever possessed. Though she wasn't widely experienced with sex, there was no doubting she'd been wrong. Not when Bram was lighting her fire with increasing regularity. Not when he was able to ignite it with the merest spark, setting her blazing like a hillside of Gold Country brush after the long, dry summer.

She knew she should have ditched him at the feed store! Instead, she'd let him show her parakeets and roosters—and then another side of himself.

But this didn't have to mean disaster, she tried reassuring herself. The reawakening of her sexuality was healthy. It was, after all, one of the steps necessary to reclaiming her life, and she'd resolved to do that very thing after the kidnapping. Why, in time she might even consider exploring these new feelings with Bram—but only if she could also consider herself one hundred percent capable of maintaining a carefree attitude toward some itch-scratching sex.

Because if she failed at that and let her emotions get involved . . . oh, that might accomplish what the kidnapping had not. It could destroy her to feel too much for a man who was, at heart, someone else's husband.

Chapter Six

*B*RAM glanced in the rearview mirror as he drove through the gate on his way to the cemetery, then caught sight of his own reflection.

Shit. He was smiling.

Unbelievable.

He supposed that proved he was still human. Human enough to smile on occasion, anyway. Human enough to feel remorse for the way he'd misjudged Honor.

And human enough, he had to admit, to feel as if he'd been stabbed when she'd told him about her kidnappers' sexual threats. For a few moments, even, dread had pooled inside him like blood.

At the cemetery, Bram parked in his usual spot, then started the climb to the highest hill. His footsteps crunching on the gravel path, he told himself he was wrong about the dread, he must be.

It wasn't possible he cared that much—no one could get that close to him. He wasn't *that* human, not anymore.

Passing his father's grave on the way to Alicia's, he paused and leaned down to brush a brown, curled oak leaf from the close-cropped grass. Though Robert Bennett had passed away from lung cancer at only fifty-five, when Bram was still in college, that death he'd understood. His father had been a heavy smoker for over thirty years.

So while Bram had grieved for his dad, he'd viewed it as a death with a cause.

Cause and effect. *That* had made sense to his engineer mind.

Four years later, though, his logical, ordered world had been blown apart by one shriek of the telephone. Just one ring, because he'd immediately picked up, never doubting he could handle whatever news was on the other end.

For a year afterward, he dreamed of letting that phone ring. Every night it shrieked at him in his sleep, but he ignored it. In his dream, if the sheriff didn't tell him about the carjacking, then it simply didn't happen. Then Alicia made it home from her excursion into town. Then Alicia came running through their door, happy and alive.

That was dreams for you.

While the wrenching, ironic reality had been that his very world had hung on the next phone call.

His mind hazy with shock, he'd unplugged all but the extension in the kitchen, illogically deciding that bad news couldn't come through *that* phone. He'd seen Alicia on it just that morning, the daffodil-yellow receiver tucked between her ear and shoulder. For three days and nights he'd camped in the kitchen by that sunny phone, merely lying on the floor when his mother pleaded with him to sleep.

He'd had additional company, as well. Dylan, the people who worked for him, other friends. The puppy had been there too, always curled up beside him.

So the room had been full when the second call came. In the woods, the FBI had found the light shirt Alicia had been wearing over a sleeveless one. *There is no blood,* the man on the other end kept repeating. *There is no blood.* With just those four words, hope soared.

His mother, Dylan, the others, they'd been there when the third, hope-crushing call came as well. But from the moment he'd been told of Alicia's murder, Bram had avoided all those who'd kept vigil with him. Touching another who loved Alicia had only flooded him with more pain, had only caused agonizing questions to whirl like dust devils in his head.

Then one day, after years of avoiding everyone, he'd realized that he'd managed to completely wall off his heart. There was a gate, but he had control of that too, only opening it once a day to release the questions that tortured him.

Though he suspected he'd built the wall at the expense of his humanity, he'd welcomed it. Because he'd finally found a way to survive.

*O*NCE it was dark, Bram returned home. As usual, his questions had gone unanswered. But he was accustomed to the dull throb of disappointment in his head and its heaviness in his chest.

Odd noises behind the house drew him to the back deck. He found Honor there, rearranging the outdoor furniture to make a place for the manse-cum-doghouse she'd bought at the feed store.

He frowned. "I would have carried that out here for you."

She jumped, swung around. "Oh. Hi. I didn't hear you come back." Her hands found the hem of her sweater and she pulled it down, as if anxious to cover more of herself.

The movement only molded the knit more closely to her breasts. Bram swallowed a sigh, though it was old news that he was also still human enough to feel lust for his heiress bride. It didn't help matters to know that underneath her sexual nerves there was a part of her that was attracted to him too. That was something else he'd learned today.

"Did you . . . did you want something?" she asked, her face coloring.

Shaking his head, he backed away from her. His visit to the cemetery hadn't been entirely fruitless. At least it had reminded him he didn't want anything from Honor. After four years of celibacy, he'd occasionally had sex, but bedding a *bride*? Nuh-uh.

So he was just going to work harder at resisting her. Starting right now.

With that party over and with her dog to occupy her, hell, they might not even need to speak again. Well, once, because he was certain he hadn't misjudged her altogether.

Any hour now she'd grow bored with small-town Hot Water and come to him to call it quits.

FOR the twenty-seventh time, Honor threw the ball down the long flagstone driveway toward the front gate. For the twenty-seventh time, her dog Joey speeded after it, his shaggy black hair lifting from his long body and winging outward, giving him the appearance of a giant-sized, supersonic dust mop. For the twenty-seventh time, he grabbed the ball in his mouth and then ran with it to a shady corner near the garage, where he deposited it, with great reverence, at the feet of a deactivated Fifo.

For the twenty-seventh time, Honor retrieved the ball herself. Joey looked up at her, praise warm in his eyes, and swiped her bare shin with his tongue.

She laughed, because after seven days it was more than obvious. "Yes, I know who's training whom." The dog leaned against her legs and she dug her fingers into his fur, hot in the afternoon sunlight. Closing her eyes, she lifted her face toward the sky, letting the warmth soak into her skin.

Joey's sudden, welcoming yelp had her eyes popping open. Bram was coming around the corner of the garage, and though he was twenty feet away, it was the closest she'd been to him in a week. Since the afternoon they'd shopped at the feed store, she figured he'd been avoiding her.

Hastily closing her eyes and lifting her face sunward again, she hoped he would continue to do so. Too many things about him tugged at her heart. The loneliness of his stubborn solitude. Those twilight visits.

And then there was the way he tugged at her body. She didn't want another test of the state of her sexuality.

"You're going to burn."

His rough voice, now close by, made her jump. Her eyes opened again and she forced herself to look at him even as her fingers tightened in the dog's fur. Instead of evading, Bram was approaching her, darn him. "Joey and I are almost ready to go back inside," she said.

In jeans and a khaki shirt rolled up at the elbows, he strolled closer. "Joey?"

"I named him after Joseph Campbell," she answered, pretending her heart wasn't starting to thump.

"You know, the man who said we should seek out our bliss."

Without thinking, she let her gaze slide down the golden column of Bram's throat to his chest, where the shirt veed to display a glimpse of black hair. Encountering the first fastened button, she came to her senses and jerked her gaze back up, hoping he hadn't noticed.

His eyes were narrowed and his nostrils flared. He'd noticed.

And just as obviously, her sexuality was already acing this latest quiz, thanks to Bram. Something about his appeal slid beneath her apprehension like a man's hand sliding beneath a silk nightgown. Just a look from his green eyes could leave her skin feeling hot and tight.

As if she were willing it, he drew even closer until he stood before her. Pulses tripped in Honor's throat and wrists as she watched Bram's hand lift, then with aching slowness reach out. Rough fingertips brushed hair off her cheek to tuck it behind her ear. The hollow there throbbed with another pulse.

"We should seek our bliss, huh?" he said.

Her voice lost somewhere, she nodded.

"Well, then . . ." His hand smoothed the hair that curved across her neck. As her skin prickled with goose bumps, his lashes half lowered. She knew he was watching them race down her neck and across her chest to disappear below the low-cut tank top she was wearing with jeans. The spandex and cotton top had a built-in shelf bra, but Honor was sure it couldn't hide how her nipples tightened in a sudden rush.

Embarrassed, she shuffled back.

His hand instantly dropped. "Damn it. I promised myself—" He halted, sighed, then spoke again. "Sorry.

I didn't mean to scare—make you edgy like that again."

He'd labeled her reaction as nerves. "Oh, no. Bram—" she started, then bit off the denial. Wasn't it better—safer for her—if he didn't know the truth? Her gaze shifted to her feet. "It's all right."

"It's not all right. I don't want you worrying about that." He spun and strode a few steps away, then spun again to face her. "I swore to myself I'd steer clear of you, but I noticed you've been half closing your door. It's not necessary, Honor."

So he *had* been avoiding her.

"You go ahead and leave your door open, and I . . ." One corner of his mouth lifted. "I just won't look."

She should be embarrassed that he brought up her closed-doors problem. And she was flushing, but she suspected it was due more to the very interesting idea of Bram looking at her than anything else.

To conceal her reaction, she propped her hand on her hip and tried sending him a saucy smile. "And how do I know I can trust you?"

But instead of sounding teasing and light, it came out sounding teasing and husky . . . a womanly, almost sexual purr. Honor swallowed as Bram stilled.

"Princess?" he said, sounding puzzled.

Honor dropped her gaze. It fell on his hand, his lean fingers relaxed against his thigh.

"Princess?" he repeated. His sandpaper voice brushed across her imagination. Suddenly she pictured him whispering in her ear, while his long fingers slid beneath her clothes, slid them away, slid all over her skin.

"Are you all right?" He stepped closer.

Appalled at how easily he aroused her, she stepped back.

He frowned. "Hell, Honor." Those lean fingers lifted in frustration. "Are you certain you shouldn't be seeing someone to talk about this?"

He'd noticed her retreat and once again attributed it to sexual apprehension.

Pressing her hand against her chest, she willed her heart to slow. "I don't want to talk to another therapist."

"Me, then. Tell me." An odd expression crossed his face. "It might help."

"I told you, I'm done talking." She took another step back, this time to get away from his mention of the kidnapping. Reciting the details served no purpose to anyone.

He made an impatient sound and advanced on her. "Honor—"

"I'd think you'd understand," she interrupted, feeling cornered. "It's not as if you can talk about your wife."

"*You're* my wife," he pointed out dryly.

"You know what I mean. *Who* I mean." On the defensive, Honor threw the name down between them. "Alicia."

Bram rocked back on his heels. "I can talk about her," he said calmly.

Honor didn't know why she pursued it, unless it was to drive home to herself that her ridiculous desire for him was out of place when Bram belonged to someone else. "Go ahead, then."

"All right." But instead of starting immediately, he shoved his hands in his pockets and slowly headed up the driveway.

Honor followed. He took the footpath that led toward the narrow bridge that crossed the stream. At the arch of the bridge, he paused, resting his elbows on the wooden railing to look down at the water rushing by in happy gurgles and splashes.

"We were high school sweethearts." His face settled into its usual, unreadable lines. "Though I'd known her my whole life, of course. Then one day, instead of being that pesky Alicia with her big brown eyes and freckled nose, she was . . ." He shrugged and glanced over at Honor. "She was a girl, I guess. *The* girl."

The girl. Honor swallowed. "You must miss her," she said, then blushed at her incredibly inadequate words.

Bram didn't seem to notice. "Sometimes I smell something, taste something, hear a snatch of a song, and I can almost touch us again. We were so young, though, and it's been so long. . . ."

He was silent a moment, and then his mouth curved. "She was the quintessential hometown girl, knowing everybody, loving every tradition and every piece of town history. She grew bushels of vegetables she shared with everyone, but she wouldn't tell even her closest friend the best place to pick wild berries. She loved kids and birds and she had this hearty, happy laugh."

Looking away, Honor blinked rapidly, then cleared her throat. "She had a place to call home and a place in someone's heart. That's a lot to be happy about."

Bram grunted. A few quiet minutes passed, then he looked over at her. "See? I told you I could talk about Alicia."

Honor had forgotten she'd all but dared him to until

she caught the answering challenge in his voice. "But that's easier," she said hastily. "That's not talking about her kidnapping, her captivity."

Bram opened his mouth. Closed it. Then he lifted his hands in a helpless gesture.

Honor stared. Bram never struck her as helpless. Hard, cold, even cruel sometimes, but never helpless. Her heart squeezed. "Bram?"

He lifted his hands again. "Alicia was murdered, Honor. The man who held her captive was killed before being taken into custody. I know very little about the last three days of her life."

Honor's heart twisted. Of course. "Right. Sure." Again, she couldn't think of a response that seemed any better than inadequate. Her fingers felt cold and she rubbed them against her pants, trying to warm them and fighting to keep them from reaching out to comfort the shadowed man who stood beside her.

Her fingers won. They extended to touch his bare forearm, right below the rolled sleeve of his shirt. The pads of her fingers absorbed the heat of his skin and the springy texture of his dark hair. Her head down, she watched her fingertips trace a circle.

Comfort, she told herself. Comfort, not a caress.

But maybe Bram didn't see it that way, because suddenly he lifted her chin, his hand gentle. "Honor," he said in that scratchy voice. It abraded her nerve endings, making her feel hot again, and worse, naked from the heart out.

"What?"

"Never mind," he muttered, dropping her chin and turning away. Then he spun back. "Honor—"

He broke off, staring at her face. "Damn it," he said,

but the curse was soft and low. "Damn it, smile for me. At the feed store the other day I discovered that I hate seeing you sad. Tears in your eyes are worse. It's like the stars are drowning."

"I'm not crying," she said, blinking. But he was right. A tear spilled over the rim of her eyelid to trickle down her cheek.

"Oh, hell." This curse was as soft as the others. Bram lifted her chin again and bent toward her. "Tell me I'm not scaring you."

"I'm not afraid." He was going to kiss the tear away, she knew it, and another tear brimmed over to follow the first. All thoughts of avoidance, any pretense of evasion disappeared. There was no stepping back now. Her fingers gripped his arm as she braced herself for the sensation of his lips on her cheek.

Instead, he found her mouth.

Her unprepared, defenseless mouth, which he sank against, ignoring the tears that trickled slowly, one after the other, down her face.

Honor barely felt them, because his kiss consumed her attention. Soft. His lips, his kiss so soft.

He moved over her mouth, pressing against each corner and the bow on top, then focusing on the bottom lip. He kissed that one lip as if he couldn't get enough of it, slanting his head to gently touch from one direction, then the other.

When she couldn't breathe, she opened her mouth and he finally gave her more, gave her his tongue. She whimpered at the sure, wet thrust of it, at the secret knowledge that it was what she'd hoped for when she parted her lips.

There was air between their bodies, inches of space,

but Bram didn't seem interested in anything but her mouth. His hands lightly framed her face, his fingers speared through the hair at her temples, and then he tilted her head back farther and pushed deeper into her mouth with his tongue.

There was something vulnerable and exciting about that position: their bodies carefully apart but her face turned up to his. His hands crept down her cheeks and his thumbs coaxed her mouth wider for the heavy thrust and frustrating retreat of his tongue.

She tried to crowd him, but he moved back every time she moved forward, focusing only on her mouth, seducing it, using it, having it.

Honor's body was trembling, her skin quivering with the beats of her heart. Her nipples had tightened into points and the heat was hotter than ever, burning, swirling in her belly. His tongue thrust farther into her mouth and a silky wetness rushed between her legs.

Like that, she was ready for him.

As if he heard her thought, Bram jerked back. A breath shuddered into his chest. "Damn it," he muttered, shoving one hand into his pocket.

Honor stumbled back. "I'm sorry."

Pulling his palmtop out of his pocket, he looked at it. *"Goddamn it."*

Honor stumbled again, the small of her back smacking the bridge railing. "I'm sorry."

"Not you. Hell, Honor. Not you." He reached for her, but when she flinched, still confused, he let his hand fall. "There's someone at the gate."

Baffled, Honor turned her head toward the wood-and-iron barricade. Joey was rushing it, she realized now, bouncing off the logs with his front paws, then rushing it again. His excited barks should have pierced her daze, but still she couldn't gather her thoughts. "Who?" she asked vaguely.

Bram was fiddling with the palmtop controls, but then he held it up to her. "Do you recognize this man?"

In the bright sunlight, Honor blinked at the small screen. On it there appeared to be a live picture of someone standing outside the front gate, caught on one of those security cameras Honor had wondered about, she realized. She took the computer in her own hand, tilting it so that sun's glare didn't obscure the image on the screen.

Her scrambled brains finally straightening, her scrambled pulse finally slowing, she recognized the luxury cut of the visitor's suit and the bumper of the fire-engine-red Ferrari behind him. She also recognized how close she'd come to forgetting her qualms and testing her capability for strings-free sex.

"Of course I know him." Relief rushed through her. The man on the other side of the gate was a godsend. He would make the perfect buffer between her and Bram.

Anxious to get him—her buffer—inside the Fortress, she whirled and ran toward the gate, still clutching the palmtop. "Which icon do I press to let him in?" she called over her shoulder.

"Honor, wait—"

"Which one?"

"Bottom left!" he yelled over Joey's excited yelping, but it was too late.

She'd already pressed several others as well. From the corner of her eye, she saw Fifo come to sudden, snarling life and rise from his place beside the garage. As the gate rumbled, then started moving, Fifo did too, heading straight for Honor.

Picking up her speed, she kept one eye on the growl-ing robot and the other on the widening entry. The sun glinted off Fifo's fangs, but she kept going. Honor reached the gate and snapping Fifo reached her just as their visitor stepped inside. Absorbing the situation in a glance, the man grinned, then swept Honor up in his arms, not displaying the least surprise over the chaos of raging robotic guard, frantically barking furry ca-nine, and irritated husband-of-convenience bearing down on them with violence in his eyes.

His gaze alighting on Bram, the grin on their visi-tor's handsome face widened and mischief twinkled in his angel-blue eyes. He hitched Honor closer against his chest. "Well, beautiful, it looks like I got here just in the nick of time."

*J*OSH McCool didn't bother hiding his smug smile as he strolled through the house known as the Fortress, ostensibly in search of the kitchen. His lips pursed in a silent whistle, though, as he got a gander of the decep-tively casual interior. His mind instinctively switched to calculator mode, assessing the value of the furnish-ings and art objects. He'd make a hell of a contestant on a classy version of *The Price is Right*, if he did say so himself. He recognized a collection of antique fishing creels and some better pieces of primitive stoneware jugs and spittoons. The Chinese robes over the fire-place were likely only a zero or two short of priceless.

He shrugged. As Warren Witherspoon's right-hand man, it was no secret to Josh that Honor's hapless hubby had bucks. But now he had to admit that Bram Bennett knew how to spend those bucks too. If Josh were ever forced to set up permanent housekeeping in a backwater like this—and just thinking about it made him want to bite his tongue—he'd choose something similar.

Pioneer posh, that's what it was. Josh snickered, then ambled back the way he'd come to spy on Honor and her scowling man through the front windows.

And Bennett was *still* scowling.

But Honor didn't look as if she were going to let hubby's thunderous expression change her mind about the invitation she'd just issued. Josh leaned a shoulder against the wall, satisfaction washing through him. He was going to be living at the Fortress.

Goody, goody, goody.

Josh sent one last smile in the direction of the less-than-happy-looking couple, then pushed off from the wall. Loosening his tie, he turned his back on them and turned his attention toward ferreting out the kitchen.

He could use a bottle or two of Bram Bennett's beer. Catching sight of those Chinese robes again, he almost purred. The sweat of a bottle of someone else's cold, *expensive* beer always felt good against his palm.

Honor had said the housekeeper could be found in the kitchen, so he followed the sound of clattering dishes, his mind back on the bickering couple outside. At least he hoped they were bickering. But he'd make certain to ascertain exactly how things stood between Honor and Bennett. A chat with the housekeeper would be good for that.

But the oh-so-convenient invite told him something already. Happy newlyweds didn't want houseguests. And *un*happy newlyweds confirmed his suspicion that Honor and Bram Bennett hadn't married for anything as stupidly impractical as love.

Upon reaching the kitchen, Josh saw that, like every-thing else about the house, it was large and well appointed. He quickly registered the presence of an aproned female at the distant end of the room, her body half obscured by a tall, glassed cabinet door as she placed dishes on the shelves of a country French buffet.

More quality, Josh thought, his gaze caught by the buffet's gleaming wood, and he was a man who knew quality. That buffet and the matching sideboard weren't any of your cutesy reproduction, factory-distressed stuff, stuff that even then cost a shitload of money these days. This looked like real country French, from the country of France. The country of the country of France.

Again tipping his metaphorical hat in appreciation to that bastard Bennett, Josh stepped farther into the room and raised his voice. "Hello, there. You're the housekeeper, right? I'm a friend of Honor's and she told me to help myself to a cold drink."

He didn't hesitate to cross to the gleaming Sub-Zero refrigerator.

A low, husky voice stopped his movement. "There's beer in the beverage cooler in the dining room you just passed through."

Josh shrugged away a brief uneasiness. Was he so transparent? How the hell did the housekeeper guess he wanted a beer and not Evian or Pellegrino or even iced tea?

But a worthless emotion like embarrassment would never deter him from something he wanted, so he backtracked the few steps necessary to find the built-in beverage bar. Oh, yes. Nicely stocked, with one section for wine maturation and another for chilling wines and beers.

He found an opener and popped the top off a bottle

of Moretti—Italy's best-selling beer and his personal favorite—and took the first cold, yeasty swallow. He loosened his Gucci tie even more, and lifted his chin to roll the cold glass against his throat.

Half cooled now, he got down to his real purpose for coming inside by calling out genially to the house-keeper in the next room. "So? How are the bride and groom getting along?"

Like a mink and a goat, he hoped. Honor's impromptu marriage had totally screwed with Josh's own plans.

"Very well, I'm sure," came the throaty reply from the other room.

Noncommittal, throaty reply. Josh shrugged philosophically. Couldn't expect the hired help to spill all the household's secrets upon first request. Not when Bennett's check paid all the housekeeper's bills.

Bennett. Damn, just thinking about Honor's husband could make Josh's blood boil. For months he'd been working on a wedding to Honor himself, slowly laying the groundwork, slowly building her trust and friendship. The kidnapping had ruined everything.

Remembering the fury and frustration of those weeks churned his stomach too. When he'd learned that Honor was being held for ransom, he'd been hot to find the bastards and kill them himself. Warren, of course, had raged as well.

But after Honor's safe return and the arrest of her captors, her father had expanded the field of blame. Focus shifted to one Josh McCool, who, after the kidnappers themselves, Warren had decided was responsible for Honor's kidnapping.

According to Warren, Josh should never have suggested Honor work at that particular company in Santa Monica—even though it had been her father's idea. Furthermore, declared Warren, Josh had rolled over and let Honor refuse a full-time bodyguard—something the old man had never succeeded in getting her to agree to either.

Warren being Warren, however, the punishment he'd leveled on Josh had been subtle. But very painful.

Knowing full well that Josh wanted Honor for himself, Warren had let her marry Mr. High-Tech Security. And then, wily bastard that the old man was, he'd now sent Josh to Hot Water to "sort out" the "minor" problems Enigma Company was facing in the expansion that Warren was planning. He'd wanted to rub Josh's nose in what he'd lost.

But Josh was wily too, and he planned to make lemonade out of the sour circumstances his boss had thrown him into.

He strolled into the kitchen, prepared to work his charm on the housekeeper. Certainly she would have the lowdown on the newlyweds.

Josh found her at the sink. With her back to him, the afternoon sun streaming through the bay window she faced created a golden nimbus around her aproned body.

His palms suddenly itched.

Startled, he drew up short. According to family legend, the McCools had a way with money. Not a way of actually *getting* any, unfortunately, but a way of knowing when money was close by. His grandmother, devotee of the nickel, dime, and quarter slot machines, swore she could grab the handle of a one-armed bandit and know there was a payout imminent by the little tickle in her palm.

Problem was, Granny rarely had enough coins in the pocket of her housedress to win that "imminent" cash flood. Time after time—Josh had witnessed it himself—just when she'd pumped in her final silver piece and been forced to move off, another old lady in a faded dress and scuffed house slippers would drop a couple of bucks in that same slot machine and get a couple hundred back.

Josh had never experienced the tickling, money's-close sensation himself, but now it was all he could do not to rub his palms against something.

The housekeeper stepped to the side, moving out of the light and half turning toward Josh.

He instantly thought about rubbing them against her.

Did he make some movement? Probably, because the young woman jumped, then whipped around to face him, her back pressed against the edge of the countertop. "Oh! You scared me."

"I'm sorry." He tried smiling, but knew it fell right off his face, as surely as he felt like he'd been knocked on his ass. "I . . ." His hand gestured and beer spurted out of the bottle he was holding to splash on the floor. He stared stupidly at the mess.

The housekeeper went into action. In seconds she was crouched at Josh's feet, wiping up the spilled beer with a rag, then drying the floor with another.

He gazed down at her glossy black hair. It sprang from a very precise, almost childlike side part and then waved heavily down her back. Below that, her lush hips curved and he could appreciate just enough of her round tush to feel sweat gather between his shoulders.

When she finally straightened, he got a closer look at her face. She took a backward step, but he made a grab for her, two fingers hooking into the waist-high pocket on the front of her apron.

"Wait," he said, his gaze running over her face. She was young, early twenties, he guessed, with skin the color of apricots. Black brows and lashes emphasized eyes that were big and brown. Her lips were full and deeply colored—a delicious shade between cabernet and claret. The only mark on the apricot beauty of her flesh was a tiny mole, à la Marilyn Monroe, on her left cheek.

Like her body, her face was lush, its colors so warm they jacked up the temperature in the room.

Pulling his hand free of her apron, Josh jolted back. "Uh, sorry." He was here for *Honor*, he reminded himself, not to get caught up in wasteful fancies about some local chick.

A wave of color rushed across the housekeeper's face and she spun away from him. "No problem."

Did she think he'd rejected her? As if he'd stepped on a cat's tail or stolen a kid's toy, shame gave him a surprise stab. Telling himself he was crazy for feeling guilty, he crossed to the butcher-block island and pulled out a stool.

He'd never hurt an animal in his entire life. The first and last kid he'd stolen from was Danny Crawford. The little bastard had thought he was God because he'd lived in a four-bedroom house with a pool while Josh bunked in a single-wide at the Sandy Acres Trailer Park. After a year of forfeiting his lunch money to the bully, Josh hadn't felt a shred of guilt for stealing the brat's prized Ninja jungle watch and chucking it into the Nevada desert as far as his ten-year-old arm could throw.

He sipped at his beer and tried to get his mind back on the task at hand. "Honor's an old friend of mine. I work for her father. I'm sure he'll be pumping me for a full report on how the marriage is going."

"Oh." As she wiped down a countertop, the house-keeper flicked a glance at him, then looked away. "How nice of you to stop by for a visit." Her gaze darted toward him again, her face flushing once more. "I'm sure Honor appreciates it."

Josh wasn't surprised at her blushes or her little peeks at him. He was a good-looking man—Granny had called his the face of a do-gooding devil. He considered the asset a fortunate accident of birth that went some way toward making up for those *un*fortunate accidents that had resulted in him being dumped in the Nevada desert, left to be raised by an old woman who was more devoted to gambling than her own grandkid.

His face was the first thing that had given him the confidence to walk away from the Sandy Acres Trailer Park. Holding positions two and three were his brains and his ambition.

He wanted money, big money, and he was smart enough, and handsome enough, to get it.

"Are you . . ." The young woman hesitated, flashing him another look from those deep brown eyes. "Um, staying for dinner?"

Josh smiled. "I'm staying for a while. I have some business over at Enigma, and the Bennetts have been kind enough to offer me the use of the guest cottage."

"Oh." He saw the housekeeper swallow. "I should go air it out, then, and, um, change the sheets."

Josh's smile died, imagining that lush body moving around his bed. God, moving *in* his bed. Moving under him, over him, his hands filled with the soft flesh of her hips, his mouth tasting that apricot skin. "Don't do anything special on my account."

He thought of the women he usually socialized with. Women who weren't soft and shy like this one, women who were hard and thin. Because they had the money for spa vacations and personal trainers, he reminded himself. Because they had prosperous trust funds. Or prosperous, passed-on husbands.

"It's no trouble to take care of the guest cottage," the young woman said. "It's my job."

"Yeah." Her job, Josh mentally repeated. She was a housekeeper in some backwater nowhere, while he lived for big cities and bright lights, money and moneyed women.

He slid the lapel of his Armani jacket between his fingers, mentally comparing its clean lines and luxury fabric to the brightly flowered apron that little Miss Clean-and-Dust-It wore. No match there. Honor was the one who fit his bill. Honor.

Savoring the sensation, he fingered the lightweight wool of his lapel again. He knew what he liked. What he wanted. He wanted more things like this suit. It pleased Josh, befitted him, good Italian stuff did. Armani. Dolce and Gabbana. Ferrari.

Struck by a chilling thought, he straightened. "What—" He had to clear his throat. "What's your name, by the way?"

She glanced over at him. "Mia. Mia—"

"That's enough," he said, holding up his hand. "I don't want to know any more."

Because Mia was bad enough. It was an Italian name, of course. God, he'd have to be stupid not to realize that her vibrant beauty screamed a set of healthy Mediterranean genes. Mia. And in Italian, *mia* meant "my."

Mine.

Chapter Seven

*A*t the cemetery, Bram slowly trudged up the highest hill. On a knoll nearby, he spotted an acquaintance, but the other man quickly averted his gaze. Bram wasn't surprised. It was rare for anyone to speak to him during his evening visits. Right after Alicia's death, all of Hot Water had respected his need to retreat. Eight years hadn't changed that.

The fact was, though, his time with Alicia seemed more like eighty years ago. As he'd told Honor, he remembered it now from a distance, as if it were a movie he'd seen. On occasion he revisited their life together by rerunning the memories in his head, but both Alicia and the Bram that he had been were long gone.

He accepted that now. But at first, the pain had been unbearable. He couldn't find comfort in his friends, and even with the puppy on the pillow beside his he didn't sleep. Unable to share his feelings even with his mother, the bleakness of his solitary mourning had finally driven her to move away from Hot Water.

With time, though, with that strong wall around his heart, he'd gotten past—if never over—losing Alicia.

Reaching her grave, Bram shoved his hands in the pockets of his jacket and closed his eyes. A breeze shivered the leaves of the surrounding oak trees. In the adjacent city park, that same wind jostled an empty swing. Its lonely creaking was his only company in the darkening cemetery.

Taking a breath, he released the gate in the wall that guarded his heart, letting the questions break free. As the twilight transformed into night, they swirled around him.

During Alicia's three days in captivity, what had she thought? What had she felt? Had she called for him? Had she despaired? How could this have happened to her? Why?

Why?

Like people needed a body to accept the death of a missing loved one, Bram needed those answers, that explanation, to finally bury his grief and find peace.

He dug his fingernails into his palms, waiting for a response. *Willing* it. But once again, no ghosts rose from the ground, no answers floated on the breeze to explain why a random, senselessly violent act had taken the innocent woman he loved.

At dark, his heart went heavy as the questions sucked back inside, lodging deep. Then the gate clanged shut, leaving the familiar dull headache echoing in its wake.

THERE was no peace to be found back at the house, either. Honor met him at the door. Her gaze didn't meet his, though, and her obvious discomfort only made it clearer that he shouldn't have kissed her that afternoon. But she'd been standing there with those wet-starlight eyes, looking at him with sympathy and concern, and then suddenly her mouth had been beneath his. He'd wanted to give her reassurance and comfort and finally just . . . sex.

Five more minutes and he would have fouled up even further by tugging down that tight little top she'd worn, to taste her tight little nipples that had pushed toward him so greedily. He shoved his hands in his jacket pockets, pulling it forward to disguise his hardening body. "What do you want?" he asked abruptly.

"I was wondering if you'd eaten dinner." She lifted her chin and the light from the foyer fixture shone on her face.

Sunshine had washed over it this afternoon. Though he'd sworn to resist her, he'd been drawn to that pretty face. Then, after thirty seconds in her company, he'd been touching her again. Bram, the man who'd avoided touch for so many years.

"Dinner?" he repeated warily.

She glanced over her shoulder. "Because, I, well, Josh thought you might like to join us for dinner."

Josh. Josh McCool, Warren Witherspoon's assistant and Honor's longtime acquaintance. "McCool wants me to join the two of you?" he asked in disbelief. The covetous gleam in the other man's eyes had made Bram think that what McCool really wanted was Honor.

Before she could answer, the blond man was in the foyer too, as if he'd been eavesdropping from around the corner. "Of course we want you to have dinner with us." He put his hand on Honor's shoulder. "We were just about to sit down."

Bram gritted his teeth. He had no idea why he'd

protested letting McCool stay at the guest house earlier today, just as he had no idea why the man's proprietary hand on Honor's shoulder now made him want to offer McCool a serving of his fist. If Honor's friend lured her back to L.A., Bram should consider it a favor, right?

He opened his mouth to decline the dinner invitation, but just then McCool's fingers squeezed Honor's shoulder in a friendly—no, familiar—way. "I'd be happy to sit down with you two," Bram said instead.

He said it because . . . well, because a man like himself, a man desperate to get his solitary bachelorhood back, would *use* this opportunity to encourage his temporary wife's departure, that's why. Getting her out of his house by November fifteenth wasn't enough. He wanted her out of his town.

So it was with good intentions that he followed the pair into the dining room. And it was certainly a cozy meal, he thought darkly as they gathered around the candlelit table. He and Honor played host and hostess at each end, while Josh, the charming snake, sat in the middle, looking as smug as Satan at a sex orgy as he served himself Bram's food and opened a bottle of Bram's best wine.

"Hey, sport." Josh smiled at Bram like a Redford-esque Gatsby. "I can't thank you enough for your hospitality."

"Thank my wife," Bram replied. Perhaps he sounded surly, but it wouldn't do to make Josh think his task would be too easy.

Josh grinned. "Oh, I plan to." He cast a speculative glance at Honor, then returned his attention to Bram. "Did she tell you we dated a time or two?"

The play of flame and shadow from the candles on the table hid her expression from Bram. He lifted an eyebrow at Josh, still posing as the protective husband. "Should I break your nose for breaking her heart?"

The other man's eyes went wide. "Oh, quite the contrary. It's my heart that was smashed to bits when Warren told me about the wedding."

Honor smiled at that. "Josh, darling, you have no heart."

Josh, darling.

Bram tamped down a rise of irritation. Not because of those words, he assured himself, but because of that easy, breezy smile. It was the same smile he'd worked his ass off to inspire when they were at the feed store last week. The same he'd asked her for this afternoon. It was just one of the many distracting things about Honor he was eager to rid himself of.

So he grabbed the wine instead of Josh's throat and allowed the other man to devote himself to entertaining Honor, reminiscing about a round of events they'd attended together. Bram tuned the details out but scrutinized the woman, noting her relaxed posture, her witty responses, the shine of candlelight on her mouth.

Her obvious enjoyment of Josh's blather about society weddings, art gallery openings, and divorce celebrations confirmed once again the kind of life she'd led and how different it was from what Hot Water offered. Bram had some experience with that life and those who lived it. He'd built an international company that had introduced him to people with enough wealth and power to have out-of-the-ordinary security concerns. But the rich and famous included the pampered and jaded as well.

Honor was one of them, right? After all, getting exactly what she wanted was why Bram had been forced to marry her. So no matter how pretty her smiles, no matter how affecting her tears, he definitely didn't want a spoiled heiress like this one intruding on his life any longer.

Faintly smiling, Josh finally turned toward Bram. "Sorry, sport. I'm being rude, cutting you out of the conversation by going on about people you don't know."

And things you know nothing about went unsaid.

Bram bared his teeth, even though it didn't matter how much Josh and Honor had in common and how little she and Bram did. "Don't apologize. Not when I've learned so much about *you*, McCool, from your socialite and charity ball gossip. I've never met anyone before who knows so much about . . ."

Shrugging, he let *so little* hang in the air.

Honor choked out a half-amused cough. "Um, Bram—"

"While I," Josh said over her, "had a technogeek roommate just like *you* at USC. He didn't have much use for parties and women either. Every month or so when we dusted off his computer screen we'd dust him off too, and then take him out to find a girl."

Honor was coughing again.

Without looking away from Bram, Josh pushed her water glass into her hand. "He never managed to keep one, though."

Meaning Bram couldn't keep Honor. His fist tightening on his fork, Bram struggled for the right response, torn between wanting to defend his ego and wanting to encourage the other man's hopes of wooing his wife.

He flicked a glance at her. Her coughing had caused a tear to form on her lashes. In the light of the candle it glittered, then fell to her cheek.

Just like that, Bram's mind spun back to the afternoon. To the bridge, to the kiss. Her body had hummed beneath his palms. But he'd been gentle with her, not yanking her close as need clamored for. The restraint had, strangely enough, intensified his desire. Her taste—

"Bram?" Honor said.

"What?" He jerked back to the present, pissed at how his thoughts had gotten away from him. "Did you ask me something?"

Josh snickered. "And here I thought a devoted husband hung on his new bride's every word."

Cursing himself for a fool, Bram forced his gaze off Honor's mouth. Aware he'd lost that round, he clammed up and allowed Josh the prize they'd been playing for—Honor's undivided attention. Hell, he probably *was* dusty, Bram thought, and damned if he wasn't perfectly satisfied that way.

But by the time Josh ran out of stories to keep them at the table, Bram was more than ready for the evening to end. Both he and Honor walked their guest to the kitchen door. Before the other man left for the guest cottage, he sent Bram another of his bastard-bright grins and bent to kiss Honor's lips.

She reacted with a laugh and shoved Josh out the door. Then, to Bram's surprise, she turned to the business of rinsing plates and silverware and loading them into the dishwasher. He'd been avoiding the house at mealtimes in order to avoid *her,* and so had missed this domestic side of her.

Which brought his mind back to their dinner companion. Annoyed to find himself almost annoyed that the last lips to touch hers weren't his, Bram crossed his arms over his chest. "Bet you didn't end too many evenings doing dishes when you were dating ol' Josh."

Sending him an amused look, she reached for another plate. "Bet you didn't think I even knew *how* to do dishes."

"You're right."

"Summer camp." She continued to efficiently rinse and load the dishwasher. "Every one of them required a minimum two weeks of KP."

He thought of slick Josh and the glittering L.A. life she'd led. "It's as hard to imagine you chopping vegetables as it is to imagine you tromping through poison oak or telling stories around a campfire."

"I'll have you know I make a mean hobo stew and can sing every verse of 'Kumbaya.'"

He shook his head, not wanting to believe a word of it. "Summer camp at Saks Fifth Avenue, maybe."

She shut the dishwasher with an action just short of a slam, then turned toward him. "Is that what you really think?"

Bram shoved his hands in his pockets. "Something had to prepare you for your adult life of champagne slurping and sequined-dress shopping."

Her mouth tightened. "I've spent the last five years sleeping in a succession of company condos, putting eighty-hour weeks into getting my advanced degree in the Witherspoon empire. Believe me, there wasn't much time for champagne and sequins."

He didn't know what to say and she didn't wait for him to figure it out. With long strides, she started out of the kitchen, the violet-colored dress she wore floating behind her.

To leave the room, she had to pass him, and the rush of air that surrounded her headlong movement was filled with the perfume of wealth and woman. His hand shot out to grab her upper arm, halting her.

Sucking deeply of Honor's scent, he looked down, discovering the vee neckline of her dress revealed a torturous glimpse of the pale, creamy rise of her breasts. Wrenching his gaze away, he found her watching him with those silvery, almost clear eyes, no evidence of sexual nerves in sight.

"What do you want?" she demanded.

Better not answer that one, he decided. Better remember that he should be encouraging her interest in Josh. It was the only word he managed to get out.

"Josh?" she repeated.

Bram cleared his throat. "What's with him?"

She flushed. "I know he didn't make a good first impression on you. Josh is a little too . . . confident for his own good, I suppose. And maybe a bit—"

"Superficial?" he offered. "Shallow?"

Her cheeks flushed darker. It brought more color to her lips too, and he couldn't tear his gaze off them. His fingers flexed on her arm as their kiss burst into his memory again. Had it made her as soft between her legs as it had made him hard?

"Bram . . ." Wariness entered her eyes.

Damn it. He shook his head, trying to clear it, trying not to recall that this afternoon his kiss had seemed to allay her nerves. McCool wanted Honor, let McCool take care of her hang-ups too. "What about the two of you?" he made himself ask.

"Josh and I? Josh and I, we're . . ." She hesitated and then half gestured with the arm he held, causing his knuckles to brush against the plump heat of her breast.

The sexual jolt was brutal. So then he would be too; he had to be, damn it, because hadn't he promised him-

self to do whatever it took to get her out of his life? "I
know exactly what you and Josh are," he finished for
her. "Two of a kind."

Her spine jerked straight as she instantly understood his message—his less-than-subtle insult. Then
she stabbed him with one frozen look from her crystal
eyes and broke from his grasp, clearly angry.

Relieved that at least one of them could walk away,
he watched his troublesome bride march off, touch-
me-never in every stride.

"Hey, sport," Josh's voice boomed through the garage
bay Bram used as a workroom and where he'd been
tinkering with Fifo since dawn. He set down his screwdriver and glanced over at the younger man, who was
looking L.A.-slick in a dark olive suit and blue-and-
white tie.

"Do I need a secret spy ring to get in and out of this
place?" Josh asked, smiling genially.

"You need me," Bram replied. "To get out *or* get
back in." He knew he sounded hostile, but he hadn't
slept the night before. The instant he'd closed his eyes,
he would see Honor's face, her expression half angry,
half hurt.

Josh's brows rose. "One-man security system?"

But Bram knew he'd done the right thing by pushing her away. "One man *controls* the security system
and everything else in regards to this house and my
life," he said.

"Hope you don't imagine that includes your wife."
Josh looked amused. "I just had morning coffee with
her and she seems a little . . . steamed. If I were you, I
wouldn't try to control her, let alone chat with her
right now."

"That's not your concern, McCool."

The humor on the other man's face died. "She's not as tough as she acts, you know."

Bram clenched his teeth. Tough enough to sashay into Hot Water and then pry open his life. He slid his palmtop out of his pocket. "Did you say you were leaving?"

"Yeah, I'm off to Enigma," Josh answered. He nodded at Fifo stretched out on the worktable. "New product?"

"We'll see." His contract with Enigma gave the company the right to license any new devices he invented. "I'm still testing."

"An additional product line means we'll need the new facilities more than ever," Josh muttered, shaking his head.

Bram gave him a sharp look. "Problem?"

Josh's slight frown instantly eased into a grin. He straightened his already straight tie. "Come on." His smile turned sly as he lifted his arms away from his body. "Do I look like the kind of man who lets anything or anyone stand in the way of what—or who—I want?"

There it was again, Bram thought, his jaw tightening. The gauntlet. Josh was making it perfectly clear that he was after Honor. The wife Bram had never asked for.

But though he wanted her out of his life, he was no longer certain he wanted her in Josh's arms instead. "Ah." Bram could smile too, even charmingly when he wanted to make a point, a very sharp, lethal point. "But you've never tried to get through someone like me . . . *sport.*"

Josh only laughed, then left. Bram watched him

drive out the gate, then pressed the controls to close it. Then he switched the palmtop to surveillance mode and, through the view of the wall-mounted security cameras, saw the brazen-red Ferrari speed away.

Several hours later, though, Josh's analysis of Honor's mood continued to echo in Bram's head. *She seems a little steamed.* Toward late afternoon, he found himself stalking back to the house. Merely intending, he told himself, to see if she was . . .

Still mad?

Still sticking with their marriage?

But his own assessment of her state of mind had to wait. Though he tracked her down to her room, she was curled up on her bed, asleep.

Standing in the open doorway, he ran his gaze over her relaxed body. She was wearing those hip-hugging jeans again. Facing away from him and with her knees drawn up to her chest, a wide patch of perfect, pale skin was exposed at the small of her back. Her feet were bare too, and he supposed it was the childlike shell-pink she'd painted her toes that made her look so young and so breakable.

On impulse, he entered the bedroom and immediately noticed the piles of papers on the dresser and the reports strewn across the desk. The top sheet of a lined yellow pad was filled with notes in the perfect handwriting of a teacher's pet. Or, he thought with sudden insight, someone who'd spent her school years doing everything perfectly in an attempt to fit in.

The work had worn Honor out . . . or perhaps she'd slept as badly as he the night before. Guilt grinding at him, Bram approached the bed and reached down for the soft blanket folded at the foot. He drew it carefully over her curled body. Then he allowed himself one more moment to run his gaze from the silky darkness of her hair, over her feathery eyelashes, and past her pretty mouth to that small dent in her chin.

He wanted to press his finger there, his lips, his tongue. He wanted to mark her himself.

She was a beautiful handful of contradictions that made him horny as hell, that was certain. But he was just as certain he couldn't afford acting on his biological urges. So he retreated. Bemused by his glimpse of Beauty sleeping, he automatically closed her bedroom door as he left.

Though his office was tranquil, his mood was not. He headed for his desk, then flipped on his computer. With a few mouse clicks, the letters ENIGMA tore across the screen, followed by the black-cloaked figure. Trying to lose himself in the game, Bram raced the player around corners and down passageways.

But his distraction was his downfall. Within seconds, a poison-tipped arrow darted across the player's path, piercing him straight through the heart.

The cloaked figure screamed, high and chilling.

Bram froze, confused. While he'd programmed the player to succeed or fail, he'd never programmed him to *feel*.

The scream sounded again.

Honor.

His pulse rocketed. He shot to his feet and sprinted from the room and down the hall. Under his hand, her bedroom door flew open and he leaped toward her.

She was sitting up, her eyes wide open but unseeing. The blanket he'd covered her with was tangled around her legs and she was fighting its light weight, her breath sucking in and out in harsh, heavy gasps.

"Honor." Ignoring her thrashing movements, Bram

dropped to the bed and gathered her in a gentle embrace. "*Honor*. You're dreaming. I'm here, you're safe."

"No!" She twisted her body, trying to break free of his arms. Her wide, unblinking eyes remained focused on a nightmare that only she could see. She twisted again, then sobbed.

The sound sent an arrow into the center of Bram's own chest.

"Honor!" Ignoring the pain, he slid his hands to her shoulders and turned her to face him. A little shake made her blink. The second made her gaze jump to his face. The third stopped her next sob in her throat.

She swallowed it back down as the fight went out of her. He drew her now-limp body closer and cupped her head, pushing it against his chest.

A breath shuddered through her.

"I'm sorry, baby," he said against her hair. He was sorry for dozens of things—for causing her nightmare, for insulting her out of his own weakness, for the experience that had marked her so deeply. And then, with her delicate, desirable body in his arms, he was, just for a moment, very sorry for the barriers that would forever be between them.

She still trembled and he rubbed his cheek against her silky hair. If he could find a way to let go of her, he'd throw his fist through a wall. How could he have been so thoughtless? How could he live with the image he had of her now, terrified and trembling?

Vulnerable.

"I'm so sorry, baby," he said, his heart banging against its protective wall. "I wasn't thinking. I shut the door."

She struggled again, but lightly now, and he didn't let her go. Despite all the reasons that he should, he couldn't. Not when he needed her in his arms to calm *him.*

*W*ARMTH took a long while to seep into Honor's bones. It was Bram's warmth she was stealing. She leaned into it, into him, grateful for something solid. Her own strength would return in a minute. In just a minute she wouldn't need him.

If she took just a minute, she wouldn't do anything with him she'd regret.

Bram was murmuring to her, but she didn't listen to the words, instead letting them wash over her and wash away the vestiges of the nightmare. There had been words in it too, frightening, sick whispers that tried to stick like leeches to her peace of mind.

She burrowed closer and tilted her face, so that her cheek, her nose, her mouth pressed against the hot skin of Bram's neck. He stilled and his fingers tightened on her back.

"Baby," he whispered.

The hoarse word penetrated her consciousness. "What?" she replied, her mouth moving against his flesh. "What is it?"

He groaned.

Alarmed, she drew a bit away and looked up. Green eyes met hers, then they came a lot closer as his mouth lowered.

She stiffened at the first touch of his lips, the nightmare recent enough to make another grab for her. Crude words echoed in her head, hands fell upon her body as they'd threatened to do so many times. But then the echoes faded, the imagined fingers disappeared. It was afternoon, in the golden light of her bedroom, not a dark cellar. And it was Bram kissing her.

Bram.

The very man who'd cast unsubtle aspersions on her character the night before. She jerked away and broke the kiss, but his arms tightened around her, preventing her complete retreat.

"Damn," he muttered, half frowning. "Scared?"

"Scared?" She shot him a disbelieving look, the nightmare disappearing in the wake of her annoyance. "No, I think kissing you is called *stupid*."

His eyebrows drew together. "What?"

She placed her palms on his chest. "Or maybe 'shallow' and 'superficial.' " Then she shoved at him.

He didn't take the hint. Instead, he sighed, leaning closer to touch his forehead to hers. "Honor, I'm sorry. I shouldn't have said what I did. I didn't mean it, I don't believe it."

It was a long, most unexpected apology. She swallowed. "Then why?"

As he lifted his head, one side of his mouth kicked up in a wry smile. "To prevent this." Then he kissed her again.

It was another gentle kiss, smoothing over her mouth, soothing her mood. And all Honor wondered this time was why anyone would want to prevent something so very, very delicious.

She lifted her hands to his head, her fingers sliding through his thick hair. Needing to hang on to him, she dug her nails into his scalp. He groaned against her lips and she opened her mouth to feel the vibration against her tongue.

His lips opened then too. When she dragged her tongue across his, he dragged her onto his lap. She slid her tongue into his mouth again, but when she tried to retreat he bit down lightly, trapping her.

Her skin prickling with a burning rush of goose bumps, she shuddered.

He lifted his head, his breath ragged. "I'm sorry. Sorry. But you taste so sweet." He hesitated. "Please. Let me hold you. For just a minute let me hold you."

Honor struggled to hear him over the thick, rapid pounding of her heart. He'd done it again, taken her from zero to sexy in the space of a kiss.

When she didn't answer, Bram shifted, swinging his legs onto the mattress. *Hold you,* she remembered him saying. He did that now, stretching out on the bed, stretching her over him, closing his arms lightly around her.

She trembled.

"All right?"

She didn't know what to say, she didn't know how to—or if she should—tell him that it was passion, not nerves, that shivered within her. Especially when they'd apparently both been trying so hard not to get this close.

He lifted her chin, forcing her eyes to meet his. "Do you want me to leave?"

She shook her head, voiceless.

He smiled a little, and the sight was still so rare that her breath caught. His hand slid behind her head and he cupped it, then pushed her cheek against his chest.

"Good. Your nightmare has left me a little . . . undone, baby. I hate you being frightened," he said, his low voice rumbling against her ear. "So let me do this. Just comfort . . . that's all. Let me comfort us both."

He wanted comfort? No more kissing. Comfort.

Okay, she decided, trying to relax against him. That was safe. You might second-guess sex, but comfort you couldn't regret.

Yet every nerve ending was still alert and throbbing and her skin seemed to quiver with each beat of her heart. Beneath her, Bram's body was hot. She wiggled, discovering that Bram's body was hot and *hard*.

Her pulse leaped, but then Bram whispered. "Take it easy," he said to . . . her? Himself?

He slowly ran his big hands down her back from shoulders to hips, a calming movement. He let out a relaxing breath, then stroked her back again, as if in complete control of himself.

Complete except for that erection, that is.

Still keyed up, Honor wiggled again. His hands paused and his heartbeat kicked against her breastbone before he stroked downward once more. At her next squirm, his hands halted longer before moving on.

Afraid he would stop touching her altogether, Honor stilled and let herself be petted. Despite her arousal, her eyes drifted half shut as Bram made a slow, gentle, nearly unsexy exploration of her body.

With her draped over him like a blanket, he was able to draw her hair off the nape of her neck. His fingers stroked the skin there, pushing into her hairline to caress the indentation at the base of her head. Then his hands wandered lower, finding the rounded neckline of the simple T-shirt she was wearing. One fingertip curled under it, tracing a line between her shoulder blades.

Just that fingertip against her bare skin caused goose bumps to rush down her back and she shifted restlessly. He instantly halted the skin-to-skin contact, going back to running his palms over her clothes. Honor squeezed her eyes shut against her disappointment. But this touch was good too, in its slow, patient way. He wasn't taking, he wasn't giving, he was *finding out*.

And for so many years, all her life, no one had ever taken the time to know her, to find out about her. She was the new girl or Warren Witherspoon's daughter or tawdry tabloid fodder.

Or ransom.

Others—men especially—had always seemed to assume they knew who she was and what she had to offer to them.

So Honor held still for Bram. She let him set the pace of whatever it was he thought he was doing. To her, it was seduction. Simple, sweet seduction, in the golden afternoon light of Hot Water, the place that had come to represent everything normal and good after being trapped in soul-sapping darkness.

But it was more than Bram's touch she found seductive. It was *him*, the dark loner, the man who made her feel womanly and wanted in a normal way again. Maybe for the first time ever, really.

His touch moved lower, his hands running over her bottom in twin caresses that awakened even more nerve endings. Her legs drifted a little apart. Beneath her jeans and her T-shirt her flesh chafed against the fabric, every inch begging for a chance to feel a naked pass of those hard, big hands.

Though Honor was holding herself still, there was no holding back her inner reaction. On another of those slow, so-arousing movements of his hands, Bram's fingertips inadvertently brushed between her parted legs. Through the thin denim she wore, she knew he would sense the dampness and heat.

The muscles of his body hardened to stone beneath hers. His hands froze, curled over the back of her thighs, fingers edging inward. "God."

Honor's face burned, but she tried sounding cool

and sophisticated. "Did you think you were putting me to sleep?" she asked lightly.

She felt him swallow. "The nightmare . . . I thought you didn't . . . you wouldn't . . ."

The uncertainty in his voice eased her own self-consciousness. "Bram . . ." She lifted her head to meet his gaze.

Words died.

Everything dissolved except for the look in his eyes. It wasn't uncertain. It was intense. Thrilling. It was desire. Need. Want.

"Have," she thought she heard him say, as if he'd read her mind and was correcting her. Then he spoke again, clearer now. "I have to have more."

Those maddening hands drew upward again, but she didn't have time to curse his restraint, because then he slid his fingertips beneath the waistband of her pants. Her body jerked, heat flaring where his skin touched hers.

"You feel so good," he whispered. "So good."

Then he insinuated his long-fingered hands inside her jeans, sliding smoothly under her satin underwear too. His presence pulled the thick merge of denim seams against the throbbing knot of nerves between her legs. Her breath caught.

His palms cupping her bottom, he pulled her higher, so that her heat, that knot of seams, and that knot of nerve endings rode his erection. She moaned.

He caught the sound with his mouth.

Their tongues tangled. He rocked her against him and pleasure shot through her. Sense and self-consciousness spun away. Regret was a worry for other women, not for Honor. Not when she was learning how the right touch from the right man could rocket her so high, so fast.

His hot mouth dragged across her cheek. He bit her ear.

Honor flinched, but it was with pleasure, and then more pleasure when that jerky movement brought her against Bram in perfect alignment. Their mouths met again and he used his hands to rock her against him in a rhythm that matched the thrust of his tongue in her mouth.

She couldn't breathe. She didn't want to breathe. She didn't want to take the risk of slowing the twisting climb of her desire.

Then the angle of the sun changed and the room, almost in an instant, darkened. Bram froze.

He tore his mouth from hers. "I've got to go." His words sounded raw and almost desperate against her ear. She shifted to look at him, but he used her movement to slip his hands from her skin, then twist away. Between one blink and the next, he was off the bed.

Confused, Honor stared at his back as he escaped across the hall. When his bedroom door shut, she automatically drew up the blanket lying in a heap near her feet in order to retain some of her quickly dissipating heat. The air was cooler, now that it was nearing sundown.

Ah.

She suddenly wasn't confused anymore. Bram had left Honor's bed, left Honor and what they'd done behind, in order to visit Alicia.

Grimacing at her own stupidity, Honor turned her face into one pillow and pulled the other over her head. She'd known something like this would happen, she just hadn't known how unsatisfied and . . . unworthy it would make her feel. The only good thing about the whole embarrassing event was that she needn't bother regretting their brief intimacy, no indeed.

Because Bram already did.

Chapter Eight

Josh guided the Ferrari along a narrow road outside of Hot Water, occasionally glancing at his scrawled directions. Passing one of the few businesses in this mostly rural section of the county—a gas station-minimart that touted in gold glitter that LOTTERY PLAYERS WIN BIG HERE!—he considered stopping.

Not for a ticket—Josh knew better than to leave his fortune to disinterested fate—but for a box of Reynolds Wrap. Then he could fashion a tinfoil beanie as brain protection from whatever damage might be done by the goofy guru he was on his way to meet. Or maybe he could duplicate Granny's homemade antenna by wrapping the silver stuff around a metal coat hanger. Granny had pulled in a station from Prescott, Arizona, with her contraption. Maybe Josh could use his to tune in to the local yokel's out-of-this-world wavelength.

When Warren had called from his ambassador's digs four thousand miles away to put Enigma's problem on Josh's plate, he'd thought it a joke. But thirty minutes at the Enigma offices this morning had cleared that up. Some crackpot was claiming contact with a UFO. Not only that, he was running around telling everyone and the Internet that the mother ship was to return in a few weeks . . . at the very property slated for Engima's expansion.

The old duff and his buddies had visited the Enigma offices several times, trying to convince the company to build on a different piece of land.

As if. The plans were in and approved, the construction company was revving up the bulldozers. And as Josh had told Bram, nothing and nobody got between Josh and what he wanted.

He shifted uneasily on the buttery leather seat. Bram seemed a determined sort too, which made this problem at Enigma even more critical. If Josh's Plan A—winning away Honor—somehow failed, then his Plan B would have to go off without a hitch. That meant getting the Enigma expansion launched smoothly. That would get him back in Warren's good graces and back in line for the megabucks promotion-plus-stock-options that his boss loved to dangle by Josh's nose.

Checking the directions again, he made the next left. Up ahead, a silver mailbox shaped like a flying saucer told him his quarry was near. It told him that maybe the old geezer had a sense of humor too.

Josh turned into the private drive, his tires speeding along the new pavement. Thank God for smooth blacktop. He would have cried if forced to steer the Ferrari down the gravel-over-dirt that too often passed for roadways around here.

Naah. He wouldn't have cried, come to think of it. He would have walked the entire quarter mile leading to the house before intentionally letting one loose pebble pit the finish of his prized car.

Saved from that, he was feeling pretty cheerful as he parked, then trotted up the steps of the small, nondescript cottage to knock on the front door. Its fresh coat of paint made Josh look back at the spanking-new pavement, which then made him wonder about the income potential of playing Paul Revere to a bunch of loony-moony UFO believers.

Then the door opened and the sight of the woman standing on the other side kicked every last thought from his brain, each one landing with a *kerplunk* at his feet. "Y-you," he managed to stutter out, rubbing his itchy palms against his slacks.

You was Bram Bennett's luscious, curvaceous housekeeper, Mia.

She flushed, and God, that faint tinge of red looked gorgeous against the apricot tone of her skin. So gorgeous that he backed down a step before he did something stupid. "I must have the wrong house."

A smell wafted through the doorway behind her. *Oh, please God, no.* "Definitely the wrong house," Josh said. But he couldn't stop himself from sucking in more of the mouthwatering, oh-so-right smell of simmering tomato sauce.

"You weren't looking for me?" she asked. Her hands fluttered at her sides, smoothing her striped apron over her curvy hips.

"Absolutely not," Josh said honestly.

She jerked back. "Well, then. Good-bye." Her hand closed over the doorknob to swing it shut in his face.

"Wait!" He had no idea why he said it, he only knew he wanted to look at her a moment—or hour—

longer. "I must have taken a wrong turn. Do you happen to know where a man lives—a man named Beau Caruso?"

That's when the encounter turned even stranger. Amusement washed over Mia's face, and she pulled the door completely open again. "Come inside," she said.

He backed down another step. "No." From here he was eye level with her ankles, strong, yet elegant, *bare* ankles, their skin the same apricot-gold of her face. Heat surged toward his groin.

He tugged on the hem of his suit jacket. "I have to see this Mr. Caruso."

The corners of Mia's mouth twitched. "Yes, I understand. But my father's not home right now. However, I expect him back any minute."

Damn. Hell. Son of a bitch. Josh mentally spit every curse that Granny had ever taught him, and then some that even *she* considered beyond the pale.

"Come inside," Mia repeated. Her beckoning hand caused the scent of that simmering sauce to curl around his taste buds and yank him forward.

Josh landed in the Carusos' small kitchen, his mouth gasping for air like a just-caught fish. He fell into a plastic-cushioned chair pulled up to a small table, its rectangle top a white-with-gold-grain fake marble just like the one bolted to the wall of the trailer he'd grown up in.

He leaned his elbows on the table, and as he shifted, the plastic cushion under his ass wheezed, just like Granny's seat cushions used to do. His head dropped into his hands. "So let me get this straight. It's your father who thinks he was abducted by aliens?"

Mia was standing at an outdated stove, stirring that

to-die-for-smelling sauce simmering in a big black pot. "That's right."

"And . . ." Josh let the word trail away, for all his usual glibness unable to think of a smooth way to lead into his next question.

Mia glanced over at him. "And do I myself believe he was abducted?" Her eyebrows lifted over her deep brown eyes.

He leaned back in the chair, trying to regather his usual savoir faire. "A natural question, don't you think?"

She knocked the wooden spoon against the edge of the pot and then set it on a small plate beside the burner. With an expert movement, she adjusted the flame beneath the sauce, then turned to face Josh.

Her looks slammed into him again, like a fist straight to the gut. Her passionate coloring and innocent, almost shy demeanor made for one intoxicating sauce of its own. Just looking at her made him feel half drunk.

"I know my father believes he was abducted," she said. Her eyes shifted to the wall at her right, where a framed photograph of a bride and groom hung above a calendar advertising a gourmet food shop. "My mom died sixteen months ago, after a long illness. This is the first thing he's really cared about since."

Josh glanced at the photo. The bride wore a generic white dress and veil. Rental tux on the groom. But there was a special glow on their faces as they looked at each other. Josh shifted on the wheezing cushion, impatient with the brief, sentimental thought. He didn't believe that a photograph could capture a picture of true love any more than he believed there was such a thing.

When he returned his attention to Mia, he caught her studying him again. Her gaze instantly jumped away and Josh started reciting another litany of mental swear words. It would be better for them both if she didn't look at him as if he were an ice cream she wanted to lick all over. It would be better if he didn't find that idea so damn appealing.

He cleared his throat and tried to get his mind back on business. "So Dad has a new hobby now, is that right?"

Mia shrugged. "It's more serious than a hobby. I know some people think he's crazy, but I'm happy he's interested in living again."

"He has a bunch of new friends too," Josh put in wryly, thinking on all that he'd learned about Beau from the front office at Enigma. "That dandy website of his has attracted enough avid believers that every day your father and his groupies are looking less like a club and more like a cult."

He ignored Mia's frown, eyeing her coolly as he asked his next question. "How does he pay for that fancy site and those slick brochures he sends out anyway?"

That struck a nerve. "It's nothing like you're insinuating," she replied hotly. "My father doesn't take money from those people. He doesn't need to."

"Okay, okay." Josh held up placating hands. "But it's getting serious here, Mia. He and his jolly band of merry men are causing headaches over at Enigma, and those headaches are *my* responsibility."

She sighed. "I know. That piece of property. I've tried to talk to him about it, but he's just so certain he's right. . . ."

"And you don't want to be the one to point out he could be wrong."

"After Mom passed away, my dad was drinking heavily. The night he says he was abducted was the one-year anniversary of her death, and maybe what happened . . ." She hesitated, her face flushing again. "Maybe what happened was partly my fault."

"Your fault?" The only thing Josh imagined Mia could be blamed for was how dangerously she distracted him.

She lifted a hand, let it fall. "It was a difficult day for me too. I was thinking about my past, considering my future. I left the house on an errand of my own, not realizing my father was heading for a bender."

Hell, she'd be breaking his heart, if he had one. "Mia, this isn't your doing."

She spun away from Josh and picked up the spoon to stir the sauce. "But the fact is, he hasn't touched a drop of alcohol since that night. So I've supported him in any way I can. Before this came along I was sure I'd be burying another parent very soon."

Josh found himself on his feet. He found her shoulder beneath his hand. He found himself gently turning her to face him. "Mia," he said softly. "I'm sorry."

She seemed fascinated by the knot of his tie. "You're sorry for what?"

"For the loss of your mother. For your worries about your father. For . . ."

Her thick eyelashes rose, as if it took an effort to lift them. Her brown eyes looked straight into his. "For?"

For the fact that though he was looking at her like he wanted to kiss her and she was looking at him like she wanted him to kiss her too, he wasn't going to. Josh took his hand off Mia's shoulder and stepped back. The woman for him was Honor.

They got along well, they always had. Sitting back on the squishy plastic cushion, he reminded himself that he and Honor appreciated the same kind of lifestyle too, her temporary fascination with this rustic backwater aside. Once he plucked her out of Bennett's clutches, they'd settle in L.A. Someplace classy, Brentwood or Bel Air, maybe. Even better, San Marino.

He could see himself belonging to the country club there. Hell, just *belonging* there. For once and for all he'd have left behind that tacky aluminum shoe box at the Sandy Acres Trailer Park, no longer helpless against the shame of being poor and parentless.

His gaze wandered to the wall and that happy wedding photograph. He'd do his damn best to make Honor happy too. It wasn't his intention to disrespect her and their friendship by cheating on his marriage vows.

Mia looked like her mother, he decided idly. That same glowing beauty and pure-hearted expression. He wished— Jerking his mind from the thought, he looked away from the photo and back at the tabletop. Plan B. He was here to make progress on Plan B

"It's my job to make sure your father and his friends don't interfere with the Enigma expansion," he said. "I'll do whatever it takes."

Mia hesitated. "I understand," she finally said.

Then why did he feel so effing miserable?

As he stewed in the juices of his own bad mood, several moments passed in silence. A sensation rippled over his skin and he looked up to find Mia's eyes on him again.

"Damn it," he said through clenched teeth. "What are you doing?"

That hot color rose on her face once more. "Oh. Forgive me. I . . ." She made a helpless gesture with her hand. "You're just so . . . pretty." The flush burned brighter.

Josh closed his eyes. "*Goddamn it.*" He shoved his chair back and jumped to his feet. "I'm not going to kiss you, do you hear me?"

She blinked. "I didn't expect you to. Honest." She made that helpless movement with her hand again. "You're a BP . . . you're you, and I'm—"

"Irresistible," Josh ground out, not understanding a word she'd just said. He stepped forward, grabbed her shoulders, then snapped her against him. Surely— please God—she wouldn't taste as good as he imagined.

Instead of Mia's shoulders, he should have put his hands on his own head. Because one brush of her soft lips nearly blew off its top. His fingers tightened on her, then he shoved her back before he forgot himself and dove inside her mouth for the kind of kiss he really wanted.

"Mia." All words deserted him again, except one. *Mine.*

She crossed her arms over her waist, the color gone from her face. *Damn damn damn.* She thought he'd rejected her. He'd hurt her already.

Josh groaned. "Mia, I need to tell you about me. I need to explain . . ." His words trailed away as she turned her back on him and picked up the wooden spoon.

Oh, good, he thought. *Maybe she'll hit me with it.*

Instead, she stirred the sauce in the pot, releasing another cloud of the mouthwatering fragrance of garlic, tomato, and basil. Could he ever eat Italian again without thinking of her? Could he ever make love to another woman without wishing it was Mia's mouth, Mia's body beneath his?

That's what got Josh to leave the house, Plan B or no Plan B. He nearly ran from it, terrified by the thought that Mia Caruso had messed with things as vitally important as his top two pleasures in life.

A week after her nightmare and Bram's defection, Honor made a round of the great room at the Fortress, teapot in hand. She topped off china cups set at the elbows of the members of Hot Water's Hooks & Needles Club. Smiling at the comfortable, feminine chitchat rising around her, Honor returned the teapot to a nearby tray and picked up a plate of cookies.

As she offered a lemon bar to the ladies sitting on one of the love seats, she almost dared to declare the evening a complete success. It was the first of the needlework group's monthly meetings she'd ever hostessed. It was the first she'd ever attended too. But now that the business portion of the evening had concluded, she only had to smile, serve, and somehow learn to crochet.

Kitty Matthews had been almost the last woman to arrive, but she'd immediately pulled Honor aside. To Honor's delight, Kitty had confided that an invitation to join the Hooks & Needles was a provisional invitation into the town's female social structure as well. Though the evening was a test, according to Kitty, Honor shouldn't worry too much. She'd already earned extra credit points for volunteering to hold the meeting at the Fortress.

The thirty women crowding the room was their biggest turnout in a long while, Kitty had gone on to say. The members were agog to visit Bram's house and had nearly fainted in collective excitement at the offer.

Honor figured Bram himself would faint too if he ever found out about it.

"Where is the man of the house tonight?" a fiftyish, matronly Mrs. Shea asked, her knitting needles clicking with brisk efficiency.

"Oh." Honor fluttered a hand that she hoped communicated *Somewhere about* rather than *I have no idea.* Since their interlude on her bed, he was rarely home.

What exactly he regretted about that afternoon—intimacy in general or intimacy with Honor in particular—she refused to wonder about. As a matter of fact, since that day she'd worked hard at putting the man and his moods from her mind. It would only be easier after tonight. A perfect meeting would cement her place in Hot Water, giving her other people and events to concern herself with.

"You know men always make themselves scarce when it comes to a crowd of females," another woman asserted, glancing up from her piece of cross-stitch. "You'd think they're afraid we'll attack them."

A younger woman, daughter-in-law of the Kemper family who owned the local grocery store, let out a lovesick sigh. "Well, *I* might attack that beautiful Josh McCool. I met him for the first time at Pearl's Diner on Tuesday and then ran into him in the driveway tonight."

That this Kemper-by-marriage was something like ten and a half months pregnant and was knitting the cutest, teeniest pair of booties ever convinced Honor that Josh was safe enough.

"What a face. What a body," the bootie-knitter continued, rolling her eyes in appreciation.

"I'll fight you for him," challenged the woman beside her—the mother-to-be's very own mother.

The crowd in the room laughed. But, catching the

matching gleams in the eyes of the mother-daughter pair, Honor didn't. Maybe Josh *wasn't* safe.

On the couch near the fireplace, a gray-haired lady leaned toward Mia. "What about you, dear? I think you might be one of the few truly available young women here tonight. Does this Josh person blow the wind up your skirt too?"

Honor grinned at the evocative expression, so apt for Mia and her Marilyn Monroe figure.

But instead of smiling too, Mia scowled. "I don't like him," she said. Then her gaze jumped to Honor's face in horror, as if she suddenly realized she'd spoken aloud. "I'm sorry, I know he's your father's assistant and your friend. I—"

"Don't worry about it," Honor replied, and laughed, though her stomach was churning. Had Josh done something to Mia? If so, she was going to kill him. Slowly. Not only would Hot Water blame Honor if someone from the Witherspoon camp hurt a local girl, she'd hate *herself* if he toyed with Mia's emotions. "I'm sure Josh will survive without the admiration of *every* female in the world."

Despite her light words, an awkward silence descended on the room. Nerves pinging, Honor quickly tried filling it. Unfortunately, only subjects of earlier speculation and discussion came to mind. "So the high school kids are really keeping their Homecoming theme top secret?" she tried anyway.

There were no takers on that one, just a few confirming nods. The Argonauts' upcoming football game had already been hashed over as she'd handed out cups and saucers.

She swallowed, her tension coiling as social disaster during her first attempt as a Hot Water hostess loomed.

"And I'll get the booth schedule sent out to everyone first thing in the morning."

Babble, she knew that's what it was, but couldn't stop herself. "Hour shifts from six to ten P.M., four members to a shift, two to sell the hot drinks, two to sell the baked goods."

Of course, that didn't stimulate conversation either. The fund-raising booth the club ran during the Homecoming game had been the first and only item on the meeting's business agenda. Their in-depth discussion of it had ended half an hour before.

Honor's face burned and she felt fifteen again, when her attempts to join any of the cliques at the Beecham School had failed so miserably.

But then Kitty came to the rescue, bless her, with a simple "How's business?" directed at the pregnant woman's mother.

That lady's instant enthusiasm revived the mood in the room. Apparently she managed one of the several bed & breakfasts in town, and she was more than pleased that her establishment was completely booked. "Best fall we've ever had," she said.

Thanks to the attention the alien abduction and predicted UFO return was netting, she explained, the town was filling up with believers, curiosity-seekers, and the press. "If we can keep these folks happy," she concluded, "my place and every other B&B, hotel, motel, and restaurant in town will be flush come winter. Not to mention how the good publicity will encourage more tourism in the future."

Honor released a sigh and settled in her chair as the talk took off in this new, happy direction. A ball of thick yellow yarn in her lap, she studied the uneven chain of crochet stitches that Kitty's great-aunt had helped her get started. With more determination than dexterity, she focused on making another link.

"Don't be so hasty to count your chickens, Greta." A new voice entered the discussion. "You're forgetting Enigma."

Honor froze. Enigma. Bram's company, now her father's.

"I can't go into detail." The woman talking wore an efficient business suit and was knitting something the color of army socks. "But there's a conflict between Enigma and the alienseekers. If it comes to a head, the press will be giddy to cover that too, and the town might not end up smelling so sweet."

Several of the club members groaned.

"Don't even think it!" said another.

Honor's blood ran colder. She didn't want them thinking it either. Worse, what would Hot Water think about *her* if her father's company somehow managed to tarnish the town's reputation?

As debate rose hotly in the room—some women pro-alien, some pro-Enigma, some with economic stakes in both—Honor tossed aside her crocheting. Thinking fast, she scrambled to her feet.

"Who needs more tea?" she called out. "Cookies? And I have hand-dipped chocolates in the kitchen."

Thank goodness, the mention of chocolate ended all the acrimony. The candies on the platter she passed around quickly disappeared, and when the chatter began again, it was unheated conversation at several separate locations around the large room.

Breathing easily once more, Honor set the plate on the small table beside her own chair. Then she returned to her hook and yarn, frowning at the loopy, wiggly stitches. Hoping a sugar rush might make some sense of the handiwork, she reached for a leftover chocolate and popped it in her mouth whole.

Its presence made it impossible for her to speak when, an instant later, Bram shoved open the front door. As he stalked inside, his gaze swept the crowded room and then landed on her. Her chocolate was only at half-melt when he reached her chair. "What's going on?" he demanded.

Some of the gossip being exchanged must have been good, because the ladies didn't immediately go quiet. Honor had time to jump to her feet, one-handedly clutching her crochet hook and yarn to her chest. She even had time to wrap her free fingers around Bram's wrist in preparation for tugging him someplace private. Someplace where the ladies couldn't overhear their conversation and then guess at the thorny nature of their marriage.

"Bram Bennett!" Kitty's great-aunt Cat managed to conclude her previous conversation before Honor could pull him away. "How wonderful to see you, and how lovely of you to allow us into your home."

Honor swallowed the last of the chocolate in her mouth as she watched the expressions that chased themselves across Bram's face—anger, bafflement, frustration.

"I. Uh. It's good to see you too, Cat." Then he looked down at Honor's hand, still grasping his arm. "Excuse me, ladies. I need a minute with . . . my wife."

Honor's pulse jumped at the ominous way he said those last two words. They apparently signaled strain to the rest of the group too, because knitting needles ceased clicking and gazes fixed on them from every corner. Honor managed to send out a reassuring smile, though, even as he plucked her hand off his wrist and towed her through the dining room to the kitchen.

His expression grim and his hand still hard on hers, he confronted her the moment they were out of eyesight. "Now. What's going on?"

"Keep your voice down," Honor whispered, trying to slip from his hold. She bobbled the ball of yarn, her hook, and the pitiful worm of stitches she still gripped in her free hand, dropping all three.

He didn't release her as she half bent, half knelt to retrieve them from the floor. His implacable gaze didn't release hers either, so she groped blindly for the items, dropped them again, grabbed them up a second time, then stood.

"What's going on?" he repeated.

She swallowed. "Just a meeting."

His mouth flattened. "Damn it, Honor, you know I don't let people in."

"But they were very happy to come."

"But I'm not happy to have them here," he mimicked her tone through his teeth. "This isn't a social hall."

"And you're a man who doesn't want a social life. I get that." Honor tried pulling free from him again, but he didn't let go. "Have you thought that maybe *I* do?"

"What, your playmate Josh isn't keeping you entertained, princess?"

Playmate. Princess. She glared at him. "I told you, that's what I think *husbands* are for."

His eyes narrowing to slits, he hauled her closer. Heat radiated from him as well as more of that irritation. "Is that the problem? You want more of what we started the other day?"

She wanted to smack his face for leaving her on the bed that afternoon, feeling like a fool. She wanted to stomp on his toes for bringing it up now, when she was close enough to him to vividly recall how it felt to lie over his big body, when she could remember with pulse-tripping detail the pleasure of his long fingers on her bare skin.

Her fingers tightened on the ball of yarn and she ignored the heat crawling up her neck. "I don't need any more of your brand of pity, thank you very much." If she'd thought about that afternoon at all, which she *didn't*, she'd thought that pity must have motivated his kisses, his caresses. His pity for her nightmare and his pity for the fears the kidnapping had left behind.

"*Pity?*" His hand released her and she took a hasty half-step back. Then he closed his eyes, his mouth moving.

Counting, Honor deduced, reading his lips.

At ten, he opened his eyes and took a deep breath. "Okay. Let's start over." His voice was calmer now, his emotions apparently leashed. "Tell me why the women are here."

"It's a meeting of the Hooks & Needles Club."

He blinked. "And what exactly *is* the Hooks & Needles Club?"

Whatever women had been in his life during the past eight years, they apparently hadn't been women deeply entrenched in Hot Water's social world.

For some reason, it made her feel almost sunny. "It's a secret organization of women intent on infiltrating the lives of gloomy, boring, brooding, cranky men."

"Very funny. And I'm not cranky."

"*Au contraire.* You should have seen your face when you walked in tonight. Definitely cranky."

"I was suffering from the sight of the front gate standing open and broken . . . *again*." His eyebrows lifted. "Would you happen to know anything about that?"

"Well . . ." Honor avoided his eyes by focusing on the angle of his right cheekbone. "I had to let the ladies in, of course."

He groaned. "How *did* you let them in?"

With her free hand, she felt for the inner pocket of her long skirt. Coming up with nothing, she tried transferring the yarn and crochet hook to her other hand. They slipped in her suddenly sweating palms and dropped on the floor again.

Inwardly cursing her nervousness, she quickly swept them back up, then located her other pocket and pulled out the palmtop stashed there. "Mia told me where to find this and which buttons to push to unlock the gate."

He snatched the computer from her hand. "Buttons to push," he muttered. "You don't need any advice in that regard, believe me."

Honor was surprised into a half laugh. "I think you almost made a joke."

He scowled. "I wasn't trying to be funny."

Honor laughed again. "Even better."

She saw his mouth move in a silent *One, two, three.* Then he rubbed the back of his neck with his free hand. Sighed. "So what time does your Society of Evil Intruders conclude their meeting?"

"You're not going to kick them out?"

"What kind of man do you think I am?" Holding up a hand, he grimaced. "Don't answer that. In any case, rest assured that tonight I'm not going to stand in the way of your social acceptance."

Honor stilled. He understood. He might not know what the Hooks & Needles Club was, but he realized how important being part of it was to her. Something warm rippled through her heart. "Thank you," she said. "Thank you very much."

As if he couldn't help himself, he reached out and brushed a lock of hair off her cheek. His thumb lingered at her chin. "Now, is there anything else you've neglected to tell me? A parade you've scheduled to pass through? A rodeo on the back deck?"

Guilt gave a little pinch. "N-no. Nothing." What she had yet to tell him was nothing like that.

He nodded and let his hand fall. "All right. This one time we'll let it go. But you know I don't want a crowd here ever again."

She knew, so she nodded.

His shoulders shifted as if he were about to turn, then he paused. Sighed. "Honor, about the other day. Can't we let that go too?"

Let that go. Forget about it, he meant. Forgive him for not wanting her enough to stay. Forgive him for feeling more pity than passion.

"This marriage—even as temporary as it is—doesn't need any added tension," he continued. "Wouldn't you agree?"

He had her there. And he had also been awfully understanding about the Hooks & Needles. Not to mention there was that small problem she hadn't told him about yet. She probably owed him something for that alone. "All right."

"Good." He curtly nodded again. "We don't need to tangle over everything." With that, he turned and took a step away from her.

A step that landed him flat on his face on the hardwood floor. The fall jerked the ball of yarn out of Honor's loose grasp and it bounced away as she yelped in surprise.

"Bram!" Dropping to his side, she realized her earlier distracted bumbling had ensnared his ankles in yellow strands.

He pushed onto his forearms and looked over his shoulder at the yarn wound about his feet. Then he turned resigned eyes on Honor. "About us tangling. I take it back. It must be inev—"

He broke off, his gaze drifting over her shoulder to snag on something she'd half hidden in the darkest corner of the kitchen. "What is that?" he asked slowly.

She pretended not to know what he was talking about. "What's what?"

He flipped over and speared Honor with his eyes. "What happened to Fifo? I remember leaving it on guard when I left tonight. How did your ladies get past it?"

Honor swallowed. He was so oddly attached to the metallic thing and she couldn't think why, especially when her sweet and silly Joey was so much warmer, friendlier, not to mention *alive*. "I deactivated him."

In a manner of speaking.

With jerky movements, Bram uncoiled the yarn from around his ankles. Then he rose to his feet, towering over Honor like a threat before striding to the shadowy corner. He swiped away the crocheted afghan she'd borrowed to hide—er, cover—Fifo.

Bram's gaze whipped toward her. "You didn't deactivate Fifo. You *decapitated* it."

"No! No! Just his ear came off, that's all." She hurried to Bram, digging into her deep skirt pocket, then holding out the piece of metal. "And his nose." She reached for that too, handed it over. "This is one of his teeth, I think."

Bram accepted the parts, all the while shaking his head. Then he bent and tenderly picked up Fifo's remains, cradling the dog against his chest.

"I'm very sorry," Honor said.

He brushed past her, then paused in the kitchen doorway. "And I was very wrong. I *am* cranky, princess. I'm very, very cranky."

Her stomach sinking, she watched him stalk off in the direction of the visitors. She'd wanted so much to make the perfect impression on the women. But what would the Hooks & Needles make of her now? How would her "test" be scored after her husband denounced her as unwanted wife or robot-ruiner or both?

Chapter Nine

"Sit. Lie down. Roll over." In the after-lunch sunlight on the back deck, Honor worked with Joey, which had degenerated into her pretending she was commanding the dog to perform exactly what he was doing naturally. "Wiggle in ecstasy. That's right. Good boy."

Shaking her head, she laughed at herself and again at the silly animal, her heart going to mush when he ran over and swiped her bare knee with his tongue. Then a shadow moved in her peripheral vision and she smoothly slid back into training mode. "Good, Joey. Sit. Scratch your ear. Lie down. Lick your—"

"Face facts," she heard Bram say, his voice dry. "That's your idiot dog's one and only talent." As he came to stand beside her, his arm brushed hers.

Her flesh twitched, and she edged away to avoid more contact. Sparks of one kind or another flew whenever they rubbed together. "You'll be sorry," she replied, "when you have to bake him four dozen dog biscuits from scratch."

She allowed herself a glance at Bram, noticing the way his short dark hair glinted blue fire in the sunlight and that he was actually half smiling as he watched Joey cavort about the deck another moment before madly dashing into the untamed stand of trees just beyond.

"Still thinking too small, princess."

"Eight dozen, then." She forgave him the royalty crack. There wasn't any real barb in the word this time and she had reason to be tolerant. Last night when he'd left the kitchen, she'd been braced for disaster with the Hooks & Needles. Sure, he'd promised not to get in the way of her social progress, but that was before he knew about the Fifo damage.

Yet, surprise, surprise, he'd merely wished the ladies a good evening. And by the end of it, Honor knew that the women had truly enjoyed themselves. As a matter of fact, several less-than-subtle hints had resulted in her offering to host the next meeting, scheduled November sixteenth, at the Fortress. The mayor's wife—the leading town matron—had even sworn to rearrange another obligation so she wouldn't miss it.

Which meant that Honor would have to broach the subject with Bram at some point. Though she was supposed to be out of his house by that date, she'd yet to make any progress on the issue with her father. Living half a world away only made it easier for him to ignore her feelings, it seemed.

But she didn't want to worry about anything today. Not when there was last night's success in forging community ties to savor. Even her relationship with Bram appeared peaceful at the moment, just another milestone to celebrate.

Honor peeked up at him again. "This must be some kind of record."

He lifted an eyebrow. "Yeah?"

"Two minutes together and we're both still in a good mood."

"You're right." He nodded. "There must be something in the air."

Honor crossed her arms over her chest. "Well, it certainly couldn't be the company."

"You've got that right, princess." His lips twitched.

Hers did too. "I know I do, grouch."

They exchanged level looks. Then, apparently as satisfied with their exchange as she, he turned back to gaze out at the woods.

Honor didn't blame him, because she couldn't grow tired of the view herself. Dark green pines bristled beside the yellow-and-red-dressed sycamores and maples. Here and there industrious, fat-cheeked squirrels raced across the twisted arms of oak trees.

She sucked in a long breath of autumn air, its taste part tangy and part comforting, like lemonade and buttered toast. "What a glorious day."

"Yeah."

A fizz of pleasure bubbled through her bloodstream. Could a real marriage be so much better than this? Two people enjoying the scenery around them. Two people who were coming to an understanding of sorts.

Effervescence shot through her again. It had been a hundred years since she'd felt so alive and happy. She sucked in another breath of delicious air, almost drunk on the beauty of the world and the simple joy of being part of it.

A light breeze whispered through the trees, and from high above, a bit of twig fluttered down and caught in her hair. Bram plucked it away before she could.

"Thanks," she said, smiling at him.

He slanted her a look. "Eight minutes, including an expression of gratitude. Definitely a record."

She laughed, more giddy bubbles coursing through her bloodstream. "You look awfully pleased about it," she added, stepping back to study him.

"I am pleased." His mouth curved and he reached out to tap her nose with his forefinger. "But it's because you did me a favor last night."

"I did?" Astonished, Honor hooked the stem of her sunglasses with her pinkie to gape at him over the pink-tinted lenses.

His knuckle nudged her chin. "Close your mouth, princess. You really did. When I was reattaching Fifo's facial anatomy, I found and fixed a glitch I wouldn't have known about otherwise."

"Wow." She didn't know what else to say.

It apparently was enough, because his face brightened and he whipped his handheld computer out of his pocket. "Do you want to see?"

"Oh. Well . . ." The robotic dog made her nervous, and her track record with the metal thing was dismal. But Bram was awaiting her response with the eagerness of a little boy about to share his baseball cards. "Sure."

He held the palmtop out. "I'll let you—"

"No." Honor couldn't stop herself from refusing. "You *know* Fifo doesn't like me."

"I know nothing of the kind," he said, but the look he gave her was indulgent. "That was the malfunction— now fixed—not a reaction to you."

"Whatever you say," she replied, trying to sound as if she believed him.

Stepping near, he slid his arm around her waist and

spun her to face the house. Then he fiddled with the palmtop to summon the dog. "You'll see."

At the distant hum and clackety-click that signaled Fifo on the move, Honor shivered and instinctively stepped closer to Bram. His hand tightened at her waist, his fingers finding the inch of bare flesh between the band of her knee-length skirt and the knotted ends of her cotton blouse.

"Relax," he murmured.

"Easy for you to say," Honor mumbled back, goose bumps breaking across her belly. His hand was warm and his fingertips slightly rough.

But Bram didn't seem to notice her reaction as he focused his attention on the robot rolling through the open door of his office and onto the deck. The metal dog stopped several feet from them, his body at rigid attention. Watching the animal warily, Honor held her ground, but then something strange reached her ears. "Don't tell me he's panting?"

As if embarrassed, Bram averted his gaze from hers and half shrugged. "Consumers like the real touch."

Oh. She suspected *Bram* liked the real touch and the idea made her heart ache. He worked so hard to keep aloof and to camouflage his feelings, but then he'd do something that made her see straight through to his soul. "It's very nice."

"But you haven't even seen what I fixed." Without waiting for her reply, he called out to the dog, "Come, Fifo. Come to Honor."

"Bram, no—" But it was too late. Fifo's legs scissored and he started for her.

Her eyes glued on the advancing animal, she drew nearer to Bram. This was when disaster inevitably happened. Fifo would start snapping his jaws and then she'd accidentally cause him harm, and then—

Then the dog stopped, eighteen inches from her feet. With his amber eyes glowing, he slowly lowered to his haunches. *Pant pant pant.*

Honor stared up at Bram. "What happened to snarl growl snarl?"

"I told you. I fixed the problem."

Honor looked back at the dog. His sitting posture appeared particularly rigid. His eyes glowed particularly bright too, his stare fixed on her. An idea niggled at the back of her mind. As an experiment, she slid her foot toward the beast.

In a flurry of jerky action, he skittered back.

Honor tried it again; again Fifo skittered away from her.

"See?" Bram said. "Fifo's fine."

"Fine?" Honor glanced up at Bram, then back at the dog. "If you ask me, Fifo's afraid."

There was a beat of surprised silence before Bram responded. "Of what?" he scoffed.

She swore she could see the truth in the metallic creature's unwavering, wary eyes. "Of me."

"What?" Amusement in his voice, Bram curled both hands around her waist and turned her to face him. "You can't be serious."

She glanced back at the dog. "I think I am."

"Come on, Honor, what do I have to do to prove it to you?"

The humor in his voice wasn't on his face, though. Looking up at it, Honor stilled, because he wasn't wearing the cool, remote expression she was used to either. "Prove what, exactly?"

"That Fifo doesn't have feelings."

She thought it was an almost-desperate tension on his face and now in his voice. Her pulse skipped, and she wondered if she understood why Bram had left her on the bed that day after all.

Maybe it wasn't because he hadn't wanted her enough. Maybe he'd wanted her *too* much.

"But . . ." Suddenly it seemed vitally important to know if she was right. She gazed into Bram's eyes. "But every time he's around me, I'm positive he feels something."

"No, he doesn't." He shook his head. "He's not that way."

Honor's pulse skipped again. Bram's hands were still at her waist, his thumbs against her bare flesh. Was he aware that they were gently moving in small circles, caressing her?

She fought against betraying a shiver. "Are you sure he feels nothing at all? Not even pity?"

His hands stilled. "Nothing close to pity. Hell, Honor, you can't be so naive as to think that."

She shrugged a shoulder. "One minute snarling, the next minute panting. I never know what to think."

"Let me do the thinking for both of us."

He was thinking to keep his distance from her, but his thumbs restarted those maddening little circles on her flesh and her pulse flared. That *I'm-alive!* fizz of pleasure surged through her body. "Leaving me the only one with feelings, I suppose."

Bram's jaw tightened. "It's not one-sided, if that's what you're getting at."

So he could admit to desiring her, she thought. But he *was* wary. Why else would he lock himself away in the Fortress if he wasn't afraid of feeling too much?

Her heart squeezed. What would it be like to have a second chance on that bed with him? At the thought, another intoxicating rush filled her.

Honor's heart sped up in excitement. She was young and the world was beautiful. More, she desired a man, this man, proving she was truly, finally, really alive.

Alive.

All at once, she found herself impatient. And reckless.

"Bram, I . . ."

The rest of what she might say—what *would* she say?—caught in her throat. "Why can't we . . ." she started again, stopped.

Then another, stiffer breeze shook the trees. A shower of leaves fell on them, around them, big drops of autumn red, orange, and gold. A second brush of wind brought more leaves raining down and now they were surrounded in swirling, drifting, dancing color. Honor laughed out loud, because no moment, nothing, had ever felt so right.

With everything to do with Hot Water going so well, why was she hesitating to take the rest of what the world had to offer? Why not embrace it with arms and heart open?

She looked up at him, her pulse thumping in her ears. "Listen, Bram."

He abruptly released her and stepped away.

"*Bram.*" He made her want to stamp her foot like the spoiled princess he'd once thought she was. She moved forward and grabbed his arm. "Listen—"

"Hold that thought."

Hold that thought until when? Right now she sensed chinks in the walls around him! She couldn't give him a chance to refortify them, or herself a chance to chicken out.

"No," she said, giving his arm a little shake. "Now."

Bram pulled away from her. "Honor, Josh is calling."

Then she heard the other man's voice floating through the house, getting closer. "Hang Josh." She waved her hand. "I'll tell him to leave."

"There you are." Josh strode onto the deck, Mia trailing behind him. "I need—"

"Go away, Josh." Honor kept her gaze on Bram's face. "We're having an important conversation." Nothing, she thought, surprised by her own vehement certainty, was more important than this. She couldn't conceive of a single thing that would take a backseat to it.

"There's Enigma trouble," Josh said grimly. "Mia thinks maybe for the town too."

Honor froze, that fizz of joy, the recklessness, instantly ebbing. Nothing was more important except for that. *Trouble for the town.*

*F*OLLOWING Josh's Ferrari, Bram turned his SUV down Gold Dust Road. "I'm not the owner of Enigma anymore," he warned, looking over at Honor, then catching Mia's eye in the rearview mirror. "This problem with the alien groupies isn't mine to solve."

Honor made a small sound.

He looked at her again. "What?"

Her clear, clearly anxious eyes cut his way, then dropped. "Nothing." The hands resting on her thighs curled into fists.

Bram squeezed his own around the steering wheel to stop himself from reaching over to touch her. Why was she so hard to resist? The two of them were so damn different. She read phantom emotions in Fifo, for God's sake, and Bram suspected she imagined emotions in him that were nonexistent too.

Annoyance and lust were the only two feelings he'd ever felt toward her, he assured himself. Even the annoyance came and went. She'd effectively evaporated his last burst of that emotion—when he'd discovered all those women had invaded his home at her invitation—by expressing her laughably misguided notion that he'd touched her, kissed her, nearly had sex with her, out of *pity*.

The motivation for that had been pure lust. And he'd left her on her bed that day to prevent breaking his own strict rules and sleeping with her. Damn, he was only trying to do the right thing for both of them, but she continued to entice him at every turn.

To remove himself from further temptation, he should have refused to be part of this little expedition. But it was too easy to see that then On-the-Make Mc-Cool would have used his Hollywood-handsome face and practiced charm to recruit Honor as sole member of his private troubleshooting team.

For reasons he wouldn't examine, Bram refused to give the slick bastard the satisfaction.

Oh, he'd still keep out of the Enigma problem and he'd keep his distance from Honor—but he'd make sure Josh McCool kept his distance from her too.

A few miles down Gold Dust Road, Josh's car swerved to the right. Bram braked behind him. "We're here, ladies."

The four of them climbed out of the vehicles, then paused, staring in dismay across the road at the acres of weedy fields owned by Enigma. Cyclone fencing had once restricted access to the property, but a section had been cut and pushed aside, leaving an opening wide enough for large vehicles to pass through.

And pass through they had. Eight large RVs were planted on the weeds, each flying the Stars and Stripes from flagpoles on their rooftops. The largest camper was center stage and additionally bore a banner in neon blue-and-green that read, simply, WELCOME BACK.

Adding to the festive camp atmosphere were several large beehive tents as well as various one-man contraptions. Propane stoves were in evidence and Bram noticed a half dozen picnic tables set end to end under a series of tarps that provided shade.

Back at the house, Josh had said that Beau and his believers had moved onto the Enigma site determined to prevent the construction. It looked as if he was right. Bram shook his head, wondering exactly how his ordered existence had suddenly become so bizarre. "How many are camped on the property?"

Josh shrugged. "I haven't taken a head count."

"More are due to arrive," Mia put in. "I didn't know my father was planning this, but I heard Gil say they expect a large group to show up in town this weekend."

Josh ran his hand through his hair, then glanced at Mia. "Will your father listen to you? Can you convince him to send everyone home?"

Looking down at the ground, she shook her head.

"Damn it!" Josh's usual urbane charm fell away and his eyes hardened. "Do you mean he won't listen to you or you won't try to convince him?"

Mia flushed. "I—"

"Lay off, Josh," Honor said, crossing to him and putting her hand on his arm. "This isn't Mia's fault."

The blond man inhaled a long breath, then the lines

of his face relaxed. He covered Honor's small hand with his and smiled at her. "You're right, sweetheart. Sorry."

Bram narrowed his eyes. "That apology belongs to Mia." He walked over and grabbed Honor's wrist, tugging her away from Josh.

"Where are we going?" Honor asked, trotting to keep up with him.

Bram sighed, realizing he was leading them toward the encampment. "To see just how serious Beau and his followers are, I guess."

Several people came out of their temporary abodes as Bram and Honor walked onto the property, trailed by Josh and Mia. Some of the groupies looked like college students in the typical dress of jeans, T-shirts, and hiking boots. A few baby-boomers in corduroy and oxford cloth descended from the most luxurious of the RVs. The flaps of one of the big tents was tossed back, emitting otherworldly flute music as well as a ragtag bunch of people dressed in long robes of red fabric.

"They look serious," Honor murmured.

Bram rolled his eyes. "They look seriously nutty." The door of the center RV swung open and Mia's father, Beau Caruso, descended the aluminum steps.

In a pair of worn white overalls and a flannel shirt, he looked just like what he was, a semi-retired painting contractor. He beamed as he strolled toward the four of them. "Would you look who's here! Visitors already. I recognize Bram Bennett and my own little girl, of course."

Honor stepped forward, her friendly smile tipping Beau's mouth higher. "And I'm Honor Witherspoon, er, Witherspoon-Bennett. Bram's—"

"Josh McCool, sir." Josh's shoulder rubbed Honor's

as he stuck out his hand. "Assistant to Mr. Witherspoon, the man who owns Enigma now."

Beau shook hands. "And did you come to join us, Mr. McCool?" he asked, as if delighted by the idea.

As Josh stuttered in response, Bram found himself stepping up to flank Honor's other side. "Beau, we're here to find out what your group wants."

The older man scratched his thick head of graying hair. "We want to welcome our extraterrestrial visitors."

Gil, the skinny young man who had been at Dylan and Kitty's party and then again at the feed store, trotted down the steps behind Beau. "And to protect the site of an event of historic proportions. The aliens were here once and will return November fifteenth. So you see, we can't allow the land to be changed in any way."

"Well, that's too bad," Josh shot back, finally finding his voice. "Because Mr. Witherspoon can't allow your group to change *his* plans for the land."

"But wait," Honor said, her hand grabbing Bram's. It was so icy and small he wasn't heartless enough to break free. "I'm sure my father has some flexibility, some—"

"Your father wants the expansion *here*, Honor." Josh raised his voice, looking around to catch the eyes of the other listeners. "And construction is scheduled to begin shortly. This is private property. Witherspoon property."

Gil drew up his skinny shoulders and stared Josh down. "We're *not* leaving." The followers ringing them nodded in support, and though Beau didn't say anything, he didn't contradict the younger man either.

Josh's jaw hardened and he slid his cell phone from the breast pocket of his jacket. "You're giving me no choice but to call in the sheriff."

Honor's nails bit into Bram's skin, just what he deserved for letting her drag him back into more craziness, he decided.

"*Wait,*" she said again. With her other hand, she grabbed Josh's sleeve and dragged him closer.

"Honor," he protested. "You—"

"This is what Mia was worried about," she whispered anxiously to Josh. "If you do this, all sorts of things could go wrong. Someone might be hurt, the deputies or these people. Even if no one is injured, the press will get wind of any mistake and then the whole town will curse the Witherspoon name."

"This is business," Josh snapped. Then he hesitated, apparently picking up on Honor's distress. His voice softened and he smiled. "Sweetheart, this is about *money.*"

Bram gritted his teeth as Honor's tension traveled in unabated waves up his arm and toward his chest. He fought the sudden need to smooth her frown away with his fingers.

As if she sensed his struggle, Honor turned to him, her hand squeezing his again. "Bram," she said. "You know I'm right. You know if something goes wrong that Witherspoons won't be welcome in Hot Water."

Better late than never, he deliberately extracted his fingers from her grip. She was *not* going to pull him further into this. He'd sold Enigma and retreated to his house to avoid entanglements.

Come to think of it, if he supported anyone's position, it should be Josh's. Getting the groupies out of Hot Water would reduce at least *some* of the chaos in his little corner of the world.

His mouth opened. "Josh, why can't you wait a while before calling in the sheriff?" was the wrong thing that came out of it.

"What? Why?"

Bram found himself stepping back, drawing Honor and Josh away from Beau and Gil so they could have some privacy. "Maybe we can come up with a solution that isn't so confrontational," he said, all the while cursing himself. "Even better, perhaps the groupies will get tired of camping and leave of their own accord."

"Yes." Honor's shoulders relaxed. "That's perfect. There's still some time left, right, Josh? I'm sure Beau and company will get tired of roughing it before construction begins."

When she looked over at Bram and mouthed, *Thank you*, he felt ridiculously . . . relieved. Yeah, that was it. Even though he'd let himself be drawn into suggesting a solution, he'd at least managed to keep his distance from her, right?

Mia stepped forward for the first time, her husky voice nervous. "Please, Josh."

For a moment Josh closed his eyes. Then he shoved his cell phone back in his pocket and sighed, avoiding all their gazes. "Oh, hell. Fine. I'll give it some time."

Bram was surprised by what happened next. Shy Mia lifted on her tiptoes and kissed Josh's cheek. Since he wasn't looking at her, Josh didn't see it coming. When Mia's lips touched his face, he jerked away.

"I'll second that." Honor moved toward Josh too, her pretty lips puckering.

Oh, hell, indeed. Bram hadn't gone this far to give Josh any satisfaction *now*.

Dismissing distance and any other sensible thought, Bram grabbed Honor's arm and hauled her back. Damn it. She was shooting every one of his good intentions to hell.

He bent to her mouth. If it was the last thing he ever

did, he thought the moment before the taste of her kiss took over his mind, he was going to find a way to pay her back.

A breeze blowing through the passenger window brushed Honor's cheek as Bram drove away from the Enigma property. She smiled a good-bye at Mia, who had opted to stay for a visit with her father. Josh was standing by his Ferrari, looking disgruntled, but Honor cheerfully waved at him anyway.

The enounter at Engima had ended peacefully, thanks to Bram. Despite his professed unwillingness to get involved, he'd been the one to suggest the solution that appeased Josh.

With a pinch of guilt, she realized she hadn't hesitated to turn to Bram when she'd needed him. It seemed she just kept asking him for things. First marriage, then solving the Enigma problem. Not to mention she'd almost demanded he take her to bed too.

She slid him a glance, feeling more guilt. He'd even had to steal the kiss she'd intended for Josh, though it was Bram himself who had saved the day. Maybe he had good reason to consider her spoiled.

"Let me do something for you," she offered on impulse.

Bram glanced over. "What?"

"Let me buy you something," she said.

His gaze slid to her again, his green eyes unreadable. "Exactly what did you have in mind, princess? A pony? A plane? Maybe my very own golf course?"

She shrugged. "I don't know. Let me buy you lunch."

"I've already had lunch."

"Then a beer. Let me take you into town for a beer.

It'll be fun." When he looked over this time, she was ready for him, her most winning smile stretched across her face. She owed him, she knew that.

His face went stony and he refocused on the road. "We have beer back at the house."

Honor suppressed a sigh. Who wanted to go back to the house? Every time the heavy gate shut behind her she had to quell a surge of claustrophobia. Worse, she could tell the Enigma situation had put Bram in a dark mood. If they returned to the Fortress he would disappear somewhere, leaving her feeling even more guilty.

"Bram . . ." There must be some way to entice him to just relax and play for once. He needed that way more than he needed lunch, a beer, or her in his bed.

A hand-lettered sign nailed to a fencepost gave her an idea. "Let me buy you a pumpkin."

"A *what*?" He shot her a look.

"A pumpkin." There was a second sign staked farther along the road, advertising a pumpkin patch ahead. She pointed to it. "When was the last time you carved a jack-o'-lantern?"

"I—" He frowned. "I don't know."

"I never have." She smiled just at the idea of changing that.

"Princess, never tell me your fancy boarding schools were so strict," he said dryly. "Were they worried your fairy godmother would turn one into a carriage and whisk you away to a prince's ball?"

"You're making jokes again." Her eyes widened with pretend shock. "It's a whole new, very interesting side of you."

There wasn't even the barest hint of laughter in the green gaze he sliced her way.

"Really," she insisted, knowing full well he didn't

like to be teased, but thinking he probably needed it. "Very attractive. Very . . . entertaining."

"Honor," he warned. "You're playing with fire."

She waved the idea away. "Right now I think we need to play, period. And we need pumpkins. You probably don't get any trick-or-treaters, out in the wilds like you are." *As if you'd let them in anyway,* she added to herself. "But still, Bram. Let's have some fun. Let's go pumpkin-picking."

After a brief moment of long-suffering silence, he grunted.

Despite what she interpreted as agreement, she was still a bit surprised when he actually turned off onto a road that led to a dirt parking area. Between the parking lot and a large field was a split-rail fence. A couple of kids were sitting atop it, swinging their feet and licking Popsicles.

Orange-colored juice ran down their arms and dripped on their bare legs. Even though she and Bram were the sole customers, it looked as if the children were having the best day Honor had ever dreamed of in her life. On the dirt beside them was a kids' primary-colored cash register and in the shade of a nearby oak sat a red-and-white cooler. Another hand-lettered sign priced Popsicles at fifty cents and pumpkins "VARIUS."

Honor reached into her purse and jammed some cash into her pocket before sliding out of the car. She smiled back at the kids—boys? girls?—whose shaggy haircuts, unisex clothing, and jumble-of-big-and-baby-teeth grins made gender-identification tricky.

Extending a dollar bill to the nearest child, she requested two Popsicles. After casting them a shrewd glance, one of the kids handed over the somewhat mushy treats: green for Bram and red for Honor. Then they were pointed toward the field.

After unwrapping her Popsicle, Honor ducked between the fence rails to study the situation. Rising from flattened nests of thick vines and broad leaves, fat orange pumpkins dotted the field's dusty surface. Smaller ones grew close to the parking lot, while Honor could see larger squashes in the distance. Setting off for Goliath territory, she concentrated on her melting Popsicle.

From the corner of her eye she kept track of Bram's progress. He was following her, looking half bemused and half puzzled by the uncooperation of his green, melting-fast "Ice Rocket." His mood might not be improving, but watching his growing frustration with the dripping Popsicle was tickling *her* funny bone.

Things so rarely got the best of him, Honor thought, suppressing a snicker. A lowly frozen treat had to be especially maddening.

She had to snicker aloud when he was forced to chase a drip down his thumb with his tongue. His gaze cut her way, blasting her with a fierce look that lost a lot of its effectiveness when the person sending it had lime-colored lips.

"What the hell are you giggling at?"

"You." She didn't even bother stifling her next laugh as he advanced, still trying to fry her with that look.

"What about me?" He was an arm's length away.

Honor shrugged, trying to remember she was supposed to be making this fun for him too. "Your bluster isn't very, uh, blustery, I'm afraid."

Holding her hand away from her body, she bent to take an emergency lick of her own Popsicle, then drew her tongue downward to catch the juice gathering near the stick. "Your lips are an incredibly sickening shade of chartreuse."

"Your lips are red."

His voice was suddenly quite near.

Honor's head jerked up; her eyes met his. He'd taken another couple of steps closer to her, close enough for her to get lost in the multifaceted green that was always such a competent camouflage of his thoughts.

For some reason she remembered his fingers on the bare skin of her waist. She swallowed. "Warm out here, isn't it?"

He ignored her comment. "Let me see your tongue."

Mouth going dry, she opened it.

His voice was soft, almost dangerous. "Red too."

For a long moment she stared at him. She heard her heart in her ears, the beat kicking up to a fast thump-thump-thump-thump. This wasn't relaxing. This didn't feel like play.

"Let's get the hell out of here," he said abruptly, turning away from her.

"We can't go yet," she protested. Not when she was supposed to be giving something back to him. Some fun. "We don't have what we came for."

He bent. *Snap.* With a flick of his wrists he broke the stem on the nearest pumpkin. "There. Take this one."

She hesitated, disappointed. "Is that all there is to it?"

"What do you mean?" One of his eyebrows rose.

Her gaze roamed over the hundreds of pumpkins in the field. "There's got to be some sort of method for choosing the ripe ones."

He opened his mouth. Then he closed it and rubbed his hand across his chin for a long moment. "Well . . . hmm. You're right. But . . . but it's kind of complicated."

She thought she saw a new spark in his gaze. It wasn't exactly playful, but at least it was interested. Maybe he *was* starting to enjoy himself. "Complicated, you say?"

"Yeah." He swung around, perusing the field with sober eyes. "There's a little system to it."

"Okay." Honor had heard the ladies of the Hooks & Needles Club arguing over the best way to select eggplant just the night before, and she was willing to try anything for the man she owed so much to. "What do we do first?"

"First, find a likely candidate." He glanced at her. "Go stand beside one that strikes your fancy and we'll see if it's any good."

"All right." After a few minutes of wandering, her gaze snagged on a pumpkin that was knee-high and that she'd barely be able to fit her arms around. A deep orange color, it looked very ripe and very just right. "This one," she said, moving to it.

"Okay." Standing a ways off, he rubbed his chin again. "I'll try not to make this too technical."

Honor's stomach sank. "Aren't you an engineer?"

"Mmm. Degrees in electrical and mechanical engineering."

Thinking of his coffeemaker, her stomach dipped lower. "Still," she muttered. "It's just a pumpkin."

He must have heard. "True. But you want the perfect one, right?"

She nodded, took a breath. "All right, I'm game."

He cleared his throat. "It's based on the same principle you use to select a watermelon."

Since she'd never selected a watermelon either, she shrugged. "What do I do now?"

"You have to kind of hunker down around it." He made a vague gesture with his hand.

It was a little hard to maneuver in her straight skirt, but she managed to bend her knees and get closer to the big pumpkin. "Like this?"

"Exactly."

It wasn't a particularly comfortable position. "Now what?" she asked, frowning at him.

"Oh. Now, now you . . . uh, sniff it."

"Sniff it?"

He drew the back of his hand over his mouth. "It has to smell right."

Honor gave up on the "hunkering down" and dropped to her knees. The dirt was soft and powdery against her skin as she obediently bent her head and put her nose near the pumpkin. She drew in a breath, then looked up at Bram. "What's it supposed to smell like?"

"Uh . . . pumpkin?"

She shot him a suspicious look, but he appeared as frozen-faced as usual. "I suppose it smells like pumpkin. Is that it?"

"No!" He tempered his voice. "No. Now you have to thump it."

She made a face. "What do you mean by that?"

"Thump it. To, uh, determine the seed-to-rind ratio." His unwavering gaze met hers. "Place both palms on top of the pumpkin, then smack it with one hand and see if you feel it in the other."

Honor did as instructed, smacking the top of the pumpkin with her right hand.

"Did you feel it in the other palm?" he asked.

"I . . . guess so."

"You have to do it more than once. As a matter of fact, it's better if you try it with both hands. Sometimes you have to loosen the seeds a bit to determine if a pumpkin has uh, prime jack-o'-lantern potential."

She tried it with her right hand again, and then her left. "I don't think I'm getting this. Maybe you better do it."

"No, no. You've almost got it, I can tell." He hesitated. "If I could suggest one thing more, you might try to get a little rhythm going. You know, think of the pumpkin as a bongo drum. As I said, it's a good idea to loosen the seeds before we pick it."

It sounded crazy, but what did she know? Honor shrugged, then started hitting the pumpkin with the flats of her palms.

"Keep going, keep going," Bram encouraged her. "Faster."

She increased her speed, concentrating on— "Hey, what am I supposed to be feeling again?"

"Oh, you'll know it when it happens." Bram's voice sounded thick. "Just keep going."

Without stopping her rhythmic smacking—bongo, he'd said—she looked up again. "Keep going?"

"Now the magic word. Now add the magic word." When her hands hesitated, he batted at the air. "Like this. Keep going like this. And then when you're ready, just yell out the magic word. Sing it, even. It's babaloo."

"Huh?" Honor was thumping for all she was worth. "Babawhat? Baba—" All at once understanding, she clamped her mouth shut on *loo,* stopped her stupid bongoing, then jumped to her feet. "Funny, very funny."

He was collapsed on the ground, his head bent over his knees.

"Bram!" She leaped forward, then at a second look skidded to a stop. Her arms crossed over her chest. "I believe this is what they call convulsing with laughter."

Though he wasn't making a sound, his shoulders

were shaking. Heck, his whole body was shaking. He mutely held up his hand.

After a minute she grasped it, supposing he needed help up. But as she leaned back to haul him to a stand, he pulled forward, tumbling her into his lap.

He buried his face against her neck. "I'm sorry, I'm sorry." Then he shook his head, his hair tickling her chin. "No, I'm not."

"Just as long as someone's having fun," she replied, trying not to sound sulky.

He was still silently laughing. When he lifted his head, humor was brimming over in his eyes and it made him look younger and even more handsome. Almost . . . carefree.

Honor's breath caught. Carefree.

Maybe she'd managed to even the score between them after all.

Chapter Ten

*M*ia pressed a roll of cash into her father's hand, kissed his cheek, and then turned to look for Josh, who had volunteered to drive her home.

"Daughter?"

Smiling, she glanced back. Then her eyes widened in alarm at his expression of concern. "What is it, Papa?"

"Are you going to be all right by yourself at the house?"

She relaxed and her heart melted to the consistency of warm brownies. *Thank you*, she thought, sending out a grateful prayer to the once and future aliens, in case they truly existed. Until his "abduction," Beau Caruso's only concern had been drowning his grief in the next drink.

"Of course I'll be all right," she said, moving close again to kiss his other cheek.

He sighed. "You're a saint of a daughter."

"Papa—"

He held up a hand. "This all seems strange, I know,

but I'm certain, certain *here*"—he put the hand over his heart—"that something important will come from this."

It was enough for Mia that he was interested in living again. "Then I'm sure you're right, Papa."

He dipped his head to catch her gaze. "And you promise, you *promise*, you don't mind staying at the house alone?"

She grinned at him. "I'll be *fine*, Papa. I'll probably enjoy the solitude so much you'll have to live in the RV permanently."

Her father didn't grin back and he sighed again. "Oh, little girl, you should have lived alone or at least away from home by now. I'm afraid your mother and I didn't encourage you to get out enough."

"No." Mia shook her head. "You and Mom didn't do anything wrong." As a plump and quiet only child, Mia had stuck near home out of shyness. Usually overlooked by her classmates, especially the popular, confident ones—the Beautiful Persons, or BPs, she'd called them—Mia hadn't made close friends.

Then, shortly after high school, the onset of her mother's illness had absorbed all of Mia's time and energy. "You know me, Papa, I'm just a homebody through and through."

He shook his head. "We should have made you take more chances."

Now Mia had to laugh. "Well, I did that once, didn't I?" Four months ago, on the same night that her father had seen his UFO.

He smiled too, though he still shook his finger under her nose. "Yes, but then you scuttled straight back to your shell."

"Good luck can be overwhelming, Papa." *Fright-*

ening might be an even better word. "It's made me very careful of what I wish for."

He patted her cheek, his eyes soft. "As long as you're still wishing, little girl."

Mia merely smiled and left her father to find her ride home.

It didn't take long to locate Josh. He stood beside his low-slung red car, dusting the gleaming finish with a white handkerchief. She forced a few deep breaths into her lungs, trying to offset her silly, intense response to his phenomenal good looks. There was no point in a woman like Mia getting hot and bothered over a BP.

It was embarrassing that he had read her reaction to him last week. In her kitchen, she'd practically begged him for a kiss and he'd make himself sick laughing if he knew how many fantasies that brief touch of his lips to hers had fueled since.

This time she was going to stay safely put in her shell. If she didn't have a hope of attracting Josh, at least she could maintain her dignity by making it clear she understood and accepted that fact.

With a final deep breath, she strode through the camp toward him. Though she tried appearing casual and calm, she found herself fidgeting, self-consciously shoving her hand against the small of her back to push the man's vee-necked T-shirt she wore deeper into the waistband of her jeans.

It slipped right back out, of course. As always, she needed a belt to cinch in the waist and, as always, she'd forgotten to wear one. When a woman had wide hips and thighs, buying the right-sized pants for *those* parts meant that she bought the *wrong*-sized pants for her waistline.

Mia sighed, resigned to the ironic unfairness that

she couldn't even fully appreciate the one slender thing about her body.

As she started across the street, Josh turned away from the car to watch her approach. Mia sighed again. No doubt about it, he was the BP of all BPs, from his precisely cut golden hair to the highly polished, fine-leather shoes on his feet.

Nearing him, she cleared her throat and kept her face expressionless. "Thank you for waiting." Without even thinking about it, she shoved at the hem of her T-shirt again, trying to tuck it tighter at the back, then the front.

"Shit," Josh said, closing his eyes.

Mia froze. "Pardon me?"

He looked at her again. "Get in the car. It's nothing." He closed his eyes, shook his head. "Or, God, I wish it was nothing," he muttered.

Mia slipped her hands in her back pockets, hoping the pose appeared relaxed. "I—I can get a ride with someone else if you don't want to take me."

"Yes, I want to take you, damn it." Josh sounded angry. "Just get in the car."

Mia slowly obeyed. She didn't have a lot of experience with men, and *no* experience with BPs, so how was she supposed to handle his sudden irritation?

By not handling it, she reminded herself. She was a naturally quiet person and the car ride home could be as silent as a tomb, for all she cared.

She shut the passenger door, only to find Josh in his seat, looking at her again. Staring, really. She opened her mouth to ask why, but then didn't think she could unknot her tongue. The purr of the engine was the only thing to fill the void as he finally started the car and pulled away.

"You're not, um, wearing an apron," he mentioned after a few minutes.

She blinked. "No."

"I don't think I've seen you without an apron before today." He glanced over at her. "You look . . . different without an apron."

"Different?"

He glanced over again and lifted his hand off the steering wheel to make a vague gesture. "More."

Mia felt her face burn, thinking of the enveloping, neck-to-knee garments she usually wore over her clothes. This was his first real look at her plump body, he meant. The knot in her tongue tied tighter and she tried to sink into the bucket seat.

"It's . . . I . . ." Josh made another vague gesture.

She didn't even try interpreting that one. Instead, she let long, silent moments go by while she imagined herself as a hermit crab, alone and unbothered in her snug little home.

Josh choked out a frustrated sound. "Listen, this is ridiculous, don't you agree? Don't you think we should just talk about it? Clear the air?"

"What?" The hermit crab in her was suddenly shaken out of its shell. Talk about "it"? She thought she'd been doing pretty well not giving anything away regarding "it." "What are you talking about?"

"This . . . thing." He glanced over.

Thing. It. Ridiculous. Her face heated.

Josh's long-fingered hands tightened on the steering wheel. "Look, the problem is, it's distracting. You make it hard for me to focus on what I'm doing and why I'm here."

Her face burning hotter, Mia wanted to disappear through the floor of the car. Her every look, her every gesture, must betray how he made her body restless and her skin tingle. "I'm sorry," she said, her voice hoarse and miserable-sounding. "But I . . . I don't know how to stop it."

"Maybe I do," he muttered grimly.

Though she waited for him to continue, only a tense silence followed as he turned onto the main road leading to her house. The car jumped forward, displaying just how eager Josh was to get rid of her, she thought.

After a few minutes more, he cleared his throat. "I saw you give money to your father."

She blinked at the unexpected turn of the conversation. What did this have to do with controlling her feelings for him? "Well . . . yes."

"You should be looking out for yourself, you know. Housekeeping can't be a lucrative job—"

"I can afford to give my father money."

"You're not interested in using your extra cash for yourself?" he asked, his blue eyes flashing her way. "To get yourself out of the boondocks, say."

"Leave Hot Water?" She shook her head. "I can't imagine living anyplace else."

"Okay." He nodded as if he liked that answer and even some of the tension in his shoulders appeared to seep away. "And you've never considered living in L.A.?"

"Los Angeles?" Was he worried she might follow him to southern California to distract him with her "ridiculous" responses there? "No. That's much too big a city for me."

"You're sure?" He threw her an odd look. "Think. You could open a restaurant. Some people would give up sex for that manicotti of yours I ate the other night."

That startled Mia into a little laugh. "You think?" But she could see he was serious, so she shook her head again. "I *do* like to cook, but a restaurant? No. I'm not very good with a crowd."

"You could call it Bella Mia," he went on, as he turned into her driveway. "They'd come for the food the first time and then the men would come the next time and all the times after that just to see you."

Now she laughed more loudly, straight from the belly. It was either that or cry.

Josh glanced over. "What?"

She shook her head, still chuckling.

"You don't believe me? You don't believe a man would choose a restaurant because of the beautiful woman he might see there?" He stopped the car in front of her house and turned it off.

Mia instantly curled her fingers around the door handle, the laughter inside of her dying. "You need to believe *me*. I hear you loud and clear, Josh." She gazed out her window at the little home where she'd grown up, the little home that was looking more shell-like and sheltering by the second. But she had to make something clear to him before her escape.

"You don't have to worry about me bothering you in L.A.," she said. "You don't need to placate me with stories about men finding me beautiful. I'll be sure to keep away from you from now on."

"What the hell are you talking about?"

His harsh tone startled her into looking at him. She licked her lips. "This ridiculous and distracting *thing* I have for you. You don't want it. I've known that from the very first. You couldn't want me."

Now more than ready for her retreat, she pushed her

door open. But he was quicker than she, reaching across her to pull it shut again.

"Why wouldn't I want you?" he demanded.

Her face burned once more. He was a BP and she was sturdy in the age of svelte, womanly in the era of waifs. "It goes without saying."

He stared at her long moments more; then, closing his eyes, he thumped his head against the back of his seat. "I'm a bastard. A selfish SOB. But even I can't let you think whatever stupid thing you're thinking." His eyes opened and he rolled his head against the cushion to look at her. "This thing I was talking about was a *mutual* thing. Yes, I know you feel a thing for me. And I feel a thing for you too."

The heat on Mia's face drained, only to spread over the rest of her. She stared at him.

"No," she finally choked out. "You can't. You don't. I'm . . . I'm too, I'm . . ." Her hands fluttered feebly in front of her body, trying to explain what was wrong with her.

Josh's eyes widened in understanding, but then rolled heavenward. "God, I'm begging you. *Begging* you. Please deliver me from women's body issues."

"That isn't funny," Mia snapped.

"No." His jaw went hard and he straightened in his seat to stare her down with flame-blue eyes. "And how I'm feeling right this minute doesn't amuse *me*. I'm hammer-hard, Mia, and I've been that way since the moment I saw your face in Bennett's kitchen. Today I got my first real good look at your breasts and you're lucky I didn't strip you on the spot and lick you all over. You're lush. You're voluptuous. I sweat just thinking about rubbing against all those curves."

Mia couldn't swallow, couldn't breathe, couldn't think.

"So don't whine about being this, that, or the other thing, because you're not going to get any sympathy from Josh McCool. You're definitely a problem. You definitely distract me. But fuck me, Mia, you also just *smell* right to me, and if that's not something to whine about, then I don't know what is."

On the heels of that angry, frustrated, and downright incredible speech, he left Mia on her doorstep. She had no idea if she'd climbed from the car or if he'd tossed her out of it.

Mind still numb, she watched him recklessly reverse down her driveway, then peel onto the road, wheels screeching. Even from a distance, she thought she saw tire marks smoking on the pavement.

When she could move again, she bent to reach for the key beneath the clay pot of chrysanthemums by the door. As she straightened, she also plucked a frothy-headed dandelion from among the cinnamon-colored flowers. Biting her bottom lip, she hesitated. Then, after inhaling a breath, she made a wish. One blow and the dandelion fairies danced away in the afternoon breeze.

It wasn't hope she wished for. She had that now. It was courage.

*B*RAM walked through the open door of Honor's bedroom, a load of firewood in his arms. With the sun down, the night air held a winterlike chill. Kneeling on the narrow hearth abutting the fireplace, he used his knee to nudge aside the smallest of the pumpkins she'd brought home from the patch that day and then dropped the logs on the stonework.

He couldn't help grinning, remembering her hunched over the biggest pumpkin. He'd concocted the idea to get a little of his own back, and it had worked. When was the last time he'd laughed like that?

"What are you doing?"

At Honor's voice, he glanced toward the bedroom door. Smile fading, he stared. Dressed in a huge pair of blue flannel pajamas decorated with green flamingos, she looked about twelve years old. Twelve years old and guilty of something.

"What happened to that red satin nightgown?" he asked, feeling both disappointed and strangely suspicious.

"What? Oh. That." Her shoulders moved up and down, though her hands stayed behind her back. "I don't wear that kind of thing to bed very often."

Thank God. He wouldn't have been able to walk out of the room—like he was going to right now—if she had. Standing, he noted she still held her arms in that odd, behind-the-back manner.

His eyes narrowed. "What are you hiding?"

"I'm not hiding anything!"

Right. He stalked toward her. A little laughter didn't mean he should let his guard down. She tried to side-step him, executing a little half twirl so that she wouldn't expose her back.

He merely grabbed one arm above the elbow and tugged. "What did you do to Fifo this time?"

"Nothing!"

He tugged again and she resisted, backstepping toward bed. His movements tracked hers and they half danced, half stumbled closer to the mattress. "Show me."

"No."

They tug-of-warred a few more minutes until he lost patience and snaked his other arm around her to pluck from her grasp whatever it was she was holding.

He stared at the box. "Dog biscuits?"

She answered him with a strange, strangled sound.

He glanced up. "What?"

"Nothing." She plopped onto the bed, meeting his gaze with one that was filled with equal parts defiance and innocence. Fake innocence.

Then she made that strange, strangled sound again. Except her mouth wasn't moving.

Bram followed the line of her body to her bare feet, which were in the act of pushing something beneath the bed. But even as she did, a few inches away the something popped back out. A black nose, a long furry snout, two brown eyes that were fixed on the dog biscuit box. Honor's dog Joey emitted another quiet but plaintive whine.

"Why is that dog in here?" he demanded. He should have known this would happen. "You promised you wouldn't let him in. That's why we bought that castle you like to call a dog house."

"I know you don't like dogs, but—"

"I never said I don't like dogs." An old memory tried to resurface, but he gritted his teeth and shoved it back down.

"Yes, you have," Honor pointed out. "Several times."

He shook his head, frowning at the canine in question. "It's just that this dog, *your* dog, is so worthless."

Honor flushed and she jumped to her feet. "You're going to hurt his feelings."

"That's right, unlike Fifo, which can actually *do* something, Joey here is just full of feelings." Bram snorted. "And if that puddle of drool on my floor is any indication, he's developed a really strong feeling for dog biscuits."

Honor glanced down at the dog and most of the fight went out of her. She laughed. "Okay, I'll admit that. But truly, Bram, Joey has great potential."

"As a salivating throw rug?" The dog had completely edged from under the bed and was belly-down at Honor's feet, his brown eyes lifted in whiny reverence for the biscuit box. Bram gazed on him in half bemusement, half impatience. "Are you aware that we were wrestling a few minutes ago and he didn't do a single thing to protect you?"

"And why should he?" Honor crossed her arms over a flock of green flamingos. She lifted one eyebrow, her starry, sparkling eyes full of challenge. "Were you going to hurt me?"

A silent moment passed. "Never."

Bram hadn't planned to say the word. But it came out of his mouth, softly, hoarsely, and those two syllables changed everything. In an instant, the atmosphere in the room turned electric. A quick move and the air would crackle.

Her arms slowly dropped to her sides. "I know you won't," she said, her voice as low as his. "I'm not afraid of you, Bram."

He didn't think she was truly afraid of anything. He thought of her delight in her dog and in the ridiculous pumpkins. He remembered catching her one day with her face lifted toward the sun and then he recalled how radiant she'd looked that afternoon with the autumn leaves falling around her.

Later, she'd made him laugh for the first time in forever.

All at once his hands started shaking with the sudden desire, the need, to plug into all that energy, into all that warm life.

And why shouldn't he? What was the point of resisting when she dragged him closer to this point each day? Lust wasn't even an emotion, after all, but a biological urge that wouldn't touch his heart or soul. His few encounters over the last four years were proof of that.

"Since Alicia died, I've never gone to bed with anyone I'll see the next morning," he blurted out.

Honor went very still, except for the pulse at her throat that was revealed by the notched collar of those outrageous pajamas. It quickened as he watched, the flutter speeding to a wild throb against her pale skin. It took only that, just the sight of her delicate flesh being buffeted by the telltale beat of arousal, to bring him to a full, aching erection.

"On the occasional business trip I've occasionally . . . met someone," he continued. His voice was tight as waves of desire washed against the careful wall he'd built.

"Never to see them again."

"Yes," he said.

Honor swallowed. "Sounds lonely."

He shrugged.

"But if we . . . do, I'll still be here in the morning," she pointed out, her face slightly flushed.

He nodded. "And if we . . . don't, so will this." He gestured between them. It was the only persuasion he would allow himself, just that one plain fact that the sexual electricity that was surging from her body to his and back again wasn't going anywhere either.

It was sex, he told himself. Just sex. And she would shortly be gone from his life. November fifteenth. Sooner.

Her fingers curled into fists, and her pajamas were so big that her hands disappeared beneath the wide cuffs. "I'd be stupid to care too much for someone still hung up on his dead wife."

He didn't deny it—neither that it would be stupid nor that he wasn't still hung up. But that pulse beat continued to thrum insistently against her skin, so he didn't leave the room, either.

It was sex. Just sex was safe enough.

"We could be careful, then," he suggested. "We could be careful that you don't care too much." There was no question that he would.

Honor looked away. "I don't even know for sure that I can go all the way through with it, you know. I want to, but maybe I can't. I . . . I'm worried that their sick whispering is still in my head."

That broke him. He tossed the box of dog biscuits to the nearby dresser, then his hand shot out to cup her hot cheek, his chest tightening at the thought of anyone, anything, wounding her like this. His heiress would get bored with Hot Water and leave soon enough, but he'd send her away without that one fear.

She bit down on her bottom lip but he gently, insistently disentangled it with his forefinger. He kept the pad there, brushing across her mouth, left, then right. "Honor," he whispered, hesitating one last time.

She met his eyes. "Let's not look back," she murmured. Then, without giving him time to respond, she reached up and pulled his head down to hers.

Chapter Eleven

When Bram broke the kiss, Honor staggered, the back of her thighs bumping against the quilt-covered mattress. She glanced at it over her shoulder, her breath jamming in her lungs even as her dizzy head cleared.

The bed. She and Bram were finally going to bed. *He'd* asked *her*.

She swallowed, wiping her suddenly damp palms against the flannel of her oversized, boy-cut pajamas. Her head bowed as she absorbed that too. On the night the sexiest man she'd ever met was serious about seduction, she was wearing green flamingos.

God, maybe the one with weird sexual hangups was *him*.

She swallowed again, edging away from Bram. "Maybe . . . maybe I should find that red satin nightgown."

"Don't bother about that."

Her heart pounded against the goofy green birds. Seriously, what kind of man came on to a woman dressed like this? She peered up at him, half expecting to be able to read nothing in his usual reserved, stoic expression.

Instead, she saw that his pupils were dilated and that there was a faint tinge of red across his cheekbones. His breath was ragged. His mouth was wet. From hers.

Her heart slammed against her chest. Prickles of excitement lifted her skin under miles of fuzzy fabric.

He touched her face. "Nervous?"

She hesitated—there was that little warning that she should be careful not to care about him—then shook her head. That euphoric fizz was back, that reckless, alive feeling that had pumped through her blood this afternoon.

"For a minute there I was worried you have some kinky fetish for flannel," she said. "But now I'm pretty sure I don't care if you do."

His eyes widened and then he laughed. A real, honest-to-God, out-loud belly laugh.

Fascinated, Honor stared at him. Even at the pumpkin patch today, he'd held in the sound.

Catching sight of her face, he laughed harder. "Jesus, Honor, *I'm* afraid you might be right." His fingers curled over the lapels of her PJs, and he hauled her up to her toes and against him. His chest was hot and hard, and what was pressed to her belly was hot and hard as well. Her breath jammed in her lungs once more.

"Flannel fetish." He shook his head, then lowered it. "I suppose we better find out," he murmured against her lips.

Honor melted against him. Even if he had a flannel fetish, she asserted again, that wasn't so bad when he kissed so good. Oh, he kissed so, so good when he wasn't trying to keep apart from her.

His tongue plunged inside her mouth.

Honor bowed, the cradle of her body pressing hard against him. His hands moved down to clamp on her hips, his fingers spreading wide. His tongue retreated, and she moaned, pushing against him until he was back in her mouth.

Her skin was on fire. One of his palms slid up her spine and fisted in her hair to drag back her head. His mouth left hers to drift over her cheek, then down her chin, until his tongue found the notch of her collarbone.

He licked her there, then he flattened his tongue against her pulse. Honor jerked into his body, but he held her steady, one hand tangled in her hair, the other flexed into the flannel-covered skin at the curve of her hip.

The pajamas were too hot. Too darn hot. She tried to tell him, but only funny little panting sounds came out of her mouth. She tried to wiggle out of them some-how, but he was still gripping her, holding her at the mercy of his marauding mouth, and she didn't think she wanted to end that yet either.

Her mind still bent on baring flesh, though, she grabbed the back of Bram's soft knit shirt and yanked it free from his jeans. Then she skimmed beneath the hem. Her palms found the sleek, hard heat of his back. He bit down on her neck.

She gasped.

One moment she was pressed against him, his body, her body, his mouth, her skin, and in the next he was holding her away, his hands gentle on her shoulders. His breathing sounded harsh in the room. "I'm sorry," he said.

Honor blinked, trying to recover her equilibrium, then gave up, preferring the slaphappy glow of desire to anything else she'd felt in a long, long time.

"I'm sorry," Bram repeated.

"It's okay," she said, still dazed. "I suppose you need to breathe." Though apparently she didn't. "As long as you go back to doing that thing again with your teeth."

Maybe her problem was not breathing so much as getting the oxygen to her brain. Because Bram was staring at her with the strangest expression and she couldn't for the life of her figure it out.

"I'm sorry for hurting you," he said slowly. His gaze slid from her face to her neck and he touched the spot he'd bitten.

Oh. *Oh.* With a little smile, Honor lifted her hand and ran the backs of her fingers against his jaw. It was bristly, so much like Bram. But if she had her way, he'd leave more than just one bite.

While still distracting him with her caressing fingers against his face, she switched their positions so that he was the one standing with his legs against the mattress. Then she lifted on tiptoes and sweetly fit her mouth to his.

He accepted the almost-chaste kiss, his hands down by his sides. What a sweetheart he was, she thought on a wave of unexpected affection. His gentle acquiescence made it easy as pie to then flatten her palms against his chest and with one shove topple him onto the mattress.

But the sweetheart was sneakier than he looked, because his fingers had apparently been gripping the hem of her pajama top. His fall became her tumble too, and she landed on top of him on the bed, nose to nose.

"Honor," he whispered. "What did I do to deserve you tonight?"

She smiled, her heart leaping right over his last word. "Not enough. Not yet anyway."

He chuckled and then pulled her head down to meet his kiss. She let it take her, she let him have her. They exchanged kisses: hard kisses, soft ones, then soul kisses, the kind of kisses that had her writhing against his big body. The kind of kisses that made the flannel of her pajamas feel rough against the aching sensitivity of her nipples.

He shifted them and rolled. Honor landed on her back, her head on the pillows. Half on his side, Bram stared down at her, his weight propped on one elbow.

She blinked up at him, the light from the bedside reading lamp haloing his head so that his face was cast in shadow. With one finger she found his mouth, though, and traced his damp lips.

He caught her finger with his hand. "The flannel has had its moments, honey, but . . ."

Honor shaded her eyes with her free hand, wanting to see the smile she could hear in his voice. "But?"

For an answer he kissed her again. Her mouth opened against his. He released her hand and she felt the heavy hot weight of his drop to the last button of her pajama top. Beneath it, her belly quivered in anticipation.

He lifted his head again, his gaze on her face as he unfastened that one button. To watch him, she narrowed her eyes against the glare cast by the lamp.

He murmured something—"Let me help," maybe. Then he reached behind him to turn off the lamp, plunging the room into darkness. Honor stilled.

It's okay, she told herself, battling the urge to run. *It's okay.* The black shadow beside her was Bram. Bram. Bram.

She heard Bram breathing.

Male breathing. Harsh. The man moved closer.

Then there were echoes all around her, mutterings, whispers, vile things, crude, scary words. Sick threats that had no place to go in the lonely darkness except inside her head, inside her soul. Burying themselves like worms.

A big hand touched the bare skin above her navel.

She screamed.

Standing on the driveway within the walls of the Fortress, Honor threw the ball for Joey, hyper-aware that Bram was slowly approaching. She pretended not to see him, hoping he would go away and leave her alone.

She hated the way he was treating her. Even a week after her humiliation in her bedroom, he hadn't relaxed the attitude he'd adopted toward her that night.

He was *nice* to her.

Nice made her edgy. Just as she'd come to expect trouble with the cliques in boarding school, since adolescence she'd come to expect that men would be unfailingly nice to her. But she wasn't a stupid heiress. She had rarely believed in their niceness, just as she rarely had faith in men.

The sad, cynical truth was that part of Bram's initial appeal was that he hadn't liked her. It might have been insulting, but at least it had been honest. And now . . . well now that he was nice it wasn't so much that she thought he was being *dis*honest.

It was that his damn pleasantness was so damn impersonal.

She watched Joey retrieve the ball, only to drop it like a special gift at the feet of Fifo. Bram couldn't help but notice the same thing, she knew.

"I think you're getting somewhere with him, Honor," he said, though, pee-wee-coach-pleasant.

Behind her sunglasses, she rolled her eyes. "Thank you."

What a weakling, she thought, disgusted with herself. Not only couldn't she manage a normal sexual encounter with a man, but she couldn't bring herself to *be* herself and yell at Bram for all his walking-on-eggshells kindness.

Maybe because she'd seen the look on his face after she'd screamed the other night. Part sickened, part stricken, his expression had only served to emphasize her sense of failure. Humiliation. Disappointment.

After that, she'd wondered if she'd ever have the guts to try to make love again, with anyone.

Bram bent down to pick up the slimy tennis ball at Fifo's feet himself, tossing it to her from the safe distance he was always at pains to keep between them now. "I took a message for you. Someone from the Hooks & Needles Club reminding you of your shift in the concession stand at the Homecoming game tonight."

"Okay. Thanks." She looked down at the ball in her hand. "Maybe later you can write down the directions to the football stadium for me."

"I'll take you."

Her head jerked up. "You don't need to. Josh—"

"Will be with us," Bram finished smoothly. "I ran into him this morning and he told me you two had plans to attend together. Now all three of us do."

"Oh. Well." Honor blinked, at a loss for words.

It went beyond remarkable to think that Bram was volunteering to take leave of his stronghold to attend the Hot Water social event of the autumn season. Not to mention the shock of him including Josh in his plans. Was Bram finally ending his isolation? To do something with her?

The idea made her smile, for the first time in days her spirits rising to execute a little short-skirt-and-white-smile cheerleader jump. If Bram was stepping away from his refuge of his own free will, then anything, just about *anything*, could happen.

But as it neared halftime that night, Honor realized that even in a football stadium holding thousands of people, Bram could find a way to detach himself from the rest of the world. The spectators on the Hot Water side of the stadium were dressed in black and gold, the team colors of the Argonauts. Honor had known the importance of that, and consequently wore black jeans and a black sweater under a shearling jacket. Josh had bought her a corsage at the entrance, a white chrysanthemum sprayed gold and tied with a black ribbon that she'd pinned in her hair.

Bram, on the other hand, was in his usual blue jeans and scuffed boots, a khaki expedition jacket over his plain fishermen's knit sweater. It wasn't just his clothing that set him apart. Though their seats were on a lower row of the grandstand, something about his rigid posture and the way he didn't meet anyone's eyes or call out to friends effectively sequestered him from the crowd.

She also now knew why he was attending. Not for her, but out of obligation. The game program made clear that not only had Enigma installed, free of charge, a state-of-the-art security system for the recently renovated football stadium and adjacent athletic facilities, but Bram himself had also made a considerable cash donation.

He was nothing if not dutiful, she thought morosely, remembering that his same sense of obligation to Hot Water had gotten them married.

Josh dropped to his place beside her and passed her a cup of coffee. "If I knew you liked football, lovely lady, I'd have bought us 49er season tickets. We could have flown the Witherspoon jet from L.A. to San Francisco on game days."

"It wouldn't be quite the same, don't you think?" Her gaze roamed over the excited crowd. Families sat together in large groups made up of every age from toddlers to grandparents, sharing popcorn and sodas and the excitement of small-town football.

Sitting nearby were Mr. and Mrs. Shea, in a noisy group that included Pearl and Red Morton. Next to them was the Honorable Mr. and Mrs. Ames, the mayor of Hot Water and his wife. Mrs. Ames caught Honor's eye and smiled.

Honor sucked in a bracing breath and smiled back, lifting her mood through sheer force of will. After her kidnapping, she'd promised herself that no one would have the power to steal her freedom or her sense of well-being again. That included Bram.

So there would be no more dwelling on that incident in her bedroom, that was all there was to it. True, she hadn't been able to overcome her nervousness that night, but plenty of people had fulfilling lives that didn't include sex. Buddhist monks. Nuns.

It would be sufficient to belong to Hot Water. That would make her normal and happy enough.

"There you are, Honor!" Breathless, Mia clambered between two kids sitting on the row in front of them.

"Hi!" Honor grinned, because Mia didn't look older than high school age herself in a ski sweater striped black and gold under a pair of overalls. "Sit down." Honor scooted closer to Bram and patted the space she'd created between herself and Josh.

As Mia slipped onto the bench, she darted an incredibly radiant, incredibly hopeful smile at Josh—a smile he patently ignored.

Honor's stomach tightened and she spoke quickly to cover his gaffe. "You're looking for me?"

"Yes." Mia slid another look at Josh, one so full of yearning that it almost hurt to see. "I just finished my shift in the Hooks & Needles booth. Mrs. Kemper asked me to find you and say they could use you in fifteen minutes, if you don't mind starting early."

Honor nodded. "No problem."

"Oh," Mia added. "And would you tell her I found plenty of insulated cups in the supply shed marked 101? That's the security passcode too, you just key it in on the pad beside the door to open the lock."

Nodding again, Honor muttered to herself. "Passcode 101, Shed 101."

"It's in the building across from the large overhang where they're hiding the halftime floats." Mia laughed. "When I got a peek at this year's Homecoming theme, I decided not to go back and report to Mrs. Kemper. I don't want to miss the parade."

Her face flushing, she half turned to Josh and smiled again. "Wait until you see it. It's going to be great."

"I can hardly contain my excitement." Josh's voice was dry, almost biting. Then, ignoring Mia's crestfallen expression, he leaned across her to address Honor. "This is like old times, isn't it, beautiful? Of course, it's not the VIP grandstand seating we had on Colorado Boulevard for last year's Rose Bowl Parade."

Honor shook her head, appalled by his thinly veiled rudeness. "Did you have a bad day or something?"

"Don't," he muttered, sitting back to gaze out at the field. "Don't remind me."

Mia cleared her throat. "My father told me you'd been out to see him again."

"I said, don't remind me," Josh repeated, his jaw tightening. "That group of crazies is getting larger by the day. And not any more cooperative."

Honor felt a pinch of alarm. "There's still time, Josh. Plenty of time for another solution besides calling in the sheriff."

Josh groaned. "Give me a break, okay? Let's not discuss it tonight. Tonight I need to think about something other than UFOs and the nuts who believe in them."

Honor saw Mia smile crookedly, but then a cannon boom sounded, announcing the end of the second quarter. The crowd around them erupted in a cheer— the Argonauts were leading their rival, the Colton Cougars, 3–0—and Honor cheered with them.

A temporary stage was rolled onto the field and in a few minutes mikes were set up. The Argonaut marching band gathered on the grass, and when they struck up the school fight song, everyone in the stands sang along.

Honor's eyes stung. It was so small-town perfect, she thought. So absolutely *good*. She listened hard to understand the words. When it came to the last chorus, she sang as loud as she could, aware that both Bram and Josh were staring at her. Too bad.

After her abduction, three days passed before anyone reported her missing. Three days until her father had returned from Europe to open the ransom letter. The company where she'd recently started working hadn't raised an alarm. When she'd failed to show up one morning, they'd assumed the Witherspoon heiress had taken off on an unscheduled vacation.

That wouldn't happen again. By wrapping herself

up in the life here, by becoming a part of the fabric of Hot Water, then she could never be overlooked again.

When the last drumbeat died away, Bram was still staring at her over Mia's head. She turned to meet his eyes, their expression as remote, it seemed, as always. "What?" she said, for the first time in a week letting her irritation at him show.

"You're . . ." He lifted his hand, let it drop.

Her eyebrows rose. "I'm what?"

He opened his mouth, but before he could get anything more out, his name was called over the loudspeaker, along with those of other townspeople who had contributed to the stadium renovation. "I have to go cut a ribbon or something," he said, rising. His hand dropped to her shoulder, squeezed. "I'll be right back. Don't go anywhere without me."

As Bram left for the stage, Josh slanted a look at Honor. "Quite the possessive husband you have there."

She shrugged. Bram's impersonal niceness made his protectiveness feel just as dispassionate. Just another obligation.

While the Homecoming court was being introduced, Josh leaned across Mia again. "You know what, Honor? You don't belong here."

A tremor of nerves skittered down her spine. She frowned. "What makes you say that?"

"This hick town is full of hick shit, and you know it. It's not what you're used to. It's not what you want."

She skewered Josh with a look. "You don't know what I want."

"I think I do."

The soft, certain way he said it made another cold skitter of doubt rush down Honor's back again. "Oh, yeah?" she said, trying to smile. "And what's that?"

"Listen. We're birds of a feather, Honor. We want to fit in. But you're never going to fit in *here* and you're never going to be happy, not even hooked up with the Head Hick down there." Josh turned his head and nodded toward the stage.

Honor followed his gaze. There were half a dozen town leaders gathered around the microphones now, accepting plaques commemorating their contributions. Far outside their circle, Bram stood in the dimmest corner of the stage, his aloof expression a fortification as strong as the rock wall surrounding his home.

It was the same way he stood, the same expression he wore, when he visited Alicia's grave, Honor remembered. Before moving to the Fortress, she'd seen him there several times herself. The people of Hot Water still saw him there, every evening.

Honor's throat went suddenly dry. "You can't know I'll never be happy here," she told Josh.

"Sure I can." He smiled. He was a beautiful man, as was his smile, so it was funny how much pain it could cause. He pointed at Bram. "And the reason why I know you won't be happy, lovely lady, is because *he* isn't."

Her legs felt stiff as she jumped to her feet. She didn't look at Josh, but she didn't look at Bram either, because she *didn't* need him to be safe, to feel normal and happy in Hot Water. She'd already decided that.

Her movements felt clumsy, though, as she slipped past Mia and Josh. "Excuse me . . . my shift . . . I belong somewhere else right now." Hearing her own words, she cringed.

*F*EELING as if he'd sprouted four more legs, Josh watched Honor stumble as she almost ran down the grandstand steps. Yes, definitely six legs total, Josh decided, because he was as low as a bug. A cockroach.

Mia swung toward him, her face furious. "What did you say that for?"

He ignored her anger, because, hey, even cockroaches needed to survive, and he was sick of watching all his financial opportunities slip through his fingers. Plan A was still married to someone else. Plan B was going to hell too, judging by the increasing number of squatters on the Enigma property.

"You can't blame a guy for trying a play when the big cat's away," he said mildly. "Bram knows that I'm after his wife."

"You're *what*?" Mia croaked out.

He couldn't look at her. "I told you. You're a distraction because I'm here for Honor. She's going to come to her senses any minute now. When she does, I'm going to take her back to L.A. and marry her myself."

A shocked silence welled. "You're . . . you're a snake," Mia finally hissed.

"A cockroach," he murmured. But hell, a *really* bad guy would have seduced the woman sitting beside him. There was no doubt Mia would have been willing. A really bad guy would have had all that luscious flesh beneath his hands, would have buried his head between her breasts and buried his cock between her thighs, and then *still* tried to widen the gulf between Honor and her hubby.

From the corner of his eye he saw Mia swallow, and then he saw angry color rise up her delectable, golden skin.

"You're not the man I thought you were."

He laughed at that. "Unless you thought I was a

greedy selfish bastard, then you're right. I'm not the man you thought I was."

She turned her head away from him as if she couldn't stand the sight of him. He ignored the small pain that caused and surreptitiously lifted his hand to lightly stroke one finger over the ends of Mia's glossy hair that were trailing along her sweater.

"What if—why shouldn't I tell Honor about this?" Mia's voice had tears in it.

A strange rush of . . . pity flooded Josh's gut. "You can't tell Honor anything she doesn't already know."

"What does Honor already know?" A harsh voice interrupted. Bram Bennett's voice. *"And where the hell is she?"*

Josh jerked up his head, surprised by the other man's vehemence.

"At the Hooks & Needles booth," Mia said. "Her shift."

Josh couldn't look away from the intensity on Bennett's face. It tickled his memory, reminding him of something.

"She was supposed to wait," Bram ground out, then abruptly took off.

A fanfare from the band on the field redirected Josh's attention. Just as the first parade float—depicting a spaceship drifting toward a map of California that highlighted Hot Water—entered the stadium, the mayor of Hot Water stepped up to the mike. Then he gleefully announced the kept-secret-until-this-moment Homecoming theme.

"Welcome to the E.T. Phone Homecoming!"

Josh groaned, even as the spectators around him applauded wildly.

Dressed in black-and-gold uniforms, but wearing

something like antennae on their heads, the members of the drill team ran onto the field. The band struck up the theme to *Close Encounters of the Third Kind.*

The crowd in the grandstands cheered.

Jesus Christ, Josh thought, stunned. The whole damn town loved the idea of being visited by little green men. Or they loved the idea of the idea of being visited by them. A hell of a thing to discover just when the success of his Plan B was whisker-close to requiring a call to the sheriff. A call that would instigate kicking Mia's father and his groupies' kooky hides out of the county.

Mia's father. Suddenly Josh recalled Bram's expression when he'd asked about Honor. And he recalled what it reminded him of, too. Not in its quality, exactly, but in its power. It reminded him of the way Mia's father looked at Mia's mother in their wedding photograph.

Ah, shit, Josh thought. The entire situation was worse, much worse, than he'd thought. And he didn't have a Plan C.

BRAM half walked, half ran toward the dozen colorful concession booths lining the main entrance into the stadium. Logic told him he'd find Honor cheerfully serving coffee, but she'd set his protective instincts on full alert the other night.

Just remembering how she'd screamed at his touch made his gut coil.

The signs above the concession stands indicated the food they served, not which community organizations were staffing them, so Bram pushed through the line at the first he encountered to ask for Honor. She wasn't there.

She wasn't at the next one either. Or the next.

By the time he reached the booth serving cinnamon rolls, brownie sundaes, and slices of apple pie, his temper was steaming. Honor should have waited for him, as he'd told her.

He shouldered aside the people at the front of the line to confront a server on the other side of the counter. "Have you seen my wife?"

Kitty Matthews blinked. "Well, hello to you too, Bram."

He sucked in a breath. "Sorry, sorry. I didn't even notice it was you. I'm looking for Honor. Is she here?"

"She was." Looking amused, Kitty turned to the older woman serving beside her. "Where did Honor go?"

The older woman glanced vaguely over her shoulder. "She isn't back yet?"

Bram clamped down on his frustration. "Back from where?"

"I'm not sure. June!" The older lady raised her voice. "Where did Honor go?"

A voice drifted through a doorway at the back of the stand. "For more cups, but that was a while ago. She isn't back yet?"

"No, she isn't back yet," Bram bit out. "Where *are* the damn cups?"

June Kemper poked her head through the doorway. "She said they were in Shed 101. She even knew the passcode for the security keypad."

Passcode? Security keypad? Bram's impatience washed away in a flood of uneasiness. Christ, if Honor was playing around with passcodes and keypads, he'd probably have to rework the stadium's entire security system.

He turned. Out on the field, the marching band's

loud snare drums recommenced beating. He started running.

By the time he reached the storage area, he'd passed a handful of parade participants, all wearing oversized rubber heads with oversized eyes and undersized mouths, as well as a larger group with their faces painted green and wearing pointy ears. But neither sight gave him the jolt that something else did . . . a gold chrysanthemum—like the one Honor had been wearing in her hair—lying crushed and dirty beside the metal door of the shed marked 101.

His heart slamming against his chest, he looked wildly about him, seeing no one but a few more teens in out-of-this-world costumes. Then he noticed the readout on the keypad beside the door. Instead of displaying the steady red "armed" signal, all the indicator lights—red, green, yellow, blue, and white—on the pad were lit and flashing, signifying nothing that made sense, nothing except electronic chaos.

Honor.

Just then the marching band wound down, the snare drums concluding with a final energetic rat-a-tat-tat. When the last echo died away, he heard another burst of sound. The sound of a fist against the inside of the metal door marked 101.

God. Jesus. Honor.

He leaped for the doorknob, wrenching on it. "It's Bram. I'm right here. Are you all right?" The door didn't move.

There was a muffled sound from the other side.

He leaned closer. "It's me. I'll get you out in a second. Can you open it from your side?" The system was supposedly designed so that the door couldn't lock with someone inside.

For answer, he only heard another thump of fist against metal, a fist-thump that sounded decidedly indignant.

"Right, right," he muttered. "If you could open it from your side, you wouldn't be in there." Stepping to the keypad, he tried clearing it, but the damn thing only mocked him, the row of lights flashing faster. EROR EROR EROR swam across the narrow LED. Christ, even the mistakes were screwed up.

The fist-thumping started up again and he yelled, hoping she could hear him. "I'm going to get help!" Frustrated and pissed, hating his helplessness and hating leaving her, he slammed his palm against the keypad.

The device gave an electronic belch. He heard a hum, a click, then the indicator lights blinked once, went off. The red "armed" indicator lit.

"Just another second, Honor," he yelled. Holding his breath, he keyed in the passcode. The pad lit green, the lock clicked, and then he jerked the door open to find—

His gut slithered to his knees, even as he reached for one slender wrist.

Honor was on her feet. She was in one piece, if you didn't count the paleness of her face and the near-shock in her eyes. She'd been locked all this time in that small shed, a space bigger than a car trunk but smaller than a wine cellar, *in the dark.*

Chapter Twelve

*B*ram paused in the hall between their bedrooms and looked into his wife's still-pale face. "Honor, tell me the truth." He reached out to touch her—God, he needed to touch her—but instead let his hand fall back to his side. "Are you all right?"

She rolled her eyes at him. "I've told you a hundred times."

"Make it a hundred and one," he said.

Once he'd pulled her from that pitch-black storage room—when the door slammed behind her, Honor had been unable to locate the half-hidden light switch in the blackness—he knew he wouldn't breathe easy until he got her home. Which meant his breathing had been messed up for hours, since Honor had insisted on working her full shift at the booth and then watching the remainder of the football game.

"For the hundred and first time, then, I'm okay."

"Still, you didn't need to serve pie and coffee." He'd made her drink a cup of it, though, dosed with several packets of sugar. "You didn't need to stay for the end of the game."

"Of course I did," she said. "I made a commitment to the Hooks & Needles. I had an interest in the outcome of the game."

When he shook his head, still not understanding her stubbornness, her voice turned fierce. "I *can't* let the past stop me. I *won't* let it stop me from living and enjoying my life."

Big brave words. From the day she'd high-heeled her way into his life, she'd been like that, big smiles, brave attitude. It conned a man into thinking she was bigger and tougher too. But he couldn't forget how she'd appeared that night when she'd screamed, and then again tonight, when he'd pulled her from the shed. Beneath the bravado and those rich-girl airs she cloaked herself with was someone damnably young and fragile.

He tried to put the images out of his head. He tried to detach himself from his raw frustration. But damn it!

It tore at him, that such a stupid thing like that malfunctioning lock, something that would be a random misfortune to someone else, had been for Honor a flashback to fear.

He half turned from her, still trying to get control of himself. "This world sucks," he muttered.

"No."

He found himself turning back, his voice hot. "Why should *you* of all people get locked in like that? It's not right."

She bit her bottom lip, then reached out to briefly touch his arm. "It gave me time to realize a few things."

His eyes narrowed as he noticed that color was starting to bloom on her cheeks now, pretty pink color that reminded him of the rose-colored lenses of her sunglasses. His mood eased a little. "You realized what?"

Her black, stub-toed boot dug into the hardwood floor. She watched it, apparently fascinated. "Should I say? It's about you." The corners of her mouth tugged upward.

The little sexy smile changed his mood again by instantly setting fire to his veins. He gritted his teeth, cursing the wild, inconvenient flames. No matter how disastrous their attempt at sex had been, the wanting of her hadn't gone away. How could it, when even now her scent was tickling his nostrils, that rich, feminine scent that had wound its way throughout the whole lonely house, and maybe into his very pores?

"I don't want you thinking you're hot stuff," she added.

"I believe it's safe to assume I won't get overconfident," he said wryly. No matter the level of his own desire, a woman screaming when you touched her could take a man down a peg or two.

She was still studying her boot. "I'm sure I looked like I'd been climbing the walls when you opened that door."

"You looked like hell."

Her mouth pursed in a dissatisfied pout. "Hey, on *that* compliment, maybe I should withhold my own."

He leaned against the doorjamb of his bedroom and crossed his arms over his chest. "What's all this hemming and hawing about, Honor?"

"It wasn't as bad as I expected, being locked in there," she said slowly. "I knew you were going to find me."

He waved a hand. "Of course I was."

"I trusted that you would." She looked up and met his gaze. "I trust you."

Something cracked inside his chest. He sagged against the wood behind him, hoping like hell he looked relaxed instead of poleaxed. Hoping like hell he would figure out someday why hearing her say those three words could both hurt so bad and feel so good at the same time.

"That trust made me realize something else too," she said, her gaze not letting go of his.

He cleared his throat. "What?"

"That if there's anyone who can help me overcome this apprehension I have, this apprehension of . . . sex, it's you."

So much for not appearing poleaxed. Bram's legs gave out and his spine slid down the doorjamb until he was sitting on the floor. "No, Honor."

She hunkered down beside him. "Yes. Please. I thought I didn't need to heal that part of me. That I would be happy, feel normal, without . . . without being with a man. But when I was locked in the darkness again, I realized that I *have* to totally reclaim my life. I can't do that unless I can do sex too."

It was too tempting to let his own desire for her melt his doubts. Already it was happening, his body burning hotter, his hands itching to reach for her.

But then he thought of her scream. "What if—"

"We have a perfectly amazing time? You know I want you, Bram. *I trust you.*"

She swallowed and he could see that fast pulse beating in her throat again, the one that had been the signal of his fall a week ago. He lifted his hand and touched it with his middle finger, remembering how it had beat against his tongue. She shivered. Hot, staticky energy surged from her skin through his finger.

It was too late to hold back. Not when he hated her to be afraid. Of darkness. Of sex. Of anything.

She trusted him.

He rose to his feet, grasping her hand to draw her up with him. Then he nudged open his bedroom door with his foot, just as he had the day she'd moved in. She'd said then she had it all figured out. He'd been certain he had. He'd been certain he was going to boot the inconvenient heiress out of his life, no muss, no fuss.

Hah.

The only light in the room came through the half-open bathroom door. He walked backward toward the bed, pulling her with him. "Do you want more lights on?"

She shook her head. "I trust you," she repeated.

Oh, God. He swallowed hard again, and sat down on the mattress, pulling her into his lap. He nuzzled his face in the sleek darkness of her hair.

She trusted him to make it right. He tightened his arms around her, tightening down on his lust for her at the same time. Making it right for her meant keeping control of himself. It meant making sure he didn't frighten her again.

Perfect. Because the one thing he *wasn't* going to do was lose control around Honor. That way he could make it good for her without risking losing something of himself. This was *still* just about sex, he reminded himself. Just sex.

He bent his head and lightly rubbed his cheek against hers. "Give me a few minutes," he said. "Let me shower and shave so I don't scratch you."

"I don't care," she said.

"But I do." It would give him a few minutes to think too. He smiled. "And I want you in those flamingo pajamas again."

Her head came up and she looked at him, half amused, half aghast. "No!"

Yes. She'd be more comfortable getting close to him slowly. "Ten minutes." He kissed her and his head spun with the taste of her soft, heated mouth. With a groan he lifted her to her feet and swatted her little round butt. "Make that five."

*F*RESH from her own quick shower, Honor lay between the covers of Bram's bed, wearing her flamingos, per request. Listening to the *shush* of the water coming from his bathroom, she tried to remember why she'd thought she could do this. She considered rushing back to her room and diving under her own bed, snuggling to sleep with Joey instead of a man.

But that would be more than a little odd, wouldn't it?

And then she recalled exactly why she'd approached Bram in the first place tonight.

She wanted to feel normal. No, she needed it.

When he walked out of the still-steamy bathroom, though, dressed only in a pair of baggy sweatpants, she found herself wanting to run again. Holding the covers tightly to her chest, she admitted to herself that while she wasn't afraid of *him*, she was afraid it wouldn't work out again.

She was afraid it was her last chance too.

As he approached the bed, the meager light coming from the bathroom gleamed on the sharp angles of his cheekbones and left his eyes dark, mysterious pools. His mouth looked fuller than usual, and below it was miles of his naked chest, its swells and ripples high-lighted, then shadowed, highlighted, then shadowed in the half darkness.

She'd invited herself into this man's bed, without even a kiss to sweeten the request. A wave of embarrass-ment washed over her and she tightly closed her eyes.

"Have you changed your mind?" he asked.

She made herself look at him. Though he'd pulled back his side of the covers, he merely sat on the edge of the mattress, watching her with that enigmatic ex-pression.

"Have you?" she countered, still clutching the sheets and blanket. "This is so cold-blooded."

"Cold-blooded?" He tilted his head, studying her face. "Is that how you feel . . . cold?"

She swallowed and dropped her gaze. It snagged on a drop of water poised at the very edge of his heavy shoulder. As she watched, it fell, sliding down his smooth skin, then rolling over his well-defined pec-toral muscle to catch in the dark hairs scattered around the circle of his nipple. She wanted to gather that drop with her tongue, taste the water, warmed by his skin. Taste his skin.

"Honor?"

She shook her head, looked up. "I'm not cold."

"Good." He swung his feet onto the bed, pulling up the covers so they gathered at his waist. Then he leaned closer to her and drew his knuckle down her cheek. "I've been thinking."

It was an opening for a snappy, sophisticated come-back. "Oh?" The smell of soap on warm male skin had scattered her wits.

"Before, you heard voices, right? It's remembering the things those bastards said that bothers you."

She licked her lips, nodded.

"Well, this time . . ." His knuckle moved again, and he drew it across her damp mouth. He trailed it in the opposite direction, then pushed it inside to rub against the tip of her tongue. "This time, the voice you're going to hear will be mine."

Her skin tingled. She grabbed his wrist and pulled his distracting hand away from her mouth. "What do you mean?"

He slipped free of her grasp to run his fingertips down the side of her face, from her temple to her jaw. His thumb stroked over the center of her chin. "I'm going to talk. I'm going to tell you what I think, what I feel, as I undress you. Slow words, hot words, the *only* words you'll be able to think about will be mine."

He leaned closer yet, his mouth moving over her forehead and downward as he spoke. "You'll only be able to think about *my* words, *my* kiss, *my* bite. . . ." His teeth closed on her earlobe, delivering a sharp, sexual sting. "*If*, honey, you can think at all."

She already wasn't thinking. There were no thoughts, there was nothing but Bram, his big body pressing against the side of hers. She was trembling already too, her fingers tight on the edge of the covers she clenched at her chest.

He bent, his breath hot against her fingers. "Your hands are so pretty," he murmured against them. She felt his mouth move over the knuckles. "I watch you pet Joey and I want them on me." The tip of his tongue edged the tight seam between her pointer and middle finger, then pushed. Her tense grasp relaxed, and he rewarded her by sliding wetness along the channel of sensitive, inside skin between them.

Honor's other fist loosened from the covers too and

she ran her palm over the sleek dampness of Bram's hair.

"Yes," he said. "Touch me."

His lips slid over her forefinger, completely enveloping it in wet heat. He sucked, and Honor clutched his hair. His eyelashes lifted and he met her gaze as he pulled on her finger with his mouth.

Then he let it slide down his tongue to release it, catching her hand in his as it fell. "Your skin is so smooth. Your fingers, your face." He took her other hand, holding them both between his. "Remember when my palms slid beneath your panties? You're so soft there too, Honor. I want to touch you there again. Kiss you."

Her skin burned. There, where he'd touched her that day. Everywhere.

Spreading her arms, he placed her hands flat on the mattress. Then he touched the bunched covers at her chest. "But here, Honor, now I need to know how soft it is here." Without breaking their linked gazes, he pushed down the sheet and blankets. Then his big palm settled over one flannel-covered breast.

She sucked in a sharp breath.

He sucked in a matching one and looked down at the hand cupping her. "Your nipple is hard, honey. So hard. And your breast is swelling into my hand."

Swelling? She was swelling everywhere. Her skin felt puffy and full and she ached. Her breasts ached, her nipples, between her legs. But he didn't move to do anything about it.

Instead, he was staring down at his hand on those dumb flamingos, his breath moving raggedly in and out of his chest.

Honor swallowed, desire spiking higher as she

waited, longing for him to hurry and take the next step. "This is going really well, Bram. I'm good. So good, in fact—"

He squeezed his hand. She moaned.

"It stabs right into my palm," he said. "As if it wants something."

Honor thought she was going to scream. Of course it wanted something! Maybe she needed to show him, she thought. She reached out her hand and brushed his chest, her fingertips stroking over his hard nipple.

He closed his eyes and gently squeezed her breast again. "So soft."

Honor thought she might die if he didn't move it along. "Underneath the flannel," she said, coasting her fingers over his chest again. "Underneath there it's soft too."

He smiled. "Is that right?" He caught her wandering hand and placed it back against the mattress. "Let me see."

The five buttons took five years to unfasten, especially when he took such pains to keep the edges of the pajama top together until he was completely done. Honor squirmed and he smiled again. "Itchy?"

If she didn't like to see him smile so much, she might have slapped it right off his face. "You're teasing me," she accused.

His smile turned sly. "That's how it works, honey."

She should have known he'd do this with the same cool control as he did everything else. But then she forgot her irritation as he put his hands on her midriff, sliding them underneath the pajama top. He moved them higher so that his thumbs met over her heart and the vees created by his forefingers rested below the lower swell of her breasts.

"You're right," he said, his voice rougher than ever. "You're soft here too."

But he hadn't touched her *there*. He hadn't bared her breasts either, and with each ragged breath she took, the flannel rubbed against the aching points of her nipples.

"*Bram.*" She hoped she sounded every inch the spoiled princess he'd once thought her, because she wanted him to obey. "Please. More." Quickly, before the past could step in and ruin the mood.

His hands rose from her skin.

"No—" she protested, but then his movement lifted the sides of the flannel top up, and away, baring her breasts.

For a minute or two he was speechless. Her hand rose to his shoulder and she stroked his hot skin. "Bram."

He grabbed her hand and put it back on the bed. Then his chest rose and fell with two heavy breaths, and he dragged his gaze away from her newly naked skin to her face. "Honor. You're so pretty."

He curled his fingers and cupped one breast. "You're so sweetly . . . pink," he added. His thumb ran over the erect nipple.

Honor gasped, the caress brushing heat across her breast to flow down her body.

"Sweet," he murmured again, then bent his head and took her nipple into his mouth. He sucked it, sucked just as he'd done her finger, his tongue curling over it as his mouth pulled.

Honor closed her eyes, moaning. Everything about her was tightening or loosening. Contracting or expanding. Her muscles, her breasts, the place between her thighs. An urgency ignited in her belly. She moaned again, the sensation of coiling in some places and un-raveling in others intense and almost overwhelming.

"Bram." She stroked his back, his muscles bunching beneath her hands as he shifted to delicately lick at the nipple of her other breast. "Bram, please."

He lifted his head, looking at her with eyes that were dark and knowing. "Please what, honey?"

"Please." She didn't know what to say, except that the insistent, demanding pulse in her body needed to be met, assuaged, taken care of. She panted, because his thumbs were stroking both taut nipples as he waited patiently for her answer.

"I'm pretty sure we can get on with it now," she managed to say. "More than sure. I'm going to be okay." When they made it through this without her balking again she'd feel normal.

His forehead pleated, his thumbs keeping up their maddening strokes. Back and forth. Exquisite torture. "Get on with it?"

There was a heaviness between her hips and she squirmed, trying to relieve it. "You know." She panted again. "Get *on* with it."

He frowned, his hands stilling. "This isn't a race, Honor. We have plenty of time."

"I'm ready *now*." These feelings were so good, so nerve-tingling, skin-jitteringly good, that she was desperate to finish it before something jinxed the perfection.

His eyebrows rose. "But honey—"

"*Now*."

Something about her urgency must have communicated itself to him. "Honor, why are you so anxious?" His eyes narrowed and his hands stilled. "Tell me you've done this before."

All the lovely heat was still washing over her body. Just looking at Bram's mouth made her want to beg. "Of course I've done this before."

He rubbed his thumbs over her nipples, sending her mind spinning. She arched toward his touch.

"With who?" Bram said.

She blinked. "With what?" she answered vaguely.

He pinned her with his gaze, then deliberately lifted his thumbs to his mouth and licked the pads. Honor's breath stuttered in her lungs. She knew what he was going to do with those wet thumbs.

He touched them to the very points of her nipples, painting tiny, light circles. Honor moaned.

"You've had a lover before, you're sure?" he asked again.

She moaned again, willing to tell him anything that would satisfy him, answer any question as long as he would abandon this too-light caressing and return to those hard, more delicious touches. "Of course I'm sure! Stucky Mitchell when I was twenty-one."

Bram froze. "You had a lover named Stucky Mitchell when you were twenty-one," he repeated, his voice expressionless.

Honor could feel her blood pulsing through her, could feel her nerve endings waving, each one trying to entice Bram's notice.

"Yes. And we did it several times, as a matter of fact," she said, growing both more desperate and more annoyed by the second. "And I might have to revise my opinion of his technique if you're going to leave me feeling frustrated and unsatisfied too!"

"Stucky Mitchell," he murmured, shaking his head. "We're going to have to talk about him—"

"Bram!"

"—later. But for now, let's move on to this." His fingers curled beneath the elastic waistband of her pajamas and yanked.

Honor's pulsebeat shot high as her pajama bottoms went low. *Finally. Please. Now.* She couldn't stand any more of this waiting or wondering. Worrying that she wouldn't be able to go through with it this time.

But Bram wasn't through with her.

He wanted to look at everything, talk about everything, touch her everywhere until her skin was as hot from embarrassment as it was from arousal.

His fingertip explored her navel. "Did you know how sexy this is? Just a glimpse of your belly button makes me hard."

He was hard now, his erection pressing against the outside of her thigh through his sweatpants. Honor pressed back, rubbing her thigh against him with small strokes.

Then his hand moved still lower. His body tensed against hers when his fingers discovered her wetness. He rubbed there lightly, always just missing the sensitive point and the aching entry. "You're so soft and hot, Honor. You really do want this, don't you, baby?"

She wanted it enough to overcome her nerves and even another wave of embarrassment as he hitched one of her knees higher, opening her more fully for his touch. He leaned down to her mouth and she bit at his, trying to let him know how ready she was.

"Please, Bram," she said against his lips.

His finger slid inside her.

She gasped, her hips arching off the bed. The way slick and easy, he withdrew, then slid in two.

Honor started to shake. "Bram." Her mind was

spinning away, and, closing her eyes, she tried to grab it back.

She needed to hold *herself* back, she thought suddenly. Anxiously. She couldn't let him make her feel so helpless.

Bram's voice broke through the burgeoning panic in her mind. "Oh, baby. You're so tight. Your body is like a fist, gripping my fingers. Look and see how pretty it looks, my hand on you, inside you, your body clasping mine. Look, Honor."

The words painted a picture so vivid and erotic and his voice was so commanding that Honor opened her eyes. Her body was open to him, exposed, she saw, her thighs splayed. There was a flush across his cheekbones, visible even in the dim light, but other than that his face was stone-hard, his eyes trained on her.

"Look, Honor," he commanded once more. His fingers slid out slowly and she felt her body grasping for them, opening immediately and closing back down on them as he breached her again. "Look."

He was playing with her body. Playing with her.

His fingers slid out, slid in again, and then his thumb found her clitoris. He toyed with it, nudging it, rolling over it. A new tension entered her body, streaks of heat centered on that one place, paralyzing her. He had her ensnared.

She felt Bram's other hand tighten on her hip. He had her trapped.

"No." Panic and passion warred within her. She shook her head, digging her heels into the mattress to break away from his hypnotizing, helpless-making touch.

She needed to fight the helplessness. She'd been

helpless in that cellar, helpless against the kidnappers and the cheap thrills they had taken at her expense. "No, Bram, no," she managed to choke out, though the desire was still singing through her blood. "I don't want this."

He froze. "Oh, baby."

She shook her head again. "I can't do this. I won't."

"The voices?"

"No, no." His fingers still penetrated her, pleasured her. The tight knot of nerves that was the focal point of her sexuality was still pulsing against his thumb, but she couldn't let herself climax.

"Please stop." Her skin was hot, her voice hoarse. "I'd rather go without sex than feel this helpless."

His eyes closed. "Honor," he whispered. "Trust me."

She shook her head wildly.

Without saying more, he slid his hand away and she wanted to scream with frustration and cry with relief. Then he shucked his sweatpants, gathered her close to his nakedness, and drew the covers over them both.

He was hot and big and she could feel his heart pounding against her cheek. "I couldn't do it," she said. "I'm sorry."

"Shhh." He ran his hand over her shoulder and down her hip. It was a gentle stroke, but her flesh was still so sensitized that she trembled in reaction.

He continued stroking her, almost impersonally running his hands over her sides and her back. With a little shove, he pushed her onto her back and petted her some more. His fingers combed her hair off her face. He traced her eyebrows, her nose, her mouth, with the pad of his fingertip.

He kissed her mouth, gentle and nonthreatening. A tear leaked out of the side of her eye and he found it, knuckling it away and then kissing the spot at her temple.

As he touched her, the frightening vulnerability and almost painful passion she'd felt dissolved, leaving her feeling tired, then warm and languid. Then almost relaxed.

His next touch snuck up on her. One minute he was caressing her shoulder and the next he was palming her breast. But the touch was so light, so warm, that she didn't protest. He leaned over and kissed her again, his tongue floating into her mouth, soft and sure.

She sighed, rubbing against his body, rubbing her tongue against his. He groaned, a soft vibration against her mouth, and then his palm slid down her torso to rest against the mound at the apex of her thighs.

He pressed there, and though she thought about protesting, she didn't. It was so good, the need that touch awakened, not that desperate need of before, but something sweeter and less lonely.

When he removed his hand, she almost grabbed it back, but then he shifted her so that she sprawled on top of him. They'd lain like this before and it felt almost familiar. His erection pushed into the softness of her belly, but his hands were unhurried as they slid up and down her back.

She turned her cheek against the hard muscles of his chest, almost drowning in a warm, pulsing haze.

He shifted her again, and she felt his erection between her legs now. She started to tense, but he skimmed his palms over her back again, up and down, up and down. She relaxed, letting her thighs fall on either side of his hips, letting the head of his penis nudge against the still-wet heat of her sex.

"This is good," she whispered.

"Yeah?" His voice was tight.

She looked up at him, but he urged her head back down with a calming stroke against her hair. The petting continued and she closed her eyes at the pleasure of it. He started rocking his hips a little, wedging himself tighter against her. Honor liked that too.

Before she realized it, he was at the opening of her body and then it was pushing inside her, degree by degree, stretching her with each delicious rock of Bram's hips. He kept moving, inching slowly until he was fully within her.

He stilled, his breath laboring in and out of his chest. "Honor. Honey."

The sense of fullness didn't threaten her. It was so good, so much what she needed. She was connected to someone. To Bram.

She lifted her head, feeling like it weighed a thousand pounds. Her eyelids felt weighted too and she lifted them only the slightest in order to see his face. "What?"

"Sit up," Bram said. "Bring your knees along my thighs and sit up."

She didn't think she could move. She didn't want to, when this was so perfect.

"Please," he whispered.

Honor's eyelids drifted back down, but then she did as he asked, almost drowsily drawing up her legs. Gathering her energy, she lifted her torso and shifted to sit up.

His erection thrust farther. Stretching her.

Honor gasped. "Bram." The heat was back at once, the heat and the helplessness. She tried pushing off him.

He gripped her hips. "No. Don't go. When we're like this, you're the one who makes it happen."

She stilled.

Then, using his hands, he showed her how to lift up, push down. At first she resisted, barely moving, but then she bit her bottom lip and tried it again, changing the angle so that she was leaning slightly over him.

He groaned.

A shiver ran down Honor's spine, curling toward the place the two of them were joined. She moved again, loving the pleasure of his body filling hers, loving the way she could press against him so it was just right.

The tempo increased and he dug his fingers into her hips, pushing up toward her with his pelvis. Heat washed across her body and then he lifted his hand, finding her breast and rolling her nipple between his thumb and forefinger.

Heat flashed over her again. Pleasure jolted her system.

That sense of vulnerability jerked her up. Paralyzed her. "Bram, Bram." *Help me,* she wanted to say.

"Stay with me, honey," he said. "Stay with me."

His hand slid down from her breast and found her clitoris again. Honor flinched.

"Stay with me." He stroked her hip, soothing. He stroked the knot of nerves, not soothing at all.

Her body tensed, everything sexual warring against everything sensible, both desperate for release from their own sides of hell.

"Let go, honey," Bram said, his voice rough, his gaze focused on her face.

"L-let go?"

His hand was still stroking and he was pushing up with his hips again, filling her, coiling all that jagged but pleasurable tension.

"Step away from the edge, baby," he urged her. "Let go, Honor. Let go for me. Come for me. *Trust me.*"

Unguarded, unprotected, she did as he said. Heated ripples moved outward, then gathered high, becoming one wave of burning, crashing bliss. She rode it out on his body, hearing him groan and then feeling him pump into her with his own release.

Sliding bonelessly back to his chest, she turned her cheek against him. *Trust me,* he'd said.

Her heart stuttered against his.

Because she had, and now she wondered if she'd ever be "normal" again.

Chapter Thirteen

*B*ram had parked his SUV at the bottom of the front porch steps. He sat on the hood, rolling his palmtop over and over in his hands as he waited for Honor to awaken. When the morning light had washed across her sleeping form, he'd left her in his bed, needing to clear his head before facing her again.

From its sitting position by the front door, Fifo suddenly jerked from its haunches to its feet. As Honor pulled open the door and stepped onto the porch, Fifo's LED vision sensors flashed and the dog rolled hastily backward. Bram grimaced, frustrated with the dog's lingering glitches.

Then another of them caused Fifo to emit an unexpected electronic bleat, and Honor's gaze darted toward the robot. Catching sight of it, she cringed, and if Bram didn't know better, he'd say Fifo cringed too. Eyes fixed on the dog, Honor sidled away from it and toward the steps. "I tell you," she said, "he's afraid of me, and he still doesn't like me."

Bram sighed. "You're letting your imagination run away with you."

She reached the bottom of the steps and stood at the car's front bumper, holding up the handful of autumn-colored sycamore leaves he'd gathered that morning. "Yeah?" She smiled. "But maybe I'm not the only one. Wasn't it you playing Hansel and Gretel with me?"

He looked away from her sunny face and stared at the solid, cool palmtop in his hands. There was no logical explanation for the impulse that had caused him to gather the best of the red-and-gold leaves dropped about the grounds. No reason either for why he'd then scattered them in a trail from the bed to the front door, instead of leaving a simple note about where to find him.

Despite that, he found himself muttering. "No flowers this time of year."

"Oh," she said softly.

He looked up. "Oh," he echoed, for the first time absorbing the details of her appearance. It seemed she'd raided a pirate's clothing chest this morning for a frilly, thin white blouse that she wore with a long denim skirt. She'd robbed the swashbuckler again for her footwear: a pair of low-heeled suede boots that softly wrapped her lower legs and then were held there with several smooth leather straps that buckled over her insteps, her ankles, and her calves.

It was a trendy, rich-girl outfit that didn't belong in Hot Water any more than she did. He needed to remember that.

Bram let out a breath he realized he'd been holding since he'd awakened at dawn to find her snuggled in his arms. For a startling, uneasy moment he'd thought maybe she belonged with *him*.

But now he was able to freely breathe again, even smile at her. "Sleep well?" She was nothing more than a beautiful woman, temporarily in his life, who'd asked him for simple, emotion-free sex.

It was her turn to look away as a blush rushed over her face, reminding him of the orgasmic flush that had bloomed across her pale, perfect breasts as she rode him. His body remembered too, and he shifted his position to ease the new, uncomfortable fit of his pants. Obviously he was nothing more than a horny man who'd gone too long without a woman.

She'd asked, he'd acted.

There was nothing complicated, nothing special here that was going to affect his behavior or his life.

Nothing special about *her*.

He jumped off the car. "How would you like to go to Pearl's Diner for breakfast?"

Her eyes widened. "Is this really you? Yesterday Homecoming, today breakfast out. You're willing to venture into town for a social event two days in a row?"

He frowned. "It's *breakfast,* not a debutante ball. Do you want a cheese omelette and homemade muffins or not?"

"Oh, I want. I definitely want."

His mind hung on Honor's words. *I want. I definitely want.*

Lust roared through his body as snapshots of the night before kaleidoscoped through his mind: her kiss-bruised mouth, goose bumps rising on her belly, his fingers breaching the burning wetness between her pretty thighs. But she was already opening the door and clambering into the passenger seat, completely unaware of how those five words had eradicated his morning-after satiety.

He told himself that was nothing special either, though, as he started the car and drove through the gates. Honor's pliant body and her gratifying, passionate climax might have made him come like Vesuvius, but his bed partners had been few and far between. He had good reason for sex to be burning in his mind.

It wasn't *her.*

Honor was quiet during the drive into town. He should have been glad, but instead the silence chafed at him. For her sake, he hoped it wasn't the silence of second thoughts, but damn it, he wasn't going to probe. He worked hard to maintain his barricade and he respected her right to have her own.

Upon their arrival at Pearl's Diner, though, he kicked himself for complaining, albeit silently, about that uncharacteristic quiet. There was a crowd standing around outside, all waiting for a table. It was a boisterous crowd too, thrilled not only with the night before's Homecoming win, but with the unexpected boom in town business due to the alien groupie invasion.

Bram shouldn't have complained about Honor's quiet because, hell, he'd complained too soon—she wasn't quiet now. She flitted among the people like a pirate-booted butterfly, smiling, chatting, and laughing with them. He seemed to be the only one struck by the strange, exotic species in their midst, though. The fact was, the citizens of Hot Water appeared more surprised by *his* presence than hers.

Though he trailed her at a safe distance, he still found himself dragged into the kinds of conversations he hadn't had in years.

"Yes," he agreed, dutifully bending over a wallet-sized photo of a shriveled peanut wearing a cap. "Your granddaughter certainly resembles you, Mrs. Ha."

Albert Sterling gave Bram a rundown on the specs of his brand-new Jeep and he even agreed to take a test drive with the older man at some later though unnamed—thank God—date.

Then there was the play-by-play rehash of the Argonauts' win. That wouldn't have been so bad, except the rehash was with the team's coach and resulted in the man handing Bram two tickets to the next game and extracting a promise from him to stop by the locker room to take part in the pregame pep talk.

Honor gazed at Bram as the coach's name was called and he and his wife followed the restaurant's hostess inside. "I didn't know you were the high school quarterback."

He grunted.

"I didn't know that you led the team to the state championship when you were a senior."

"We lost." He glanced down at her upturned face. "It was your good buddy Dylan who took the team to the state victory two years later."

She blinked. "And you're still mad about it."

"I am not!"

"Jealous, then." She looked amused.

He froze. No one, no one had ever guessed that carefully buried secret. That it took Honor about two and a half seconds to figure it out was nothing special, though, he hurriedly assured himself. It was just some stupid, lucky guess on her part. Grabbing her elbow, he dragged her away from the milling crowd. "I'm not jealous either."

She stuck that princessy little nose in the air. "Well, you shouldn't be. When we were locked in that cellar together, Dylan talked a lot about you. I know you two were best friends, but I think you were his hero too."

"I wasn't either his hero," he grumbled, then shot her a look. "So he talked about me?"

"Mmm." She brushed unseen lint from her skirt.

Bram cleared his throat. "Besides the friends stuff, what, uh, else did he tell you?"

"He said you were brainy."

"Brainy?" For God's sake, what the hell was Dylan thinking? What kind of way was that—*brainy!*—to describe a friend to a beautiful woman? "Are you sure he didn't say something different? 'Brawny,' maybe?"

She shook her head. "Brainy."

Bram grimaced. "Gloomy, boring, brainy. I'm beginning to feel like a twisted version of the seven dwarves all rolled into one."

Her lips twitched. "You forgot nerdy, cranky, and brooding."

He rolled his eyes, lifted a hand. "There you go."

She peeked at him from beneath her thick lashes, her sexy mouth curving up at the corners. "He did say a few other things too."

"Yeah?" This sounded somewhat more promising.

"Yeah," she echoed, and then went silent.

He held out for three-quarters of a minute. "So, um, what . . . what did you think about those few other things?" He couldn't believe he'd asked.

"What did I think?" She shrugged. "I made the poor man talk for nearly ninety-six hours straight. He told me about so many things, about so many people."

"Meaning you don't remember thinking anything about me in particular."

"That's not what I said."

He set his back teeth and remained silent, refusing to give her another opportunity to pull his chain.

Finally she laughed, then stepped closer. Putting one hand on his chest, she went on tiptoe to bring her mouth near his ear. Her breath was warm, her breast was pressing against his arm, and he forced himself not to grab her as sex once more swamped his brain.

"If you really want to know . . ." Her voice was artless and sweet. "I thought you sounded like a scrumptious lay."

He froze, his heart slamming against his chest. He knew she was kidding. *Of course* she was kidding. Those ninety-six hours with Dylan had come right on the heels of two weeks of terrifying captivity with a gang of sexual thugs.

Yet even after the kidnapping, Bram thought, even after last night and all that had happened between them, she could still tease and have fun with him. Have fun with life. Another snapshot flashed in his head: Honor, her mouth open as she belted out the Argonaut fight song.

He swallowed and wrapped his hands around her upper arms. "A scrumptious lay, huh?" he repeated, trying to match her light tone, though this tough, soft, valiant, funny woman had just poleaxed him again. "Better than Stucky Mitchell?"

A potent mix of heat and laughter flashed in her starry eyes. That little smile played at her mouth again. "Oh, yes. *Way* better than Stucky Mitchell."

Bram drew her closer to him. "Honor," he whispered, his gaze trained on her lips. Then, almost too late remembering she was supposed to be nothing special to him, he dropped his hands and backed away.

"I can't believe my luck!" an unfamiliar voice rang out.

Both Bram and Honor spun toward the door of the diner as two men stepped through and approached them. Bram moved closer to her again. "Do you know them?" he asked her quietly.

"Of course she knows us," one of the men boomed in answer. In a safari jacket and khaki shirt that strained over his paunch, he looked overfed and over-happy to see them. "The name's Gordon Gregg. *Celeb!* magazine." His hand stretched out.

Bram didn't respond.

Gregg only smiled and switched his attention to Honor. "You've been hiding from us, sweet pea." He chuckled. "I'm here for the Martian invasion, but my boss'll lay a mondo bonus on me for an exclusive one-on-one with you about your mystery marriage to the mystery man."

Honor shook her head. "No, thanks," she said pleasantly. "You'll only twist my words."

The man shrugged, obviously uninsulted. "Maybe, but your other choice is we'll just make them up."

Bram stiffened. "Hey—"

"Don't rise to the bait, Bram," Honor said quickly, curling her finger around one of his belt loops.

The fat asshole smiled again. "Listen to the lady. She's an old hat at this, Bram." His eyes narrowed and his gaze shifted to Honor. "So this *is* Bram Bennett, then? We reported that Daddy Witherspoon bought you a husband, but nobody's seen the two of you around town together."

Honor didn't answer.

"Oh, don't go pouty on me, sweet pea. I only want to know how much Daddy paid to get you off his hands."

Anger surged from Bram's gut to his fists. "Leave her alone, damn it."

Honor slid her arm around his waist. "Don't respond to him."

"But maybe he has something to say," the reporter remarked, giving Bram a between-us-guys, smarmy smile. "Maybe he wants to tell us what it's like to marry an heiress—and what's wrong with you, sweet pea, that made Daddy have to buy you your man."

Bram lunged for the jerk, but Honor pulled him back. "Don't." She wrapped both arms around his waist. "This is nothing to them but a way to get you on assault charges, or worse, on a page of their magazine in an unflattering photograph."

God, Bram thought, even now she could smile.

Gordon Gregg, the slime, grinned too. "She's right. But hey, it's nothing personal. It's not about her at all, really. There's nothing special about sweet pea here, except her daddy's worth billions."

"*That's it.*" Bram broke free of Honor's hold and grabbed the slime's lapels to drag him close.

"Hey, hey, hey. Take it easy." Gregg glanced over his shoulder at his buddy. "Where the hell's your camera, Ray?"

"I have one thing to say to you, and feel free to quote me." Bram shook the other man. "There's more special about a freckle on her toe than you could imagine with that flea-sized brain of yours. But right now what's most special about this woman is that she's my wife and you're in her face. So beat it."

Released, the reporter instantly backed off. "Fine, fine," he said. "You don't have to be rude about it."

Bram clenched his teeth but didn't take his eyes off the reporter and his companion until they climbed into a sedan and sped away. Then he looked around him, noting the fascinated gazes of the people still waiting outside Pearl's.

He groaned inwardly, but couldn't think of anything else to do but turn and face Honor.

She merely lifted an eyebrow. "A freckle on my toe?"

He couldn't even appreciate her good humor now. "Damn fucking straight."

*T*HAT afternoon, Honor lay on her side, her cheek cupped by her pillow, her hand toying with hair silky and dark. She ran her fingers over it, savoring its warmth. "Bram," she said, staring into the eyes across from hers while struggling for a tone that sounded casual yet sophisticated. "I think it would be best if we don't continue with this sex, uh . . . thing, don't you?"

The one she'd questioned leaned closer and gave her a big wet kiss on her cheek. His tail swung, thumping in a steady rhythm against the nightstand. His front paws, propped atop the mattress, executed a brief but tricky dance step. He licked her face again.

Honor gave Joey a weak smile and sat up. "I *do* hope that's not Bram's reaction." She rubbed his long ears. "Though I appreciate the opportunity to practice."

Joey bounded off the mattress and raced to the French doors leading to the back porch. He whined.

"They're out there, huh?" She envied the animal his eagerness. *He* wasn't dreading a heart-to-heart, the lucky dog.

She walked to the French doors and hesitated, ignoring Joey's excited prancing. She was going to have to flat-out make her statement to Bram, that was all there was to it. Of course, there still remained that small problem of naming what they'd done the night before. *Sex, uh, thing* didn't seem quite right.

Sex leading nowhere?

Sex without commitment?

Good time, good fun . . . what?

Once she figured out how to label it, she'd make clear she didn't intend to experience it again.

Last night Bram had restored her sexuality. And whether it was testament to his technique or her own rejuvenated passion, she wanted to be with him again.

She'd wanted him when she'd woken up alone in his bed. Again, when she'd caught sight of him sitting on the hood of his car. Right this instant.

She thought of the night before, of his tongue on her fingers, his mouth on her breasts, her body leaning over his and taking him in. An echo of climax shivered through her and she wanted the real thing even more.

But more intimacy with Bram was too risky. She knew that.

There was no predicting how Bram would react to what she had to say, though. Last night she had asked him to help her overcome her fear of sex, and he'd done that. And before last night he'd told her that he hadn't slept with anyone more than once since his wife's death. Did he expect last night to be both beginning and end of *their* sleeping together too?

His behavior this morning had been typically enigmatic, leaving no real clue to the answer. There had been that romantic trail of autumn leaves, then his withdrawn attitude on the drive into town. His almost embarrassed defensiveness when she'd teased him about being jealous of Dylan, followed by his zealous championship of her with that annoying, though harmless reporter.

It was something foolish and female inside her that made her consider that shadowy complexity of his appealing. But it was something wise and womanly that recognized when it was time to beat a hasty retreat from it.

The more times she slept with him, the more she risked coming to care about him.

Determined to get the conversation over with, she twisted the knob of the door. Joey raced out into the late afternoon sunlight, then she shoved her hands in the pockets of her skirt and headed after him.

The sun was warm on her shoulders as she crossed the wide redwood deck. In the distance, she could hear a rhythmic thumping that sounded louder as she trailed Joey through the wooded grounds behind the house. The footpath she followed led to the detached four-car garage and then beyond it to the rustic-styled guest cottage where Josh was staying.

Upon reaching it, the thumping was even louder and she walked around the side of the little house to discover a small clearing. Her heart tripped and her feet stumbled. Bracing her hand on the wall of the cottage, she halted. Fifo was posed at one side of the clearing, Joey cavorting around him. His back to her, Bram was chopping wood.

Shirtless, wearing only jeans and heavy work boots, he moved in a rhythm that was as unfamiliar to her as it was hypnotizing. She'd never seen a man do something so . . . well, physical. Her gaze slid over his back, watching the play of heavy muscles between his wide shoulders.

They lengthened as he bent to retrieve a chunk of

tree trunk, then place it on the chopping block. The muscles shortened as he forced a wedge-shaped piece of metal into a crack in the surface. They bunched as he swung the ax over his head, then smoothed as the log split with one powerful stroke.

He tossed the pieces on a nearby pile and then started the fascinating process all over again.

She'd watched the European men's ski races in Gstaad. Clapped in appreciation over a well-fought tennis match at the Bel Air Country Club. She'd tallied lacrosse points, praised sailing trophies, even admired a masculine form or two astride sweating polo ponies.

But a primitive emotion rose from deep within her as she witnessed a man's muscles work at something useful. As she continued to watch, the woodpile grew higher, and that odd emotion, part satisfaction, part comfort, part something primal and *un*comfortable, grew with it.

Then, as if he sensed her, Bram suddenly turned and caught her staring.

It was too late and she was too bewitched to make it look as if she'd just arrived. He slowly walked toward her, pulling a bandanna from his back pocket, then wiping his face with it as he approached.

Honor didn't move, taking the opportunity to run her gaze over this side of him. The skin of his chest was smooth and tan and now she knew how he came by his well-defined pecs and biceps.

He stopped a few feet from her, tilting his head and frowning. "You have a funny expression on your face."

I'll bet, Honor thought. She swallowed. "I think I just had an out-of-time experience. Watching you work, I was suddenly a woman from the 1800s, a woman who felt a distinct, visceral thrill at the certainty of plenty of wood for winter."

He glanced back at the pile of freshly cut logs. "It'll take more than that to keep the fires burning."

Oh, I think my fires will burn just fine, Honor thought, her gaze resting on the spot where his low-slung jeans cut across his rippling abdomen, a little heat kindling in her own belly already.

"There you go with that funny expression again." His voice softened as he stepped closer. "What's going on inside that beautiful head of yours?" His hand reached toward her face.

Honor snapped to attention.

She snapped back to the present.

She jumped away to avoid his touch. *Foolish, foolish, foolish.*

"I wanted to talk with you." She cleared her throat of its telltale huskiness.

"Yeah?" He lifted one eyebrow.

She tried focusing on it, instead of the interesting path a bead of sweat was taking down his bare chest. "Yes." The bead accelerated, dipped into his navel, and then—

Her gaze jerked up. "I won't have sex with you again," she blurted out.

That eyebrow inched higher. "Is that right?"

She nodded. "Yes."

"I thought you said I was a scrumptious lay," he said mildly.

"No. I said I *thought* you were a scrumptious lay. Before I knew you. Before I ever met you."

"Ah. So I'm not 'way better' than Stucky Mitchell, after all?"

"Stucky Mitchell was a mistake."

"Honor"—his voice was amused—"why you would think anyone with the name 'Stucky' *wouldn't* be a mistake, particularly when it comes to sex, eludes me."

She flushed. "*Stuckford* Mitchell. You know, of Stuckford Products?"

"Tobacco, pharmaceuticals, cereals—"

"Cookies, paper goods. You name it, Stuckford Products has a finger—no, both hands and feet—in it." She grimaced. "I had sex with Stucky because I thought he was safe."

Bram tilted his head. "I'm trying to follow you, honey. You thought Stucky of Stuckford Products was safe because he'd have easy access to condoms or . . ."

"I thought he had money. Lots of money. And I was right about that."

"But wrong about what?"

She pressed her lips together and shook her head. "This has nothing to do with us."

"I thought you just told me there wasn't going to be any more 'us.'" His voice was amused, his eyes watchful. "So tell me about Stucky."

"Last night, I wanted to feel normal, all right? You did that. Thanks. Thanks very much." She whirled. "Let's leave it there."

Bram caught her arm and swung her back. "I don't think I can leave it there."

"Let me go." Her skin went hot beneath his hand.

"Tell me about Stucky, and I will."

She frowned. "You're fixated on Stucky."

No," Bram corrected. "I think part of the problem here is that you are."

Frustrated, she sighed. "Stucky Mitchell is the only person I ever met whose family has more money than mine. And he seemed to really like me, okay? Get it?"

"I'm trying to, Honor, by God I am," he said gently. "But . . ."

"I'm not stupid, Bram. And those boarding schools didn't mince words as the daughters of wealth reached young adulthood. I was very cautious about entering into a . . . relationship because I always wondered if a boy—or a man—liked me for myself or for my—"

"Money," he finished.

"My *father's* money," she corrected. "Occupational hazard of the poor little rich girls of the world." She said the words before he could.

"Honor—"

"By the time I was twenty-one, apparently my reputation for caution made me into quite the attractive conquest. And Stucky Mitchell liked to gamble. Not that he needed me to pay off his debts . . . he just needed me to win the bet that was going around our set of so-called 'friends.'" She studied the circle of Bram's hand on her arm. "He made fifty grand off my virginity."

"Fifty thousand *dollars*?"

"Yes."

"Bastard."

"Yes." She looked up, into the icy hardness of Bram's green eyes. "I thought we had a real relationship. I'd been sleeping with him for several weeks when a mutual acquaintance let it slip. Once I found out, I threatened to tell his grandmother—she's the one who holds the keys to Stucky's trust fund—unless he gave me the entire amount he'd won."

She surprised a harsh laugh out of Bram. "No."

"Yep. I found a shelter that rescues abandoned pot-belly pigs and donated the money to them in Stucky's name—making him their biggest one-time benefactor. Now he figures prominently in all their literature and I believe he's still receiving monthly solicitations." She tried to slip her arm from Bram's grasp, but it only tightened. "So that's Stucky."

"And you steered clear of sexual liaisons since?"

She lifted her chin, remembering the humiliation. "Yes. Do you blame me?"

"Hell, no. I'm only more surprised about last night." He swallowed and his eyes darkened. "You really trusted me."

"That's right." She nodded. "Especially because you don't like me."

"*What?*" He stared at her.

"Or didn't like me. Whatever." She shrugged one shoulder. "Unlike some—most, maybe—you've never faked how you feel about me."

Dropping her arm, he cut his gaze from hers.

"So"—she shrugged again—"I wanted to restore my sexuality with someone trustworthy. You. Thanks."

"With someone who wouldn't 'fake' it." His voice sounded cool—dangerous, even. "With someone who wouldn't pretend with you."

"Exactly." She backed up a step. Another.

His hand snaked out and grabbed her arm again.

"Hey!"

His posture, his expression, his words were tense. "You want unfake feelings? Then let me tell you. I always wanted you, Honor. I wanted you the moment I laid eyes on you."

Her pulse leaped. *Foolish, foolish, foolish.*

"I want you now."

Heat softened the place between her thighs. She

madly shook her head. "No. I don't need you any-more."

"Because you're all better, you say." His eyes looked dangerous now.

She swallowed. "Yes."

His fingers tightened on her arm. "Then you can see yourself having sex with someone else?"

"No! Yes!" Too late, she realized he'd trapped her.

He smiled triumphantly and pulled her close. The damp warmth of his bare chest seeped through the thin fabric of her shirt. He smelled like his soap and sweat, a deeply male scent that reawakened that primal, un-comfortable, jittery feeling in her belly.

"And I do like you, Honor. I think you're sweet and funny and smart and"—he touched his mouth to hers—"delicious."

She swallowed a moan. "Thanks very much, but—"

"Let's go to bed." His big body moved, herding her in the direction of the house.

"Now?" Honor blinked, startled by the thought.

"Now."

"But . . ." But she was still worried that getting close to him again could be disaster! He was hung up on his dead wife, and Honor was—

"*Now*."

Honor was someone who'd vowed to live life to the fullest. She was an optimist who believed that things would always work out for the best, whatever way that was. Her resistance melted in a runny rush. "*Carpe diem*," she murmured. "Seize the day."

Bram kissed the words off her lips.

They didn't make it to the bed. The real beauty of that outside wall, Honor thought hazily, was that it made the grounds of the Fortress as private as a bedroom. By the time they reached the house, her blouse was hanging open and he'd unfastened the front clasp of her bra. His fingers had teased her nipples to tight, aching points.

Once she climbed the stairs to the back deck, he turned her. With his feet on a lower step, his mouth was at the perfect level. He fondled one breast with his hand and took the other in his mouth, sucking on the nipple with greedy hunger.

Honor cried out, the wet heat of his mouth matching the wet heat between her legs. She reached for his bare chest and he jerked, then caught her hands in his free one, holding them off his skin.

His mouth lifted from her breast and he looked at the wet tip. Then he bent forward to lick it again, as if he couldn't help himself. "Delicious," he murmured, before moving to the other one and pulling on it with the same eagerness.

Honor's body bowed toward his. She wanted more. She wanted it all. Just for today, if that's all she could have. "*Carpe diem,*" she murmured again.

He released her breast and dragged her toward her bedroom. They kissed wildly at the threshold of the French doors, and then he pulled her inside and pulled her onto the floor. With the door still open, the cooling evening air flowed over them, but it didn't abate the heat.

In seconds Bram had her out of her blouse, bra, and skirt. She sat up to unbuckle her boots, but he smiled at her, a wolfish smile. "Leave them. You're my bounty, baby, just like this."

He pushed her back and shoved off his pants and

shoes. Then, though she was still wearing her boots and panties, he used his clever, clever fingers to make her come.

For the first time that night.

And just as the day darkened into evening, he ripped her panties aside and entered her. He groaned, and then his long fingers gripped her hips and angled them to push even deeper.

"Not *carpe diem*," he said harshly. "But *every* day, every night. That's what you owe me for how I helped you. For marrying you. Every night and every day until you go."

She squeezed shut her eyes. He wanted her, like this, until they were free of each other. *Foolish, foolish, foolish,* her wise self said. *Don't promise that.*

"Look at me."

She obeyed his command. It was dim inside the room now. Outside too. He pushed into her, hard and deep, and she saw stars. Stars behind his head, in the evening sky.

Day was gone. Night was here. Bram was too. Not at Alicia's grave.

"Say it, Honor."

She felt the power gather in his body and her own release coiled again, preparing to strike.

"Say it, Honor." His body reared over hers, the stars brilliant behind him.

Seize life. "Yes, yes, yes."

His head dropped to her breast and he pumped into her. She shuddered, her inner muscles gripping him, in her climax her body acting out her other, more frightening desire to hold him to her forever.

Chapter Fourteen

*J*osh stood at the edge of the Enigma property with the "committee" of four he'd assembled— Honor, Bram, the mayor of Hot Water, and the mayor's wife. With one hand, he gestured toward the groupie camp, which had quintupled in size since his first visit. Dozens of tents and tarps and other sorts of temporary shelters littered the field.

"See?" he said, his voice filled with disgust. "It's become a Ripley's Believe It or Not! revival meeting."

Honor let out a laugh, then, catching Josh's eye, quickly swallowed the sound. Her husband thumbed the dimple in her chin and the look the two exchanged only heightened Josh's foul mood.

"They even have Porta-Potties now," he pointed out. "Though how the hell they convinced anyone to place portable toilets on property they don't have the slightest claim to is beyond me."

Mayor Ames cleared his throat. "I might be able to explain that." He cleared his throat again. "Beau gave me a call at the end of last week, concerned about the lack of facilities out here. I put him in touch with my brother-in-law." He cast a look at his wife.

Josh would have loved to glare at the old battle-ax, but she bore an uncanny resemblance to the principal of his junior high. Just looking at her smoothly coiffed hair and the pearls around her neck made him want to babble out some lame excuse for cutting third period.

"Naturally," said Mrs. Ames, smiling at her husband, "as mayor, Art is concerned about the comfort of anyone staying within the confines of town. He told my brother it was all right to deliver them."

"But it's not the town's dime," the mayor assured Josh. "Beau's paying the bill."

Josh ground his teeth, fuming. First a website and glossy flyers, now portable toilets. If he ever figured out who was funding the freakin' fantasies of some half-crocked Italian house painter, he was going to send their ass into outer space, that was for damn sure.

He sucked in a calming breath. "The point is, I wanted both you and Honor, sir, to grasp how outrageous this situation has become. Then I think you'll agree with me that it's time to call the sheriff in."

Neither Mayor Ames nor Honor met his eyes. Instead, both of their gazes slid away from his to survey the encampment.

Let 'em look, Josh thought. *Let 'em take their time.* But there was no doubt they'd come around to his side.

His hand on her shoulder, Bram leaned close to Honor and murmured something in her ear. Josh watched responsive color rush across her cheeks, and his temper burned brighter. Brighter still, when he saw Bram take note of that telltale flush and observed the satisfied, knowing expression it put on his face.

Smug bastard, Josh thought. Well, it didn't matter

how pleased with himself Bennett was, not as long as Josh got the go-ahead to drag out his cell phone and make that call to the sheriff, free of guilt.

"Josh, have you talked to Mia?" Honor asked.

"What the hell does she have to do with this?" he shot back, his voice hot. "I don't need her permission."

Everyone's eyebrows rose.

To hell with them, Josh thought, stomping toward Beau's RV. To hell with all of them, including Beau's stacked, brown-eyed daughter, who was the one who made him feel guilty in the first place.

Guilty! That had to be wrong. The real, citified Josh McCool didn't possess enough scruples to feel guilty. Thank God.

"Josh." Honor hurried after him and caught his arm. "Don't do anything rash."

In an abrupt move he swung toward her, only to meet a clear warning in Bram Bennett's icy eyes. "Yeah, McCool," Bram said softly. Menacingly. "Don't do anything rash."

"For God's sake," Josh bit out. He didn't know what pissed him off more, this ridiculous—and unwarranted!—attack of conscience, or the idea that Bennett thought he'd do anything to hurt a woman.

But then his mind leaped to Mia and the thick sound of disillusionment and tears in her voice at the Homecoming game. *You're not the man I thought you were*, she'd said. Pain twisted once again in his solar plexus.

Well, he wasn't the man he thought he was either, he told himself, ignoring the uncomfortable ache. Not if he couldn't kick the kooks off Enigma's property without first salving his conscience by getting Honor and the mayor to agree.

He opened his mouth to tell them his mind was made up. "Do you have a better idea?" came out instead.

Honor shrugged. "Maybe. Let me and the mayor talk to Beau again before you do anything."

Josh closed his eyes and sighed. "I'm going soft," he muttered.

Honor smiled at him brilliantly and patted his cheek as she passed him by. "You're so much nicer that way."

Josh sighed again, and followed her. What man cared for nice when he wanted to be rich?

The five of them had to wait to speak with Beau until he finished his interview with a reporter from the high school newspaper, a straggly-haired girl with a backpack bigger than she was. Then the old coot was called away to take a telephone call from a local TV reporter. Josh barely clung to his patience as Beau's self-styled assistant served them coffee from a huge pot that sat on a table in the shade cast by the RV.

"Face it," Josh said for Honor's ears only. "This will be a circus in a few more days when the media attention heats up."

Honor's gaze roamed the area, moving over two scholarly-looking men huddled around a chessboard set up on a card table, a group of young people lounging on side-by-side sleeping bags sharing newspapers, the nearby cooking tent where three huge pots were steaming over butane stoves.

"It's certainly colorful," she admitted.

"It's crazy, Honor. You know I'm right about this. Your father charged me with smoothing out this problem and I'm sure he isn't too happy with how long it's taking me." Further jeopardizing Plan B, Josh thought grimly. And it was the only halfway viable plan he had at the moment, considering the casual yet possessive way Bennett was resting his palm on Honor's ass.

Josh grimaced. If he didn't ensure the Enigma expansion wasn't delayed, he'd have nothing to show for all the years of working for Warren Witherspoon except a closetful of high-priced suits. Even the Ferrari belonged to the corporation, not Josh.

"Believe me, lovely lady," he said, trying to charm her when all he felt was desperation, "it will be easiest on everyone if we clear them out of here before the crowd grows any larger."

Apparently overhearing, the mayor and his wife turned. "However, the town is profiting from the notoriety this crowd brings, Mr. McCool," the older man said. "If Beau and his friends move someplace else, I'm afraid Hot Water won't be very happy."

Josh clenched his teeth. "Yes, but—"

"You might not understand our ways," the mayor interrupted, "but I do. We have a long history of tolerating, even appreciating, eccentric people. As the descendants of gold seekers, we particularly sympathize with those chasing a dream."

Mrs. Ames nodded and she looked over at Honor. "We have long memories too. We'd like to think kindly toward the Witherspoons."

Josh nearly groaned aloud as Honor's face froze. She clutched his arm with rigid fingers. "See, Josh? You need to think more carefully about this. We don't want to foster a town grudge against Witherspoons."

He shook his head. "Honor . . ."

Her voice tightened. "If we can get a sign of cooperation out of Beau, then you have to promise me you won't call the sheriff."

"Honor . . ."

He was saved from any further pressure by the appearance of Beau himself, who appeared as affable—no, downright delighted—as he always did. Josh stepped back and let Honor and the mayor meander through a conversation that seemed as far from the point as Josh was from his favorite martini bar in West L.A.

Suddenly his palms went itchy.

He turned his head, certain who he'd find. Mia. He watched her walk toward them, and that unfamiliar sense of shame he'd felt since the football game redoubled. He wished she'd never discovered what a selfish, heartless, scheming bastard he was.

Ignoring him, she drew nearer. In an ankle-length soft skirt and clingy, long-sleeved top, every luxurious curve was lovingly delineated. It made him remember the rich, bony females he'd dated before. Their skinny butts and fake, hard tits seemed an abomination to womanhood now.

Mia was probably wearing that outfit to punish him.

When she got closer, he caught her scent, something lemon-and-basily, and he *knew* she was punishing him.

He grabbed her arm as she passed, yanking her close.

She looked at his hand. She looked at his face. She was looking at him as if he were the scum on pond scum, but even a sneer on her lush mouth appeared gorgeous.

"Don't interrupt," he told her, nodding toward her father.

"Who made you the boss of me?" she snapped back.

Despite everything, Josh smothered a grin. The last time he'd heard that question, it had come out of his own fourteen-year-old mouth and Granny had casually backhanded him for his sass, her mind already on the quarters in her fist that she should spend on food but wouldn't.

"Mia . . ." Then he paused as he tuned in to what Beau was telling Honor.

". . . I was walking there," he said, pointing up the road in the direction of town, "when a dark mass hovered over me. Scared me sober, I'm not embarrassed to say. I started running, but the dark ship kept up with me, tracking my every move. When I ran into this field—there wasn't a fence then—it followed. A green mist suddenly covered the ground and I tripped and fell. The ship hovered over me again, and then from it a light beamed down."

"Jesus," Josh whispered to Mia, a chill rolling down his spine. "Have you heard this before?"

"Of course."

Her words, her acid tone, shamed him again. Of course she'd cared enough to listen to her father's story. Not like Josh, who only listened to himself and what he thought he wanted. Who only listened to the people who could give him those things.

Beau was talking again, his voice hushed. "The light was bright, strong, like sunlight, but the silver color of the stars. At first I was terrified, because my body felt so heavy and my mind dizzy. Then I heard a hypnotic, insistent voice. I heard it in my mind, you understand. 'Don't be afraid. Don't be afraid.'" He shrugged. "I wasn't any longer."

Several of the people in the encampment drew closer, as if Beau's story itself were hypnotic. The similar, almost yearning expressions on their faces creeped Josh out. Without even realizing it, he drew Mia against him, as if to protect her.

"Tell what happened next. The linking," one of the groupies prompted.

Beau nodded. "I felt that . . . a linking with them. It wasn't really an abduction in the physical sense, but an out-of-body experience of unity. As if they drew me to them and we were one. They told me things."

Then Beau seemed to look straight at Josh. "We have so much to learn. So much we should appreciate and find beauty in."

A second chill prickled Josh's skin. Mia must have felt him shiver, because she turned and looked at him with scorn in those chocolate eyes. "What's the matter? You can't be bothered by something you're so certain is nonsense, right?"

He shook his head, stopped himself, nodded. Of course it was nonsense.

"Then, somehow, I knew they were going," Beau concluded. "I didn't want them to. I begged them to stay, because it was so warm in the light and everything was so *clear*. Not to worry, they said in my mind. They told me they'd return soon."

A silence fell over all the listeners. Honor was the first to speak after the long quiet. She cleared her throat. "Well, Mr. Caruso, I'm wondering. Why are you so certain the ship will come back to this exact location?"

Oh, here she goes, Josh thought, rolling his eyes.

"Well, because this is where they found me," Beau answered.

"Yes." Honor smiled at him. "Exactly. Found *you*. It seems to me that it's not this location that's the draw, but you."

Beau's puzzlement was reflected on the faces of all his followers. "I'm not sure what you mean."

"It found you on the road out there, right? And it was you who ran onto the Enigma property. The ship stopped when you did. It stopped for *you,* not *here.*"

"Well," Beau said, blinking. "Hmmm. That bears some thinking about."

There were murmurings among the groupies as they mulled that new thought over. Honor half turned and shot Josh a triumphant look. "Maybe you should think about it," she suggested gently, turning back. "Maybe your location doesn't matter at all. And if that notion starts to make sense to you, Bram and I would most certainly welcome you at the Fortress to discuss an alternate site for your next, uh . . . meeting with them."

She flicked a glance over her shoulder again, making Josh acutely aware that he still held Mia against his body. "And I'm sure I speak for my father and Josh"— *Josh, who is riddled with guilt over the lust he has for your daughter and the callous way he's treated her,* her next quick glance his way seemed to say—"when I tell you you're welcome to remain here until you've had a chance to think that over."

By the time Honor, Bram, and the Ameses had left the encampment, Mia could tell that Josh had shaken off the uneasiness brought on by her father's story. He'd replaced it with frustration.

"I'm going to kill Honor," he fumed, stalking toward Mia. " 'I'm sure I can speak for Josh.' That nutty woman neatly painted me right into a corner."

A butcher-style apron wrapped securely around her, Mia stood at a long table in the encampment's makeshift cooking area. She didn't look up from loosening the foil off one of the three restaurant-sized lasagnes she'd prepared and baked at home. "That's not a very nice way to talk about the woman you plan to marry."

He halted in front of her. "What in the name of all that's holy is that?" he asked, pointing to the pasta dish she'd uncovered.

Mia kept her eyes down. It was best not to look at him. Perhaps it didn't say much about *her* character, but the fact that she knew how flawed *his* character was didn't suppress the desire that burned low in her belly at even the briefest glimpse of his male beauty.

"Answer me, Mia," he demanded.

She calmly removed the next foil covering. "Lasagnes, of course. I would think a sophisticated, worldly man like yourself would recognize them." Her forefinger indicated each large pan in turn. "Italian sausage here, this one's veggie—eggplant. The third is made with ham and a cream-asparagus sauce."

There was a long moment of silence.

"Damn it," he finally ground out. "None of this is Honor's fault after all. It's you. We've been counting on the rustic camping conditions to discourage the groupies. But who in their right mind would leave here when they're getting fed like this?"

Instead of answering, she merely scooped a portion of the first lasagne onto a paper plate and handed it to Josh along with a plastic fork. Through her lashes, she watched him take a bite.

"Oh, my God." The words were muffled but soulful, his anger at her supplanted. He shoved another huge bite into his already-full mouth, his slick manners forgotten, apparently, in his lust for the dish. "Where have you been all my life?"

Mia's dumb heart heard the words and she couldn't help herself from lifting her head. Josh was looking at her, his plastic fork in midplunge, a dab of sauce caught in the corner of his mouth.

Without even thinking, she leaned across the table and wiped the sauce away with her thumb. Josh froze, and his eyes darkened, their bamboozle blue turning to a color that was as honest as it was hot.

Just with that, Mia found herself convinced he hadn't been lying about his attraction to her. She'd wondered, after the football game, if he'd talked about the attraction as mutual merely to amuse himself. But now she believed it.

Really believed it.

And on the strength of that single flattering conviction, Mia leaped out of her shell for only the second time in her life.

Her gaze fixed on Josh's, she slowly opened her mouth. She extended her tongue. She sensuously licked the smear of sauce from the pad of her thumb.

She saw him swallow. Then again.

He carefully set the plate on the table. "I have to go."

"Me too," Mia said calmly, reaching to untie the apron bow at the small of her back. Then she lifted the canvas fabric over her head and half turned to toss the apron behind her. As she'd hoped, when she turned back Josh was still standing before her, his eyes still that deep-heat blue.

"Would you drive me home?" she asked, hoping he wouldn't ask her what was wrong with her own car.

"I don't think that's such a good idea." But he didn't move.

"It's a fine idea," Mia said, coming around the table. "Liberating, even."

"I might be a lower life-form," he said, retreating a step, "but I'm not an idiot. You're scaring me, Mia."

But *she* wasn't afraid any longer. The old Mia had hidden behind her plumpness and her parents and waited for luck, for life, to approach *her*. But what was that adage? You can't win the lottery unless you buy a ticket? That made perfect sense to Mia now.

You could never have a man like Josh unless you tried to get him.

She stopped in front of him. Smiled innocently. "I'm only asking for a ride home, Josh," she lied. For good measure, she drew in a cleavage-enhancing breath, following it up with a raised eyebrow.

It worked.

He cleared his throat, shoved his hand into his pocket for his car keys. "Just a ride home."

The Ferrari purred all the way to her house. Mia nearly did too, because it was completely obvious that Josh's usual urbanity had left him somewhere between his first bite of lasagne and her deep breath. Braking the car before her front door, he shoved his hand through his hair, leaving it untidy.

"Here you are," he said, making no move to switch off the engine.

So Mia did it for him. She reached over, and with a quick flick of her wrist, the car was off. "Come in," she said.

"No." He shook his head. "I'm not the man you thought I was, remember? Nothing's changed about that."

"Maybe I have." That wasn't such a big lie. On the basic issues, she hadn't made an about-face, but in other ways she was different. The old Mia would never have gotten even this far with a man like Josh.

She put her hand on his leg above his knee, slid it up the lightweight wool toward his crotch. It was thrilling, both the instant tightening of his muscles beneath her hand as well as the unignorable hitch in his breath.

Inches from dangerous territory, he caught her hand beneath his. "I'm selfish."

"In bed?" She performed that delicious eyebrow raise again.

He blinked. "No! I—" He broke off, obviously frustrated. "You don't know what you're asking for."

Oh, but I do. I know what I'm hoping for, anyway. Because her heart couldn't accept that "selfish," city-slick Josh couldn't want her in the same way—all the ways—that she wanted him.

She lifted her chin, prepared to say whatever she must to have her chance with him. "Maybe I'm shallow too. Selfish. Because I think you're beautiful, Josh, and it makes me want you. I want you enough to push you. That's a new one for me." Beneath the heavy weight of his hand, she still managed to caress his leg. "I think I like the feeling."

His eyes narrowed. "Even if you're fooling yourself, you're not fooling me. You don't want what I have to offer. Which is nothing. Nothing more than a toss or two in your bed."

Panic fluttered in her belly, threatening to override all the wonderful desire. He couldn't leave her. Not now. "Don't be so high-minded, Josh."

" 'High-minded'?" He obviously detested the word.

"Mmm," she agreed, studying his reaction. "And noble. You don't have to be so noble."

His eyes went hard. "That's it." His voice was tight. "You asked for it. Just remember that. You asked for it."

Before she could absorb what was happening, he

was out of the car and then pulling her out too. His hand was hard on hers as he towed her toward the house. "I'm tired of playing do-gooder," he said. "I'm sick of feeling guilty for saying no and I'm sick of feeling horny because I won't say yes."

She didn't know how he found her bedroom, but he did, shoving the door open with the flat of his hand. He halted beside her bed and grabbed her shoulders. "I'm going to bed with you because I take what I want, do you understand?" His eyes were still hard, still hot.

He gave her an almost-rough shake, heat pouring off his skin. "I'm a bad, bad man and you'll give me what I want. *Do you understand*?"

Mia was sure she did. For an answer, she took the small step necessary to bring her body—the body that she'd always deplored in varying degrees—against the most beautiful man she'd ever seen. He shuddered.

She lifted to her tiptoes, desire swamping any residual nerves as his hands settled on hips she'd always considered too wide. She fit her mouth to his, pressing her lips fiercely to his. His fingers flexed, biting into her flesh.

Bad, bad man, she heard in her head. Over and over the words sounded, like a pulse, like a heartbeat. The sound of pure excitement. Her body quivered, anticipating the bad, experienced man's next move.

He took over the kiss.

Gently. Tenderly.

His mouth softened against hers. He wooed her with his tongue, letting it creep up on her, sleek and wet, so that when it tickled the underside of her lower lip she was so needy for more that she instantly widened her mouth and moaned.

But he refused to give her what she wanted. Instead,

he moved his lips over her face, tracing her ears, running the flat of his tongue along her jawline.

She wanted more, she wanted to be lost in lust, in passion. She tried to capture his face with her hands, but he stepped away. He gazed at her with eyes now dispassionate, his mouth wet and his breath moving fast in his chest. "Strip," he said, his voice almost angry.

Strip? But it was daylight. And she was . . . Mia. She wanted to believe she'd left her shell behind. She wanted to believe all her body issues had evaporated too, and maybe they would have been, if it was dark. Or if he would just kiss her, touch her, make her mindless with want so that she couldn't remember that her hips were too fleshy and that her breasts needed the euphemistic "eighteen-hour" support.

If she'd known Josh was going to show up in her life, maybe she would have spent some money on cosmetic surgery.

"Strip," he said again, but his pose relaxed a little.

He didn't think she would do it, she realized. He thought Mia would run scared from the "bad, bad man." But she wasn't going to be careful of what she wished for, not anymore.

Determined, she crossed her arms, her hands going to the hem of her long-sleeved knit shirt. Then she hesitated once again. She'd been the first one in her grade to wear a bra. She could remember the deep embarrassment of trailing her mother into the lingerie section of the department store in the next town over. How loud her mother's voice had sounded as she asked for help in selecting a bra for her nine-year-old daughter. At that moment, shame had infused Mia's body and never left.

She remembered trying to hide from other shoppers

behind a rack of stretchy body shapers. Even now she could see the sign above them. It had showed a line drawing of a rounded fertility-goddess-type figure that in a second drawing was tamed to supermodel slimness, merely by the addition of one excruciating-looking, elastic "Curvebuster," absolutely "guaranteed to take off twenty pounds in an instant."

She'd been plumpish then, not too bad, really. Her mother had tried to reassure her that those chubby pounds would someday turn into womanly curves. Mia remembered the conversation now, during the "ladies' lunch" they'd shared after that first, humiliating bra-shopping excursion.

Mia hadn't listened. Instead, she'd hunched in her chair, terrified that everyone in the small café could tell she was wearing a bra under her blouse. She'd worried that the kids at school would notice. She'd wondered where those twenty pounds the Curvebuster instantly removed actually *went* while you were wearing it.

And all that terror, worry, and wonder had turned an average—if early-ripening—little girl into a self-conscious mouse. It had created a teenager who hid behind her shyness. And because she'd bought into every airbrushed advertisement since, because she'd believed the fashion magazines when they found six-foot fourteen-year-olds and held them up as ideals after making them up to resemble adults, she'd become a woman who brought a gorgeous man to her bed but who still hesitated to embrace him because her body might not be good enough.

Hadn't she promised herself to live, really live, on the one-year anniversary of her mother's death? She hadn't followed through with that very well.

Mia yanked off her shirt and threw it on the floor.

Her hands shaking, she reached behind her and undid the five hook-and-eyes necessary to a bra with all-day support. She let it drop, feeling her breasts sway forward, pendulous—no!—glorious.

She didn't dare look at Josh, though. She wanted to trust him, but . . . instead, she kicked off her shoes, then shimmied out of her elastic-waist skirt. Without even taking a breath, she pushed down the long white slip that was supposed to keep clothes from clinging too closely to her hips, her belly, her too-round rear end.

Her panties were ugly. She'd always admired the pairs that were cut high on the thighs, but always thought she had too much thigh to expose like that. Closing her eyes, she shoved her pair of utilitarian Jockeys down her legs and stepped out of them.

This is me. Taking a deep breath, she opened her eyes. Still too chicken to look at Josh, she sent a quick, sidelong glance to the long mirror in front of her.

She blinked, looked again.

Without her clothes, she looked different. Without her clothes, there was nothing to measure herself against except . . . herself. Without her bra binding her breasts, they seemed to find their place, find their shape, even, standing out beneath her square shoulders with the fullness of a fifties centerfold. Without the ugly underpants, her body curved like a woman's body was made to curve: rib cage narrowing to waist, waist widening to hips that were on the same scale as her breasts. Mia saw that her thighs were strong and muscular from standing at a stove and tending to a house.

She looked normal. Good. Normal and . . . and more.

Why, Mia thought, amazed, naked she was . . . beautiful.

She slowly turned toward Josh. It didn't matter what she saw on his face, because she knew all she needed to already.

But he didn't disappoint her. As a matter of fact, he looked as if she'd hit him straight between the eyes.

He shook his head as if to clear it. "You're too good for me," he murmured hoarsely.

Mia grabbed the end of his tie and pulled him toward her naked, voluptuous curves, not willing to waste an instant in case this body-beautiful feeling didn't last forever. "You just might be right."

But still, he made love to her. Like an angel. Like a devil. He made her feel like a sinner and she whispered hallelujahs to the clever hands, worshiping mouth, and passionate body of the bad, bad man.

When evening came and the bedroom turned dark, Josh was gone. They hadn't talked. He hadn't bothered to take a look around her room. He'd only looked at her.

Now alone, Mia still felt beautiful.

Chapter Fifteen

*H*onor threw open the curtains that covered Bram's office window and peered out the glass. "Have you noticed anything strange about Mia lately?"

He grunted, squinting against the sunlight that glared on his computer screen. He would have drawn the curtains by pressing the code on his palmtop, but when he'd tried that yesterday they'd gone haywire, zooming nonstop back and forth until he'd been forced to take a screwdriver to them.

And then there was something so pretty about the warm sunlight washing over Honor's face.

"Something's different about her," Honor said, frowning now. "I've seen her talking to Josh an awful lot."

Bram figured he knew what was going on between Mia and Josh and he also figured it was none of his business. Mia was an adult and at least McCool had stopped bird-dogging Honor. "Did you come in here to gossip?" he said, trying to sound impatient.

Apparently it didn't work, because she merely left

the window and then wormed her way between his desk and his chair to plop into his lap. Her arms wound around his neck. "I came in here to make you smile."

He didn't take his eyes off the screen. As if he weren't right this minute hardening beneath her squirming, cute little butt, he reached around her to continue typing on the keyboard. One of them had to keep the upper hand and he was determined it would be him.

But he knew he was smiling already.

She rewarded him with a light kiss that slid from his cheek to the corner of his mouth. At the touch of her lips to his, his stiffening erection twitched.

From the corner of his eye he saw *her* smile.

He didn't let it panic him. The fact that they were sleeping together—and that he'd made her promise to keep sleeping with him until she got bored and left Hot Water—wasn't surprising.

The chemistry was good between them. Hell, every time his fingers sank into her, every time he found her wet and hot, the pleasure of it jolted him like an electric shock. From that point on, he always refused to let her arousing fingers touch him. If he was going to keep control—and he was—he had to constantly remind himself to keep the sex tempered too.

She wiggled again on his lap, and he cast her a forbidding look. "Don't you have something else to do?"

"I was thinking about tomorrow night. Halloween. I was thinking we should dress up." She grinned at him.

He shook his head. "No point. We won't get any trick-or-treaters out here."

She shrugged. "So?" Her grin turned sly. "We can take turns asking each other for candy."

His fingers slipped on the keyboard, putting a garbled sequence of letters on the screen that looked like comic strip cusses. "You're dangerous, do you know that?"

She laughed. "Not to you, I'm sure."

Oh, but yeah, she was. Because she made him want to indulge her, pet her, play with her in every sense of the word. Despite his protective wall, he was still afraid she would infect him with that smile of hers. He was afraid she would send her *joie de vivre* germs rushing like champagne bubbles through his bloodstream. And if she did, what would his withdrawal symptoms be like when she left?

"Who should we dress up as?" she asked.

He shook his head. "Seriously, Honor, we won't get anyone out this way."

"Then we'll go out." She gave a little bounce against his knees. "We'll go into town and trick-or-treat ourselves."

"We're *not* going into town."

Her lower lip pushed out in a pout that he knew was entirely for his benefit. "Fuddy-duddy."

"Brat."

"Bore."

"Princess."

They were smiling at each other again. Bram caught himself, sighed, and forced his attention back to the computer screen.

Honor wasn't giving up, however. "We could go historical. Antony and Cleopatra. Romeo and Juliet."

Tragic, star-crossed lovers.

The notion washed coldly over him. With firm hands, he lifted Honor off his lap and rose himself, walking to the window to manually draw the drapes. The dimness soothed him some. Without the dual dazzle of the sunlight and Honor in his arms, he could think more clearly. He could remember not to let his guard down and let her get too close.

"I can tell by your expression you'd like something more contemporary." She pursed her lips, obviously thinking.

It wasn't all Honor's fault, he admitted. He needed to loosen his hold on her as well.

"Can you think of a more modern married couple?" She shoved her fingertips in the front pockets of her hip-hugging pants, dragging the waistband down to bare her tight, sexy little belly button.

She was doing that on purpose, Bram decided, feeling himself beginning to harden again. He edged farther away from her and crossed his arms over his chest. "Bill and Hillary?"

She narrowed her eyes at him. "Ew."

"Lucy and Ricky?"

"Oh! Don't remind me," she said, advancing on him. He retreated until she had him backed against the long worktable.

He breathed in and out her rich-girl perfume, promising himself that starting today he'd encourage her to take some solo trips into town. She was perfectly safe in Hot Water, she'd said it herself, and he could use more solitude.

"Let me think . . ." Honor said, then brightened. "Sonny and Cher!"

"*Sonny and Cher?*"

"Sure." She leaned against his chest and looked up into his face. "You'd be a perfect Sonny."

"Sonny?" Now he was annoyed with her for an entirely different reason. He circled her upper arms with his hands. "You think I'd be a perfect *Sonny*?"

She laughed and, hell, just as quickly as it had come, his irritation dissolved. He lifted her toward his mouth. Another kiss, more sex, neither meant a permanent break in his barricade. Later today, he'd send her on an errand into Hot Water.

"How about Tommy Lee and Pamela?" he murmured against her mouth.

"Who—"

Distant barking halted Honor's response. They both turned their heads. "It's Joey." She made to break away from Bram.

"No." He kept her arms in his hands, because he could also hear Fifo, on alert by the front gate, snarling. "Let's see what it is first."

With Honor right behind him, he crossed to a closed armoire on the other side of the room. Opening the doors, he heard Honor's, "Oh."

"The live feeds from the security cameras come into here," he said, tapping at a keyboard with one hand and using the other to flip the switches that brought the three small color monitors to life.

Images bloomed on the screens, two different angles of the front gate from the outside, and another picture of the front gate from the interior. Both dogs pressed close to the peeled-log barrier. While Joey was barking in excitement, his front feet braced on the timbers, Fifo had assumed his "armed and dangerous" pose—low on his haunches and growling.

On the other screens, two men were pictured, one with a video camera resting on his shoulder. Bram groaned. "Damn, it's that reporter and cameraman we ran into at Pearl's."

Honor sighed. "I'll go out there and get rid of them." She started for the door again, and again Bram halted her with a hand on her arm.

"I can do it from here." He tapped a couple more keys to activate the mike, then raised his voice. "No comment."

Over the dogs' noise, the words boomed out in a harsh, menacing tone.

Honor jabbed Bram in the ribs and he looked over to catch the puzzled expression on her face. "Was it just me, or did that sound like Darth Vader?"

He shrugged one shoulder, suppressed a grin. "Voice synthesizer."

The reporters' heads had lifted and they glanced around—nervously, Bram thought with satisfaction—until apparently realizing the voice had projected from a hidden speaker built into the rock wall. "Bennett, Honor," one of the men began. "We want to know what you think—"

"No comment," Bram interjected again, his voice sounding raspy and evil through the speaker.

Honor murmured in his ear, "New idea . . . Dorothy and the Wizard of Oz."

Sliding her a quelling look, he leaned toward the microphone again. "Now get lost." His hand moved to flip off the monitors.

"So you have nothing to say about the possibility of Kenny Adams coming here?" the reporter shot out.

Bram shook his head in disgust. "I don't know any Ke—"

Honor touched his back. Even through his shirt her fingertips were icy. "I do," she said.

He glanced at her face. His heart stopped beating.

He clapped his palm over the mike so his voice

wouldn't carry to the reporters. "What is it?" he demanded. "Who the hell is it?"

"Kenny Adams is the ringleader of the men who kidnapped me," she said, her voice as wooden as the expression on her face.

"Shit." Bram pulled his hand from the speaker. "What's this about Adams?"

The son-of-a-bitch reporter had the nerve to casually slip his hands into his pockets. "Why don't you let me in and we'll talk about it?"

"Why don't I come out there and kick your ass?" Bram snapped, Honor's frigid face scaring the hell out of him.

The reporter gave a half-smile, but nothing else.

Pissed, Bram flipped off his mike and the monitors, then swung away from them. "I'll get the information myself," he muttered. But Honor gave him pause again. She was staring off into space, her arms wrapped around her slender body.

The phone on the desk started ringing, but Bram let it go. Mia would pick it up, or even if she didn't, whoever, whatever could wait. "Baby," Bram said softly, gently tugging on Honor's wrists to open her stiff body to his. He stepped against her and enfolded her as closely to him as he could.

"Baby," he repeated, his cheek against her hair. "It's going to be all right. It's probably nothing. A slow day and they're here to create some hype."

The phone had stopped pealing. Joey had quieted too. Only Fifo was still making noise. The robotic animal's deep-in-the-throat growl went well with the uneasy expression on Mia's face when she showed up in the office doorway, Josh behind her.

"Dylan called," she said. "He's on his way. But he

wants you to know that several hours ago one of Honor's kidnappers escaped from prison."

"Fuck." Bram's arms tightened on Honor as a tremor rolled through her.

Mia reached back and caught Josh's hand. He pulled her against him. "He said to lock everything down," Mia added quietly. "He said you shouldn't let Honor out of your sight."

𝒥ℕ the living room of the Fortress, Honor sat between Mia and Kitty on one of the golden-toned, cut-velvet couches. Josh sprawled on the one facing it. Dylan had propped a hip on the arm of a chair, his posture communicating a calm readiness—his special agent stance, Honor thought.

Only Bram was moving, pacing with fierce strides around the room as he punched the number for the ambassador's residence several time zones away. Guilt gave her a little pinch. She hadn't called her father to try coaxing herself out of the marriage in days and days, and November fifteenth was fast approaching.

"Kenny Adams didn't actually escape from prison, Warren," Bram said after getting through. "He managed to walk away from the local hospital after convincing the guards he was having an appendicitis attack on the way to a court hearing. From there . . ."

Bram's free palm ran over his short hair. "They don't quite know how he got out, but he did. They have security video showing him leaving the hospital in a pair of green scrubs. Yes, they're sure it's Kenny Adams."

Honor closed her eyes and tried to tune out the rest of Bram's conversation. She didn't want to hear that name again. She didn't want to think about what had happened before and what everyone thought could happen again.

She opened her eyes and looked straight at Dylan. "Even if he kept up with the tabloids to know where I am, he's not coming here. Why would he try to kidnap me again? That would be stupid."

Dylan nodded. "You're right. That would be stupid, especially when we're going to make sure you're safe until Adams is reapprehended."

That name again. Honor took a fortifying breath. "He'll go to Mexico. No, overseas. Remember? All four of them planned on living off the ransom money in Europe." He would not come to Hot Water. Nothing bad could happen to her here, she was convinced of that.

Still, just hearing that name made the walls close around her. She looked over at Mia, then Kitty. "Let's go in the kitchen and act busy. Make tea. Bake cookies. Open something alcoholic and drink ourselves into a stupor."

Kitty smiled. "I drank myself into a stupor once before." She glanced at Dylan and her smiled deepened. "It didn't turn out half bad."

At that, the other women followed Honor into the kitchen. Once inside, she took a breath and faced them. "This is a kidnapping-free zone, okay? We won't talk about it, all right?"

Mia gripped her fingers together. "We're ready to listen, though," she offered, her brown eyes full of such sincere concern Honor nearly wept.

Nearly. "No," she said, shaking her head to keep her resolve firm. "Let's get drunk and . . ." She looked around the bright kitchen and her gaze snagged on the pumpkins she'd grouped at one end of a countertop. "Carve some jack-o'-lanterns."

Honor fetched three beers while Mia spread newspapers across the long butcher-block island in the center of the kitchen. With great solemnity, the women clacked their bottles together.

"To . . . thinking of other things," Honor said.

Happier things. Heck, why be so picky? *Anything*.

Choosing which pumpkin each woman would carve and finding pens to first draw the faces took a few minutes. Honor benefited from the expert advice of Kitty and Mia, who had apparently made dozens and dozens of jack-o'-lanterns in their lifetimes.

Mia looked stunned to discover Honor's novice state in pumpkin-carving. "Not once?" she asked again.

Honor shook her head. "I was at boarding schools in Europe for several years. Brussels, another in the mountains of Luxembourg, a tiny school in Monaco where the princesses had studied. No pumpkin-carving there."

Mia gaped. "Monaco?"

Josh strolled into the kitchen. "Not everyone was born chewing on a piece of hay, Mia." His voice was cool, almost cutting. "Some were born with silver spoons in their mouths."

Honor wanted to smack him. "What's with—"

"It's okay," Mia said, catching her eye.

Kitty sent him an acid look that should have curdled him where he stood.

Instead, Josh's charming smile slid over his face as easy as a woman's sigh. "Did I say something wrong?"

Without answering, Honor opened a nearby drawer and handed Mia a long knife. She passed another to Kitty and took up a third for herself, then shut the door with a slam.

At the sight of the three women armed, Josh smiled

again, this one degrees less charming, degrees more sincerely amused. He held up his hands. "Hey, no offense."

"Josh's point is that he belongs in the city," Mia said.

"And some others want a simpler life," he added.

Kitty bristled. "I hear an insult in 'simpler,'" she said. "Mia could go anywhere she wants, belong anywhere she wants. For your information—"

"Mia would like to drop the subject," Mia interrupted. "Please."

Kitty opened her mouth again, glanced at Mia, then closed it. "Fine," she muttered.

"Help yourself to a beer, Josh," Honor said, trying to defuse the atmosphere. "And would you take a couple more to the living room for Dylan and Bram?"

When he obligingly ambled out, Kitty leaned toward Mia and hissed, "You're making me nervous. I thought he was supposed to be Mr. Savoir Faire. Well, if you ask me, he's a snake and you're letting him get his coils around you."

Worried too, Honor studied Mia's face. "Is everything okay?"

Mia hesitated, a blush reddening her cheeks. "We're sleeping together."

Kitty's hand tightened on the hilt of her knife. "Should I murder him?"

Mia laughed.

"Or Dylan will do it," Kitty said. "He's always telling me he knows interesting ways to kill people. Maybe, if I ask nicely, he'll oblige."

"Kitty, no," Honor responded, half amused, half alarmed. Dylan was besotted with his wife. Who knew what he'd do to keep her happy? She turned to Mia, sighed. "Do you know what you've gotten yourself into?"

Mia seemed to think a moment, then sighed herself. "I haven't a clue. This is going to sound crazy, but I . . . I trust him."

"Trust him?" Kitty practically yelled, obviously aggravated all over again. "He's just some slick, rich, too-spoiled-for-his-own-good person. A person like that . . . like—"

"Me?" Honor interjected.

Kitty stopped. "No. Not like you, Honor." Her gaze cut away, but then she looked over again, meeting Honor's eyes squarely. "I admit I distrusted you at first too. Wealthy, citified strangers who try to make Hot Water their own have a way of getting the backs up of most of us who live here."

"But you're different. You married Bram," Mia said, smiling. "You fell in love with him."

You married Bram. You fell in love with him. Honor avoided the other women's eyes by turning her attention to her jack-o'-lantern. Mia and Kitty did the same, and the talk thankfully turned to pumpkin guts. The other two women traded techniques for roasting the seeds.

After a time, Honor stared at the orangish mound of stringy pulp and plump seeds beside her pumpkin, then at her slimy hands. "This takes longer and is messier than I expected."

Mia lowered her voice. "You know, that's exactly what I think about sex."

Honor and Kitty froze. Then they looked at each other, looked at Mia.

She was blushing again. "Well, actually, I *expected* it to be messy. But the time aspect . . ." Her voice faded and her face flushed even redder. "I don't have anyone else to talk about this with," she finally finished.

Honor felt she should speak up, since in a round-about way she was the one responsible for Josh's presence in Hot Water. "What exactly did you want to talk about?"

Mia took a swallow of her beer. "You two might not understand this. But when I used to look at myself in the mirror, I *never* looked face-on. I always turned to the side and sucked in my stomach so hard that it hurt."

Kitty grinned. "You want to compare bad body parts? You should see me flat on my back. Instead of breasts it looks like eggs-over-easy sliding off a plate."

Two pairs of eyes turned to Honor. After a moment, they narrowed. She jumped. "Hey! Don't look at me like that." With a frown she returned stare for stare. "I have to suck in my stomach *and* I'm flat when I lie on my back."

Mia and Kitty rolled their eyes at each other.

Honor tried not to panic. But until now she'd felt as if she were making friends with these two women. She'd liked it and needed it as much as anything else she needed to find here in Hot Water. "Listen, when I have a yard of blond hair and a mile of legs like you, Kitty, or the body of a sex goddess like you, Mia, then we'll talk."

Kitty waved the compliments away. "We were just kidding you, Honor."

Mia flushed again, but kept her gaze steady. "But that sex-goddess-body thing is what I wanted to talk about." She hesitated, then continued. "I never saw myself that way."

"Until Josh?" Honor guessed. "I'm glad for that, at least."

Mia looked up from her pumpkin. "That's what I

mean about trusting him. You don't think it's just his . . . patter?"

"No," Honor answered. "How can I explain Josh? You know how some people have a skin of sincerity but are actually baloney to the soul?"

Mia nodded quickly.

"Josh is the exact opposite of that, I think. He has this charming, slick way about him that goes about one-quarter inch deep. Though he tries hard to pretend otherwise, the rest of him is genuine."

Kitty looked skeptical. "He's too good-looking to be nice."

"I didn't say he was nice, exactly," Honor replied. "Because that sounds uncomplicated. I'm just saying he doesn't want to *try* to hurt Mia."

Mia nodded slowly, as if that concurred with her own opinion. "Still, why does he only want to give me that one-quarter inch?"

"How do you mean?"

Mia returned her gaze to her pumpkin. "Well, um, when we make love, for example. He works very hard at keeping under control."

Honor's stomach lurched and she squeezed the handle of her knife.

"I think I'm starting to get the picture," Kitty said.

Mia pulled a wedge of pumpkin rind clear of her jack-o'-lantern's face. "When we're together," she went on, "it's great, but I feel like I'm getting more than my share. He watches me so closely, to see where I am, how I'm feeling, but in an almost distant way."

"He's holding himself back," Kitty declared. "Protecting himself from letting you get too close."

Honor's stomach lurched again and the tip of her

knife slipped, making an unplanned stab in her pumpkin's face.

"I think you're right," Mia said slowly. "I think he's afraid to care too much about me."

Honor bent her head over her jack-o'-lantern, focusing on finishing her carving. Yet still she heard Kitty's next remark, worry apparent in her voice.

"Fun and games in bed are one thing," she said. "But Mia, you're not falling in love with him, are you?"

You married Bram. You fell in love with him.

"What do you think, Honor?" Mia said. "Would that be so bad?"

Would that be so bad?

Noticing that they'd all laid down their knives, Honor avoided answering the question by bustling around the kitchen, rolling up the newspaper, and washing the utensils.

"Honor? You didn't answer."

But she was saved from whatever lie she might have come up with when Josh, Dylan, and Bram chose that moment to walk into the kitchen. Bram strode straight to her, his green eyes hard and intent. "We have to talk."

Her pulse leaped and she held him off with a sudsy hand. "No. Not now. This has been declared trouble-free territory."

He gave a brief shake of his head. "Honor."

She sent a look toward Kitty, who immediately stepped in. "You heard the lady of the house, Bram. The only thing you guys get to do is talk about our jack-o'-lanterns. I know . . . we'll let you decide which one is best."

With a flourish, she spun her pumpkin so it faced the three men. Honor got her first good look at it too.

Kitty's pumpkin had big round eyes and a small pursed mouth, no teeth in sight. She'd cut some sort of curlicue between the jack-o'-lantern's eyes that looked like a baby's curl.

As a matter of fact, the pumpkin's entire face looked like a baby's.

Dylan appeared a little queasy. "That thing looks like an infant. You aren't, uh, trying to tell me something, are you?"

Kitty blinked, spun the pumpkin back her way. "Oh. I see what you mean." She laughed. "The only thing I'm aware I have to tell you is that I'm not giving up my day job. I was actually going for scary."

Dylan grinned. "Hey, diapers and two A.M. feedings *are* scary. Who's next?"

"Mia." Kitty reached over and twirled the younger woman's pumpkin their way.

They were all silent a moment. Then Josh spoke. "It's perfect," he said. Then, as if embarrassed by saying something nice, he looked away and took a long draw on his bottle of beer.

Honor leaned back against the counter. Mia's *was* perfect. The jack-o'-lantern grinned, showing just the right number of missing teeth. Its eyes were wide and devilish in a thoroughly wholesome type of way. Once again, Honor pictured Mia with armfuls of children, little ones who scampered through her kitchen snitching cookies and kisses. Little ones who sat, good as gold, in the church pew on Sunday mornings and who listened to their granddad's stories of alien abductions on Sunday afternoons.

She laughed to herself, then sobered, because she couldn't put Josh in that picture.

You're in love with him.

Would that be so bad?

"Honor's next," Kitty called out. She sidestepped to reach the last pumpkin and turned its face toward Honor, Mia, and the men.

Mia gasped.

"What?" Kitty peered over the top of the jack-o'-lantern, then walked around the island to get the same view as the rest of them. "Yow."

Nobody else said a word.

The face of Honor's pumpkin wasn't gruesome or evil or scary-looking. Not funny like Kitty's, not classic like Mia's. Her carving had started out innocuous enough, but then she'd cut outside the lines she'd drawn while she and the other women were talking. The mouth and nose were nothing of note, but the eyes were large and startled-looking. Below them, she'd disguised a miscut or two by carving teardrops into the flesh, so that it appeared to be crying.

Her pumpkin, Honor realized with a start, looked afraid.

Dylan gazed seriously at Honor but took Kitty's hand. "It's going to be all right. You're safe."

Mia moved nearer to Josh. "I'm so sorry."

Josh grimaced, then drew Mia close to drop a kiss on the top of her head.

"Oh." All at once Honor realized they thought the pumpkin reflected her fear of the kidnapper who had escaped. "Oh, no. It's not—" She caught herself, unable to explain what it *did* reflect.

Her fear of the certain knowledge that she'd fallen in love with Bram.

Chapter Sixteen

*A*s the group started to move back into the living room, another round of beers in hand, Bram slipped through the kitchen door to the back deck. He stood in the near-darkness, the kitchen windows, lit like TV screens, on his left. Facing the inky shadows of his back woods, he didn't turn to see who opened the door and stepped out to join him.

"So you remembered our old signal?" he asked.

"Of course," Dylan replied. "Though I think the last time we used it was to ditch those extra laps after football practice."

Bram shoved his hands in his pockets, touching the comforting, hard shell of his palmtop. "We need to talk." He was going to get Honor out of Hot Water and he would need Dylan's help.

"Sure," Dylan said. "But first, how are you doing?"

"She'll be fine," Bram answered shortly.

"I asked about you."

Me? I'm ill at ease and working my way toward worried sick. Bram inhaled a long breath, yearning to run away to the cemetery and his solitary twilight ritual. Even those damned eternal and unanswerable questions seemed more bearable than this.

"I want my old life back," he found himself admitting.

"Hmm," Dylan said after a moment. "Which one is that? The life of brash and confident Bram who came back from M.I.T., married his childhood sweetheart, then began on his childhood dream of building his own company?"

He shook his head. Those times and that Bram Bennett were impossible to recapture.

"Or then there's the life of Bram-the-recluse," Dylan continued, "who spent the last eight years hiding from everyone but his dead wife."

Caught unawares by the surprise attack, Bram snapped his head toward his old friend. "Harsh words from a man who left town and didn't come back for those same eight years."

"Maybe that makes me the man who can say them."

Bram tightened his grip on his palmtop. "Damn it, you don't understand." No one could understand the helpless rage and despair he felt in the face of the world's senselessness. The only refuge from experiencing that was in isolating himself. "I don't want to have to worry about anyone again."

Dylan shrugged, then pointed toward the kitchen windows. "Don't you think it's a little too late for that?"

Bram looked in the direction his friend indicated. Honor was moving between cupboards and countertop, preparing a tray of cheese and crackers. As he watched, she gave a surreptitious glance over each shoulder, then beckoned in the direction of the dining room. That ridiculous dog of hers came bounding into view, leaping up to slurp at her with his tongue.

Bram shook his head. Every time he reminded her to keep the worthless mongrel outside, she promised—cross her heart!—that from now on she would.

Her expression going stern, she picked up a slice of cheese and held it high. He could read her lips as she commanded the dog. *Sit. Sit.*

Joey pranced in front of her, his tongue lolling, his blank face uncomprehending. Honor grimaced and waved the cheese in front of his furry snout, apparently trying to get the dog's attention.

It got Joey's attention, all right. His eyes followed the cheese, then his gaze jumped from the small bit Honor was holding to the large platter of stacked slices on the countertop. In the blink of an eye, he leaped, swiping a tall mound. Then, pleased as can be, he sat in front of her to gulp the huge mouthful down.

Honor gaped at the mutt, her bribe chunk of cheddar still held high. Her obvious chagrin surprised a laugh out of him.

"See?" Dylan pointed out. "She makes you laugh."

She was kneeling now, her hands buried in the dog's coat, her cheek against its neck. With a pang, Bram remembered the feel of the puppy's fur against his face.

He forced the memory aside and looked away. "There's nothing funny about her situation, though. We need to do something." Dylan would be the one to take care of it. To take Honor away.

"Like what? Adams is most likely on his way out of the country. His parents had a thousand excuses for his criminal behavior and never accepted he was the mastermind behind the kidnapping. They'll give him money and whatever else he needs. It wouldn't make sense for him to come anywhere near Honor."

None of that was good enough for Bram. "Her father's been paying for weekly reports from the prisons where the men are being held. Warren says Adams enjoys the papers, including the tabloids."

"So it's possible he knows where Honor's living right now." Dylan let out a low whistle. "Always a resourceful guy, that Warren."

"Yeah. He knows how to get what he wants." Bram hesitated, then told the truth, knowing it would help persuade Dylan to take Honor off his hands and away from Hot Water. "As a matter of fact, Honor and I . . . well, it's not a real marriage."

Dylan was quiet a moment. Then he said, "What part of it, exactly, is phony?"

The question tightened around Bram's throat like a noose. He thought of her glow, her princessy airs, the laughter she'd brought to his house. Why hadn't he refused to have sex with her that first time? Why had he then done it a second time and a third and . . . *Shit*! He swallowed. "It's just temporary."

And finally over, thank God. Now he had a good, logical reason to get what he'd been after since the day she'd moved in—Honor moving out. Since the kidnapper was loose, it was necessary for her to disappear from Hot Water. With Dylan's help, Bram would stash her someplace where the press couldn't follow and Adams wouldn't find her.

By the time it was safe for her to emerge, she'd have lost her interest in the town. And Bram.

He closed his eyes. It was going to be a damn relief

to have her out of his life and out of his house, especially when the alternative was locking her in. Wasn't it just hours ago that he'd promised himself to put more space between them?

He swallowed and opened his eyes, determined to get the plan rolling. "Dylan . . ."

"Yeah?" The other man was staring up at the night sky. "You ever wonder if ol' Beau really *did* see something up there? Hell, it's a vast darkness. Stands to reason there's things in it we don't know."

Bram snorted. "I remember you saying that very same thing when you were ten years old."

Dylan laughed. "You're right. And I'm sure it's not the discussion you brought me out here for. I take it you have a plan?"

"Yeah." A sensible plan. Bram rubbed his forehead, trying to focus on it even as Dylan's words, *vast darkness* and *don't know*, echoed in his head. When Bram sent Honor away, he wouldn't know how she was—if she was safe, if she was sad, if she was still nervous in the darkness. *Damn, damn, damn.*

"Bram?"

He sighed, mentally waving good-bye to his so-sensible first idea. Damn him, but he couldn't send Honor away. "Do you think you can get me a few good, digitized photos of Kenny Adams?"

"Easy. I'll take Kitty home right now and make a call. My former boss at the L.A. FBI office will e-mail them to you."

"Perfect." His mind already on the new enhancements he planned for Fifo, Bram started walking toward the door that led into his office. "Tell Honor I'll be working tonight, will you?"

"Uh, buddy." Dylan hesitated. "I hate to interfere in

your, um, 'temporary' marriage, but don't you think she might need you right now?"

Bram thought of her clinging to the dog and something inside his chest hurt again—the pins-and-needles pain of blood rushing back to a body part long asleep. It made it only more imperative that he hurry for the sanctuary of his office to distance himself from it. "I'll be doing what she needs most."

You didn't come to bed last night," Honor said, trying to keep the tension out of her voice. She didn't look at Bram, pretending instead to be engrossed in the previous day's edition of the *Gold Country Gazette* she'd spread open on the kitchen counter.

"No. I worked until late, then caught a few z's on the couch in my office." As Bram walked behind her, the clean scent of his spicy soap wafted past.

Honor closed her eyes and breathed it in. She'd missed that scent, his warmth, *him* beside her in bed last night. After yesterday's events, especially after realizing she'd been so reckless as to fall in love with him, she needed reassurance. She needed to know their relationship hadn't been changed by his concerns for her safety and by her unspoken feelings.

"What the hell?"

Honor glanced over her shoulder and stifled a smile. Some things would never change. Clutching a mug, Bram was standing in front of the coffeemaker. Every light on the appliance's panel was flashing and every two minutes or so it emitted a series of high-pitched peeps, all of which Honor had been ignoring.

"I programmed it last night, as usual, to brew automatically. What could be wrong with it?"

"If I had the explanation for that," she murmured,

"I'd also have a Nobel prize." Suppressing another smile, she turned back to the newspaper as Bram began grumbling to himself and punching buttons.

A few minutes later, he slipped a mug of coffee beside her elbow, prepared with a dash of milk, exactly as she liked. The simple gesture soothed her raw nerves. "Thank you," she said. "I . . . I really missed you last night."

He looked away. "Honor . . ."

Her stomach twisted, tension retightening. "Guess what?" she said, desperate for him not to voice whatever it was that made him unable to meet her eyes. "The newspaper took a poll about our imminent alien invasion. Thirty-eight percent of those they spoke with think Beau might be right and that we'll be greeting otherworlders in a few days. Pretty optimistic, huh?"

His gaze returned to her face and her heart thumped in relief as humor sparked in his eyes. "Optimistic? Where've you been, honey? Not watching the Sci-Fi channel, apparently. Think *Day of the Tripods*. Think *Mars Attacks*." He stepped closer to her and tapped her nose with one finger, his mouth curved in a crooked smile.

Smiling back, Honor reached for his hand and laced their fingers. "Maybe Beau's extraterrestrials are the peaceful type. Maybe they're no threat to us."

"Yeah, maybe." The humor deserted Bram's face and he slid his hand out of her grasp. Then he lifted his mug and took a long swallow of the hot coffee. "Honor, we have to talk."

No. Talking would spoil everything, she could feel it. She shook her head.

"We need to do some things differently until Adams is recaptured."

"No," she whispered.

Bram ran his hand over the back of her hair, but it was cold comfort. "It's for the best. Josh is moving out of the guest cottage. Mia will stay away too, to eliminate all comings and goings through the gate."

Meaning no visitors to the Fortress. No Mia and no Kitty, who were starting to feel like real friends. "On Wednesday I have a meeting in Old Town with the Hot Water Preservation Society."

"If he's not back in custody by then, you'll cancel it. The security system at the house will be in full operation twenty-four hours a day. And if Adams does show up, Fifo will be able to recognize him."

"*What?*"

"That's what I was working on last night," Bram said. "Enigma has some software I developed that's nearly through beta testing. I installed it in Fifo. By digitizing Adams's face, Fifo can now pick him out, even in a crowd."

Honor wrapped her arms around herself. "I still don't think there's a need for any of this! Surely Ke—" she stopped herself from saying his name. "Surely he's left the country." Hot Water was her safe place.

"Maybe." Bram hesitated. "Honor, I think we should talk about your kidnapping too."

"*No.*" That was her one solid rule. That experience wasn't going to touch here, touch *her* here, any more than it already had.

"Honor . . ." His face wore that odd expression it always did when he brought it up.

"I won't. That's past. This is now." She raised her eyes to his. "Please. I don't want things to be different. Can't we forget about all this?"

His green eyes were implacable, cool. "No."

She swallowed. Of course he wouldn't. He didn't forget anything, preferring to hold firmly to his own past and his love and grief for Alicia. How could Honor ever compete with that?

"There's another choice." Bram's voice was cooler than his eyes and without inflection. "Dylan can help you disappear, if you want to leave me."

If you want to leave me.

The words rolled around inside her mind for a moment, then she almost laughed. Of course she didn't want to leave him. She loved him. And she was foolish optimist enough to keep hoping that he could sometime, somehow, someday love her back.

"How it's been with us . . ." she began. They could build on what they already had, she was sure of it. She would bring out Bram's laughter and bring him into the world, little by little. "I don't want that to change."

"Sorry, princess." He shrugged. "You've got to see that everything's changed."

STANDING on the linoleum in Mia's kitchen, Josh rinsed the soap suds off the dimestore dinner plate. He tried to dredge up a healthy distaste for the cheap stoneware, but it was actually an inoffensive creamy color, with an attractive design of raised ivy leaves around the edge. More important, it was large enough to hold the massive helping of Mia's incredible version of penne with zucchini and ricotta he'd just consumed.

Pissed at how easily his standards had lowered, he gritted his teeth and handed the plate over to her to dry.

"You seem a little tense," she ventured.

Tense! Christ, there was an understatement. He'd been playing house with Mia for days and the easy, seamless transition into sharing her home was scaring him shitless. He picked up a pot and scrubbed it angrily.

This, for example. He'd fallen right into doing the dishes. On his very first night in her home, he'd automatically reached under the sink to find the plastic tub she used for soapy water. The sink in Granny's trailer had been small too. Plastic tub on the counter for soapy water. Sink used for rinsing.

It hadn't seemed odd to hang his thousand-dollar suits in Mia's coin-purse-sized closet either. Furthermore, without even thinking he now showered with his elbows close to his sides to keep them from banging against the too-narrow walls.

Why was it so easy to be here? Even the tub/shower combo in his condominium in L.A. was big enough for a threesome, if he'd wanted to have one. In his not-too-far-in-the-future dream home he planned to have a shower large enough for an orgy and closets sized for a football team.

"Josh?"

He started, realizing he'd been rinsing the final pot for the last five minutes. With a distinct lack of elegance, he shoved it at Mia, then ripped a paper towel off the roll to dry his hands.

There was no doubt about it. The time had come to end this with her.

He didn't look at Mia until she'd stowed the pot away, dried her own hands, and neatly rehung the dish towel. When she reached behind her back to undo the apron she wore, he tossed out the first line of his planned speech. "Have you ever thought of opening a restaurant?"

She paused. "You've mentioned that before. Are you sure it isn't *you* who wants to open one?"

"Too much risk, not enough reward. Anyway, I don't cook."

She tilted her head, her glossy black hair falling over one shoulder in perfect waves. "Yes, but *I* do."

Was she hinting that the two of them could open a restaurant? Together? He steeled himself and coolly met her eyes. "I was thinking about what you might like to do once I leave Hot Water, Mia."

She stilled. "Ah."

He found he couldn't meet her eyes anymore. Hating himself for his weakness, he pretended an interest in the tassel on his Ferragamo loafer. It was stupid to feel so lousy about this! They'd both always known he belonged in the fast-moving, fast-living circles of L.A.

"I could visit you there," she said softly.

"*No!*" Damn it. He hated the emotion that one word had given away. It wouldn't be right for her to get the wrong idea and think he'd regret leaving her. She'd gone into this eyes open, hadn't she?

For God's sake, she hadn't wanted him to be noble! So she'd gotten what he was instead.

He put a bit of a snicker into his voice. "You think you'd fit in, Mia? We're talking movie people, finance people, *beautiful* people." The implied insult made him sick, so sick he couldn't manage the sneer his words required.

"I suppose not." Mia pulled her apron over her head, revealing the snug jeans and long-underwear top she was wearing. Without a bra.

Josh nearly fell onto his knees to beg forgiveness as he stared at their voluptuous weight swinging free while she hung the apron on a nearby peg. She went braless, occasionally, for him. He'd asked her to, in the close darkness of his second night in her bed, his hands overflowing with all that hot, sleek flesh.

Her bed was so small they were always close, her skin only a tongue's-reach away. While he might curse the small size of the rest of Mia's residence, her bed was just right.

As were her breasts. He couldn't stop thinking about them. He couldn't stop remembering the scent of her skin when his face was buried between them.

He jerked his gaze away from her and tried to find something else to look at. The blissful wedding photograph of her parents was a definite no, so he skipped past it to the Madonna figurine in the niche by the back door. There. That should cool his lust.

Except the innocent loveliness of the statue reminded him of Mia. In his mind's eye he could see her as a mother, holding an infant in her arms. She'd feed the baby herself, of course, and he imagined a blond head cradled against her lush, milk-swollen breasts—

He groaned.

"What's the matter?" Mia asked, pausing in the act of straightening the spices in her many-shelved rack.

"I'm not good enough for you."

She raised one eyebrow in that unsettling way she had. "You've said that before too."

But oh, God, just for a second, just for one spineless moment, he'd wanted to be.

He pulled out a kitchen chair and sank into it. The wheezy noise of the plastic cushion helped. It made him recall those years in Granny's single-wide and how he couldn't wait to tap the sand of that cheesy trailer park off his shoes.

"Did you talk to Honor or Bram today?" Mia asked, unaware of or ignoring Josh's inner turmoil.

"Nothing's changed. No word on the kidnapper from the southern California authorities and no sign of him around here either."

"And Bram still doesn't want anyone going near the Fortress?"

"Yeah." He shot a look at her. "That includes you. I want you staying away from there, Mia. I mean it."

At his proprietary tone, she raised that eyebrow.

I'm an idiot. "Of course, you're free to do whatever you like," he muttered. "Go wherever you want."

She tucked her hair behind her ears. "Today I went to the Enigma property. My father said you'd been by earlier." In the first sign of apprehension all night, she sucked her bottom lip into her mouth.

He closed his eyes.

"You noticed the press lined up along the road?" she asked hesitantly.

Josh shrugged. "November is sweeps month." It was also the month the bulldozers were supposed to start moving. He'd tried one last time to get Mia's father and followers to agree to leave the property.

"He was surprised to hear you're staying here," Mia said.

Josh stared at her. "You told him?" He'd considered snitching on himself, thinking it a fine way to get an Italian papa off someone else's property and back into the house where he could keep an eye on his lovely, desirable daughter.

In fact, Josh's mouth had been open to utter the words. He'd been prepared to take a fist in the face or the gut or wherever else Beau thought it appropriate too. But he hadn't been able to go through with it.

Not to protect himself, but to protect Mia. To protect *them* and to keep private what they'd shared in this little home. Josh cleared his throat. "What did your father say?"

"That I was old enough to make my own decisions . . . and my own mistakes."

"Mmm." He tried to look away, but her big brown eyes wouldn't let go of his.

"Is that what I did, Josh?" she asked softly. "Did I make a mistake?"

"Of course." His laugh came out sounding strangled. He put his elbows on the fake marble tabletop and stared at the gold veins running through the plastic. It was definitely time, he thought. Right now he would tell her it was over, then leave.

"Damn it," he said instead. "I grew up in a dump of a town in a dump of a trailer across the road from the town's dump. Granny—my grandmother—got stuck with me when my parents took off."

Mia merely looked at him.

"The TV was on, twenty-four/seven. She'd make me watch those glitzy eighties dramas with her—you know, *Dynasty* and *Dallas*. *Knott's Landing* too, though even then I knew that the suburban, cul-de-sac shit was second-rate. Granny would go on and on about how I could have some of that myself."

" 'That' . . . ?"

He hesitated, trying to put it into words.

"Family?" Mia prompted. "Community?"

This time he did laugh. "Nice try, sweetheart." Why had he cared about putting a fine point on it anyway? "Money. And money. And lastly, money."

"Not to mention sequins, shoulder pads, and big hair," Mia murmured.

He laughed again. For all her small-town shyness, for all her break-his-heart innocence, she wasn't slow. Not his Mia. He grinned at her.

"So." He still smiled as he gestured vaguely. "You see."

She lifted a shoulder. "You dreamed of being rich. But I—"

"Don't tell me. I don't want to hear about your dreams." Josh's moment of good humor died an instant death. He couldn't stand to hear her tell him of the kind of life and the kind of man she'd always wanted, because he knew exactly how short he'd fall from the mark.

For the first time that evening, her face showed hurt. "No?"

"No. I . . ." He leaned back in the chair. "I don't care that much."

Her head ducked.

What a bastard he was, Josh thought. He'd never seriously asked her about herself, her past, or her plans because he hadn't wanted to get sucked into caring about her.

But, damn it, it had been the right way to play things. *Tell her it's over,* he thought. *Then go.*

"Mia—" He stopped to give himself another mental pep talk. *Just two little words,* he told himself. "Come here."

Of course, those weren't the ones he'd intended, but he held out his hand and repeated the command all the same. "Come here."

Her fingers were warm against his. She was always so warm. He scooted his chair from the table and drew her into his lap. "Let's not talk," he said huskily, hoping that this next idea would work. "Let's have sex."

He braced himself for her slap. At least for her to

leap up and yell at him for not wanting to listen to her. For just wanting her body and not her soul. That would give her a fine reason to hate him and give him a fine reason to walk out on her.

"What are you up to?" she asked slowly.

He slid his hands beneath the bottom hem of her thermal top and moved them upward, lingering on her rib cage. "Isn't that obvious?"

She narrowed her eyes. "You're picking a fight."

"I'm not picking a fight!" He said it too defensively, he realized. He lowered his voice and inched up his hands. The heavy weight of her breasts brushed the back of his knuckles. "Why make war when we could make love?"

Jesus, he thought, he sounded as corny as the Dean Martin impersonator in the casino lounge down the road from the Sandy Acres.

She crossed her arms over her chest, trapping his hands beneath her breasts. Blood rushed to his cock, already half hard.

"Don't give me that," she said. "You're up to something."

"Damn it!" He jumped to his feet, Mia falling out of his lap. He slid his hands down to steady her at her waist. "You're so suspicious."

"What I'm not is gullible."

"Then you know what I am too, Mia. The kind of guy who asks just one thing of you. Who wants just one thing of you."

"Josh—"

"Fine." He threw up his hands. "If you're tired of it, if you're tired of me just taking and taking from you, why don't you just say so? I'll be out of here. Tonight. Right now."

He studied her face, desperately assessing her reaction.

She laughed.

"What the hell is so funny?" Now he was mad.

"I recommend that you don't ask any of your beautiful, movie-people friends for a screen test. You're a terrible actor, Josh."

He glared at her instead of strangling her like he wanted to.

Her face still showed amusement as she recrossed her arms over her chest. She tapped the toe of one sneaker. "You're going to have to do it yourself, Josh. If you want to break up with me, then you have to say the words. You're not going to goad me into them."

A panic-coated anger rose up within him. " 'Break up'?" he repeated, his tone mocking and nasty. "This isn't fifth grade, Mia."

She flushed, but held firm. "I don't know how else to term it. I didn't have a boyfriend in fifth grade or anytime since."

Because she's mine. Because she'd been waiting for me. Josh hated the possessive heat that burned in his blood at those thoughts.

"Fine," he said, his voice hard and angry as that panic threatened to overtake him again. "Mia, I—"

Even now he couldn't end it like that. Not with manufactured anger and trumped-up sarcasm.

He sucked in a breath and met her eyes honestly, on the one hand hating to tell her, on the other knowing this last card he held would make the break inevitable for both of them.

"You know the bulldozers are supposed to start work next week," he said. "Well, I'm not waiting any longer. I called the sheriff after I left the property today.

Your father and his squatter groupies will be arrested and thrown in jail if they're still there the morning of November fifteenth."

Before the evening of November fifteenth, with its anticipated alien encounter that was her father's dearest dream.

She did throw him out, as he'd known she would. She didn't cry, though, which oddly made him feel more the bastard. It was as if she'd expected him to fail her all along.

Chapter Seventeen

*B*ram swung the ax, pausing in the downstroke as movement in the surrounding woods caught his eye. He lifted his head. Joey was loping toward him through the trees. Behind the dog, flashes of blue jeans shifted around and between the trunks of oak, sycamore, and pine. Honor.

He dipped his head and refocused on the metal wedge. The log split with a satisfying *swack*. He tossed the halves on the woodpile, reached for another log.

Joey raced up to sniff Bram's boots. Then the dog raced off, most likely to scout for Fifo. In seconds Joey was back, whining.

"Brainless dog." Fifo had been positioned at attention by the gate for days, but Joey could never find the robotic dog on his own. Bram sighed, then gestured toward the driveway. "That way," he instructed. "Go that way."

Joey cocked his head, let his tongue loll, then ambled off in the opposite direction.

Honor had made it to the clearing now, but Bram

didn't speak to her. The air around her was speaking enough—it was almost sparking with electric energy. The continued isolation was causing her restlessness to grow.

As did the woodpile, because Bram escaped to it whenever the atmosphere in the house turned unbearable.

There were other ways to work off the tension; dreaming of them woke him up at night, hard and aching, but he hadn't slept—or had sex—with Honor since learning of Adams's escape. Convinced they both needed distance, he was catching the occasional hour of sleep on the couch in his office. He told Honor he was working late hours on a new project.

He didn't know whether she bought the excuse. She continued to spend every night in his room, while he spent the dark hours counting all the reasons to separate himself from her. There was no point in becoming accustomed to a woman in his bed when she was a high heel away from losing interest in rustic Hot Water. There was no sense in making room for her in his life when it was solitude that he valued most.

Swack. The overly forceful blow of his ax sent the next two pieces of split wood flying. One landed at Honor's feet. He could feel her gaze on him as he stepped close to retrieve it.

"I can't live like this indefinitely," she suddenly declared. "I think we have to pick a day. If he hasn't been recaptured by then, we assume he's left the country."

The strained edge to her voice tugged at him. Trying to ignore it, he bent and grasped the log. His gaze swerved to her feet, those damn pirate boots she was wearing a magnet to his eyes and his memory.

Honor naked, just inside the French doors of her bedroom.

Her skin goosefleshed from cold or from his touch, but the place between her legs slick and hot. His hand running up the suede to the satiny flesh of her inner thighs. He'd almost lost his control that time, instantly, when the tips of his fingers found her center already so wet. His fingers, painting her folds with her own sexual essence, then touching that knot of nerves that made her jump, as the sweet scent of her arousal nearly undid him.

". . . what do you think?" she was saying.

He snapped back to the present. *Distance*, he reminded himself.

Bram straightened and turned away from her. What had she been saying? She wanted his opinion on what? Oh, yeah. A day when they decided the kidnapper was no longer a threat.

"What day did you have in mind?" he asked, aware that it might, indeed, come to that.

"Today."

"No!" He spun to look at her. Big mistake. He wanted her more than ever, with that frustrated pink flush across her cheeks and the bright glimmer in her silver eyes. "No way," he said. To her. To himself.

She lifted her arms, flapping them so that her jeans jacket and the light blue sweater she wore beneath it slid up and down on her rib cage. "I'm going crazy!"

He felt that tug of sympathy again. "No, honey."

Her chest rose on a swift inhale and she looked a broken fingernail away from a temper tantrum. "I'm not kidding, Bram."

His lips twitched and he tossed the log to the top of the pile. "Thanks for the warning, princess. I'll break out the straitjacket when I get back to the house."

He'd hoped for a laugh to ease the strain. He'd thought she would smile at least. Instead, she stalked toward him and rose on tiptoe, grabbing his shirt in her fists to bring his face close to hers.

"I'm"—she visibly struggled to calm herself—"feeling claustrophobic."

"Oh, honey." Then, hearing himself, Bram shuffled out of her grip, trying to rally his defenses against the clear desperation in her eyes.

But she pounced on his evident weakening. "Let's go into town. I need to see people. Talk to someone face-to-face besides Joey and you. Please. Just for a few minutes. We can get lattes or ice cream or something."

Smiling now, she came close again, nearly dancing with enthusiasm. She grabbed his arm and started towing him toward the house.

"No, princess." He dug his feet into the ground. "Honor. It's not sa—"

The rest of the sentence dried up in his mouth as her half-turned position gave him a new, startling view. "What the hell are those?" he asked, ogling her pants.

Clearly puzzled, she looked down. "Jeans."

He disentangled their arms and took a giant step back. Still staring, he twirled his forefinger. Honor hesitated, then followed his unspoken order and spun 360 degrees.

"Zipper," he said, trying to find a way to explain his own bafflement.

"*Oh.*" The confusion on Honor's face cleared. "The brand is Ya-Ya. Cool, yes? The zipper slides front-to-back."

He choked on his own tongue. At first glance, her jeans were just your average, everyday lightweight denim with a slight flare at the bottom. But that zipper—"the zipper that slides front-to-back"—did just that. It started at her waist and then curved between her thighs so that the zipper tab rested on the sweet curve at the small of her back.

He took off at an almost-run for the house.

"Hey, wait!" Honor started after him. "Where are you going?"

"*We're* going. For a drive. I've gotta get out of here." Before he forgot his good sense and his vows of distance and unzipped those Ya-Yas into two halves in order to uncover *Honor's* ya-ya. Their fake marriage had evolved into a hot fling, but it had been wise of him to end it. He needed to remember that.

An icy shower later, he bundled her into his car, hardly noticing that the gate nearly jammed again and his dashboard clock was running two hours and eighteen minutes late. With the dangerous privacy of the house behind them, he unrolled his window a couple of inches and turned the car toward town.

"Thank you, thank you, thank you." She bounced on her seat.

"Don't do that." Bouncing made him think of that zipper again. Bouncing made him think of wanting her to bounce on *him*. He groaned silently, angry at himself for not holding firm.

He groaned again, shifting on his seat. He was firm, all right.

As he sped away from the house, he decided to drive through town. It would give them both the change of scenery they needed and Honor could at least have the opportunity to *look* at other people, though he didn't want to take the chance of letting her get close enough to actually talk to any of them.

His brain must have migrated south, though, because when they approached the outskirts of town, he didn't notice the unusually slow speed of the cars in front of him. It took a few more minutes for him to suddenly—make that tardily—realize they were stuck in a traffic jam in the middle of the main street in downtown Hot Water.

"Goddamn it," he said. A long line of cars idled at a standstill in both directions on the narrow blacktop. As if it were the busiest of summer weekends instead of tranquil November, people crowded the sidewalks that abutted the two-story, Victorian-style storefronts, moving in and out of the cafés, antique stores, and specialty shops.

Prickles rose the hair at the back of Bram's neck. He pressed the switch that caused his window to roll back up. For good measure, he punched the button to automatically lock the already-locked car doors.

Honor peered out her window, looking as unprepared as he was to be stuck in gridlock in a town of two thousand people. "What's going on?"

One of the teenagers of the entrepreneurial Kemper family wandered by the front bumper of their car. He wore a T-shirt that demanded TAKE ME TO YOUR LEADER! and a headband that sported a pair of glittering silver antennae. He carried a box that held more T-shirts and headbands. A price list marked on the cardboard indicated the shirt was $18 and the antennae headband $10. If the kid's grin was any indication, sales had been brisk.

Honor craned her neck to see what was happening on the other side of the street. "This is incredible."

"But not surprising," Bram added, shaking his head as he caught sight of some little kids hawking photographs. Of the UFO, he was sure. All this extraterrestrial hooey was just more chaos he didn't want in his world, but how Hot Water was responding to it was true to the town's character.

"You know who made the real fortunes during the California Gold Rush, don't you?" he asked.

Honor shrugged.

"The merchants. Would-be miners were more dream seekers than practical men. They would arrive without anything they needed to find gold . . . except cash, that is. So they'd be sold the right clothes, the right pans, any kind of supplies they needed at highly inflated prices."

Honor's eyebrows rose. "But once a miner made a strike—"

"Gold mining was rough work. Long days. A man didn't have time or a woman to do his laundry or bake his bread. So those cost dearly too. And then the clothes or the pan would wear out and . . ."

"And they'd be right back where they started." Honor rose in her seat, peering about her again.

A knock on Bram's window made them both start. He jerked his head around, then pressed the switch to lower the window a few inches. "Good afternoon, Mayor."

The older man was beaming. "Bram." He ducked his head to greet Honor too. "Mrs. Bennett. Quite a good afternoon, wouldn't you say?"

Bram cocked a brow. "I believe I just did. But it would be better if we could get moving. What's the problem?"

Apparently nothing was going to mar the mayor's affable mood. He was still smiling, looking at the crowded streets and sidewalks with an air of immense satisfaction. "A new shipment of glow-in-the-dark Frisbees inscribed with The Date fell from the back of the Ha family's truck. They'll have them picked up in a minute. They're going to sell them out at The Site. At the ice-cream shop they've been flying off the shelves." He chuckled at his own bad pun.

Honor laughed too, forcing Bram to send her a quelling look. "Don't encourage him," he said under his breath. Then he raised his voice. "The Date? The Site?"

The mayor nodded and gestured with his plump hand to indicate the mobbed sidewalks and street. "That's why The Crowd is here, of course."

He bent to catch Honor's eye through the open window. "You could have made a killing if you'd opened the living history district for the month. Or even just for The Big Weekend."

Honor bit her bottom lip. "I know. I was thinking the same thing myself. I wonder if—"

"*No*," Bram said, suppressing a shudder of panic at the thought of her opening the tourist attraction. If she got it into her head to flit around town in this mob, he would have a hell of a time getting a net on her.

The mayor gave Honor a look of commiseration. "Don't feel bad. Another time." His gaze transferred to Bram and he lowered his voice to a stage whisper. "She fits right in, you know. Though I admit I had some concerns when she arrived, you're a lucky man, Bram. As a matter of fact, that opinion was shared by all at this week's IOOF breakfast."

Bram rolled his eyes. "Honor doesn't need the approval of the IOOF, Mayor." Only because she wasn't here for the long haul, though. The IOOF—the International Order of Odd Fellows—was a fraternal organization dating back to the Gold Rush times. To this day it was the foundation of the social and business framework of the town and its environs. Anyone wanting to conduct business in the area curried the IOOF's favor.

The car in front of them edged forward, so he waved to the mayor and pressed the accelerator. Three feet ahead they came to another stop. This time, the knock came on Honor's side of the car. Apparently the pair of women were Hooks & Needles Club members, because the talk was entirely incomprehensible to him. He suspected it might have been the same for Honor, but she nodded her head sagely over phrases like "yarn weight" and "knitting gauge."

That's how they progressed for the next few blocks. Every time they stopped they were meeted and greeted by a fellow Hot Water citizen. Bram hadn't spoken with that many people since . . . since the last time he'd been out in the world with Honor. Everyone was cheerful and smiling and so damn glad to see him that *he* was feeling claustrophobic.

But they were damn glad to see Honor too, and that was what made it bearable. That and how her eyes shone and her smile radiated like a beacon.

Looking at Hot Water through her eyes, he could see how its historic tradition coupled with the small-town atmosphere appealed to someone who had felt on the outside all her life. It wasn't that he didn't appreciate the place himself, but he'd never looked at it in quite this way.

When they were finally able to regain the speed limit, he was surprised to find himself more relaxed than he'd been in days. He glanced over at Honor. "Can we head home?"

"Yes, thank you. I can breathe now." She put her hand lightly on his upper thigh and smiled at him.

With just that one gesture and with just that one smile, she was under his skin again. His muscles tensed and his blood pumped hotly through his body, but it wasn't only more of her touches he wanted. He wanted more of her smiles too. How much he wanted her, how much he wanted all of her, was starting to unnerve him.

Gritting his teeth, he turned right to head home by a less-traveled route. This street bordered residential blocks on one side and the town park and cemetery on the other. The cemetery had been established by the IOOF during the gold boom, and a century ago they'd deeded the adjacent land for a city park. Ever pragmatic, the citizens had never blinked at the unusual pairing.

"The new park sign is up," Honor said. "It looks very nice."

Bram slowed. In August, the town had dedicated the park to Alicia's memory. A new sign hung over the entrance, the letters carved into a long slab of oak: ALICIA BENNETT CITY PARK.

He braked the car, staring at it. "She would like that." Then an ache echoed inside him, a phantom pain from a part of him amputated long ago, and his eyes squeezed shut.

The back of Honor's fingers drew down his cheek. "Oh, Bram," she said, her voice soft and tender.

The ache eased, and then—and then he jerked away from her touch. Damn her, she was trying to reach deeper inside him! Pressing down on the accelerator, he sped the car toward the cemetery.

He hadn't been to this part of town since the first night he'd made love with her, and that was his mistake, he decided. If he'd continued to visit Alicia's grave every evening, he would be better insulated from Honor.

So he slowed again as he reached the cemetery. His gaze found Alicia's hill and lingered on her grave.

"Why don't you stop?" Honor suggested.

He didn't look at her, just shook his head.

She touched his cheek again. "I think you should visit her."

Again, he jerked away from her soothing touch, desperate to deny how good it felt. "How would you know what I should do?" he asked harshly, as if she hadn't just voiced his very own thoughts.

"You're obviously miserable."

He gave her a dark look.

She ignored it, her eyes squarely meeting his. "Of course, you were obviously miserable when you visited her every day too."

His temper starting to smolder, he sent her an even darker look.

She must have been feeling especially reckless, because she kept at him. "For God's sake, Bram, you shouldn't go on like this. You can't laugh about it. You can't cry about it."

That's because he didn't want to feel, damn it! But he didn't respond, focusing all his energy on not exploding.

She made a frustrated noise. "What have you been doing with your grief for the past eight years? I swear, you must soap yourself up with it every morning in the shower."

The high whine of fury was in his head. "Be quiet," he said, his voice low and tight. "*Just be quiet*. What do you know about it? No one knows."

"Explain it to me, then."

Her calm, reasonable tone turned the whine in his head to torture. He jerked the car to the side of the road and turned it off. Then he grabbed Honor's shoulders and yanked her to face him. Their faces were close. He could smell her scent and feel the warmth of her body.

"I've avoided everyone all these years because I don't want to answer questions like that. You don't get it. No one gets it. 'Go visit her,' you said. That's not why I go there, damn it. Alicia isn't *there*."

Honor swallowed. "All right," she said. "Why do you go there?"

He should let go of her, but he couldn't seem to get his fingers to obey. "I don't know where Alicia is. Maybe in the air, maybe with the angels, maybe only in the memories of those who knew her. But not *there*."

"You didn't answer me," Honor pointed out. "Why do you visit her grave?"

The fury died. Anguish welled in its place, a deep, soul-wringing ache that filled his chest. It was the painful helplessness that he had tried to survive by building that strong, well-guarded wall. But Honor kept breaking through it, she kept breaking him down. There was never enough distance to prevent it.

He released her and sat back in his seat, staring unseeing out the windshield. "I visit Alicia's grave looking for answers to *my* questions. Why did it happen to her? *What* happened? What did she think about? How did she manage in those last days? Did she despair, did she hope, did she call for me? Did she trust me to find her?"

The ache inside him deepened, and he rubbed his chest. "Closure, they call it. I beg for it every time."

THAT night, Honor found Bram in his unlit office, sitting at his computer. Stifling her own lingering uneasiness of the dark, she crossed the room without turning on a light.

When he didn't speak to her or glance her way, she edged around his chair to see what he was working on. She knew he knew she was there, because when she bent near his shoulder to look at the screen, she heard the quick catch in his breath.

But he made no other sign. Instead, he continued to play the puzzling game that was on his monitor. In a frame in one corner was pictured a darkened castle with a bright, beautiful light glowing over its topmost battlements. A firefly-sized spark was moving inside the castle walls, and it took a few minutes for Honor to realize that the firefly represented the progress of Bram's player in the monitor's center frame.

The black-cloaked figure raced about, dodging arrows and trapdoors as he sped through maze after maze. It was the oddest thing, she thought, her heart squeezing. While it would seem natural that the objective would be for the player to reach that beautiful glow above the castle, it looked as if Bram's game was all about the player going deeper and deeper into the darkness. Into isolation.

Honor swallowed, her last qualm disappearing. "Bram," she said, her voice hoarse. "I want to tell you something."

He grunted, absorbed in his game.

She waited for her heart to beat, not confident she was going to make it through this alive. "I want to tell you about my kidnapping."

His hand jerked. The player on the screen exploded, dissolving into a million pinpoints of light before the screen went dark. Bram swiveled in his chair, its high squeak the sound she wanted to make when she got her first look at his face. It was etched by wariness, all sharp angles and deep shadows.

"Why?" he asked. "You've told me half a dozen times that you don't want to talk about the kidnapping."

The half a dozen times he'd asked her about it, she hadn't understood exactly why the question was so important to him. "For you," she said simply. "I think . . . I hope it might bring you some measure of peace."

He just looked at her.

Honor lifted one shoulder. "At least it's worth a try. Don't tell me it hasn't occurred to you that I could tell you something of Alicia's state of mind."

"It occurred to me."

Yet he'd never pressured her to tell him, because she'd told him refusing to speak of the details was her way of managing her feelings about it. Then the kidnapping became something *she* had power over, instead of the other way around. But now . . . now it was time to talk.

"Come on, then," she said, holding out her hand. There were risks in the telling, but she'd walk over hot coals if she could bring him comfort. "Come sit with me."

He built a small fire in the woodburning stove and she turned on a couple of lights. Then she sat at one corner of the couch.

Bram hesitated, then dropped to the other. Resting his elbows on his knees, he rubbed his face with his palms. "I don't think I should let you do this."

"Oh, since when have you ever 'let' me do anything?" she said, softly teasing. She looked at him across the expanse of smooth leather. Of course she had to do this. She loved him. It was only a question, now, of how *well* she would do this.

She drew her legs up to her chest and hugged them with her arms. Then she took one long breath and began. "You know I was kidnapped in the parking lot of the company where I was working. I'd stayed late that night, like I did most nights. I didn't see them coming, just all at once they were there. One of them had a gun, one of them had pieces of duct tape for my mouth, my ankles, my wrists. I was in the trunk of my car in a couple of minutes, I guess."

Her stomach quivered at the memory, but she ignored the reaction and got through the basic facts. "They took me to Kenny Adams's house. His parents were on a cruise. I was locked in the wine cellar for two weeks and then Dylan was in there with me for four days before we were rescued by the FBI."

If possible, Bram's face set even harder. "Honor, I . . ." He made a gesture with his hand. "So you know, I hate what happened to you."

She nodded once. "But that's not why we're talking. It's not *what* we're going to talk about."

Abruptly, he shot to his feet, then strode over to her and reached for her hand. "I can't ask you to do this."

Shaking her head, Honor refused to touch him. "You're not asking. I'm going to talk, Bram. If you don't want to listen, that's your choice."

He closed his eyes, then went back to his position on the couch. "I don't know why you're doing this."

To find a way through barricades erected over eight years of suffering. "I'm going to tell you my feelings over those two weeks. If you have any questions, ask them."

His gaze on her face, he hesitated, then nodded.

Honor took a deep breath. She'd spoken to the local authorities, federal authorities, and then people trained in crisis counseling about the details of her kidnapping. She'd stated facts and revealed emotions. But she'd never told anyone what she was about to tell Bram.

Staring at her bent knees, she began to talk. "For the first several minutes—longer, probably—I was numb. It took quite some time for me to realize that I wasn't caught in a bad dream. I wasn't in terror, or afraid at all, actually, because it seemed so unreal."

She sifted through her mind for what came next. "When I did figure out I wasn't having a weird nightmare, I turned very practical." Risking a peek at Bram, she sent him a little smile. "You may find that hard to believe."

One side of his mouth kicked up. "I've learned not to underestimate you."

"Well." The compliment flustered her a little and she had to look away from him again so she could concentrate on getting this right. "I focused not on what was happening to me, but on where I was going and how I could describe the men who had abducted me. My head was very clear as I cataloged everything I noticed. I don't remember any panic."

"Never?" Bram asked softly.

She looked up and met his eyes. "Never." Her hands were trembling, so she entwined her fingers and rested them on her upraised knees. "There were bad moments, sure, but those came from replaying the onset of the abduction. I went over and over in my mind what I could have done differently. But Alicia . . . she knew the children were all right, Bram, so I think she would have been able to take a great deal of comfort in that. I know I would have."

"Yes. Yes, you're right."

Honor let out a breath she didn't realize she'd been holding. "On that first day, after a few hours in the wine cellar I collapsed into sleep. I know it's hard to believe that I could, but my adrenaline had peaked and then I just crashed. It was like that until Dylan ended up in the cellar with me. I'd experience periods of surging adrenaline when I felt hyper-conscious and I continued to almost coldly collect facts about my situation. Then there'd be a couple of hours of intense, dreamless sleep."

"Did you think about someone you loved . . . your father?"

Nodding, she squeezed her fingers together, hoping Bram couldn't see the reflexive movement in the softly lit room. "He was my rock. In my mind, I saw him as completely in control of the situation, and that image— that *knowledge*—was a well of confidence and strength that I continually drew from."

She looked toward the room's French doors and checked her reflection in the glass. She appeared tense, she thought critically, but that was only natural. "I was held for days longer than Alicia, Bram, and I never considered the intellectual reality that I would be hurt or . . . killed."

He leaned toward her, his gaze intent. "I find that hard to believe."

So she had to make him believe. Relaxing her hands, she untangled her fingers and let them drift to the couch. She straightened her bent legs and angled toward him. "Really, I was never pee-in-my-pants afraid. The scariest moment was when the FBI came blasting in. Hey, even Dylan jumped then."

"I imagine he did." Bram's gaze raked her face, and there was still a suspicion in his eyes. "But Honor—"

"I can't tell you why," she interrupted. And she knew that he could make his own leap to the fact that

Honor couldn't truly know how *Alicia* had felt. "But I can tell you that I hung in there, I hung strong, because *it never, ever dawned on me that I wouldn't get free.*"

Closing his eyes, he slumped against the couch.

Honor didn't try saying anything more. Instead, she listened to the nervous pounding of her heart and hoped that she'd convinced him, helped him, in some small way.

As the silence stretched, she was certain the tension in the room eased. Then Bram opened his eyes and looked over at her. Her heartbeat kicked up and something warm and sweet rolled through her.

Relief, maybe even the lightness of a burden lifted, because she'd just told Bram what she'd never before told anyone.

And it appeared as if he believed her lies.

Chapter Eighteen

*B*ram closed his eyes again and Honor suffered through another few minutes of silence, her heart still pounding loudly, her hopes still pinned on it being a good silence rather than an ominous one. She was a terrible liar, that was what had made her the most nervous about dissembling. But nothing would have convinced her to tell him the truth. He would not have been served by knowing how bleak it had been.

But she'd been truthful where she could, omitting only small details like that ninety percent of the time she'd been so scared she couldn't have *spit*, let alone pee. About the overwhelming, helpless feelings of abandonment and loneliness she'd felt in the dark. About how she'd begun to wonder if she and the kidnappers were the only five people left in the world.

Anyway, Bram already knew about loneliness. And her despair had lifted once Dylan arrived and started spinning his magical stories about Hot Water. The town, even then, had saved her.

As for the rest . . . she could only hope that Alicia *had* believed to the very last moment she would get free.

Honor studied the strong lines of Bram's face and admitted to herself what had given her the courage to lie to him. *If I had been married to Bram, I would never have given up hope of getting back to him.*

In that moment, she made another important connection—this time to Bram's wife. She'd felt unworthy compared to Alicia, but now Honor felt . . . akin to her. There was no need to compete, because they both only wanted the same thing—Bram's happiness.

After more quiet moments, he finally let out a long breath and rose to his feet. Standing in front of Honor, he gazed down, his expression unreadable as always. In her next life, she promised herself wryly, the man she fell in love with wouldn't have a face of stone.

"Thank you," he said, his voice its usual rough tone, but a softer rough, one that stroked over her skin like his callused fingertips. "I know that was difficult for you."

"Not so difficult," she whispered back.

She thought she caught a ghost of a smile curving his mouth, but then it straightened. He reached out and pressed his forefinger against the center of her chin. "Let me make love to you, Honor."

"Oh." Her heart contracted. She'd been wanting him so much. For days she'd been needing him around her, inside her, to shore up her spirits and to distract her from the strain.

Wasn't it just like him to come through for her now? No matter what reluctance or reservations he had, in the end he always did. "Well, yeah."

For sure he was smiling now, an aching-sweet smile full of affection. " 'Well, yeah'?"

"As long as it's not out of pity or gratitude or something foolish like that," she added.

Bram reached for her hand and pulled her up and against his body. "I believe I can assure you it's not out of pity or gratitude," he said, pressing his growing erection against her belly.

Once more, she could feel the atmosphere in the room lightening. She could feel *him* lightening, and that made *her* feel like she could float off the floor. She smiled, almost giddy with happiness.

"If it's not because of pity or gratitude . . ."— opening her eyes wide in artless innocence, she gave a long, wet swipe of her lower lip with her tongue and felt him twitch against her—"why is it, then?"

One of Bram's hands drifted from her waist to her hips to palm her bottom. "It's these pants," he said. A fingernail of his other hand found the starting point of her zipper at the small of her back. Then he moved his finger, bumping the nail slowly, lightly, along the tracks.

Honor gasped, desire flooding her in one instant rush, setting her nerves buzzing as if he were stroking them instead of the metal teeth. His finger traced to the damp warmth between her thighs and he made a little satisfied grunt that was nearly as stimulating as his touch.

"You like to turn me on," she whispered, the desire curling tighter in her belly with the words. "And it turns you on to turn me on."

He looked amused. "Well, yeah."

She made a face. "Smartass."

"Princess," he countered automatically, but there was laughter, not insult, in his eyes. His hands holding her against him, he shuffled his feet backward, toward the door. "Come on, baby, let's go to bed."

"Bed?" she echoed. Feeling a little smartassy herself, she arched a brow. "Fuddy-duddy."

He froze. "What did you say?"

She lifted her chin. "You heard me."

"You don't want to do it in bed?"

Honor twined her arms around his neck and plastered her body against his. "Maybe I can't make it to the bed." She kissed him.

His lips opened instantly and she pushed her tongue inside, moaning at the delicious, hot flavor of his mouth. She'd been truthful about not making it to the bed. Already her skin felt too tight, her body primed for his touch.

His hand came between them to cup her breast, and she thought her pulse would leap out of her body. Pressing into his hand, she pushed her tongue harder against his, rubbing against it like she wanted to rub her naked body against him.

He pinched her nipple and she moaned.

"How wild do you want it, baby?"

Wild? She was already wild. He pinched her nipple again and she leaned away from him to shove up her own sweater. "Please, Bram."

He laughed, a sexy, all-male sound, and his clever hands drew off her sweater, and his clever fingers unfastened the front catch of her bra so that he could take both of her naked breasts in his hands.

Her head dropped back. "You're so smart," she whispered. "Brainy."

"Oh, yeah, baby. Because I know exactly what you want." He bent his knees to wrap his arms around her upper thighs and then lifted her to his mouth. His tongue licked her breast, under, over, everywhere but the hard point that was stiff and aching.

"I take it back," she mumbled, twisting against him. "You're not so brainy after all."

He laughed again, then moved to the other breast. He tortured that one too, until she grasped his head in both hands and brought him to the point. *Her* point. He sucked on her nipple, long, strong pulls that sent delicious ribbons of heat and sensation uncoiling through her body, then coiling again.

His head lifted and he stared at her wet nipple. "Pretty," he said. "So pretty." He kissed the tip gently and then, with her still in his arms, crossed to the worktable.

A quick move of his arm shoved its surface clear. Then he laid her against the cool wood, coming down on his elbows over her. "You never told me how wild you want it."

"I wildly want you," she said, uncertain what he was asking.

He smiled, kissed her. "Just a minute, then." He strode to the armoire a few feet away and she rose on one elbow to watch him. In moments he had the doors open and had swiveled one of the color monitors so that it faced her. A couple of keystrokes, and she was suddenly looking at her own half-clothed body.

She'd always considered herself fairly sophisticated until she went "Eeek," and threw her arms across her chest. Her head whipped around, trying to locate the camera in the room.

Bram cocked a brow at her. "Too much?"

Honor hesitated. "I'm starting to remember you mentioning Tommy Lee and Pamela the other day. Aren't there some X-rated videotapes floating around the Internet made by a rock star and a busty actress while on their honeymoon?"

"Now who's the brainy one?"

"You wouldn't . . . let anyone see this, would you?" she asked.

"Besides me and you, you mean?"

Air backed up in her lungs. "We . . . could watch it?"

He nodded. "Later . . . and now."

"Oh." Oh, yes. She could watch him touch her. She could watch herself touch him. The idea of it was racy and liberating and took her so far out of the realm of what she'd ever imagined that it left any lingering sexual apprehension in the dust forever. "I take it back, you're not a fuddy-duddy at all."

His eyebrows rose again, still waiting for her answer.

Honor moved her arms off her chest and dropped them to the table. Her image on the screen did the same. A hot thrill shot from her belly, heading south. "And the truth is, I'm not feeling very princessy at the moment either."

Bram's nostrils flared and he stalked toward her. "Then let me see what other names I can come up with."

He knew a lot of variations of "shameless." He whispered each one in her ear as he took her clothes off—one pants leg at a time; the zipper seemed to fascinate him—and stretched her out on the long wooden table. Then he proceeded to prove how shameless she indeed was, because he licked, sucked, and bit nearly every square inch of her body as she watched herself react on the screen.

Then he drove her right past shameless when he pulled her to one end of the table and bent her knees. Still fully clothed, he knelt, spread her legs, and tasted her.

She closed her eyes and screamed. There was no point in looking toward the monitor because her vision was a hazy blur. There was only sensation: the intimate way he held her open for his tongue and the soft wet strokes on the soft wet parts of her body. He gave an exciting grunt of satisfaction, and then gave it over and over again, and she knew he loved what he was doing.

He turned his face to rub his whiskered cheeks against the insides of her thighs, and then he returned to her center, finding her tightest, tingliest place and flicking it with the pointed tip of his tongue.

Honor was shaking. Her muscles, her nerves, her emotions were so tightly wound that she thought she would never untangle. It was the moment that had stopped her that first time with him, that moment in which she had to choose trust or fear.

To be alone or to be his.

Bram flattened his tongue against her, once, twice. But now there was no reason to stop reaching for that sweet helplessness, she decided. No reason at all. She was in love with him.

And then she felt the first hint of unraveling and moaned at the sharp, aching goodness of it. He must have known what the sound meant because he left off with the tongue strokes and caught her in his mouth, sucked. Honor gave over to him completely, bowing in his hands as the pleasure started to play out, ripples of it that took her breath.

Then he slid two fingers inside her and bit lightly down, snapping the line taut. Sharp bliss sang along it, and she shook with every echoing and reechoing note.

When her body stopped shuddering, Bram stood and leaned over to kiss her. She tasted herself, shocked at the sugary saltiness, shocked that her body clenched in another tremor of pleasure. "You slay me," he said.

Oh, she wanted to. But she knew she hadn't, not really. He always called the shots. Until tonight, he'd always dictated the where, the when, the how. He liked control.

But he couldn't be hers until he was willing to surrender to her too.

Still slightly sex-groggy, she smiled at him and put her fingers on the top button of his shirt. "My turn."

Something flickered in his eyes. "I can do it." He tried to push her hands away, but she refused to give in.

"Just watch," she insisted. Taking his chin in a determined grip, she turned his face toward the monitor.

Their image seemed to mesmerize him. Honor quickly sat up and used his uncommon acquiescence to strip him of his shirt. She even managed to switch places with him, pushing his back against the table as she stood on the floor. Thank goodness she was birthday bare, because she suspected that's what kept him cooperative for the few more seconds it took to open his fly and draw him out, hot and hard.

He groaned, then started to sit up. "Enough, Honor."

She pushed his chest back with her hand. Then, expecting another protest at any moment, she did what a woman had to do when a man needed to know whose turn it was to take charge. She bent her head, her hair falling across his groin as she took him into her mouth.

He groaned again, and the sound reverberated through the palm she had resting low on his belly. *Helpless. Helplessly mine.*

"Honor, no." His fingers sank into her hair.

She lifted her head. "Just for a minute or two," she coaxed, drawing a finger down the wettened surface.

He groaned a third time. *Must be a yes,* she told herself.

Nervous about her ability but determined to have him truly share the intimacy with her, she bent back to him. She might not be experienced at this, but if there was one thing girls in boarding schools seemed to know a lot about, or talk a lot about anyway, it was oral sex.

So, casting her mind back to a dozen gossip sessions she'd overheard in schools from Belgium to Boston, she tried it all on him: Kitten Laps, Butterfly Tickles, Bobbing for Apples. But then something happened, she forgot all about the silly names and her untrained technique and instead let her mouth make love to him.

Through the hand on his lower belly, she felt his breathing accelerate. She glanced over once and saw that his gaze was glued to the monitor. She looked there herself and tingles burst over her skin as she watched the most vulnerable part of him slide between her lips.

But nothing was better than feeling him, satiny and slick, at the mercy of her mouth. Feeling his body tensing, his muscles straining as they waited for the next stroke of her tongue.

"Honor. Honor, stop," he suddenly said, his fingers twining in her hair and pulling her head away from him.

She looked up, saw the helpless desire on his face, loving how much he needed her at this moment. How much she *owned* this moment and him. "Trust me, Bram," she said.

Her gaze on his, she slid her palms down his shaft.

"Trust me." Curling her fingers around him, she slowly slid her hand back up.

He groaned and then his body gave a sharp jolt. Under her fascinated gaze and the command of her still-stroking hand, pleasure burst, then pulsed from him.

When it was over, he shuddered once, and threw an arm over his eyes. "God, Honor. I . . . I'm sorry. I completely lost it."

She blinked, coming out of her own state of smug satisfaction. He was embarrassed.

Not knowing what else to do, she climbed onto the table.

"Jesus, Honor." He tried to hold her off, away from what he'd released on his skin, but she took care of that by flopping against him, chest to chest, groin to groin. "*Honor.*"

"Hey, no going squirmy on me now," she told him. "Don't forget we're in this together, fuddy-duddy."

He went quiet a moment, then finally slapped her lightly on the bare behind. "Princess." He laughed, and she thought he sounded a lifetime younger. "Maybe we are. Maybe we are."

*A*FTER an indigestible fast-food dinner, Josh lay on the hard narrow bed in his room at Motel 1, twenty minutes outside of Hot Water. It was the only room to be had for miles around. It was also the worst room to be had for miles around.

Obviously Motel 1 wasn't called Motel 1 because it was *number* one, but because it was five notches below Motel 6. A thousand and five.

He sucked in another breath of insecticide-laced air. Motel 1's only luxury was that each room came equipped with its own aerosol supply of Raid. After two days his can was already three-quarters empty.

Rising on one elbow, Josh peered out the small grimy window to make sure the cockroaches hadn't made off with the Ferrari. But it was still there, parked on the dirt spot right outside his room. A bare yellow bulb illuminated a patch of the front hood and the film of filth covering the finish.

Flopping back to the skimpy pillow, he groaned. How had it come to this? With all his smarts, with all his ambition, with a Plan A *and* a Plan B, he'd landed somewhere lower than the Sandy Acres Trailer Park.

His mood couldn't be lower either.

Forcing himself out of bed, he decided a drive might cure his depression. But that notion led to only more depression, Josh realized, as he stood in the dark beside the dirt-dulled Ferrari. Since moving here he hadn't even been able to rouse himself to wash his beloved car.

When he returned to L.A. he was going to trade it in for something German, that's all there was to it. The only thing Italian he had the least interest in anymore was Mia.

He groaned softly and tried to banish her face from his mind. Failing at that, he climbed in the car and sped away from Motel 1, rolling down his window to let in the cold night air. Maybe it would blow her image from his memory or at the very least freeze his brain.

Instead, the cold wind swirled a thousand what-ifs in his mind. What if he'd been able to wrest Honor away from Bram? What if the groupies hadn't picked Enigma's property as their camping ground? What if Honor had never heard about Hot Water or had never been kidnapped in the first place?

What if Josh hadn't grown up in Granny's single-wide? What if he didn't want money so much? What if he had never met Mia?

All the questions stopped short on that one.

Josh shook his head and took stock of his surroundings. "Shit," he said aloud. Without thinking about it, he'd driven toward Hot Water, of course. He wasn't far from the turnoff to Mia's house, and he wasn't far from a gas station either, thank God, because his tank had only an ounce or two of gas left and he needed to get out of her proximity ASAP.

He turned into the one-pump gas station-minimart. He'd passed the place several times before—you couldn't miss that LOTTERY PLAYERS WIN BIG HERE! sign—but had never stopped there. As he braked, an old man came shuffling out of the store.

"We're full service," the man called as Josh started to open his door.

"All right." Josh settled back, resting his head against the seat as the old man set to work.

Full service meant the works—windows, oil, air pressure—and Josh waited out the man's slow movement patiently. He had nothing else to do, nowhere else to be, no one else to be with.

His gaze idly roamed around the small station. "So," he said as the attendant passed by his open window, "do lottery players really win big here?"

"Sure. Multimillion-dollar winner a few months back." The old guy grinned. "Got myself a nice commission too. Lottery people give a cash prize to the place that sells the winning ticket."

"Congratulations." Josh didn't remember hearing anything about it, which was surprising because it was the kind of news small-town Hot Water would chew over endlessly. He smiled to himself. He had to confess, he found the community's closeness damn near charming. "Was the ticket-buyer someone passing through?"

"Can't say," the attendant answered, leaning over to polish the driver's side-view mirror with a rag. "Confidentiality."

"Ah." Josh nodded.

The old man moved to the rear window. Josh closed his eyes and went back to contemplating the fucked-up state of his life. A blast of cold air shot through his window, stirring those what-ifs back again.

What if he'd never met Mia?

What if he'd never fallen in love with her?

In *love*?

An ecstatic, dizzying feeling swamped him, so sweet and so startling that it caused his eyes to pop open. He was in love with Mia!

He stared out the newly clean windshield at the oak-and-pine-dotted field across the street. His gaze caught on something unusual, then focused. There was a greenish fog glowing over the tops of the trees, and hovering in the middle of it was a dark, oval-shaped, air vehicle kind of . . . thing.

Josh closed his eyes, then opened them. Still there. He shifted in his seat to look through a different piece of the glass. Still there. As he watched, a beam of light shot from the bottom of the . . . thing to his windshield. A silvery glow flooded the interior of the Ferrari.

Josh froze, transfixed by the starry light. That ecstatic, dizzying feeling rushed over him again and he thought of Mia, of how he loved her, of how lucky he was to know this kind of feeling. How it prioritized everything and paled so much that he'd thought was important to him. Emotions burned inside of him with the brilliance of that strange yet beautiful light.

"Sir? Sir?"

Josh started, then opened his eyes. The attendant was looking at him with the beginnings of alarm on his face. "Oh, good," the old man said. "I thought maybe you'd had yourself a heart attack or something. Just a nap, I guess."

Or something. I guess. Josh jerked his gaze off the man to where the object had been, but there was nothing but blue-black sky and the country-bright stars. The interior of the Ferrari was dim, the passenger side barely touched by the light of the flickering fluorescent bulb in the gas pump's overhang.

He cleared his throat, trying to clear his mind at the same time. "Did you . . . did you see anything strange a few moments ago? Lights in the sky?"

The old man gave him a knowing look. "One of *them*, are you?" He jerked his thumb over his shoulder. "The people you want are a couple miles back. Take the second right until you run into them TV trucks."

Rather than protesting, Josh paid the man and then started the car. He hesitated before turning onto the road, craning his neck to look all around the sky. Had he been asleep?

Of course he had. He turned the wheel to head back to Motel 1, but then, for some improbable reason, he jerked it in the opposite direction. Toward Mia's.

What the hell was he doing? But that deep sense of well-being surged inside him again, growing stronger and stronger the closer and closer he got to her little house. He pressed on the accelerator, his heart pounding in excitement.

Once parked in his usual spot, he ran up the steps to her front door and knocked briskly. When she opened it, that well-being transmuted to a happiness as pure as the silver light he'd dreamed of in the car. His palms itched again, but now he knew why. She was the most valuable, most essential treasure of all.

Her gorgeous brown eyes flashed nasty black fire at him, however. "What are you doing here?"

Her anger didn't deter him. He knew the answers now. "I—"

"Don't bother telling me," she snapped, then reached out to grab his arm and haul him inside. "My father's here, as I'm sure you know. He doesn't believe the sheriff is coming tomorrow to kick them off. I want you to confirm it."

Josh opened his mouth, closed it. "All right," he said. "I want to talk to him."

In the small living room, Beau looked surprised to see Josh, then gave him a sharp look before transferring his attention to his daughter. "Mia—"

But she interrupted him too. "Go ahead, Josh," she said without even glancing at him. "He's right here."

"Sir. Mr. Caruso, sir." He looked at Mia because he wanted to remember this moment for the rest of his life. "I'd like to ask your permission to marry your daughter."

The color drained from Mia's face. She whirled to face him. "What? *What?*"

A trickle of unaccustomed embarrassment ran through him, and he felt his face redden. Maybe he should have insisted he talk to her alone first. Maybe he should have made sure she felt the same way he did. But then he shrugged. Hey, once an arrogant bastard, always an arrogant bastard.

He stepped forward to take her hands in his. "Listen to me, Mia." His face heated again and he marveled at how she could bring him to his knees.

So he dropped to both of them.

Oh, how his friends would laugh—no. Who the hell cared what anyone would say, when this was only between him and Mia? When this was the most important thing in the world—no, the whole damn universe?

"I've been greedy all my life," he said softly. "Hungry, I thought, for money. But you were right the other day. What I've been hungry for is something else. Someone to love. A place to belong. The empty wallet I've been trying to fill has really been my empty heart."

She was shaking her head slowly back and forth, as if she didn't believe him. "No. This doesn't happen. Not *two* wishes. I don't really get to have you as a *husband*."

He was going to spend the rest of his life making certain she was sure of him. For now, he could only squeeze her hands. "Trust me, Mia. Trust me like I trust you to feed my soul and fill up my heart."

And, arrogant bastard that he was, he took the first tear that spilled over her cheek as *Yes*.

THIS is a dream, Mia thought for the thousandth time, looking up at Josh from the circle of his arms. At some point in the last fifteen miraculous minutes, her father had slipped out of the house. They were alone.

With one knuckle, Josh tilted her chin higher. "Uh-oh. I know what you're thinking. And no, this is *not* a dream." He reached down and pinched her, hard, on the bottom.

Mia jumped. "Ow!"

He grinned. "What'd I tell you? If you were sleeping, you'd be awake now, right?" His head dipped so his forehead rested against hers. "Though I'm flattered you think me such a dreamboat."

She tried to frown. "I need to be careful. Your head's too big already."

He wiggled his eyebrows. "Part of my charm." Then he sobered and pulled her face against his chest. "Oh, sweetheart. You don't know how long I've needed you."

Mia felt another sting of tears in her eyes. She was *not* going to spend the first night of her engagement crying! Lifting her mouth, she kissed the underside of Josh's chin.

"Come with me," she said, leading him down the short hall toward her bedroom. Once they were inside, she attacked the buttons of his shirt, wanting him naked and in her bed *now*. There'd be no tears then, she knew.

"Hey, hey, hey." He caught her hands. "Wait. I don't want to rush right into that."

Mia pouted. "No?"

"Well, yes, but first I want to know about you. I want to know all the things I never let you tell me before. Your past, your hopes, your dreams."

He turned to survey the walls of her room with interest. Mia's heart leaped again. This *was* all true. Josh had never paid the least bit of attention to any of the personal items she displayed.

On the night that her father had seen his UFO, she'd stomped out of her house to take the first chance of her life. That had paid off. But it had scared her too, scared her about risking again.

And then, finally, she had. She'd risked having Josh. Though it had broken her heart when he'd left, she'd tried telling herself it was enough to have had him for even that short a time.

But now! Now she took the time to explain everything on display in her room: photos and 4-H ribbons, her cooking school certificate, her baking trophy from last year's county fair, until there was only one item remaining. She hesitated before pointing out the small frame hanging on the wall.

Instead, she looked down at Josh's golden head as he paged through an old photo album of her mother's. Suddenly he looked up. "Oh, shit," he said.

"What?" He was stopped on a wedding photograph of her parents. "What's the problem?"

"Me," Josh said. "I need to give you a chance to take your 'yes' back."

"What? Why?"

"Mia, I don't have any money. Not any to speak of, anyhow. And as for my job . . . you heard me assure your father I'll talk to the sheriff again. I won't move him and his friends off the Enigma property. So it's probably bye-bye to my current employment as well."

"I didn't want to live in L.A. anyway," Mia said, turning to lift the little frame.

"I know, and I don't want to go back there either. But we have to have *something*."

She knew exactly what they could do. "What about a restaurant? An elegant one. You know wine and food, love it, and you know I can cook. It could be here in Hot Water or the next town over or—"

"Mia." He shook his head. "That has possibilities, but the problem is we'd need some money to start with."

She tried to keep her smile to herself, but it bloomed across her face, so wide her cheeks hurt. "We have some money to start with." With a little flourish, she pushed the frame into his hands.

He stared down at it, uncomprehending. "A lottery ticket?"

"A winning lottery ticket." She ran her hand over his hair, that golden, perfect, BP hair. "I've taken two chances in my life, and boy, have they paid off. A man to love. And twenty-point-two million dollars."

"Oh, my God." Josh looked up at her, his expression stunned. "Your father's website, the portable johns . . . *you* paid for all that." He blinked. "Did you say twenty-point-two *million* dollars?"

She nodded. "Hardly anyone knows. I didn't want people to think differently about me, you know? So I've only told my father and a few others. Bram too, because I quit my job with him for about half a day. But then I didn't know what to do with myself."

"You didn't know what to do with yourself and your twenty-point-two million dollars," Josh repeated stupidly.

She wasn't sure he was ever going to recover. "Oh, I know what I want to do now," she said confidently, because it was almost scarily clear that if she wished for something, her wish came true. "Marry you and have your babies and show the world that the most valuable thing the two of us have is not the money, but each other."

Josh tossed aside the framed ticket and drew her down to him. "You didn't happen to look up in the sky tonight, did you?"

Puzzled, she shook her head. "No. Why?"

"Doesn't matter," Josh said against her mouth. "Nothing matters but you."

Chapter Nineteen

*A*fter a face-to-face meeting with an agent in the Sacramento FBI field office, Bram sped toward home. It was later in the afternoon than he'd planned to be gone and he didn't like Honor by herself this long. He'd worried about leaving her alone at all, but she'd sworn she would be perfectly fine.

It had been more than two weeks without any sign of the escaped kidnapper, and Honor and everyone else was convinced Kenny Adams was in Zurich or Zihuatanejo with a black market passport and a plan to spend the rest of his life away from the U.S. The FBI special agent he'd met with—who had kept Bram waiting for an hour—had indicated the authorities might never catch up with the man.

Yet despite that frustrating thought, Bram realized he was smiling.

Well, why the hell shouldn't he be smiling? There was a beautiful woman waiting for him. His beautiful wife.

They'd pick a date, he decided, just like she'd wanted to before. A date that declared them completely free of Adams. And on that date, they'd marry again. A Saturday afternoon ceremony in the red-brick, white-spired Methodist church located in the center of Hot Water. It was the first church established in town and had been there since 1851.

Honor would love that.

He grinned, deciding to propose the idea as soon as he got home. A few more miles flew by as he imagined her reaction. She'd know how much he cared about her then. How much he wanted her to belong to him.

All because she'd lied to him.

That had been the turning point for Bram. It was one thing for her to bare her soul about the kidnapping after swearing for weeks she wasn't going to talk about it. It was entirely another for that starry-eyed woman to try to protect him by coming up with a story that was just a tad too comforting to be believed.

He'd known at that moment that Honor was in love with him.

In the face of such an astonishing gift, he'd had no other choice but to leave his unanswered questions behind. For the first time in eight years, he thought he could.

For her.

Maybe he couldn't love her back, his heart had been walled-off too long for that, but he thought he could make her happy.

Nearing the turnoff to his private drive, he slid his palmtop from his pocket and placed it on the passenger seat in readiness to open the gate. His mind leaped from the gate to the security system to the security cameras and then to their videotaped lovemaking.

A shot of lust overrode his residual embarrassment. *Trust me,* Honor had said, and he had. He did.

She'd found her way over every barricade and through every one of his defenses, and he . . . welcomed her presence now. By God, he was grateful for it. Something heavy lifted from him and he suddenly felt buoyant. Almost weightless. It was a strange feeling, he mused, it was . . .

Happiness.

He was happy.

Grinning like a fool again, he pressed on the accelerator, more eager than ever to get home to Honor and the life they were going to have together. Happiness was still bubbling inside him when he made the turn onto his drive.

His foot fell off the gas pedal. Empty cars, dozens and dozens of them, were parked on either side of the pavement leading to his house.

The euphoric bubbles died. Bram stomped on the accelerator to speed down the curving drive toward the gate. Honor was under strict orders not to let anyone in, he tried assuring himself. She'd sworn she wouldn't.

He'd been tempted to hide the other handheld computer that controlled the security system, but decided there was no reason for it. Honor had said she was going to spend the afternoon taking another stab at training Joey.

She *wouldn't* have opened the gate.

And yet, as he neared the peeled-log barrier, he could see it was off its track again and it *was* drawn open, wide enough for a man to pass through.

Bram slammed on his brakes and jumped out of the car. A high whine in his ears, he flew forward. Once through the gate, his feet stuttered to a halt.

His home had been invaded. People were everywhere, standing in groups, sitting in lawn chairs, sprawled on blankets beside picnic baskets and playpens with babies. The crowd looked to be a mix of Hot Water residents, UFO groupies, and curious tourists.

Kenny Adams could be among them.

An icy fist seemed to grab his throat. Squeezed. *Where the hell was Honor?*

He quickly surveyed the area, ignoring the people who called out to him in greeting. Down the long stretch of driveway that led toward the garage, his gaze snagged on Joey, leaping in furry exuberance around Fifo, frozen in a position of . . . frozenness.

Honor had touched the other palmtop, all right.

But where was she now?

He ran forward, searching for her in the confusion. He dodged a Kemper kid hawking more T-shirts and antennae and then another who was trundling a cart of drinks and snacks. *Where was she?*

Then he saw her. The spare palmtop in hand, she stood calmly—*cheerfully*, even—beside the mayor and his wife at the bottom of the porch steps. Fear released its stranglehold and then relief gave way to a white-hot anger. He slowed to a stalk.

Even though she was wearing her rose-colored sunglasses against the last of the afternoon light, he knew she'd spotted him too. As he approached, she took a small shuffle backward.

"Good afternoon, Bram!" the mayor said jovially.

Bram proceeded straight to Honor. He curled the fingers of his hand around her upper arm. "What the hell is going on?"

"I . . ." She licked her lips, and her eyes darted toward the Honorable Mr. and Mrs. Ames, then darted back to his face. "We . . ."

"What the hell is going on?" Bram repeated.

"Mia's father showed up about an hour ago with his followers," she said quickly, her tone placating. "He'd reconsidered my idea that maybe his alien . . . friends would return to him, rather than to a particular place. Remember how I invited him here to discuss it sometime?"

He gave her arm a small, controlled shake. "Have you forgotten Kenny Adams is loose?"

"Of course not." She made a helpless gesture with her free hand. "But what was I supposed to do?"

"Say no," he bit out.

Apparently sensing trouble, the mayor sidled closer. "I spoke with Honor about it too. Josh McCool had called in the sheriff and then called him off, but it solves a lot of problems for everyone if tonight's gathering occurs on private property."

Honor nodded. "There was only going to be more trouble if they moved somewhere else without permission, so he thought of us."

Us. Bram pulled her a distance from the mayor, then dropped her arm. "They've got to go, Honor. Everyone has to leave."

"Why?"

"Kenny Adams."

"Bram, come on." Her eyes pleaded with him. "Kenny Adams can't hurt me, not in Hot Water, and I . . . I can't just tell everyone to leave."

Her pretty face wouldn't move him. "What do you mean, you can't?"

"All right," she said, her mouth tightening. "I won't. I can help out the town with this. We both can."

"No. Forget it. Everyone is out of here." He turned from her.

She grabbed his arm. "I invited them in. They stay."

"*No.*"

"But Hot Water—"

"I don't give a flying fuck about the town or your ridiculous hope that you'll fit in here." *She had to listen!* She had to stop worrying about the town and start worrying about herself. "I don't understand why you'd want to."

Her face had gone pale and she'd dropped his arm. Her eyes had gone pale too, and they glittered like winter sun on ice. "Let me try to explain. Some of us don't want to be sequestered from the rest of the world. Some of us don't want to live with mechanical animals instead of real ones." She gestured at the palmtop he still held. "Some of us don't want to live our lives by remote control."

Fury buzzed in his head. He could barely think over its noise and the noise of the dozens and dozens and dozens of people that she'd let into his space and his solitude. Goddamn it! Why had he ever let *her* in?

"You're acting like a spoiled brat." Panic gave his voice a razor-blade edge. "If they stay, we're through." *She had to listen.* "Do you hear me? This is D-Day, baby, November fifteenth. Unless you throw them out, we're going to be divorced so fast your head will spin."

She flinched, but then she cloaked herself in stiff, royal Witherspoon disdain. "Go ahead. Do what you must. Divorce me."

His hand tightened on the palmtop so hard the plastic case cracked. "You don't want that. You're in love with me."

She flinched again, but then she narrowed her icy eyes. "That's *exactly* why I want you to divorce me. Because I'm enough of a spoiled brat to want to be loved in return. But you won't give someone else that kind of hold over you, will you? No, you'd rather hold on to a tragic past than take a step forward and risk loving me back."

Love. He hated the word, he hated hearing her say it amid the chaos of the crowd and the chaos her stubbornness was creating inside of him.

"Love you?" he repeated harshly. "My 'tragic' past has been good for one thing, Honor, and that's to teach me it's not safe to love anyone. So you're absolutely right. I'm never going to love you. I don't want to."

Sickened by the noise, his panic, and most of all by the look of devastation on Honor's face, Bram bolted.

*H*ONOR watched Bram tear out of the Fortress, pushing past the people streaming through the gate. *I'm never going to love you. I don't want to.*

Bram had abandoned her.

Her skin went cold and suddenly the air smelled musty and dead. She was inside the wine cellar again, with the darkness pressing against her, trying to flatten her heart and squeeze her soul to nothing.

"Honor, are you feeling well?" It was Mrs. Ames, the mayor's wife.

Honor started, sucking in a quick breath of fresh afternoon air. Then she turned to face the other woman. "I'm fine. Just fine." Through sheer force of will, she gamely pasted on a smile just as she'd been gamely pasting on optimism every day since her rescue. "Is there something I can do for you or the mayor?"

There was still the town, she assured herself. It was going to be all right. *She* was going to be all right, because Bram was wrong. She *would* belong in Hot Water.

As the sun went down, she moved about the front grounds, righting a downed toddler, locating the owner of a pair of lost glasses, directing the press to the corner of the property where Beau and his group had set up to wait. Anytime she thought of Bram's defection, anytime the falling darkness tried to drape its heavy loneliness over her, she pushed it away by remembering Dylan's voice in that other darkness.

I grew up in a little Gold Rush town in northern California. . . .

Within an hour she'd been entranced, picturing Hot Water, its eccentric citizens and old-fashioned traditions. Within a day, as he continued to talk, she'd been convinced that if she was ever rescued, Hot Water was the place where she could rediscover her sense of security.

By the time she was rescued, she'd been certain that making Hot Water her home would restore her faith in the world.

As twilight descended, Hot Water was like the ghost town it had avoided becoming for over 150 years. *Because everyone's at my house,* Bram thought, his jaw tightening. A thousand things roiling inside him, he parked at the cemetery and climbed the hill toward Alicia's grave.

Standing at its foot, he pushed the heels of his hands into his eyes. "I like order," he muttered. "Logic. Cause and effect. Is there something so wrong with that?"

His hands fell, but he kept his eyes closed. "I don't understand randomness. Explain that. Just tell me how to manage this helplessness I hate. Then I can move on."

As usual, though, calm and rational netted him

nothing. Eyes still tightly shut, he shoved his fists in his pockets and tried to master the frustration and the fury welling inside of him. Then his eyes popped open and his gaze bore into the ground as if he could see straight through to hell and the devil that had tortured him for the past eight years.

"Answer them!" he shouted, as the gate inside him flew open and the questions burst forth. "Answer *me!*"

Silence.

"Answer me!"

But the only response was the whistle of the wind in the trees, the papery rattle of fallen leaves tumbling across the grass, that lonely swing creaking in the nearby park.

Defeated once more, Bram finally sank down to the cold grass and dropped his head to his upraised knees.

Then he found himself talking aloud again, but to Alicia this time, even though he'd never before felt that she was here. "You'd like her, Leesh. Oh, you wouldn't know what to make of Honor's fancy clothes and crazy shoes, but the woman inside them has such a joyous heart."

He did understand why Honor had let Beau and the mayor and everyone else in. She accepted the risk for the reward of opening herself to others.

"I can't do that myself," Bram admitted. "Leesh, I just can't."

He couldn't love anyone again because he was afraid of losing them. Eight years ago that meant keeping distant from family and friends. It meant giving away the big-footed, goofy-grinning chocolate Lab puppy that Alicia had given him two months before she died.

"Hershey ran in front of a car on the day of your fu-neral," he whispered, his throat clogging at the memory. "He was almost hit. I *had* to give him away, don't you see? I couldn't take the chance of having to bury something else I loved."

So now that meant there would be no second wedding to Honor, no sweet nights with her in his arms, no more loving looks from the silvery depths of her eyes.

The certainty twisted in his belly and he lifted his head to the sky, searching for relief in the starlight that reminded him so much of her. Against the now-black sky, the stars stood out brightly, twinkling but offering no ease. Certainly no closure. Sighing, he turned his head and looked across darkened fields and stands of trees in the direction of home.

A few miles southwest, a strange green glow caught Bram's attention. He squinted, half rising at the immediate thought of fire. But fire didn't smoke green. And the glow wasn't smoky, it was more like a fog, and rising from it to hover in the sky was a lens-shaped, dark . . . object.

He fell back to the grass, staring. What the hell—?

Then a beam of light shot from the object and found Bram. The beam pored over him, its light silver and beautiful.

His thoughts scattered, then swirled in his head. He shook it, trying to clear his vision, but it remained around him, that beautiful, Honor-bright, caring light. So he just sat in place, bathing in its calm vibrancy.

The wind blew, and it was a warm wind, like summer. It seeped through his pores, blew through the barrier around his heart, then reversed. With one powerful gust it knocked the wall down, and Bram felt himself warm from the inside out.

He opened his eyes. Realizing he was lying flat on

his back in the grass, he sat up. He rubbed his palm over his face.

I must have fallen asleep, he thought. *I was—*

He snapped his head around. He'd been staring over there, a light had shone on him—both were now gone.

"Oh, shit," he said aloud. "It couldn't have been . . . ?"

Naw, he told himself. "It was searchlights or a bonfire or . . ."

But there was no explanation. He knew that. Not a logical one, anyway. And damn it, he couldn't dismiss the *illogical* one either.

It was a crazy, chaotic notion, but when he left himself open to the idea of it, he felt—

Oh, my God. He felt . . .

Peace.

And that's when he knew, *really* knew, that he would never find the answers to the questions he'd been asking for eight years. Not in this lifetime anyway.

It was a hell of a thing to accept, that the world was random and imperfect. A hell of a thing to swallow, that there was no explanation for senseless, unfair tragedies. A hell of a thing to acknowledge, that there would never be closure for him.

And yet, that left openness.

Openness let things in.

He lay back in the grass and looked up into the night sky, aware that he'd been looking down and backward for too, too long. But if he looked up, looked out, then he could see other things. Beautiful things that also couldn't be known or explained or reasoned away— like UFOs, and silvery beams of light, and . . .

Love.

Love.

Oh, God, Bram thought. His protective wall was truly gone. And if he didn't want to lose Honor, if he didn't want to be isolated and only half alive for the rest of his life, then he had to forgive the world its imperfections and take the chance on feeling again. On loving.

Finally accepting that into the depths of his now-unguarded heart, he rose to his feet. He stood at the grave site for another moment. Then he pressed two fingers to his lips, touched them to Alicia's gravestone. "Good-bye, Leesh."

Then he smiled. "You know this stuff already, don't you?"

The certainty of that was the last thing he needed to walk away.

FROM her place on the driveway, Honor noticed the waving beam of a flashlight catch on Fifo's frozen metal hide. She grimaced, feeling guilty all over again for whatever she'd done to break him this time.

Stupid palmtop. It was resting in the pocket of her jacket, but she'd vowed never to touch it again. Leaving the crowd behind, Honor headed toward the robotic dog. The least she could do for the paralyzed thing was get him out of the evening dampness.

Easier said than done, she realized once she reached him. Fifo was too big and too awkward for her to pick up and carry off. She could just leave him there—

But no, she couldn't. Bram loved the metallic mutt, for whatever reason and no matter why. Well, she knew why. Because he could control everything about it, from its bark to its brain.

With a sigh, she slipped the handheld computer from

her pocket, deciding to try to get the dog moving again. She pressed an icon on the screen. Nothing happened.

"The story of my life," Honor mumbled. She pressed it again. Still nothing happened.

"The second story of my life." Giving it one more try, she closed her eyes and randomly stabbed at the touch-screen, murmuring "Babaloo" for good measure too.

An electronic hum had her eyes popping open. Fifo rose creakily from his haunches and his eyes flickered. Then the amber lights steadied as he seemed to look at her.

She smiled weakly and gave him a little wave. "Hi, boy. So sorry about what happened."

Fifo growled, low and vicious.

Honor swallowed and took a nervous step back.

Fifo rolled forward, and Honor took more steps, edging toward the shadows near the garage wall.

The dog had been on his best behavior with her lately, but who knew which of his circuits were fried now? "Hey," she said as the dog continued to advance, still snarling, "is this any way for the monster to talk to Mrs. Frankenstein?"

*B*ACK at the house, Bram discovered the front grounds were teeming with an even larger throng. He laughed to himself as he saw a couple of news crews dashing about interviewing people in the crowd. He had yet to shake the crazy feeling that everyone waiting here had already missed the show.

Despite the fact that the landscape lights had been turned on, it was still difficult to recognize specific faces in the darkness of the moonless night. Looking for Honor, Bram drifted among the groups, asking for her. Every so often someone would say she'd just passed by or that they'd seen her near the little bridge or by the front steps, but he couldn't manage to track her down.

It was only after he'd walked through the deserted house that he started to worry. In his office, he flipped on the monitors and clicked through the views from the security cameras, coming up with nothing.

THE robotic dog's next growl was lower, more vicious, and Honor realized Fifo's gaze wasn't *on* her, but *past* her. The hairs on the back of her neck sprang up and she whirled.

Kenny Adams was standing in the meager illumination of a dim spotlight washing up the far end of the garage wall. His head was shaved and he looked pale, almost ghostly, in wrinkled gray pants and a white shirt. He was holding something in his left hand.

He's left-handed. Her mind latched on to that single thing, turning the fact over and over as time slowed and the world around her went hazy. For goodness' sake, she thought with an odd detachment, she'd forgotten to tell the FBI that Kenny Adams was left-handed.

"Hello there," he said. "I couldn't go away without seeing you again."

Honor didn't like the sound of that. But it was hard to get too worked up about it, not when this must be a dream. Of course a dream, because she'd always been certain Kenny Adams wouldn't come here.

Behind her, Fifo was still growling. He rolled forward until he was level with Honor.

Kenny's gaze didn't waver from her face. "Weird sort of friend you have there. I'll make a better one." His lips turned up. It wasn't a smile.

Then his left hand lifted, and she saw that what he was holding was a gun.

Reality broke through the strange dreaminess trying to claim her mind. Kenny wanted to be her "friend" again. Kenny had a gun.

Kenny was here in Hot Water.

Light gleamed dully on his bald scalp as he nodded over his shoulder. "That gate the only way out?"

Yes? No? Maybe? The words spun through her brain. Was there a best answer?

"Doesn't matter," Kenny said. "We'll use it. Then I can steal another car as we leave."

We. He wanted her to leave Hot Water. With him.

Even with Fifo growling rabidly beside her, even with that ugly little gun pointing at her, numbing shock was overtaking her again. Kenny had something right, Honor thought in that funny, detached way. It *didn't* matter.

She didn't belong here.

She wasn't loved here.

And she certainly wasn't safe here.

Come to think of it, she supposed she might just as well go.

WITH no sign of Honor and panic tugging at him, Bram thought of Fifo, then dismissed the idea. The dog had appeared frozen when he'd arrived home that afternoon. Though he hadn't seen the robot on the driveway a few minutes ago, probably someone had merely bodily moved it.

Still . . .

As Bram slid the palmtop from his pocket, the cracked case caught on a thread. He tugged it free, then pressed the icon on the touchscreen to display the view from the camera mounted in Fifo's chest. The image painted down the small screen.

The night-vision facility gave the picture an orange-ish cast. Bram squinted, trying to make out whatever it was.

Legs. Pirate boots. Another pair of legs and an arm. Bram took a breath.

Then choked on it.

At the end of the arm pointing at Honor was a gun.

The scream that gathered in Bram's throat had been eight years coming. The soles of his shoes slid on the hardwood floor as he shot from the room. He caught the doorjamb in his free hand and swung his forward momentum to the right.

He didn't know where Honor and Fifo were, but the last place he'd seen the dog was near the garage. The fastest, most direct route was from the front door and there wasn't time to consider another plan.

He flew down the front steps and barreled into the mayor's wife. She shrieked, and then again when he grabbed her arm and shoved his face close to hers. "Call 911. Tell them Kenny Adams is here and he has a gun."

Then he started running again, tagging a man he recognized. "Help me," he said, grabbing him by the arm. Suddenly Josh loomed in front of him, his fingers laced with Mia's.

Bram reached out and grabbed their entwined hands. "Help me." He took off, aware the three others were right behind him.

A gunshot punctured the night. Bram's belly, heart, soul clenched. His gaze jumped to the palmtop in his hand, just as the screen went black. Throwing the useless thing aside, he rounded the corner of the house at a dead run.

In the distance, two figures standing. His heart clenched again. Honor's, small and so damn fragile. A man's, a gun raised at his side.

An unearthly howl rent the night.

Bram didn't feel the scream finally working free to tear through his throat, but he supposed it must be his.

Even as his feet pounded faster forward, a creature leaped from the shadows by the garage. Fur flying, teeth flashing, it was a mythic monster. A werewolf. A one-headed Cerberus. The Hound of the Baskervilles.

The man with the gun didn't have a chance. Joey's front paws drove into his chest, knocking him backward. The man's head hit the flagstone, his gun hand opened, and the weapon skittered away.

With a final leap, Bram reached Honor. "Are you hurt?" he asked, scooping her against him as Josh went for the weapon. Shaking her head, she closed her eyes, clung.

Dylan dashed up to check the unconscious figure on the ground. His hands went to his belt buckle. "Kenny Adams," he said grimly, his gaze flicking to Honor. With his boot, he shoved the man over, then restrained his hands with the belt. "The sheriff's on his way."

"Looks like he shot Fifo," Bram said, trying to pretend his voice and hands weren't shaking. He couldn't look at Honor again, not yet, not when the smell of gunpowder and seared metal tasted bitter on his tongue. He surveyed the heap of shattered metal on the ground while Joey stood over the remains, whining. "I programmed him to attack if Adams came within eight feet."

Dylan glanced over. "The digital photo recognition worked?"

"Think so," Bram answered. Then Honor began to

tremble against him and he looked down at her in alarm. "What's wrong?"

Her eyes were wide and dark, no light in them at all. She dropped her arms from around his waist and stepped free. "Nothing," she said, and for an instant he thought she would even manage a smile.

But then she swayed, and that almost-smile died, and her facade, that confident, optimistic, brave facade she'd been wearing since the day she'd moved in completely dropped. As he caught her, he was sure he heard it shatter at their feet.

She was too thin, he thought, running toward the house with her in his arms. The lump in his throat was heavier than she was. Damn it, the woman he'd let down his guard to love was too thin, too fragile, too vulnerable. He'd nearly lost her tonight.

He'd nearly lost her.

His feet stumbled and the lump in his throat doubled in size. Oh, God, oh, God. He knew what that shattering had been now. It was the sound of what he'd been avoiding for the past eight years.

What he'd just heard break had been his newly defenseless heart.

TWENTY hours later, Honor stood inside the locked gate of the Fortress, thankful the landscape lights were off. She was thankful too that seven P.M. in November meant the front grounds were pitch-dark. With a nervous glance toward the house, she grabbed the small toiletry bag from the suitcases surrounding her and heaved it.

It hit the gate with a *thwot*, then reversed direction. *Thwak.* It landed on the flagstone at Honor's feet. She grimaced, then, with another wary look toward the house, tried again. Then a third time. On this attempt, as the bag fell back it knocked her on the top of the head.

It knocked some sense into her too. Even if she succeeded with this little bag, she didn't have a hope of throwing her large suitcases over. And even if she managed that, how could she then scale all twelve slippery feet of peeled logs to reach the other side?

There was only one thing to do.

Grabbing the handles of her large suitcases, she dragged them to the gate. Then she shoved the largest over with her foot, stacked the second largest on top of it, then the next and the next and the next. Reaching up, she balanced the little toiletries bag on top of them all.

Quickly, she mounted her impromptu stairs one suitcase at a time. As her right foot wobbled on the bulging side of the smallest bag, the landscape lights suddenly blazed on.

A floodlight washed the gate, catching her backside in its beam. Honor froze, paralyzed by discovery.

Bram's voice, mild, and somewhat curious, sounded behind her. "After all the trouble you went to breaking *into* my life, now you're leaving without saying good-bye?"

Swallowing hard, she took her foot off the little wobbly bag and forced herself to turn and face him. He was standing twenty-five feet away, his arms crossed over his chest. Joey sprawled on the driveway at his feet. "I—I called a cab."

"I thought you were asleep."

She gave a little shrug. She'd faked the sleep just as she'd been faking "fine" since last night. Bram had gone nice on her again, conscientiously hovering from the moment she'd almost fainted in his arms until the last of the FBI agents left in the early morning hours. She'd had to do *something* to get free of him.

She stepped down to the first suitcase. "Now that you're here, perhaps you wouldn't mind opening the gate for me."

He seemed to consider it, then shook his head. "I think I would mind. At least until I hear what you have to say for yourself."

She'd *known* he wasn't going to make this easy. "It's time for me to go."

One of his eyebrows winged up. "Town lost its interest for you?"

He'd always claimed that would eventually happen. "Yes," she said.

"Liar."

She dug her fingernails into her palms. "Bore."

He laughed at that. "I've got some videotape inside that proves you wrong."

Her eyes closed. "Don't," she said wearily. "Don't jab at me anymore. Just let me go."

"That wasn't supposed to be a jab, but an enticement to stay."

"I should stay with you for sex?"

"Well, it isn't why you were leaving, is it?"

She almost laughed, because she was so, so close to tears. She'd counted on never having to see him again. "I have to go, Bram."

He walked closer to her. "Why?"

As a precaution, Honor climbed back to the second suitcase. "Does it matter?"

"Yes." He took another step.

She climbed higher. "Because you were right. Satisfied now?"

His brows drew together and he came even closer. "Mmm, maybe. But I've been right so many times. This particular one is . . . ?"

She should rail against his arrogance, but he was wearing his remote, cool commando face. It only made her heart ache, because she remembered how it could be warmed by his surprising smile or softened when he was making tender love to her.

"You were right about all of it," she said. "How's that?"

"It's very nice, but I'm still not quite sure—"

"I wasn't safe here." Her throat tried to close over the words, but she kept going, forcing them out, forcing herself to accept the truth that there was no magic place for her, that there was no magic that could restore her faith in the world. "I wasn't safe here and I don't belong here. I never will."

He seemed to absorb that for a moment. Then he rubbed his hand over his chin. "That presents a small problem, because I want you to stay."

She blinked. "What? No."

"You told me once that you trusted me because I don't pretend feelings for you I don't have, do you remember that?" He moved forward again.

He was at her feet now, and so she stepped up to the smallest, topmost bag. "I remember," she said warily.

"Then you'll believe me when I tell you that I'm in love with you."

Shocked, Honor jerked, teetering atop the precarious bag. "No. You don't. You can't."

"But I do. I can. Oh, I resisted, because I know what it's like to be helpless too. And it was hard for me to risk being helpless again to someone else's happiness, to their very life." He reached for her, but when she jerked and teetered again, he dropped his hand. "But I can't give you up, Honor, not even to protect myself. I won't let you go."

Her heart was slamming against her chest. She put her fist there, trying to calm it, slow it, trying to remind it not to make any foolish moves. "For eight years you've been so . . ."

" 'Cranky,' I believe you once mentioned. 'Brooding' was another of your words." He lifted his hand again. "Come down, Honor, and put me in a better mood. Permanently."

She stared at his fingers as if they were snakes. "No," she whispered. Her father had gotten to him. Or his conscience. He felt obligated or worried or responsible for her. "I don't believe you."

"You can, though. You should." The expression in his eyes wasn't so much remote now as serious. "I know *I* don't have any doubts, not after last night."

"W-what do you mean?"

"Last night was *my* nightmare. I came home to tell you I was in love with you, and then what happened? I almost lost you. It was a hell of a test, Honor. But look, I'm not running from you, from us, from our love. I'm here. I'm still willing to take the chance."

Stunned, Honor stared at him. He'd come back to her last night? She'd never stopped to wonder why he'd been there when she'd needed him.

"Baby, come down," he coaxed. "We'll talk."

"No. I . . ." It couldn't be true. "No."

He sighed. "I guess it's time for my ace in the hole, then." With two fingers to his mouth, he let out a sharp whistle. "Joey! Attack!"

Stunned again, Honor's gaze jumped down the driveway. From his relaxed flop on the flagstone, she saw the dog gather his furry self, stand. He looked at Bram.

"Attack!" Bram pointed at Honor.

To her shock, Joey then obeyed, racing toward her. Honor's jaw dropped. What the dog had done to her would-be kidnapper flashed in her mind, but before she could collect her wits to protest, or scream, or scramble down from the suitcases, Joey did, indeed, attack.

If you could call your lower limbs being hugged by two moose-sized, furry forelegs an attack. If you could call the teetering, then toppling he accomplished an attack. If you could call finding yourself falling into the arms of the man who just said he loved you an attack.

Bram loved her.

From this close, she saw it in his eyes, she felt it in the slamming beat of his heart. She placed her palm over it, reveling in the way it was thudding. For her.

"Bram?" she whispered.

He smiled, that warm, surprising smile. "I love you, Honor. So much."

With his gaze locked on hers, the emotion poured from him and Honor felt it wash over her, enter her. She felt it fill in the missing pieces from her lonely childhood and then repair all the cracks and dents the kidnapping had left behind. Bram loved her. He really did.

And that he could love after what happened eight years ago and after what happened last night, that he was still willing to take a chance on love—it was . . .

It was the one thing that could restore her faith in the world.

Bram pushed her hair away from her face. "Say

something, honey. At least tell me what you think about Joey's trick."

She swallowed carefully, aware the smallest thing might make her cry. "You dared me, remember? If the dog ever learned something useful, you had to do something for me."

"I've already decided what that is."

She smiled then, knowing he would see in it the hope, the love, the faith he'd given back to her.

He did, because he turned his gaze heavenward, mouthed, *Thank you*, then looked back down at her.

Taking a deep breath, he cupped his hands around her face. "Tell you what. Because Joey finally learned to do something useful, every day, every day for the rest of your life, I'm going to make sure that you know that you have a place to call home and that you have a place in someone's heart."

She sniffed.

"My heart," Bram clarified, his voice strangely tight.

Now she cried. "I love you."

And at that, her stony-faced, icy-eyed commando of a man cried too.

HONOR would have liked to enjoy the privacy of the Fortress with her husband that evening, but before they'd even made it back to the house, a car approached the other side of the gate. Bram managed to get it open after a couple of muttered curses and frustrated pokes at his palmtop. Honor merely smiled sweetly.

A smile that turned to surprise as she took note of the long line of cars on their drive. Leading the pack was Kitty, in a gleaming white minivan. Following her were a dozen or more other vehicles, all filled with members of the Hooks & Needles Club.

Honor had completely forgotten she'd volunteered to hostess the November meeting.

But no one minded (except Bram, but that was for an entirely different reason) that she was unprepared. The women crowded into the kitchen and helped make tea and coffee. They passed the time with gossip and then with congratulations when Mia showed up with both her father and Josh in tow and announced she was engaged to be married.

Maybe it was the imminent wedding, but Mia's father didn't seem the least disappointed that the aliens hadn't returned as he'd predicted. The followers had disbanded at his insistence, he said, but most hadn't been downhearted. They considered themselves heroes of a sort—they had helped thwart a kidnapping attempt on an heiress! That was their story, anyway, and they were sticking to it.

Gil was vowing to write his story down. He was planning a book about his experience. With the words "Harry Potter" or "Diet" in the title, he was predicting an instant bestseller.

Later that evening, Honor went to retrieve more spoons from the kitchen. She paused to watch her husband through the window. *I love you.* She would prove to him just how much, later tonight. But he looked content for now, sitting with Joey, Josh, and Beau on the back deck. The men slumped low in their chairs, glasses of whiskey in hand, their heads tilted back at the sky. They appeared to be talking. She couldn't imagine what those three would have to say to one another.

As she hurried back out, her eye caught on the bank

of windows at the other side of the room. There was a strange green glow. . . . As she walked closer, though, her attention was diverted to poor Fifo, propped in the far corner. A blanket covered his wounded metal hide.

Bram promised he'd soon be as good as new, of course, but Honor placed a healing kiss on his pavement-scraped snout anyway. Then she glanced over at the window and the green glow again. Odd. . . .

A burst of female laughter interrupted her train of thought. "Honor! Honor! Hurry up, you've got to hear this," a woman called from the other room.

Blowing a kiss toward Bram, she dashed back to the Hooks & Needles meeting, leaving whatever was out the window behind. Mrs. Percy was in attendance to-night and she was detailing each of her four marriages.

Honor had a very particular interest in the one that had begun with a wedding cake topped by two plastic dogs.